Praise for the n~~o~~

"Faced with a complicated set of cases that leave you
guessing until the very end, Brennan doles out just the
right amount of family drama while moving the story
effortlessly between cases. This is the beginning of a
fabulous new series from the queen of crime fiction."
—J.T. Ellison, *New York Times* bestselling author
of *It's One of Us*, on *You'll Never Find Me*

"Allison Brennan just raised the bar for private eye
fiction! *You'll Never Find Me* is complex, combustible and
convincing. Secrets, action, suspense, *You'll Never Find Me*
has it all!"
—Matt Coyle, Shamus Award–winning author
of the Rick Cahill private eye series

"Set among Louisiana's swamps and brooding atmosphere,
Seven Girls Gone is a complex mystery whose characters
are as intriguing as the storyline." —*Denver Post*

"An intense, pulse pounding thriller from start to finish.
There were so many suspects, not to mention surprises and
twists." —*The Reading Cafe* on *The Wrong Victim*

"Allison Brennan is always good but her latest and
most ambitious work ever…is downright spectacular…
A riveting page turner as prescient as it is purposeful."
—*Providence Journal* on *Tell No Lies*

"A lean thriller starring a strong and damaged protagonist
who's as compelling as Lisbeth Salander."
—*Kirkus Reviews* on *The Third to Die*

Also by Allison Brennan

Quinn & Costa Thrillers

The Third to Die
Tell No Lies
The Wrong Victim
Seven Girls Gone
The Missing Witness

Regan Merritt Series

The Sorority Murder
Don't Open the Door

For additional books by Allison Brennan,
visit her website, www.allisonbrennan.com.

ALLISON BRENNAN

YOU'LL NEVER FIND ME

mira

mira™

Recycling programs
for this product may
not exist in your area.

ISBN-13: 978-0-7783-0527-9

You'll Never Find Me

Copyright © 2024 by Allison Brennan

For questions and comments about the quality of this book, please contact us
at CustomerService@Harlequin.com.

TM is a trademark of Harlequin Enterprises ULC.

Mira
22 Adelaide St. West, 41st Floor
Toronto, Ontario M5H 4E3, Canada
www.Harlequin.com

Printed in U.S.A.

To my daughter Katie, who last year made me feel super old by making me a grandma. I'm proud of you, your new family and your career in law enforcement. Stay safe.

Sometimes if you want to see a change for the better, you have to take things into your own hands.

Clint Eastwood

Sunday

One

Margo Angelhart

Arizona State Trooper Peter Carillo had left for work thirty minutes ago. I waited down the street, making sure he didn't double back to check on his wife. Carillo's job had a lot of flexibility, so he could come home any-time during his shift, but according to Annie, he rarely returned before lunch. Still, no counting on it. The plan: in and out in thirty minutes—forty, tops.

The cookie-cutter two-story house in north Phoe-nix, in a community called Norterra, had been built up over the last twenty-some years with near-identical homes distinguished only by slightly different facings. The Carillos lived on a large corner lot. I lightly tapped my horn as I turned into the driveway. The garage door rose and I pulled in. As I'd instructed Annie, she quickly closed the door behind me.

The front entrance was off-limits because Carillo had installed a video doorbell system that would alert him every time someone approached their front porch. The one time Annie had "accidentally" turned it off she'd paid with a gut punch. I feared if we tried that today, he might immediately return home, so decided on the stealthy approach.

I set my watch timer for thirty minutes; it was now 7:32 a.m. I hoped it didn't take longer to get Annie and her two kids out of the house.

Annie stood in the doorway. Too-pale skin framed by thick black hair, dark circles under her eyes, but the firm set of her jaw and tilt of her head confirmed that she was committed.

I couldn't afford to be wrong about Annie.

Last time I thought the woman I was helping escape a similar situation had been strong enough to walk, I'd been mistaken. Mistaken? What a joke. I'd miscalculated and misunderstood the people and emotions involved, and Christy ended up dead.

You can't force them to leave, Margo. You can't drag them out by their hair, kicking and screaming, insisting that their asshole husband will change, that it's their fault, that if only they hadn't done X, Y, or Z he wouldn't have gotten mad.

Pushing Christy and failure aside—failure was *not* an option this time—I opened the back of my Jeep and pulled out a new luggage set, rolled it over to where Annie stood, dressed in jeans and a white T-shirt.

"Are you sure?" I searched Annie's brown eyes for any hesitation, any doubt.

"Yes." She nodded her head once as if to emphasize her affirmation. "I did everything you said, Margo— didn't pack, didn't do anything to draw suspicion."

"We're on the clock. Everything is in place. Where are the kids?"

"PJ is watching cartoons. Marie is stirring in her crib."

"Leave her for now. We'll start in your room."

Annie led the way upstairs.

As in many of the tract homes built at the turn of the century, the master suite was spacious. Annie had taste—everything attractive and homey—but this room didn't feel like her. While the living areas were filled with feminine touches—dried flower arrangements, tasteful and delicate antiques, and comfortable furniture suitable for toddlers, the master was completely different. Large black contemporary furniture, a black satin comforter with gold and white pillows on the king-size bed, and a wide leather love seat in front of the mounted television. The entire room was dark and overly masculine, as if Peter Carillo wanted to exert dominance over his wife in the bedroom.

I hefted the suitcase onto the bed, unzipped it. Inside was a smaller case and a duffel bag.

"Just bring what you need," I reminded her, pulling on gloves before touching anything.

When Annie looked at my hands and frowned, I explained, "If he has the place printed, mine might pop. I've never been arrested, but I'm a licensed PI so my prints are on file." Carillo would have to break the law to search in noncriminal databases. I wasn't certain he would go that far because it could come back to bite him in the ass, but no way was I taking chances.

I tossed her the duffel. "Bathroom. Grab only essentials."

Annie took the bag into her bathroom while I grabbed items from the dresser. A week's worth of socks and underwear from the top drawer. Next drawer held sexy lingerie, the lacy kind that was super uncomfortable and usually bought by a man. Skip it.

Third drawer: perfectly folded pants, jeans. I selected four, put them in the largest suitcase. Bottom drawer held running shorts, sweats, tank tops. After picking out three of each, I turned to the closet.

Annie came out of the bathroom. She put the half-filled duffel down on the bed. I called from the closet, "Pick two pairs of shoes, comfortable."

Annie came in, grabbed a pair of sneakers that matched what she currently wore, and a pair of black loafers that would go with anything. Then flip-flops. "Okay?" she asked.

I nodded as I pulled a couple T-shirts, nice blouses, and a blazer and skirt set that would be good for a job interview and rolled everything tightly for packing. Then, I added one complete change of clothes—sweats and a T-shirt—into the duffel bag. "To make traveling easier, so you can leave your big suitcase in the car." A quick glance at the countdown: nineteen more minutes. "Anything else in here that you really want?" I waved my arm around the room.

Annie stared. "It doesn't matter, does it?"

"These are just things, but some things are more important than others. Maybe something with sentimental value."

Annie walked over to a small vanity and opened her jewelry box. Like the rest of the room, the box was organized. She took off her wedding ring, put it on the table, and pulled out a black velvet pouch. "This was my mother's ring. It's the only thing I really care about."

The pain in Annie's voice hit me. She had no living family, no close friends, no one she trusted with the truth—except me, a virtual stranger she'd met only three months ago. She was leaving her abusive husband and there was no turning back. I knew it, she knew it.

"Bring the kids' things in here and I'll pack. I know they'll want toys—only take things they really, really need. A favorite stuffed animal. A few games or books for the road."

"PJ has an iPad. I know he's young, but…"

"No iPad. No phones. No electronics of any kind. Nothing he can use to track you."

Annie's lip quivered. "I—I didn't think about that."

"I did. Just get the clothes, any important papers you might need."

Now tears fell. "He keeps everything locked in his safe. I don't have the combination."

Of course he did. Damn bastard. "That's okay. I have good forgeries of what you need with your new names, but the originals might come in handy. Don't worry about that now. Go. Clock's ticking."

While Annie went to the kids' rooms, I searched her bedroom, looking for anything that I could use against Peter Carillo. Important items were likely in the safe in the closet. Bet his guns were in there as well.

Annie came back with a laundry basket filled with boys' clothes and a worn blue blanket. "PJ can't sleep without it. And his pillow."

"Good. I'll pack everything. Go get Marie and her things."

Eleven minutes left. PJ's things filled most of the smaller suitcase once I'd stuffed in the pillow and blanket. That was okay. Again, I selected a change of clothes and rolled them into the duffel, then added the blanket, which freed up room for Marie's clothes in the suitcase. When my nephew was little, he couldn't sleep without his T. rex stuffed animal. We used to tease my younger sister about her attachment to a small beanbag dog named Rosie, until she lost the dog when we were camping at the Grand Canyon and cried for a week.

Annie came in with another laundry basket of baby clothes for Marie. "Grab everything else I put on the list—diapers, medicines, ointments, whatever. Go."

Annie obeyed without question. She was strong. At least now she was; I hoped she stayed strong over time—when she was alone, scared, with only two young children as company.

Babies were messy, so I put three clothing changes into the duffel plus a handful of diapers. The rest went into the smaller suitcase, and by the time Annie came in with Marie and a diaper bag, I had everything zipped up.

I carefully searched the diaper bag for any sort of hidden tracker. Annie watched me, but didn't speak.

"Anything else? Anything important? You can't come back."

"You said no electronics, but what about a portable DVD player? For the car—it's a long drive. There's no internet or anything. PJ loves his shows, and…well… I don't know what to tell him. I don't know how he's going to handle this."

"He'll handle it if you handle it. He's almost four. He looks to you for everything." My timer went off. Dammit. I set it for five more minutes. "We have to go. Grab the smaller suitcase." I took the large suitcase and duffel off the bed and went downstairs.

PJ was standing on the other side of the child safety gate. He looked at me with curious eyes as I hauled the dark purple luggage over the railing. "Who are you?"

"A friend of your mommy's." While I'd been working with Annie for nearly three months, we never met around PJ, fearing he might say something to his dad. No matter how innocuous, even an innocent comment could put the plan in danger. Put Annie in danger.

Behind me, Annie said, "PJ, go put on your shoes, okay?"

"Where are we going?"

"It's a surprise."

"Okay!" He ran to the laundry room where his shoes were lined up in cubby holes.

"Do you have food for the drive?"

"Yes."

"And you didn't take any money out of your account?"

She shook her head. Peter Carillo tracked all household expenses, but for the last fifteen months—since she found out she was pregnant with Marie—Annie had been planning to leave. So she'd been taking cash back at the grocery store—twenty dollars here and there, not every trip. Keeping change. On her own, she'd saved up just over three thousand dollars. Hid it in Marie's room under the diaper pail lining. Brave, and a sign that I was right about Annie: she wouldn't fail me.

I inspected the portable DVD player and deemed it okay to bring. Annie pulled several DVDs from the shelf, stuffed them into the bulging diaper bag. Together we jammed everything in the back of my Jeep.

I'd wanted to be in and out in thirty minutes; it took thirty-six. I could live with that.

"This is really happening," Annie said. She was shaking.

"Don't fall apart on me now," I said.

Annie shook her head. "I'm okay."

"You're doing the right thing."

"I know."

Annie transferred the car seats into my Jeep, buck-led in her kids, and we left.

PJ had a million questions. Annie responded vaguely, but he seemed to be satisfied with her nonanswers. Marie was drinking a bottle. She was eight months old with big brown eyes that looked at everything. She didn't talk. Much easier to work with a baby than a preschooler.

I'd had my associate Theo leave the car we'd pro-cured for Annie in Tempe, near the ASU campus. Far enough from Annie's house in case we were followed. We weren't. There wasn't much traffic on a Sunday morning, so I would have noticed a tail.

I loaded the bags into the trunk of an old but reli-able Toyota 4Runner that had been donated for this ef-fort. The registration was Arizona, but the tags were in Annie's new name—April Carra. Because PJ was nearly four, he knew his name, so I needed to create identities close enough to make it easier for him to learn and adapt.

While I handled the luggage, Annie secured the car seats into the back of the 4Runner.

"Mommy, are we going on a vacation?" PJ asked. "Is this a new car? Where are we going?"

"Hold on a minute, honey," Annie said. She looked lost. "I—what if he asks?"

"He will," I said, "and you'll tell him what we dis-cussed. It's up to you how much you think he can han-dle and when. But you're his mom. He trusts you. He'll adjust. He's a good kid."

"He is. I—"

"Stop second-guessing yourself."

"I'm not. I'm *not*," she emphasized. "I know this is the only way I live to see thirty. The only way my babies don't grow up with that monster."

Good. That was the right way to think. Still, I knew the next few weeks would be the hardest.

I handed Annie a thick manila envelope. "New IDs. They're false names, but these IDs are real, not counterfeit." It helped that I knew a few people in key government positions, people who didn't mind bending (or breaking) the law for a good reason—and because they trusted me. "New last name. The kids have the same first names, but yours is now April. The address where you're going, your contact there. There's a job lined up, temporary housing, and only one person who knows what's going on. She'll keep the secret, help watch for any threats. There's also a prepaid phone. Keep it charged. Only call me if you have a real emergency. No social media, no emails, and don't ever access your joint bank accounts, credit cards, *nothing*. I know this is going to be hard."

"You warned me. I'm ready for this."

"I know you are."

I hugged her. Annie needed it; so did I. The last twelve weeks had been stressful for both of us.

"One more thing." I reached into my glove compartment and handed her a thick bank envelope.

She shook her head. "No. I told you, I have enough."

"Three thousand isn't going to last long. You'll need to find permanent housing, buy food, clothes, diapers—you name it. Take it. Really, I have a new client who will pay me twice this to prove her husband is cheating on her." I hated adultery cases, but they paid well. I shoved the money into her hands. "Go."

Annie wiped away tears. "Thank you, Margo. Thank you for everything."

I watched Annie drive off. Scanned the parking lot, made sure no one else was watching, following. All clear.

Hopefully Annie could build a real life for herself in San Antonio. I'd tried to find a place farther away from Phoenix, but had to make due with limited options.

She was safe—for now. I wanted Annie and her kids safe forever, which meant putting Peter Carillo, abusive husband, out of commission.

But how? That was the million-dollar question, and one that I'd been losing sleep over since I first met Annie. Carillo was a cop, he was vindictive, and he had emotionally and physically abused his wife. Taking him down was going to be next to impossible.

But nothing—*nothing*—was impossible. The improbable just took time. And I had all the time in the world to destroy the man.

First things first: earning back the five thousand I'd given to Annie *real* quick. My mortgage was due in two weeks, and no way in hell would I ask my mother for a loan.

I'd walked away from the family business three years ago, and asking for help now would be admitting that I had failed and needed them.

I would get out of this hole the only way I knew how: working my ass off.

Two

Margo Angelhart

I quietly slipped into the last pew of St. Dominic's Catholic Church and hoped Uncle Rafe didn't spot my late arrival. I probably shouldn't have come at all. I could easily have called Rafe with the update about Annie.

But on my way home, thinking about grabbing a few hours of much-needed sleep before tracking Brittney Monroe's super-wealthy dot-com husband, I'd spotted the cross in the distance and deeply instilled Catholic guilt washed over me. I hadn't been to Mass in three weeks, and avoided my uncle's messages while planning Annie's escape.

I could easily blame the cases I'd been working—both paid and unpaid—but the truth? I'd broken one of the Ten Commandments three weeks ago. Sure, I broke the commandments all the time. Lying. Working on the Sabbath. Unmarried sex—though, unfortunately, not recently. I hadn't killed anyone, even when I wanted to, so that was a plus, right? But this time, I'd lied to my mother, and that always made me feel doubly guilty. The whole honor thy mother and father rule? I *really* tried to obey that one.

Worse, my mom knew I was lying. And she knew that I knew that she knew I was lying. So, how could I go to church in good faith when I lied to my mom?

I'm pretty certain I'm not the only adult who felt guilty when lying to their parents, but double guilt here because my favorite uncle is a priest and I'm a borderline halfway decent Catholic. And I was pretty certain Uncle Rafe could read my mind, which would not be a good thing most of the time.

You could be home right now, Margo. In bed. Sleeping. Call Rafe about Annie later today.

Yet…there was peace here at St. Dominic's that calmed me like little else. One of the oldest churches in Phoenix nestled in the valley between the Phoenix Mountains Preserve and North Mountain, designed to look like a small California mission, but with a distinctive desert feel. Thick adobe walls, narrow stained glass windows, and a long covered veranda that surrounded the church on three sides. Established trees flanked the structure, and to the west was a K–8 school with only nine classrooms—one for each grade, thirty to thirty-five kids in each class.

St. Dominic's took up one side of a quiet dead-end street in Sunnyslope. Sunnyslope had once been an upscale suburb north of downtown but had gone downhill over the last twenty-some years. Half the community still maintained their stately streets, large lots filled with trees, and older homes that had been renovated and were now worth seven figures. Abuela and Pop still lived in their home off North 7th Street, the one they bought in the 1960s, where they raised their seven children in four bedrooms with only two bathrooms. But on the fringes of Sunnyslope, especially near the freeway, light-rail stations, and most everything on or off 19th Ave, were run-down apartments, small houses with bars on the windows, graffiti, boarded-up businesses, drug deals in broad daylight, regular shootings, and gang activity.

I blinked as the congregation rose for the Gospel. I may have fallen asleep with my eyes open during the second reading, because I didn't remember a word.

Then, as if Rafe were speaking directly to me, a verse jumped out:

"'The person who is trustworthy in very small matters is also trustworthy in great ones; and the person who is dishonest in very small matters is also dishonest in great ones.'"

That capsulized what had been bothering me ever since I'd taken the adultery case ten days ago. A nagging little lie that my client told. It wasn't a lie that needed to be told...so why had Brittney Monroe said it?

When we met ten days ago at a generic coffee shop far from where Brittney lived in Scottsdale, she'd at first seemed very distraught and forthcoming. Her husband had changed, lying to her about where he was and who he was with, and she had smelled perfume on his shirts that wasn't hers. She just "had to know" if he was cheating on her so she could "fix their marriage." I suppose that could have been true, though in my subsequent research I learned that, because of her prenup, she gets more money in the divorce if he cheats.

But her rambling about irrelevant things, like her family and college, gave me a lot of information to verify. I usually check out my clients, so when she said that she didn't want to divorce because her parents had gone through a nasty divorce that forever impacted her, it was easy to verify.

Except, her parents had been married for thirty-six years and lived in the same house where they'd raised their two kids in Colorado Springs.

I asked her about it during our next conversation— over the phone, making it harder to read if she was lying—and she said, "Well, they didn't divorce, but they separated and it felt like a divorce."

Maybe that was true. But why not just say it? Why say divorce when it was a separation? A separation that clearly hadn't lasted.

I could have talked to her parents and brother and learned the truth, but decided it wasn't important. Besides, if she had lied, then I would have a harder time accepting her money…and I really needed the money. Bored housewife from Scottsdale wanted proof that her hubby of three years was doing the dirty with someone else? Sign me up. Hate the job; love the payday.

And a small lie was irrelevant as to whether dot-com multimillionaire Logan Monroe was cheating on his wife. It just annoyed me.

If she lies about small things, is she lying about big things?

And yeah, thinking about Brittney's possible little lie reminded me of my big-fat whopping lie to my mom.

Dammit.

I sat through the Eucharistic prayer, then joined the line for Communion. Would have slipped out right after, but I couldn't avoid Rafe's warm all-knowing eyes when he handed me the body of Christ. I could practically hear him ask, *Why have you ignored my texts and calls, Margo?*

"Amen," I said and put the wafer in my mouth.

I knelt after Communion, said my own private prayers, and tried not to fall asleep in the pew listening to one of the lectors drone on and on about news everyone could easily have read about in the bulletin.

Though the church was small and the 9:00 a.m. Mass catered to the older community, everyone wanted to chat with Father Raphael.

I could have left, but I'd come here in part to talk to my uncle. So I waited outside—Arizona spring is my favorite. It would top ninety by two o'clock that afternoon, but that was fine. Until temps moved north of the hellish one-ten, I was good. Last year we had the hottest summer on earth, weeks of temperatures exceeding 110. That was just fucked, as if a vent from Hell had opened up under the city of Phoenix. But other than those blistering days, I liked it.

The lull of voices and sound of cars leaving the lot put me into a semi-catatonic state as I leaned against my Jeep and soaked in the sun.

Ten minutes after Mass ended, Rafe approached. "You look tired," he said.

"I *am* tired."

I stretched, opened my eyes, stifled a yawn. "I was on my way home when I saw the cross and guilt had me turning left instead of right."

He didn't smile, though he usually enjoyed my humor.

"I've been avoiding you—I know. Sorry. I figured if it was super important you would have said so."

I feared my mom had talked to him. That he would

try and smooth things over, and I didn't want to take out my anger and frustration on Uncle Rafe.

"I was worried about you," he said.

"I told you I had everything under control."

"I was right to be concerned. You don't look like you've slept all week."

"Juggling two cases. But Annie's safe—or, on the road to being safe."

He frowned. "I didn't say goodbye, make sure she's okay."

"She's fine. We need to be careful. I don't know if her bastard of a husband will be able to trace her to you. It's better she didn't visit. If you see him, even if you *think* you see him, call me. I'm serious, Uncle Rafe," I added when he didn't immediately agree. "I can be here in five minutes."

He nodded. "And she's really okay?"

"She will be. It's a process. You know that." This wasn't the first time we'd worked together to help someone disappear.

"I've been thinking..."

"No."

He raised an eyebrow.

"I know exactly what you've been thinking, Uncle Rafe, and I'm not dragging Jack or Josie into this. Jack isn't a cop anymore and if he knows there's a bad cop, he'll do something he'll regret. You know it, I know it. And I'm not risking Josie's career. She's barely out of training, still on probation. This is *my* case. I'll find a way to take him down."

Rafe didn't say anything for a minute, and that always made me squeamish. Even before he became a priest.

Then he said, "I brought Annie to you because I knew you'd help her."

"That's my job."

"It's your calling," he said. "I feared for Annie's life. For her kids. That was the immediate problem, but while she may be safe, her husband is still an issue. He's in law enforcement. He has friends. He has authority. Abusing his wife may not be his only crime. You shouldn't go after him alone. Without, um, what do the shows say? Without backup."

"I get what you're saying, but—"

"There is no but in this. It's not a crime to ask for help."

"If I need help, I'll ask. I have friends. Taking down Carillo is the long game. I'm telling you again: if you see him, call me."

He nodded. "I'll call you first, then I'll call Jack."

"Dammit, Rafe!"

An elderly couple using walkers were slowly leaving the church and gave me a harsh look. They'd heard me swear at a priest. A popular priest who everyone in the parish loved. I just extended my time in purgatory. At this rate, I'd never get out.

What wasn't to love about Raphael Morales? Other than the fact that he was stubborn and manipulative and noble and compassionate and usually right.

"Just call me first, okay?" I said. "St. Dominic's is so far from anything he knows that I don't think he'll put two and two together. But there's a slim possibility he'll remember that her grandparents had lived in this neighborhood, and he might come around, start asking questions. Possibly while in uniform. Maybe send over a surrogate. He's tracked her movements for years, and even though she only came here once since they've been married, he might check. Be alert."

He nodded, kissed my hand, held on. "I will see you next weekend."

A statement.

"You never ask me to come to Mass, why now?"

"I meant for my parents' anniversary party."

"Oh. Right. Yes. Of course I'll be there. I wouldn't miss it." Abuela and Pop were celebrating their sixtieth wedding anniversary. My uncle Tom was closing his restaurant for the event and there would be a huge buffet, lots of family and friends and Very Important People because Hector and Margaret Morales both came from long-time Phoenix families. Pop was a retired judge, and Abuela had raised her kids while also running a taco stand near the courthouse. A taco stand that turned into a food truck in 1978—and may have been the first modern food truck outside of Los Angeles—that turned into eighteen food trucks. She'd stepped aside nearly twenty years ago, and Uncle Tom and his son, Adam, ran the business now.

"Why didn't you think I would come?"

He didn't speak. I grew suspicious.

"Who's talking about me?"

"I know you and your mom had a falling out a few weeks back—"

"Stop. Don't. Mom and I had a falling out three *years* ago. But I never let that stop me from doing my family duty, did I?"

"I know you don't want me in the middle of things, but I am fair."

"It's not about fairness. If I thought you could solve our problems, I would have asked you to mediate three years ago. We have a fundamental disagreement. I will not budge. If that makes me stubborn and rigid, I don't care. My dad's innocence is not something I will ever stop pursuing. *Ever.* He shouldn't be in prison. I can't just walk away."

"No one has walked away from Cooper."

"Yes, they have! Visiting him every week is bullshit." I winced, but didn't apologize. "I tried to understand why he pled guilty, but it doesn't make sense, and he was wrong to do so. Mom was wrong to agree with him. She could have talked him out of it—he would have listened to her. My brothers and sisters were on *my* side until she convinced them to go along with it. And I don't see the *why.* So no, you can't mediate. The only thing you can do is convince Mom that she is wrong, and you won't do that. You think I'm stubborn? I'm Ava Morales Angelhart's daughter. I get it from her."

"I didn't mean to upset you, Margo."

I took a deep breath, needing to calm down. "I'm tired, and I have to work this afternoon, so I need to sleep. Like you said, I look like shit."

He raised an eyebrow but had a sparkle in his eye. "I don't think that's what I said."

I smiled. A truce. "Not in so many words, but you were thinking it."

He smiled, rubbed my shoulder. "I'm glad you came to Mass."

"You might see me again here next week." I hugged him. "Love you, Uncle Rafe. And remember what I said about Carillo. See him, call me."

I crashed hard for five hours and woke up at four that afternoon feeling disorientated. I hated sleeping in the middle of the day, but three hours' sleep a night for a week had finally taken its toll.

I popped a pod into my Keurig and grabbed it as soon as it was done. Took the mug into the bathroom where I showered, towel-dried my dark blond hair, dressed in cargo pants and a white tank top, then checked my messages.

Sure enough, one came from Brittney Monroe. Also several texts from Theo, the college kid who worked for me part-time. He'd given me a solid report on Logan Monroe's whereabouts today, including pictures and details. He'd done good.

Though I maintained a storefront in a tired strip mall near the busy intersection of Cave Creek and Hatcher— got a good deal on the tiny space from friends of my cousins—I preferred working at home. I sat at my desk in the second bedroom that I'd turned into my office (though if I had a guest, they could sleep on the pullout couch that, when unfolded, took up all remaining floor space).

I hit Brittney's number. She picked up on the first ring. "You don't get Sundays off, Ms. Angelhart."

I had to bite the inside of my cheek to keep from mouthing off.

"No, of course not."

"You are highly unprofessional."

I made faces that she couldn't see. I wanted to quit *so bad* but didn't, because of two things: first, reputation. I couldn't risk blowing a major client just to maintain the moral high ground. And two, empty bank account.

"I had my colleague confirm that Mr. Monroe was, in fact, at his regularly scheduled golf date this morning at nine. I have photos of the men he golfed with—they are his regular group. They had lunch at one, and right now your husband is, in fact, at your house."

"I know all that. He was in the shower when I called you and you *did not answer*."

In my most contrite tone, I said, "I am sorry for missing your call." The apology felt like dog shit on my tongue.

"He told me he's going into the office for a few hours. That's what he's been saying and I know for a *fact* that he's not going to the office. This is it. I want photos, I want the little whore's name, and I want it as soon as you know."

"Yes, ma'am." I moved my jaw back and forth and heard it pop.

"I have to go," Brittney hissed. "Just do your job and get me the proof ASAP." She ended the call.

I barely refrained from throwing my phone against the wall. Deep breath in, slow breath out. Again.

Proof. Right. There would be no proof if Logan Monroe wasn't actually cheating. He'd been acting off and lying, according to the wife—signs of *something*, but I could think of a half dozen reasons other than screwing around.

But screwing around was certainly on the list.

I dialed Theo.

"Yep," he answered.

"Where are you?"

"Parked outside their gated neighborhood."

"He's supposed to be going to the office in a few," I said.

He snorted. "You think?"

"He did last week when she called thinking he was meeting with his mistress. It's going to take me thirty minutes to get there, then you're free."

"When you paying me?"

Fuck. "I can give you half tonight, plus gas."

"You gave that mom all your money, didn't you?"

"You aren't supposed to know about her." If I hadn't needed Theo's help with getting the car, I'd never have told him.

"You're a softie, Margo."

What would be the point of denying it?

"I don't need a lecture from a twenty-year-old criminal."

"*Former* criminal. I've been clean since the day before my eighteenth birthday. You know that, sugar."

"Don't call me sugar or you won't be seeing a dime."

He laughed. Theo had a hearty laugh that made him sound older and didn't fit his tall skinny body. "You're fun to wind up, Angel."

Theo had a half dozen nicknames for me. Some of them got old real quick.

"If he leaves before I get there, tail him and call me."

"Roger that, boss."

"You can certainly call me boss."

Three

The Thief

For the last year—fourteen months to be exact—the thief had implemented a brilliant plan.

He'd created a billing fee under a hidden code that charged customers between forty-nine and ninety-nine cents per transaction. No one paid attention to cents, but he didn't want a consistent number that might be easily seen in audits. When there were over a hundred thousand transactions a month, the money added up.

It was diverted into a blind account, and he had already transferred the first million into a secure off-shore account that only he could access. He wanted another million, which he would have by the end of the summer, except for one problem.

Jennifer.

The nerdy IT bitch had downloaded logs she should never have known existed, and he had to get her computer or he would be screwed. She was the only person who *might* be able to tie the billing fee to him. *Ironic*, he thought—he'd implemented his scheme right after she started working in the IT department just in case he needed a fall guy. And now his fall "gal" was his problem.

He had a new plan he'd already put into motion, and as long as Jennifer kept acting like her awkward, weird, jumpy self, it would work.

If he could destroy her laptop.

A laptop she never left unattended, as if it were a suitcase full of cash. A laptop that had the best virus protection software on it so the virus he emailed her didn't do its job. Hence, he was here, sitting in an empty house, waiting for Jennifer to show up.

He didn't know why she had rented the house for a few days. He'd cloned her work emails and the message had come in yesterday, confirming the short-term rental, from Sunday through Thursday. Helpfully, the garage entry code had been included. His goal was simple: wait for Jennifer, release the nitrogen gas, and wipe her computer. He'd already cleaned the server at the office, so it was only Jennifer's computer that had evidence of his embezzlement. By the time she woke up, she wouldn't know what happened. Any suspicions would be just that—suspicions, unprovable.

He'd already set her up to take the fall. She *was* acting weirder than usual, so it wasn't difficult to drop whispers in the right ears that she was up to something.

Jennifer White was smart, but so was he—better, he was ruthless.

He looked at his watch. Four in the afternoon. He'd only been waiting for an hour, but already he was antsy.

Still, he waited. There was too much at stake for him to fail now.

Four

Tess Angelhart

Tess Angelhart's favorite cases involved brain work over field work, so corporate espionage was right up her alley—most of the time.

Corporate espionage.

She loved the way the words rolled off her tongue. There was something fun and diabolical about *corporate espionage*. She loved the legal aspect, the analysis, the brains behind a good white-collar scheme. Her second favorite were *heists*—not violent robberies, but a good old-fashioned *heist* where the bad guys took weeks to set up the perfect theft, often without anyone knowing until long after the goods were gone. Solving those made her feel like an old-time detective, Pinkerton or even Sherlock Holmes.

She much preferred cerebral cases, where she could spend most of her time researching and putting together information, thinking about the hows more than the whys. She'd rather interview an expert or scour a li-

brary or courthouse archive for *days*, than sit here…in
a car…with her brother…for *hours*.

She read through her notes—reviewing how she
tracked Jennifer White to this short-term rental, mull-
ing over who she would be meeting with, what exactly
she was selling, how the plan was structured. Though
she had far less patience than Jack, she thought she was
holding her own, at least until Jack spoke.

"Stop," he said.

"I'm not doing anything."

"You're fidgeting."

"Am not."

He didn't respond.

"I'm restless," she admitted. "Do you think I got it
wrong? That she's not meeting the buyer here?"

"You got it right," Jack said. "Stop second-guessing
yourself."

She didn't think she was wrong. If there was one
thing she was good at, it was research. She had been
an investigator in her mother's law firm for nearly ten
years, so she knew how to find information. But she
was used to working in the courthouse, pulling cases,
reading filings, tracking people on paper. She was good
at interviews and talking to witnesses, getting people
to tell her things they probably shouldn't.

But patience? Not her superpower.

"You should have brought Lulu instead of me," Tess
said. Their youngest sister was more patient than even
Jack.

"She has a paper due tonight."

Luisa Angelhart—only family called her Lulu—was
a college student. Late to the college scene because she
spent six years in the Marines, but got a free education

out of it. Maybe because of her personality, or maybe because of her military training, Lulu could sit on a stakeout for however long it took and never complain. Tess thought she actually enjoyed it.

The short-term rental that Jennifer White had reserved in the name of a shell corporation was located on a quiet street on the north side of the Phoenix Mountains, in pricey Paradise Valley. Tess didn't know who owned the shell corp—yet. They would have to go on-site in Nevada to pull the papers. Right now they assumed it was under Jennifer's control, but it could have been reserved by the buyer if Jennifer was guilty of selling company secrets.

She also didn't know why Jennifer was meeting with someone *here*. Why not meet at a hotel? At a bar? The trailhead of the preserve where there were no security cameras? Why *here*?

She'd brought up those questions to Jack when she found the rental yesterday; he'd told her they would follow the facts. He didn't question. He observed, investigated, learned, deduced. He had been a police detective, after all. He'd told her more than once that all answers came through gathering information, and information came from observation, interviews, physical evidence, and the experience to interpret all of the above.

The CFO had uncovered evidence that someone in-house had downloaded proprietary information. Over the last week, Angelhart Investigations had run basic background checks on every Desert West employee, plus analyzed computer logs and data. Jennifer White was the only employee who *could* have downloaded the data, though they didn't have hard proof. Based on her odd behavior of late, Tess suspected they were on the right path, but the CFO wanted solid evidence.

Yes, Jack was right: they needed to follow the facts. But did following the evidence have to be so mind-numbingly boring?

Her brother said, "Here she comes."

They were in Jack's black truck up the street from the house, tinted windows providing some degree of concealment. At this angle, no one approaching the house would be able to see them.

Jennifer's practical late model white Honda Civic pulled into the driveway and partly disappeared behind a collection of saguaros that decorated the front yard. She approached the garage door, where she typed on a keypad and the door rolled up. A moment later, she pulled into the empty garage. Shortly thereafter, the door came down.

"Now we wait to see if she's meeting with anyone," Jack said.

Great, more waiting. But Tess kept her mouth zipped. Of course, she was meeting with someone. Why spend a thousand bucks a night for a rental only twenty minutes from where you lived?

The house was locked up, blinds closed against the desert heat. There were no other vehicles on the property, but there was no way to know if someone was already inside—perhaps dropped off by Uber before she and Jack arrived. Because the house backed up to the mountain, there was a possibility that someone could access it on foot, and there was no easy way to keep an eye on both the house and the mountain. There were no cars parked on the street near the house. The houses in the neighborhood were on large lots set back from the road, with trees and walls for privacy.

Tess didn't think that computer nerds were particularly sneaky in physical cloak-and-dagger games. Online, sure, but climbing halfway up a rocky mountain when it was ninety-four degrees and rattlesnakes were basking in the sun? Nope.

Jennifer had arrived alone. What was she doing? A staycation? It was a nice place—not large, but from the photos she'd seen online, there was a pool, jacuzzi, gourmet kitchen. White could afford the place, but why when she literally lived in one of the nicest condo complexes in Scottsdale, right across from Fashion Square? Maybe the setup here was to make the buyer of Desert West data more comfortable? Or maybe she simply wanted more distance from her personal life.

Jack said, "Stop."

"I'm not doing anything."

"You're still fidgeting. If she's meeting someone, they'll be here soon."

"We have different definitions of *soon*," she grumbled.

Tess ignored the smirk on her brother's face. Jack had been a cop for fourteen years—the last six as a detective—before leaving the force. He was used to stakeouts. Waiting. Watching. Being bored out of his mind.

"I'll never understand how you do it," she mumbled. "How many times were you called into Father O'Connor's office for being disruptive in class? Mom called you the energizer bunny because you couldn't sit still."

"School was boring."

"This *isn't*?"

"I grew up. Now I mentally entertain myself."

She rolled her eyes, looked up at the roof as if asking God for understanding and patience.

A car slowly came up the winding road and Tess leaned forward. A lone driver, male. Jack already had his camera in hand and had taken several shots of the late model white Tesla.

"Model X," Jack said.

Tess knew next to nothing about cars. "Is that good?"

"Expensive."

The Tesla turned into the driveway of the target house. Jack kept the camera on the vehicle and continued to shoot photos as the driver got out.

The man was approximately six feet tall, slim, with sandy blond hair that touched his collar, dressed in khaki's and a light blue polo shirt.

"Bingo," she said.

In order to catch Jennifer White red-handed, they had to identify the man she met with. This would allow them to compile a more detailed report and hopefully uncover what White was up to. The stakes were high; the CFO had to decide whether to fire her or prosecute her for stealing company secrets. Although the evidence was circumstantial, Tess was confident they were building a solid case. The most important thing was to identify the buyer and document the money trail.

Another car came up the road less than two minutes after the Tesla. Tess first thought a resident, though there were only a dozen houses up the road from them before the street dead-ended into the mountain. There was no maintained trail access from this road, though someone fit could hike into the preserve if they cut through a yard or used a drainage ditch.

The black Jeep looked familiar. It did a one-eighty in front of the house, the faded Army decal on the rear window telling Tess exactly who was driving. Jack swore under his breath at the same time as Tess said, "What the hell?"

Their sister Margo parked two houses down, her Jeep barely visible from their vantage point.

Tess glanced at Jack. "You need to find out what she's doing."

"Let's see how this plays out."

Margo had intentionally turned her back on Angelhart Investigations three years ago. Their paths rarely crossed in business, and Tess only saw her sister at family functions, where Margo usually arrived late and left early. *Her choice*, Tess thought bitterly. She chose to walk away, and Tess wasn't going to feel bad about it.

Even if she missed her irritating, compassionate, stubborn, smart, spontaneous, independent, distrustful sister.

"Hey," Jack said.

"I'm fine," she mumbled.

He shot her a knowing look, then said, "She's walking around back."

"Why is she here?"

Jack didn't respond because, of course, he didn't know. No one knew *exactly* what Margo was up to these days.

Margo struggled because she worked too often for free, but when she did make money, it was either taking a dangerous bounty assignment or an adultery investigation. Through the family gossip chain, word was that Margo was on retainer for one of the big divorce law firms in Phoenix. Fit right in with her sister's cynical view of family and marriage. A view completely unjustified, in Tess's opinion. They had everything they needed even if they didn't always have what they wanted, and never felt unloved. And their parents had been married for nearly forty years and still loved each other.

Even though their dad was in prison.

Margo circled the house, a camera around her neck. What a miserable job, taking sex pictures. Was the man married? Did his wife hire Margo? Jennifer White was single, twenty-six. Maybe she was dating a married man, giving him company secrets.

Tess wished everything had been different. That she could just pick up the phone and call Margo, go out for drinks and talk like they used to. But three years ago Margo had burned the bridge. Tess could forgive her— that was how they were raised—but Margo would never ask for forgiveness because she didn't believe she'd been in the wrong.

Margo suddenly started running toward the back again, a determined look on her face. Tess lost sight of her.

Jack said, "Something's up."

Five

Margo Angelhart

I recognized the house as soon as I saw it. Logan Monroe had lived here before he married Brittney, then converted it to an exclusive short-term rental.

A perfect place to have an affair. No one would question why he was here—not even his wife.

I accessed my file on Monroe and flipped through the photos on this property. The best access point was in the rear—the west-facing front had small covered windows that would be difficult to open and also make it easy for a passerby to see me, but the rear had large picture windows with the mountain as the primary view. Plus, the master bedroom was in the rear.

Maybe Monroe and his lover would be having sex in the pool. That would make my job a lot easier.

Stepping out of my Jeep, I headed toward the property with unwavering determination. Despite the isolated spread of the houses, I kept a careful eye out for any nosy neighbors. A black truck was parked up the road. Short-term rentals in the area meant an influx of unfamiliar faces, making my presence seem like nothing out of the ordinary. But best to be cautious.

I halted at a locked side gate. Dammit. Irritation simmered as I weighed my options. As easy as it was to scale the fence, I hesitated. But it wasn't the first time I'd trespassed, and I doubted it would be my last.

With a deep breath, I hoisted myself up, bending my knees to absorb the impact of my landing. Muscle memory from basic training kicked in, making the jump effortless.

The house was cloaked in secrecy, every window covered. Breaking in was not an option, not when the occupants could be armed. Brittney had warned me about Monroe's 9mm, and I couldn't afford to take that risk. All I needed was a small opening, and the bedroom was the perfect target. A gap in the blinds, a quick snapshot, and I'd be out of here before anyone noticed.

I carefully navigated around the rocky terrain, avoiding the ankle-biting cacti. The only sound was the constant hum of the AC unit. I eyed the sparkling pool. It hadn't topped one hundred degrees yet, but I was hot and that water looked so inviting. Instead, I focused on my job.

Off the master suite was a semi-private patio. The blinds were drawn, so I braved the enclosed space and tried to see around the edge. No luck. Even with my ear to the glass, I heard nothing. No voices, no sounds of passionate sex, no shower. Maybe they were having foreplay in the kitchen with chocolate-covered strawberries and champagne...

Where the hell had that thought come from?

It had been far too long since I'd had a regular guy to

enjoy sex with, no wonder I embellished adultery with sexy, fun romantic gestures.

Sometimes, adultery wasn't solely about the sex. Sometimes, it was about the personal connection, talking to a person who understood you better than your spouse. Rarely ended well, but people lied to each other all the time.

Stealth wasn't going to cut it. Time to be bold.

The covered back patio, which ran almost the entire length of the house, was complete with fans and misters, both turned off. Classy but functional outdoor furniture filled the space. The patio alone was twice the size of my house.

There was no place to hide, so I assessed the area quickly. The blinds were drawn across the large picture windows. The kitchen had two sets of French doors with sheer blinds, easy to see through. The primary kitchen window, however, was bare. If I approached it at the right angle, I should be able to see inside without anyone seeing me.

I squatted and awkwardly waddled to the window in case someone was standing at the sink doing dishes—or having sex on the counter. Then slowly I stood next to the window, back to the wall, and peered inside.

It took a second or two for my eyes to adjust to the dimmer indoors. A laptop was open on the long counter that separated the kitchen from the dining area, but I couldn't read the tiny spreadsheet that covered the screen.

Who brought a laptop for sex games?

Next to the laptop was a messenger bag, flap open. A couple water bottles. Water—not wine, not champagne, and no chocolate-covered strawberries.

Plus, no people.

Where was Logan Monroe? Was he here alone? Had he spotted me lurking around? Damn, I felt like a Peeping Tom.

I headed to the French doors. Curtains blocked the window squares, but they were pinched in the middle, enabling me to see part of the interior. This would give me a clearer view, but it would be easy for someone to spot me.

Prepared to bolt, I looked inside.

Logan Monroe and a brunette woman were lying on the floor, unmoving. I stared for a good five seconds, wondering if this was a game, if they were looking for a lost contact lens, anything but what I immediately thought.

They didn't move.

"Shit!" I tried the door. Locked. I could break a window, but that seemed like overkill. Maybe Monroe hadn't locked the front door when he entered.

I dropped my small Canon EOS into the carrying case on my left hip, pulled out my cell phone and called 9-1-1 while running around to the front of the house.

"9-1-1 what is your name and your emergency?"

"Margo Angelhart. I'm a licensed private investigator currently at 9980 Thorny Rose Lane in Paradise Valley. Two individuals are unconscious inside the house. I'm trying to find a way inside."

"Are they injured? Bleeding?"

"Don't know, trying to get in. I saw them through the window in the kitchen." That sounded stalker-ish, and these calls were recorded. Maybe no one would notice.

"I'm sending Police and Fire. Stay on the line."

I tried the front door. Locked. Reminding myself that

it was only breaking and entering if you were caught, I pulled my lockpick set from my pocket and went to work, grateful this wasn't an electronic lock. There was a keypad on the garage, but not on the door. With locks, I performed magic. Electronics? Not so much.

Twenty seconds later, voila. I had no one to impress but myself.

I was duly impressed.

Only after I stepped into the house did I consider that maybe walking into a building where the occupants were unconscious wasn't the smartest move. But I had 9-1-1 on the line, and Police and Fire should have a quick response time at five on a Sunday afternoon.

"I'm in the house," I told the operator. "I'm going to check their vitals."

"Can you describe the individuals?"

"Male, Caucasian, mid-thirties, six foot one, one hundred and eighty pounds. Female, early to mid-twenties, Caucasian or Hispanic. Hold on."

I pressed speaker and put the phone down so I could kneel and check each pulse.

"Both individuals are unconscious but each has a strong pulse. I'm going to open the doors and windows in case there's a gas leak. I don't think I should move them unless you think I should."

"Do you smell gas?"

"No."

But many gases had no odor, and I didn't want to pass out.

Thanks to Uncle Sam, I had advanced first-aid skills, but unfortunately let my EMT certification expire years ago after I left the Army. Still, I wasn't going to let anyone die if I could stop it.

I opened both sets of French doors, then spent too long searching for the panel that would open the family room blinds. Finally found it—a remote on the table. The doors were glass and they, too, slid open via the remote. Sweet.

The AC was on, but I switched the fan to high, which would help (I hoped) clear out any gas from the house.

I took a peek in the master bedroom—no sign that the bed was used. No luggage, no discarded clothing, no sexy lingerie, and no champagne on the nightstand.

By the time I returned to the kitchen, Logan was stirring. He groaned and struggled to get up.

"Don't move, help is on the way."

"Wha—?" he asked, groggy, as if he'd been woken from a deep sleep. "My head."

"Stay still."

The woman was smaller, maybe she absorbed more of the drug or poison or gas or whatever it was that had knocked out two healthy people in less than thirty minutes.

To the dispatcher on the phone I said, "The male is waking up, complaining of a headache. The woman is still unconscious. She's approximately five foot three, maybe one hundred and ten, twenty pounds, tops."

Now that I knew Logan Monroe wasn't dying, I breathed deeply, trying to figure out what might have incapacitated these two. No smell, no physical reaction, no cough, nothing to suggest I had inhaled a toxic substance.

"Did you drink anything?" I asked Logan.

He stared blankly, as if trying to figure out what was going on. He leaned against the counter, still too weak to stand.

"Just...water."

"Bottled? Did you open it yourself?"

He shrugged. Okay, he was still kind of out of it, but doing better than the woman.

"What's her name?" When he didn't immediately respond, I snapped my fingers in his face and repeated slowly, "Logan, what is her name?"

"Jennifer. Jennifer White."

I tapped Jennifer lightly on the cheek. "Jennifer. Wake up. Time to wake up."

The woman groaned, but didn't open her eyes or move. I heard the dispatcher in the distance asking questions I couldn't hear, so picked up the phone again. "Repeat, I didn't catch that."

The dispatcher asked, "Did they take drugs? If so, what kind? Any alcohol?"

I asked Logan, "Are you on any drugs?"

"That's ridiculous. I don't do drugs."

"Drinking? Beer, wine, vodka?"

"Just water."

He stared at Jennifer and frowned, confused. Then he looked at the laptop on the counter.

The dispatcher said, "The fire department and ambulance are at the location. Please let them inside."

Outside, I heard the distinct whoosh of fire truck brakes.

"The door's open," I said.

Laptop, messenger bag. If they weren't having an affair, what the heck were they doing?

Because I already had my cell phone in my hand, I used that instead of my Canon to take pictures of the counter and everything on it.

"What are you doing?" Logan asked.

"Evidence. You were poisoned."

Evidence, I thought, *to figure out what you're up to.*

"Poisoned?" Logan questioned.

I had some ideas, but none that fit perfectly. The gas had to act quickly, then disperse—or it was in the water, but what poison had no taste? Assholes roofied women with alcohol or soda to mask the taste of the drugs. My brother Nico, the forensic scientist, would probably know; I'd call him later. Forensics was far outside my wheelhouse.

I heard the clomp of soft-soled boots on the tile floor.

"Back here," I called, "in the kitchen."

Two paramedics came in with their gear. Jennifer finally began to stir, but didn't open her eyes. Logan was fully alert; I avoided his suspicious gaze.

"What happened?" a paramedic asked, kneeling to check Jennifer's vitals.

I gave the basics, leaving out that I had (technically) broken in. Before anyone could ask why I was there, I stepped into the backyard, hoping I could slip away before the police arrived. There would be a broader investigation, the gas company would be called, toxicology screens at the hospital, testing the water.

I had no reason to believe they'd been drugged on purpose, it could have been an accident, yet the whole situation felt like a setup. I glanced into the house, saw the paramedics were doing their job, and both Jennifer and Logan appeared to be okay. I turned away, stared at the pool, and thought about what might have happened.

Could Brittney Monroe have already known where her husband was meeting the woman? She would have access to the house, could have planted a poison or sabotaged the gas line and sent me here. Why? To save her husband?

My head hurt thinking about every wild theory, though I couldn't stop working through the problem. Logan Monroe owned this house, but I'd been tracking him for ten days now and he hadn't come here. The rentals were handled by a management company, but he'd have a key and would know when it was unoccupied, so he could easily use the place whenever it was free. Perfect love nest.

It didn't feel like a love nest.

A flash above caught my attention—in the boulders, above the house. A reflection?

I slid on my sunglasses, grateful that the sun was behind me, and scanned the mountain.

Movement. Two men were scurrying out from the boulders, both in black—*in black when it was nearly a hundred degrees!*

No, not suspicious at all.

I ran across the yard, climbed the pool's waterfall, hopped the fence, and pursued them.

Six

Jack Angelhart

Jack entered the house moments after the paramedics arrived. He scanned the room, his eyes landing on Margo who stood outside with her back to the house. The paramedics were checking the vitals of Jennifer White and the man she'd been meeting with. Now that Jack had a clear view of the stranger, he thought he recognized him, though didn't know from where.

"Sir? Is this your house?" a paramedic asked.

Jack shook his head, was about to identify himself when the man said, "It's my house."

He owned the rental—or was he lying? Jack suspected Margo had the answers.

"Please stand aside." The paramedic motioned for his partner to bring the stretcher forward.

As they worked on Jennifer, the man who claimed to own the house remained silent and sat on the floor against the counter, rubbing his temples. Jack needed to figure out what happened and why Margo was involved.

Dammit, Margo, what are you up to?

He made his way outside to speak to his sister, but she was already on the move. She bolted across the yard and jumped over the back fence, heading up the hill into the Phoenix Mountains Preserve. Jack wasn't sure who she was running from or why, and he debated following her or tracking her down at her house tonight and demanding answers.

His radio beeped. He and Tess communicated via radio when working, a lot easier than cell phones when you were in the field.

"Yeah," he answered.

"Margo is running up the mountain!"

"I see."

"Help her!"

"What?"

"There were two men hiding behind that cluster of boulders halfway up the hill. Both wearing black T-shirts and tactical pants. She's going after them. They're headed northeast, toward the neighborhood on the other side of the ridge. She's going to get hurt!"

Jack looked beyond the boulders, saw Margo, then a hundred yards past her were two men who quickly disappeared from view.

"I got her," he told Tess and pocketed the radio. He followed Margo's path, the sun at his back, but it was too hot to be running up a mountain. What the *hell* was she thinking pursuing two men alone?

Though he was closer to forty than thirty, Jack was in good shape. He spent a lot of time both hiking and working out at the gym, so the steep hillside didn't slow him down. Yet, the heat and beating sun would quickly exhaust him.

Margo had a solid lead, but he was gaining. He loved his sister, but sometimes he wanted to throttle her.

The air was dry and still. What he wouldn't give for a monsoon to clear out the dusty air, and he hoped his pop was right and monsoon season would come early this summer.

"Margo!" he shouted. He didn't yell again, realizing he didn't know who she was pursuing or why—if they had weapons or had been responsible for whatever happened to Jennifer White and her alleged co-conspirator.

Either she hadn't heard him or she ignored him. He was gaining ground.

The men she was following dropped out of sight as they descended the other side of the mountain. They weren't on a trail, which made traversing the terrain tricky—cacti and ankle-twisting boulders were the least of his concerns. There were rattlers all over the state, and when he hiked he wore appropriate boots and looked for telltale signs.

Running across the face of the mountain was *not* being smart.

Margo should know better. When they were teenagers, she'd been bit by a rattler during a family hike along the Pima Loop on South Mountain. If their dad, a doctor, hadn't been with them, Jack wasn't sure Margo would have survived. But Dad knew what to do, slowed the spread of the venom, and a rescue helicopter swooped in and brought her to the hospital for antivenom and fluids. You'd think after that experience Margo would be more cautious, but no—she runs up the mountain during prime rattler-basking time.

Jack was gaining on Margo, but she was now on the down side and he lost sight of her. He picked up his pace, saw a trail ten feet to his left, and crossed over to it. He slipped, started to fall, but caught himself, hands scraping across the dry rocky soil.

"Shit," he muttered. "Dammit, Margo."

He reached the trail, rubbed his palms on his jeans, shook out the pain where he'd been nicked by a stubby cactus.

He made much better time on the trail. Margo came into sight—she was now on the trail right in front of him. He still couldn't see who she was pursuing, but below them the trail led to a neighborhood of multi-million-dollar homes nestled high up on the edge of the preserve. The view from here was spectacular. At sunrise, the entire valley and mountains beyond would be aglow, an awesome sight.

But in the late afternoon, the sun burned and he didn't have time to enjoy the view.

"Margo!" he barked out once.

She glanced over her shoulder, startled when she recognized him. Then she motioned in front of her and started jogging down the trail.

Two men in black emerged from the end of the trail into the neighborhood. They were making a beeline toward a dark SUV parked on the street. No way was Margo going to catch up with them.

Suddenly, she stopped, as if she just realized what Jack had. She pulled out her camera and started taking pictures of the men and vehicle. They were gone seconds later when Jack finally caught up with her.

They were both out of breath. Margo shoved her camera back into the pouch on her side, on the opposite side from her holstered SIG Sauer. Then she dropped her small tactical backpack and pulled out a water bottle, draining half of it. She handed the rest to him.

"Thanks," he mumbled and finished it. Margo was always prepared. He rarely, if ever, saw her without her pack. He would have had water if he'd had his bag, but he left it in the car.

She took the empty bottle, put it back in her pack, and said, "What are you doing here?"

"I should be asking you that."

"My job."

"You left two semiconscious people in that house—"

"With paramedics."

"What happened?"

She shrugged. "I saw them lying unconscious on the floor, called 9-1-1, picked the lock. Those guys were watching the house from behind boulders. I don't know why, but they bolted after Fire showed up. I knew I wouldn't catch up to them but I thought I recognized one."

"You recognized one of the men?"

"Looked familiar, but I never got close enough. I'll enhance the pictures. If I also caught the license plate with the camera, I can run it. Maybe they're involved in whatever happened at the house."

Jack didn't think his sister had been hired to track Jennifer White, not when his agency had been retained, so he guessed she was following the guy.

"We should head back," Jack said. "The police must be there by now."

Jack pulled out his cell phone, hit Tess. "Can you pick us up on the other side? I don't want to hike back."

"What happened?"

"They had a car, got away."

"Five minutes."

Jack ended the call and Margo said, "Tess?"

"Yeah."

"Shit."

"Truce."

Margo didn't say anything as they walked down the path toward the road. Jack hated that his sister felt estranged from their family. Margo was stubborn and loyal and independent. She wasn't going to give in, their mother wasn't going to give in, and Jack didn't know how to fix the family when he understood both sides of the argument. What he didn't understand was why Margo couldn't put this disagreement—serious as it was—aside for the sake of the family.

He desperately wanted to fix everything. With their father in prison, it was his responsibility to keep everyone together. The family, a close-knit unit, bonded and whole. As they'd always been, until three years ago. The fracture left him incomplete, always waiting, watching, worried. And deep down sad.

"Talk to me," Jack said after a moment.

"I have a job, apparently so do you. We'll each do our job, and I'll see you at the party Saturday."

"Don't you think it's strange that two private investigators were hired for the same case?"

Margo asked, "Why were you hired?"

She obviously knew he was fishing, and she wasn't going to share anything unless he gave her something. Right now, he was just glad that Tess wasn't here. She had taken Margo walking away from the family business personally and Jack didn't know how to fix that, either. They'd once been so close they could have been twins.

Hell, he had so many broken pieces in his life he felt like Humpty-Dumpty.

"This stays between us," he said.

"Sure."

"We were hired by White's employer because someone in their company downloaded proprietary information. Our investigation pointed to White, and now we're working to prove it. This meeting was out of her pattern, so we suspected she was meeting a buyer to sell the information. Basic corporate espionage. Clearly, that's your man. Because I don't think our client hired another Angelhart."

She smiled. "No."

"You?"

She didn't say anything.

"Come on, Margo, I gave ours, what's yours?"

"Adultery. I've been on it for little over a week, after three days I thought the wife was pulling the accusation out of her ass. This was the first time I thought maybe she was right."

"White could be sharing secrets with her lover."

"I don't think they're doing the horizontal."

"But?"

She shrugged, didn't look at him. Jack started to get angry. She was figuring out *something* and she wasn't going to tell him?

"Spill it, Margo. What's in that suspicious brain of yours?"

"Confidentiality goes both ways."

"Of course."

She stopped walking, turned and faced him. He couldn't see her eyes because of her sunglasses, but the set of her jaw told him she wasn't at all pleased that their individual cases had collided.

"Do you know who the guy was with Jennifer White?"

"No. But I'll find out as soon as we get back." He still knew half the guys on the force, and the other half probably knew he'd been a cop.

"Logan Monroe."

Monroe. Monroe. Did he know… "Oh!" That's why he'd looked so familiar.

"Yeah. That Logan Monroe."

"Corporate espionage? Seems like small potatoes for him."

"I certainly don't want to spread that rumor without substantive proof," Margo said. She took off her glasses and stared him in the eye. "We both know what happens to good people when they're accused of doing something illegal."

His stomach flipped. Yeah, they did.

"Okay. But if he's guilty—"

"I don't know what's going on," Margo said as she slid her glasses back up her nose. Tess turned onto the street. Jack waved at her, and she honked once.

"I hear a but."

"But nothing. We don't leak any of this unless we have one hundred and ten percent proof that Logan Monroe is stealing proprietary information. It'll destroy his reputation."

"Agreed. Where do we start?"

"We?" Margo waved toward Tess. "I don't think my big sister is going to want me involved, and I sure as hell am not taking orders from either of you."

"We, as in partnership."

"I don't know."

"Margo—"

"I don't know," she repeated. "Let me think about it. Dammit, Jack, I don't know how this will work, but I'll figure it out."

"*We* can figure it out." He wanted to work with Margo. He had since the beginning, when they first conceived the idea of a family business. But he understood why she couldn't be part of it, at least right now. Still, he saw an in, and he would take it. Wedge his foot into the crack until Margo opened the door and came back.

"Let's go to the house and see what everyone knows." She smiled at him as she opened the back door of the truck. "Maybe this will work," she said, her tone definitely lighter. "You'll get more out of the police than me. And we'll go from there. Okay?"

Jack wasn't certain that Margo wouldn't take the information and bolt, but she was his sister, and he— mostly—trusted her.

"Okay," he said, sliding into the passenger seat. "Don't make me regret it."

Tess turned and said to Margo, "You ran off after two men alone. You didn't know Jack was following you. Didn't have backup. They could have been armed, waiting to ambush you, and—"

"Hey, sis. How've you been?"

Tess whipped back around and glared at her in the rearview mirror, then did a quick one-eighty on the dead-end road and headed toward the rental in silence.

Truce, Jack thought. He hoped it lasted more than a day.

He doubted it would last an hour.

Seven

Margo Angelhart

On the short drive back to Monroe's house, I convinced Jack to talk to the police alone. I had a good relationship with the cops, but Jack had been a cop, and they'd be more open with him.

Tess and I ended up alone in Jack's truck. I leaned back and closed my eyes.

Tess shifted in her seat, her glare heating my skin. I lasted a minute before I took off my sunglasses and stared back at her. "What?"

"I saw you with the camera. Sex pics? Really?"

"Sex pays," I said. "Real well." When Tess scowled, I added, "Prude."

"Oh, please. So, you have the money shot? Going to get your bonus?"

Her snide comment irritated me.

"None of your business."

"I'm going to find out. Were they clothed or naked? Enjoying a romantic meal or getting high?"

"Yep, you'll find out."

"You don't have to be such a bitch," Tess said.

"Right back at you."

This back-and-forth with my sister was exhausting, but I couldn't stop myself. I loved Tess, but life had a way of stirring shit up, and the last three years we'd focused on our disagreements more than agreements. We shared a bedroom our entire childhood. I knew all her secrets, and she knew most of mine. Those who knew you best knew best how to get under your skin.

Jennifer White was being wheeled out on a gurney, an oxygen mask over her face and an IV in her arm. Her messenger bag and laptop were between her legs. Damn, I should have gone through them when I had the chance. But in front of Monroe? I don't think he would have stopped me, but I didn't know and didn't want to cross the line. At least, not yet.

"Margo," Tess said in her you-need-to-listen-to-me-because-I-know-best tone.

I'd had enough. I got out and headed toward my Jeep.

Jack waved me down.

Dammit. No clean getaway.

I flashed my most charming smile and turned to Jack and the cop he was standing with.

"Yep?" Did I sound irritated or innocent?

He didn't say anything, just gave me *the look*. Meaning, *don't leave*. He said something to the cop that I couldn't hear, handed him a business card.

I itched to go to the hospital and follow-up with Jennifer White. We needed information, and I couldn't exactly ask Logan Monroe, considering I'd been trying to catch him au naturel.

"So, where do we go from here?" I asked Jack when the cop went back inside the house. We were standing under a tree. The canopy of leaves offered relief from the unforgiving sun to the point that I was comfortable.

"Monroe told Officer Cameron that Jennifer was a friend and they were having a business meeting, then both started to feel woozy and Jennifer fainted. He tried to carry her to the couch, when he stumbled and fell, losing consciousness."

"How long? I was only a few minutes behind them."

"White was in the house for about ten minutes before Monroe arrived. You arrived three to four minutes after he went in."

"I spent about five, six minutes looking for a good viewpoint," I muttered. "Okay. So either she got it worse because she was in the house longer, or they both drank something and she got it worse because she's smaller."

"Logical. They're sending crime investigation out to test the air, filters, entire system. If something was airborne, they'll find out what. They'll test the water, both in the bottles and house. It'll be several days before we have answers, unless the hospital can run her blood quickly." Even then, unless the lab knew what to test for, they might not find anything.

"I have an idea."

"I'm listening."

"I can't talk to Monroe—his wife hired me. He's not going to tell me squat when millions of dollars are riding on whether he's fooling around with White. But, he might talk to you—especially if he thinks his reputation could be in the tank if he doesn't."

"You're okay with us talking to him?"

"Yep. This is the way I see it—if he's having an affair, he's going to cool it off for a while because he doesn't want his wife to find out. If he's not having an affair, he's up to something else. Illegal?" I shrugged. "Who knows."

"And you? You're just going to wait until we have answers?"

"Nope. I'm going to the hospital. I can interview White. You'd be hard pressed to do so because you were hired to investigate her."

He obviously didn't like the idea, but he didn't have a better plan, and I knew it.

"Okay, on one condition."

"Always conditions."

"I want a copy of the photos you took."

Fair enough.

I pulled out my Canon, pressed a few buttons, and sent the photos to Jack's phone. "Done. I'm not positive because I didn't see his face clearly—but I scrolled through and I think one of those guys is Frank Sanchez."

"The asshole who works for Miriam Endicott?"

"Yep."

"Why would Endicott be watching Monroe's house? Could his wife have hired two PIs?"

"Could White's employer have hired two PIs?" I countered.

"We'll confirm the identity, run the plates, see what we can get. I'll let you know."

"Appreciate it."

Eight

Tess Angelhart

"You let her go to the hospital to talk to White?"

Tess didn't know why Jack would involve their sister in their investigation. Margo had made it clear she wanted nothing to do with the family business.

"First, she probably won't get in to see her before we get there," Jack said. "Second, we have an agreement— I share, she shares."

"I don't believe it."

"I trust her, Tess."

Tess wanted to trust Margo. Despite the mix of anger and sadness, she missed her sister—her best and closest friend. Although they had their fair share of arguments, they shared countless happy memories. Hundreds of family events. Their yearly spring camping trip to the Grand Canyon, the Fourth of July weekends at their grandparents' cabin in Pinetop. Weddings, funerals, births, celebrations. Double dates, soccer games, just hanging out at the coffee shop talking. When Tess went through a tough breakup with her first serious boyfriend,

Margo was the one who picked her up, dusted her off, and convinced her he wasn't worth her tears. While Tess was in college and Margo in the Army stationed in Texas, Margo flew to Tucson after she heard that Tess's boyfriend had cheated on her, breaking her heart. They had always been there for each other, until three years ago when everything fell apart.

Margo left, not you.

Tess didn't miss Margo's stubbornness, or her tendency to rush headfirst into situations without a plan. Yet, she also admired her bravery and her willingness to stand up for the underdog. Margo could be the most self-righteous, unforgiving person on the planet, but she was also kind, compassionate, fun, and brave.

"Trust me," Jack said when Tess wouldn't give him the answer he wanted.

"I do," she said, and meant it. If Jack could look past Margo's behavior for the last three years, Tess could at least try to do the same.

Logan Monroe, the male victim, exited the house with one of the firefighters. A team was going through checking the gas and AC unit to make sure there were no leaks. Officer Cameron was waiting for the detective and crime scene investigators to arrive.

"Mr. Monroe." Jack approached and she let her brother take the lead.

Tess may not have recognized Logan Monroe on sight, but she knew the name. Monroe was a self-made multimillionaire and had created several computer gaming companies, grew them, then sold them. He had his fingers in many pies, including partial ownership of a golf resort in Scottsdale that catered to the rich and richer. But his background was software—and Jennifer

White had a dual degree in computer science and math. There had been no hint that Monroe was unethical or stole company secrets, but he would be in a position to understand the value of what Jennifer had to offer.

And if it got out, it would damage his reputation. He was probably rich enough to withstand the hit, but it would still hurt.

Monroe eyed them with suspicion. Tess didn't blame him; he'd just been poisoned. But he hadn't called his lawyer or his wife, which Tess found suspect.

Jack held out his business card and said, "I'm Jack Angelhart. My agency was retained to track down a possible security breach at Desert West Financial. How do you know Jennifer White?"

A friendly, direct tone. Jack did a good job exuding authority without being overbearing, something Tess admired about her big brother.

Monroe looked from Jack to Tess. Suspicious, but with a good poker face. "The officer said I could go, but I need to lock up. You're not with law enforcement, so I'm asking you to leave."

"Of course," Jack said. "But if you could—"

"I'm not interested in talking to you, Mr. Angelhart. If you have any questions, please contact my attorney, but since you have no authority or jurisdiction, she won't have anything to say to you, either." Monroe handed Jack a card.

Carmen Delarosa, Attorney-at-Law.

Tess knew Carmen Delarosa. She knew most of the practicing lawyers in town after working for her mom and Aunt Rita for years before becoming a PI.

Jack didn't back down.

"I'll need to report to my client that you met with one of their employees."

Monroe frowned. "Mr. Angelhart, my reputation would be damaged without cause if you spread a rumor that I was doing anything unethical. I can assure you I wasn't."

"You can assure me, but I would still like to know how *you* are acquainted with Ms. White."

Monroe ran a hand through his dark blond hair. It was a bit on the long side and curled at his collar. It made him look young.

"Jennifer interned for me when she was in college. She asked me to meet her, said it was important and would explain when she saw me. I agreed."

"You make a habit of talking to interns in a short-term rental?"

"This is my house," he said. "She wanted to talk, and felt she was being followed. The house was available, so I reserved it for her through one of my companies for a few days. When Jennifer interned for me, she was hardworking, intelligent, and I gave her a recommendation for future employment. That's all I have to say."

"What did she want to talk about?"

"We didn't get that far. I need to contact my home-owners insurance and my lawyer. If you have further questions, call Carmen and she'll pass them on to me. I'll give her a heads-up so she doesn't put up roadblocks, fair enough?"

Jack nodded and watched Monroe walk away.

"He's lying."

Tess hadn't seen that. "He sounded genuine."

"Everything he said was the truth, except they were

in the house long enough for Jennifer to tell him something—or offer to give or sell him information or software. Maybe he said no, doesn't want rumors to fly; maybe he was considering it. But he didn't tell us the entire truth."

"Was the poisoning an accident or on purpose?" Tess wondered out loud.

"Too coincidental to be an accident," Jack said. When he saw Officer Cameron, he called out, "Hey, Cam, let me know what the lab rats come up with?"

"I'll see what I can do," Cameron said.

Jack and Tess walked back to their car. "Now are we going to the hospital?" she asked.

"Should be just in time to talk to White."

Tess laughed. "Really? You think Margo can't talk, bribe, or sneak her way in?"

Jack hesitated. "Maybe. But nurses can be pit bulls when it comes to protecting their patients."

"Twenty bucks says she gets in."

"No way I'm taking that bet."

Nine

Margo Angelhart

I'd practically grown up in hospitals.

My dad was a VA doctor most of his career, so I'd visited him often, did school reports on different aspects of the hospital and had access to many people in different capacities. My favorite report was in eighth-grade science when I wrote an essay about how X-rays worked. Maybe it fascinated me because I'd already broken three bones before I turned thirteen.

And then there was Nico. My younger brother had some serious health problems as a kid that took years to diagnose as a rare but treatable bone cancer. Tess, Jack, and I took turns keeping him company when he had to go in for tests, some that required overnight stays. I usually volunteered because I have a soft spot for Nico. He's funny and sweet and sarcastic and kind without a mean bone in his body, though sometimes his wit was a bit too sharp and not everyone appreciated his dry sense of humor. To this day, some people never knew when Nico was being sarcastic or serious.

So between dad and Nico, I knew my way around hospitals. What staff did, how they managed floors, routines, rules, and schedules. Getting information about a patient you weren't related to was next to impossible, but *visiting* a patient—even in the emergency room—was a piece of cake.

At least for me.

The first part was understanding the routine of a particular emergency room. Jennifer White had been taken to Abrazo, only a few miles north on Highway 51. The paramedics would bring her in through the emergency room, and she would bypass anyone waiting in the lobby. They'd hook her up to machines, check her vitals again, draw blood, inspect her for external signs of distress or injuries. This time of day—early Sunday evening—wasn't generally busy. With the increase in urgent care sites all over the valley, emergency rooms mostly saw the seriously injured or those experiencing a major health event like a heart attack.

It would take the triage nurse fifteen to thirty minutes to process Jennifer, and depending on how busy they were, the doctor or PA might overlap. The best time to sneak in was after the initial exam while they awaited test results.

That was the one thing that still bugged me: what had they been poisoned with? Logan Monroe wasn't faking. Though he recovered quicker than White, his eyes had been unfocused and he appeared genuinely confused when he first regained consciousness. Still, I'd been fooled once by a bounty I nabbed before he crossed the border into Mexico. I'd Tasered him, took him down, pleased with myself that I'd found the bastard who'd molested little boys and bolted before his court date.

Then he faked a heart attack and it seemed so real that I called for an ambulance and took the cuffs off.

Then he hit me.

I used my Taser on him (again), took him down (again, harder), but still remembered how my jaw had smarted almost as much as my ego.

So yes, Logan Monroe could have been faking. But I didn't think so and I trusted my instincts, bounty mishap notwithstanding.

Angelhart Investigations had been hired to look into Jennifer White for possible corporate espionage. No way would my mother take an adultery case—she considered it beneath them.

Well, Mom, some of us have bills to pay and can't afford to pick and choose.

Jack and Tess worked full-time for Angelhart Investigations; Lulu worked part-time. Nico, like me, had kept his old gig—he worked at the Phoenix PD crime lab. I'd been a private investigator since a year after I parted with the Army—eight years this fall. I was supposed to join Angelhart Investigations. I'd helped my mom plan, organize, set up the office and the business. Then she stabbed me in the back. My own mother.

Dammit, I didn't want to think about all that. Jack and Tess would be here soon enough, and I needed information before they arrived. I'd share because I'd promised Jack, but I wanted the upper hand.

I tossed my backpack over my shoulder. My just-in-case bag with extra supplies like water, energy bars, phone charger, cash, Taser, personal items.

Just in case I broke down by the side of the road in 110 degree heat…

Just in case I couldn't make it home for the night and desperately needed to brush my teeth…

Just in case I needed a prop to bypass hospital dictators…

I entered the emergency room and immediately assessed the situation. Nearly empty. Three people waiting to be seen. A nurse in the triage area taking an elderly man's blood pressure. Another nurse filling out paperwork. The intake clerk sat behind a glass window.

Through double doors were the emergency bays, each separated by privacy curtains. They weren't visible from the lobby. To the right of the bays, a hallway led to additional rooms, the surgery center, offices.

Jennifer White would be in an emergency bay.

The intake clerk was likely the most dictatorial in the room. She made the trains run on time, made sure insurance papers were in order, was the first line of triage. She also knew occupancy, staffing levels, and resource availability. She wouldn't just let me walk in.

But the nurse doing paperwork at her small cubicle? That was the one.

I smiled warmly as I approached her desk. "Hi, I'm Margo. My roommate texted me from an ambulance. She was in some sort of accident—Jennifer White? She asked me to bring her a few things. I rushed over— can I just go back and give this to her?" I held up my backpack.

The nurse smiled kindly. "I just processed Ms. White's paperwork. I think the doctor is with her right now. Let me check for you. Feel free to have a seat."

"Thank you." I sat down in the chair closest to the nurse so I could eavesdrop.

The nurse picked up the phone. "Hi, Don, it's Cindy.

I have Jennifer White's roommate here with personal items. Is Dr. Patin still with her?"

Silence for a moment, then, "Okay, thanks."

I pretended to read my phone. Cindy said, "Ma'am? She's having bloodwork done, so it'll be ten, fifteen minutes."

"Thanks so much."

Bloodwork did not take fifteen minutes. They'd bring the phlebotomist to her. Five minutes, tops. I set the time on my phone. When it vibrated, I got up, paced, looked out the window at the parking lot. Sat down in a different chair—one where Cindy couldn't see me, but where I could hear her. As soon as Cindy got a call, I stood, poked my head around the corner, held up my phone. "Hey, Jennifer just texted me—I'm going to walk this back, okay? Oh, sorry," I said, pretending I had no idea she was on the phone.

Cindy waved me toward the bay doors and continued her conversation.

Piece of cake.

Discreetly, I looked into each of the bays to find Jennifer.

The first bay was empty. The second had a mom and a little kid who was crying as a doctor examined an arm that was clearly broken. Ouch. Been there, done that. Third bay was empty, but the bed was rumpled—someone had recently been here. Fourth and last bay had an elderly woman on monitors.

I rechecked the third bay, picked up the chart at the end of the bed.

White, Jennifer.

Maybe she was in the bathroom.

Except that her messenger bag wasn't here.

An orderly walked by pushing a gurney. "Hey, sir," I said, "my friend was brought in by ambulance, and the nurse said she's supposed to be here." I pointed to the bed.

"She may have gone for tests."

"Can you check for me? Please? I'm really worried about her."

"Name?"

"Jennifer White."

"One sec."

It took more than a second. When the orderly came back, he said, "She must have been assigned a room, but it's not in the system yet."

Her chart was still here; if she had been assigned a room, the chart would have gone with her.

She had bolted.

I thanked him, then walked out and spotted Jack and Tess in the lobby talking to the intake clerk. I caught Tess's eye and motioned for them to follow me outside.

"She ran," I said when they exited.

"She was in no condition," Jack said. "I talked to the paramedics, who said she was still pretty out of it when they arrived."

"Maybe then, but now she's gone. Could have exaggerated her symptoms. Logan Monroe was confused and queasy for about five, ten minutes after he came around, then he was talking and walking just fine. She could have milked it to get out of the house, away from us, so she could disappear."

"Why?" Jack asked.

"I should be asking you that," I said. "I thought you wanted a *partnership*."

"You haven't agreed."

"We already know what you're doing," Tess interjected. "You're trying to prove Monroe is cheating on his wife. Jennifer isn't married, he is. End of story."

I shrugged. "I'll find out what's going on, you know that."

Silence.

"Fine," I said and opened the Jeep door. "Do it your way. I'll do it mine." I got into the driver's seat.

Jack walked over, stopped me from closing the door. "Don't go."

"You want my information, but you don't want to share. I have my own contacts, my own resources, I don't need you."

"Okay, I'll tell you," he said.

Tess didn't argue with him, but she didn't look happy about it.

"Something is going on with Monroe and White. It might not be an affair, and it might not be corporate espionage," Jack said.

"How did you track her to Monroe's house?"

"She had a confirmation of the rental," he said, "but it was under a business name, not her name, sent to her email."

"Monroe owns the house, but it's in the name of one of his LLCs," I said.

"Yeah, I learned that today."

I wanted to ask why they didn't check property ownership before jumping to conclusions, but I didn't. Not my place.

"Money laundering?" Tess offered, then shook her head. "No, that's small potatoes. And how did someone know they would be there and why kill them?"

"No one tried to kill them," I said, my thoughts running in a completely different direction. "Whatever they were dosed with knocked them out, that's it. But I think I have more information than you."

"Right," Tess said. "In an hour, you learned so much."

"Drop the fucking attitude," I snapped. "I've been doing this a hell of a lot longer than you, Tess."

Jack put his hands up, one palm toward Tess, one toward me. "Truce. What do you know?"

I almost walked away, but knew that my anger was about everything that happened three years ago. I didn't know if I'd ever come to peace with it.

Yet, I'd promised Jack, and my word meant something. Besides, I'd been skeptical about the whole affair angle after tracking Monroe for the last ten days and finding zero proof of infidelity.

"Logan Monroe originally founded Desert West Financial with Gavin O'Keefe. Together they'd started several businesses over the years, built them up, sold them off. This time he sold his half to O'Keefe and walked away."

From the look on her face, Tess was in shock. I smiled, added a bit of snark, "Researching your target is good, but researching who you work for? Better." I turned the ignition and was about to close the door but Jack put his hand between the door and the frame of the Jeep.

"Come to the office."

"No."

"Please. We'll share everything, you share everything, and maybe between the three of us we'll figure out what the hell is going on."

I didn't want to. This felt like Jack's way of sucking me into the family business. Every few months, he'd try to sell me on the benefits of Angelhart Investigations.

I'd happily drink the free beer and listen and then tell him no, not interested.

But this was a puzzle, and I loved puzzles. Why had Jennifer White disappeared from the hospital? What was she up to? What did Monroe have to do with it?

You were hired to prove whether Logan Monroe was having an affair. He's not. Case closed.

"Tomorrow morning," I said. "If I help you, I'm billing you."

"We don't need your help," Tess said.

"I don't really care. I have plenty of work." *Not.*

"Tomorrow morning," Jack repeated. "Eight."

I looked at my brother. God, I loved him. He was a true big brother in all the best ways. Sure, he loved to tease us and he could be downright mean when Tess and I hogged the bathroom in high school. But he defended everyone in the family without question. He was the first to help in a crisis. Jack was the most honorable person I knew. Loyal. Honest.

"I'll be there."

As soon as Jack moved his hand, I closed the door and backed out.

Ten

The Thief

The thief remained in hiding for more than an hour after he heard no more voices.

What the *fuck*?

He'd waited a few minutes after Jennifer entered. Then he put on an oxygen mask and released the nitrogen via remote. There'd been a chance it would kill her, but at this point he didn't care. He was so angry that she'd gotten into his business that it served her right. But at a minimum, it would knock her out long enough that he could wipe her laptop and disappear before she woke up.

Then he heard voices. He strained to listen, but he couldn't make out the male voice. Mostly, Jennifer was doing the talking. Was she telling someone what she'd found? Who?

Then he heard, "Jennifer? Are you okay?"

A minute later, silence. He waited a few more minutes just to be on the safe side.

Okay, just a small hiccup, he'd thought, and was

about to leave his hiding spot when he heard someone come in through the front door. A woman, on the phone with emergency services. He was stuck. If he left the room, she'd see him.

Then, chaos. He was stuck in a bedroom. Fearing discovery, he crawled under the bed and waited. He heard paramedics and a few minutes later, the police. Lots of people in and out of the house. Someone opened the door, looked around the room. By the person's durable black boots, it was a cop. They walked out, but left the door open. Now he was really trapped under the bed!

The thief hadn't left any trace of himself, but if he didn't retrieve the nitrogen canisters from the vents, someone would find them. While they couldn't be traced back to him—and he'd used gloves when handling them—he didn't want to leave them behind. Now he might not have a choice.

He waited. No voices for a long time, and he was about to come out when he heard a very familiar voice. A lone man, on the phone.

"I need you to contact my homeowners insurance, and take down the house listing until we know what happened… The police are investigating, and the crime scene team will be here but I don't know when… No, I don't know if it was an accident… I don't have to stay. They left an officer out front. I gave him the garage code… Okay, thanks. I'm heading home."

That voice. He knew the voice.

The man started talking again. "Jennifer, it's Logan. How are you feeling? Call me when you get this message. We need to talk."

Logan. Logan Monroe.

Out of all the people in the world Jennifer White

could reach out to about what she found, it had to be Logan Monroe.

The thief waited. He heard the door close. The cops were outside.

He had to get out before the crime scene investigators arrived.

He counted to two hundred very, very slow. Then he eased himself out. There was no way he could remove the canisters from the vents—they were too heavy. He'd had to make three trips into the house, and that was when he had his car in the garage. But he'd moved his car down the street after unloading his supplies, so he was stuck.

He left out the back, jumped the fence, and walked through the preserve until he reached the trailhead where he had parked his car. He drove straight to Jennifer White's condo, fear and anger fueling him.

He might have to take a bolder action.

But she wasn't there.

Eleven

Peter Carillo

Peter Carillo would have been home hours ago except for the fatal wreck on the 303 where he was assigned to divert traffic until someone relieved him.

Annie wasn't returning his calls or text messages. He was livid. She damn well knew to respond to him when he tried to reach her. He wanted to know where she went this morning. The garage door opened at seven thirty-two in the morning and she had returned at eight-o-eight. Where was she for thirty-six minutes? He checked his Ring camera; no one had come to the door, but it only showed him the front door and street. Their garage was on the side of the house.

He ordered a camera for the garage door from his phone. It would be delivered tomorrow morning. He had Mondays and Tuesdays off and would install it immediately because this deception was unacceptable.

She could have run to the grocery store. When he checked her location at 8:30 a.m., she was home. And she hadn't left again all day. But not answering her phone?

He had a bad feeling that something was up. Annie had been acting…off. There was no other way he could explain it. She hadn't complained about anything for weeks. That was unlike her. As if she felt guilty about something she'd done. In fact, she hadn't even complained about morning sex in weeks.

Peter loved morning sex. There was nothing better than waking up with a hard-on and sliding it into his wife. She used to complain that she wasn't ready, that it hurt, that he came too fast—that earned her a slap. But it wasn't fun for either of them if she was dry, so he bought a tub of lubricant. His favorite thing first thing in the morning was waking Annie by sliding two lubed fingers deep inside her, prepping her for him, then pushing his hard cock into her while she was still half asleep. Half the time he came on the first or second thrust, so he would stay on top of her until he grew hard again, and they would make love. That second time, she was always into it. Peter recognized that women needed more attention to achieve orgasm, and he was willing to give that to her.

She tried to fake it once. He could tell; she made all the right sounds and motions, but it was too quick, too loud, very unlike her. He knew her body well; he knew the quiver she had when she was close. He'd told her if she faked it, that meant he wasn't doing his job. He would rather her not orgasm than pretend, which was insulting and humiliating, as if she were a prostitute. She apologized sufficiently and said she had just wanted to make him happy.

He hated his fucking job. He had applied to Phoenix PD years ago, but they'd had a hiring freeze and the only law enforcement position he could get was in

DPS. Being a state trooper was boring, and every other cop out there treated them like shit. The one thing that got him through the day was sex in the morning, and he would not be denied that pleasure because it was inconvenient or uncomfortable for Annie. He provided for the family; she would provide for *him*.

Had she been flirting again? Last time he caught her flirting with a waiter, he'd made it clear that such behavior was unacceptable. Or maybe… Oh, God… Was she having an *affair*? Was she screwing someone behind his back? If she spread her legs for another man, he would kill her.

No, he couldn't kill her. He loved Annie. He'd fallen in love with her the minute he saw her working at Starbucks when he came in one morning before his shift. She'd been nineteen, a part-time student, sweet, beautiful. He had treated her like the angel she was, courted her, proposed six months later. She had given him two beautiful, perfect children. She kept an immaculate house. She was pretty and compliant and a perfect hostess. He wouldn't kill her.

But he could make her wish she were dead.

She was already going to be in serious trouble for avoiding his calls.

As he pulled up to the house, he considered the last time she avoided his calls. She had broken the heirloom vase that his mother had given them for their wedding and knew he'd be upset. She claimed it was an accident, but he doubted that. She had been angry with him because he told her no more book club. The women were trash, mostly divorced single moms who probably made her feel like she'd be happier if she left him.

He made sure she understood that if she *ever* left

him, he would make sure she never saw the children again.

Her car was in its slot in the garage and he breathed easier. Okay, she was home. Probably punishing him because he'd made her give him head this morning. Annie knew he expected her to be in bed when he woke up on work days. If the baby woke up, she knew to be back in bed before his alarm went off. Annie damn well knew that he was happier after sex, and having to search for her in the house—she'd been in the kitchen claiming she couldn't sleep and wanted to bake muffins—had irritated him. So he made her get down on her knees on the tile floor and use her mouth until he came, and he made her swallow because he knew she hated it. Then he grabbed her by the arm and hauled her upstairs, threw her face first onto the bed, and took her from behind. "If you're going to act like a bitch, I'll treat you like a bitch."

Well, if this petty ignoring him is how she reacted, she'd be on her knees servicing him until she learned.

With a spring to his step—because remembering this morning made him horny for his wife—he walked inside through the kitchen door. "I'm home!" he called out. His favorite part of coming home was when PJ ran to him with a big "Daaaaddddyyyy!"

Silence.

"Annie?" he called.

He didn't smell dinner cooking. He didn't hear the children playing. Just…silence.

For the first time, he thought that something was wrong. That Annie was hurt, that the kids were hurt. His heart raced as he ran through the house, up the stairs, looked in the kids' rooms, the master bedroom, the bathrooms.

No one was home.

Her car was here, but she wasn't.

For a second, he thought maybe they were at the park.

He picked up her phone that was charging on the nightstand.

27 unread text messages from his number.

8 missed calls from his number.

2 voice mails.

One unread text message from a familiar number. Why wasn't Natalie Nichols's name in Annie's contacts?

Why wasn't *his* name showing on the screen?

He slid open the phone and expected to type in her passcode, but there was no passcode. His heart beat hard against his chest as he read the message from Natalie.

Missed you at the craft fair today! We sold all of our flavored oils and nearly all the garlic vinegar. Brian is super happy my idea for a second income didn't make us broke! LOL. Call me.

Brian Nichols and Peter had been troopers together for eight years, went through the academy together, became friends. Brian had been his best man five years ago, and last year married Natalie. Peter didn't particularly like the woman—too independent and too bossy—but Brian was a friend, so Peter allowed Annie to socialize with them.

Clearly, Annie was planning to go to the craft fair—though she hadn't told him about it.

But she didn't go, and her car was here, yet she and the kids were gone.

He looked around the bedroom and then he saw it. Annie's wedding ring, on the dresser, next to her jewelry box. He stared and, as if in a trance, walked over and picked it up. He didn't know how long he stood there staring at the golden circle, their names and wedding date engraved inside the band.

Annie, what have you done?

He put the ring down where he'd found it and went back downstairs. Checked the garage. The stroller was still there—she hadn't taken them to the park down the street. Her luggage was still there.

Where the *fuck* was his family?

Annie was going to pay for this. For making him scared. For making him angry. For leaving her ring behind.

He went back inside and almost called Brian— maybe Natalie came over and took Annie and the kids to her place—when he saw an envelope clipped to the refrigerator. His name written in Annie's perfect penmanship.

He grabbed it, ripped it open.

Peter:
You hurt me one time too many. I've left with the children. You will never see us again.
Annie

On the verge of hyperventilating, he pulled her phone from his pocket and looked through it, hoping to find answers as to where she was. There was nothing. She'd restored it to factory settings and only the messages that came in after eight-o-six this morning were on the phone. Every app she'd had was gone—her email, Facebook, photos, all gone.

He would find her. She couldn't hide from him.

She had taken his kids. She couldn't do that.

His wife. His kids. His life.

"Fucking *bitch*!"

Peter would find her, take his kids back, and then he would kill her.

But he had to think, be smart about it. Someone must have helped Annie. She didn't have the money, the brains, or the courage to do something so despicable.

Find that person, and he would find Annie.

Twelve

Jack Angelhart

Most of Jack's core memories growing up had centered around Sunday dinner. Between their parents careers and the busy lives of five kids—sports, theater, band, community service—regular weekday dinners were nearly impossible to coordinate. Sunday was the day for family. When they were younger they often went hiking after church, or to baseball games—especially during spring training—or took a day trip to Sedona or watched a movie they all wanted to see. As adults, they met at the house for Sunday dinner.

But when Cooper Angelhart went to prison after confessing to killing a colleague, their family night had virtually disappeared. Jack suspected it had more to do with Margo walking away—having Dad gone was bad enough, but with the family divided, dinner reminded them of loss, and the good memories faded away. Jack's marriage had fallen apart and he only saw his son every other weekend. Luisa, then still in the Marines, was stationed in Hawaii. Their dad was in prison, and Margo stopped showing up. Someone was always missing and that hole was felt by all.

Sunday was also the day that their mother drove two hours roundtrip to Eyman Prison in Florence to spend four hours with her husband.

So when Jack walked into the house just after six, Ava Angelhart wasn't cooking—she was sitting outside on the shaded patio drinking a glass of white wine and reading a book about the fentanyl crisis.

She looked surprised to see Jack.

"Hi, Mom," he said when he walked through the back door and took a seat next to her.

His mother had turned fifty-nine last month. She had never seemed old to Jack, not until his father had gone to prison. Now, the fine wrinkles that had framed her eyes and lips were deeper, her makeup more carefully applied, her hair cut and styled short, dyed lighter than her natural brown in order to better hide the gray. She was five foot four, but had perfect posture and always seemed taller.

"Jack." She smiled, but there was sadness in her eyes. The sadness was always there, but Sundays it was on the surface.

Jack had admired both his parents, but it was his mother's steadfast pursuit of justice—first as a prosecutor and elected county attorney, then as a private practice lawyer, now running the family PI firm—that had driven him the most. She was the reason he became a cop, the reason he'd done the job right. He believed in the system—though what happened to his dad three years ago had definitely shaken him. It had shaken all of them.

He leaned over and kissed her cheek, then sat in the chair next to the lounge she relaxed in.

"Have you had dinner?" she asked.

"I'm heading to the gym, then I'll get something."

"I have Rita's albondigas soup and I was going to make grilled cheese."

She said it hopefully and Jack didn't have the heart to decline.

"I'll come back after the gym, but fair warning— I'll be starving."

"I have plenty. Is seven thirty good?"

"Perfect. Thanks."

Jack knew that his mother missed family dinners as much as he did, as much as everyone. Maybe, if he handled the situation right, this case would bring Margo back—to the business and the family. They could reclaim Sunday dinners and find what they'd lost three years ago.

"I wanted to give you a heads-up that Margo is coming to the office tomorrow morning."

Ava marked her place with a bookmark and put the book on the table next to her. She didn't say a word. He knew his mom well, but times like this he couldn't read her.

"It's about the Desert West case," he said. "We traced Jennifer White to the short-term rental and she met with a man there."

"A buyer?"

"Doubtful. Logan Monroe."

Her brows lifted in surprise. "The entrepreneur?" She sounded impressed.

He nodded. "They were only in the house for a short time before Margo showed up. She was hired by Monroe's wife and had been thinking sex, not corporate espionage."

"Oh. It would explain a lot if she was having an affair with Monroe. Though why would he want Desert West's proprietary information? A rivalry?"

"According to Margo, Monroe cofounded Desert West and sold his half of the company to his former partner last year. But that's not even the big news." He told her everything they knew from the time Margo found Monroe and White unconscious to how White slipped away from the hospital. "White's vehicle is still at the rental house, so Tess is sitting on the place."

Ava smiled. They both knew how much Tess detested stakeouts. "How long will she stay there?"

"I'm taking over at nine. I don't know how long I'll stay, but my gut tells me she'll return after dark to retrieve her car, if she returns at all. She may have been spooked by today's events."

"And what does this have to do with Margo? Other than she is tangentially involved."

"Margo identified two unknown men watching the house from the preserve. She pursued, got photos of them, their vehicle. She shared them with us, and I asked Luisa to enhance them. Margo thinks she recognized one of the men, but we need to confirm."

"Margo is *cooperating*?"

She sounded like she didn't believe him, though Jack shouldn't be surprised. Ava had once said she and Margo were oil and water; that was wrong, though Jack wouldn't contradict his mother. Most of the conflict between his mom and Margo stemmed from the fact that they were too much alike: stubborn, smart, driven women who always thought they were right. They usually were. So when they disagreed on something, it was explosive.

"I asked her to work with us on this case. She agreed to let me chat with Monroe."

"She couldn't very well do it since his wife is her client."

"And," Jack said, ignoring the snide undertone of his mother's comment, "Monroe claimed that White called him, asked to meet in a private location to share something with him. He claims he doesn't know what specifically, that they passed out before she could show him whatever it was."

"Do you believe him?"

"No."

"Buying information?"

"I couldn't say."

"And Margo agreed to assist?"

"She's thinking on it. I asked her to come to the office at eight. She'll be there."

"We have to tell the CFO about this meeting," Ava said. "Mr. Monroe is familiar with their industry, understands their business, would benefit from inside secrets."

"Except," Jack said, slightly uncomfortable, "I don't see why he would be involved with corporate espionage at a company he probably knows more about than anyone else."

"Did you confirm Margo's information?"

"I have no reason to doubt her."

"Margo bends the rules. She's probably correct, but we need to verify. And just because he used to own the company doesn't mean that he isn't still involved." She thought a moment. "Though, it seems unlikely."

"I want Margo back," he said.

His mom looked sad, defeated. "She never worked for us, Jack."

"And you know why."

At the beginning, the idea for Angelhart Investigations had come from Jack and Margo, and they convinced Ava. It didn't take much—Ava had been burnt out as a lawyer, and private investigation was a natural career shift. Plus, since she was still a licensed attorney, she could take legal cases when she wanted.

Margo had the vision. She'd built her own small successful one-woman practice, but having a staff to handle research and background checks would free her up to be in the field more, to pass off the detail work to Tess who thrived on research. They planned to open the doors as equal partners—the four of them—Ava, Jack, Tess, and Margo.

But Margo assumed their first case would be investigating the death of Dr. Devin Klein, who their father had confessed to murdering. Ava said no.

Your father sacrificed himself for this family, and while I hate with all my heart and soul that he's in prison, his life—all of our lives—would have been at risk if he went to trial. At your father's request, we are not touching anything surrounding Klein's murder.

At the beginning, Jack had agreed with Margo— and he had been just as frustrated that their mother refused to explain the risk to the family. They would have taken any risk to clear their father's name and bring him home.

Ava wouldn't budge and that's when Jack realized that there was something more at stake. Though neither of his parents explained, they wouldn't have asked them to stand down if it weren't important. Jack didn't like it, but he could live with it. He'd always been a dutiful son.

Margo felt betrayed, that it was her against everyone. She refused to join Angelhart Investigations and their mother let her walk.

Though Ava had never said, Jack suspected his mother thought Margo would return in a few months. When she didn't, Ava continued to dig in her heels and Margo grew more distant from the family. Over time, Jack realized that they had taken business from Margo. Because of Ava's reputation, some of the lawyers who had once hired Margo, now hired them. Not because Margo wasn't capable, but because with Angelhart Investigations they had a team of licensed private investigators, a dedicated research staff, access to experts and legal consultants.

"I would love for Margo to join our business. She is a smart, shrewd investigator," Ava said. "But she would never agree to all of my terms."

"Which are?"

"I'm sure she'll avoid the unpleasant, scandalous cases—she detests adultery investigations as much as I do. And I could probably overlook her rule bending. But she'll never stop looking into Klein's death. She lied to me, Jack. Three weeks ago she told me to my face that she hadn't interviewed Klein's former intern. She's putting a target on her back, and it terrifies me that she's going to get hurt."

"Maybe Margo will surprise you."

Ava drained her wine. "I know your sister, Jack. Better than she thinks I do. It pains me every day that Cooper is in prison. But it would kill me if I have to bury my daughter."

Thirteen

Margo Angelhart

I didn't want to meet with Brittney tonight, but the woman gave me no choice, claiming she couldn't talk on the phone. So at nine Sunday night, I drove to Beverly's in Scottsdale. From the outside, the bar looked like any other popular hangout in old town Scottsdale. Patio seating—which would have been fine tonight because temperatures dropped after the sun went down and it was a comfortable seventy-five degrees. A yellow vault door led inside where upbeat jazzy rock played under the hum of multiple conversations.

It would be a great place to hang out with friends, if I were in a social mood—worn brick walls filled with books and heavy decorative knickknacks. A dark speakeasy vibe. Classy table lighting and deep red, curving leather seats arranged along the dark walls for private conversations, but plenty of high-top tables were scattered around to stand at or sit on stools. Lots of nooks and crannies to people watch or have a semi-quiet conversation. They even had a basement, though you needed reservations most of the time to get a table down there. Yeah, I would have loved it except for two things: the price of the drinks (nowhere in my world would I pay eighteen bucks for a drink; call me cheap,) and it was known as a place to be seen.

Why Brittney wanted to be seen in public with her hired PI made no sense to me. But I'd taken her retainer, and liking my client wasn't a requirement for presenting a report. If Brittney wanted the report verbally and in public, that was her call.

Brittney had a table reserved downstairs, but "Mrs. Monroe hasn't arrived yet." The hostess, in a black blouse and matching pencil skirt that skimmed her knees, offered to escort me, but I preferred to wait at the bar—a large raised platform in the center of the joint. The wood was sleek and polished; spotless wine, martini, and cocktail glasses in an assortment of sizes hung upside down from racks. Two bartenders—one male, one female, each wearing black slacks and black T-shirts with the gold Beverly's logo—moved smoothly as they prepared drinks. One barkeep immediately came over and asked what I wanted.

I'd never acquired the taste for whiskey or vodka or even wine. But beer? Loved it. Especially microbrews. Beverly's had one of my favorite local breweries featured, so I ordered the Church Music IPA. I'd expense the drink, plus a very nice tip. I'd been a bartender for nearly two years after I left the Army while building my PI business. It could be a great job, but you also dealt with a lot of shitheads, so tipping well was a must in my book. It would take a majorly rude server and multiple mistakes to get zip from me.

I paid for my beer and kept an eye out for Brittney,

while also being an observant detective and checking out my surroundings. If there weren't so many people trying hard to be noticed, I might have enjoyed the atmosphere. Maybe I'd come back on a slower night. Early in the evening, middle of the week.

I did a double-take when I saw my brother Nico and his boyfriend, FBI Agent Quincy Truman, walk into the bar. They looked around and Nico waved to a small group in one corner. Quincy saw me before my brother did.

I'd love to have a beer with Nico; unfortunately, I detested Quincy. There were many reasons for my distaste, but primarily he was an arrogant, mightier-than-thou, authoritarian federal prick.

To be fair, Quincy wasn't a jerk to Nico. Otherwise, I would have been far more vocal in my dislike of the man.

Quincy whispered something to Nico, who turned and saw me at the bar. He lit up and I smiled. Nico was like that—he always made me smile. The family mediator, the glue that kept us from taking swipes at each other when we were forced together over the last three years.

Quincy went over to the group they clearly knew, but Nico came to me, arms outstretched for a hug. "I wouldn't expect to see you here," he said. "I love this place, but it doesn't seem to be your vibe. Too crowded, too expensive."

Nico knew me well. "Meeting a client. And I've been here a couple of times."

"Voluntarily?"

I laughed. "Hardly. It's not a bad place. Just too many pretty people who spend more time documenting their drinks and eats with their phones than enjoying the company."

Nico slowly surveyed the room, nodded his agreement. "You want to join us?" He motioned to the table of his friends. "It's not going to be a late night. Work tomorrow. But Quincy has had a rough week and needed to get out for some fun. And you'd like these people, I promise."

"Probably."

I didn't want to know about Quincy's rough week, so I didn't ask.

"You canceled dinner with us twice."

"Don't start."

"I know you guys got off on the wrong foot, but—"

I cut him off. "He expects me to apologize for doing my job. *Never.* And I know he's not going to apologize for doing his—even when he tried to have me arrested for no valid reason. Just look at him over there—glaring at me."

"He's not," Nico said, but I caught him glancing to make sure. Quincy was watching us. Maybe not *glaring*, but I could read between the eyes.

"Thanks, by the way," I changed the subject.

"For?"

"Bringing on Theo as an intern this summer."

"No need to thank me. It's part of the program."

"Yeah, but I know most interns don't get to choose which department they work in. I'm glad he's learning from you."

"You've done a great job with him. He's kept his nose clean for two years, taking the right classes, putting in time and effort. He's a smart kid."

"A smart ass," I muttered.

Nico laughed. "So are you, sis. Now, about dinner—"

"Quincy is about to come over and rescue you, and I'm not in the mood to be nice, so go."

"Margo—"

"I'll be at Pop and Abuela's party next weekend, on my best behavior, okay? And as long as you're happy with the arrogant fed, I'll bite my tongue until it bleeds."

Nico shook his head, then kissed me. "Love you, sis."

"Love you more, brat."

Nico walked back to his table.

I'd known Quincy Truman for years, had butted up against him several times when the FBI overstepped and I'd been hired by a defense lawyer to review discovery evidence as well as corroborate witness statements. Twice I'd found witnesses that helped the defense— witnesses that the FBI hadn't even bothered talking to.

I didn't like working for defense lawyers—most of the people who hired them deserved to do time. But some people were innocent. Some needed a fighting chance. I *really* didn't like when the government went after people who couldn't afford to fight back. Sometimes, innocent people got railroaded because they had no one to help them navigate the process. A fair playing field was necessary: if the defendant was guilty, throw him in jail. I had no tears for them. If the defendant was innocent, he shouldn't have to pay tens of thousands of dollars to prove it. And when the feds stacked the deck against someone? I would knock that house of cards to the ground every chance I got.

Nico and Quincy had met through mutual friends and hit it off—Nico didn't know that Quincy was the asshole fed that I often complained about. Probably because I used the nickname Not-So-Special Agent Dickhead. I'd hoped that once Nico knew about all the times

Quincy Truman screwed with me, he'd break it off...
but he didn't. And he made it clear that if I couldn't say
anything nice, zip it.

No way would I lose my brother over anyone, especially his boyfriend.

Five minutes later, Brittney walked in—I'd been ten
minutes early; Brittney was fifteen minutes late. She
stopped in the middle of the bar, standing out in a bright
white sundress with black piping. She smiled, chatted
with people, but either didn't see me or ignored me.

I ordered a second beer and took my drink downstairs to where Brittney's table was reserved.

It took her ten minutes to make her way down the
stairs.

"Whew! I thought I would never make it through
the crowd," she said with a half smile and fake laugh.
Everything about this woman was fake. I really, really
didn't like her.

But her retainer check cleared, so that was a plus.

Almost immediately, a cocktail waitress came over
and took Brittney's order. After the woman returned
with a mojito, Brittney said, "Can I see the pictures?"

"I told you on the phone that your husband was not
in a compromising position."

"So you didn't take *any* pictures? How do I know
you're telling me the truth? Logan could have paid you
off."

That angered me. "You hired me. We have a contract." I took a folder from my bag and slid it across the
small table. "This is my report. Every place your husband went for the last ten days. I have not caught him
in a compromising position."

"But he *did* meet with another woman today!" Brittney

flipped to the last page, read the paragraph under today's date. "Jennifer White? That's the woman he's sleeping with?"

As calm as possible, I said, "They were fully clothed and appeared to be having a business meeting."

"At the house he lived in before we married. *Right*."

"Have you spoken to your husband at all today?"

"Yes. We had a bite to eat at home, then he said he had calls to make and I left him in his home office."

It was interesting that Logan Monroe hadn't told his wife he had been rendered unconscious by a yet-unknown substance. But it wasn't relevant to why Brittney had hired me, so I didn't put those details into the report.

"Who has a business meeting at an empty house?" Brittney demanded. She read the paragraph again. "They were inside for thirty minutes? Then they left? Together or separate?"

"Separate," Margo said truthfully. "When I ID'd the woman, I learned that she had been an intern for Mr. Monroe at one of his companies a few years ago."

"Why were they meeting?"

"They were looking at content on a laptop that Ms. White brought to the meeting, but I couldn't see specifically what they were looking at."

Brittney didn't say anything for a long minute. She sipped her drink and frowned at the report.

"I want pictures."

"There are no pictures of your husband in a compromising position with anyone, man or woman."

"Keep following him."

"I've been tailing him for ten days. When he's not at home, I know where he is, who he's with, what he's doing. I've caught dozens of cheating spouses, and it's never taken me longer than a couple days to prove it. If he is having an affair, he hasn't been physically involved with her since you hired me."

"You can't quit."

I can do whatever the fuck I please.

But I didn't say it.

Brittney read the report again, this time in greater detail.

"This doesn't make any sense," Brittney said after a few minutes. She slid the report back toward Margo.

"What specifically?"

"Logan has changed. Longer hours, not at his office when he says, being aloof. I hired you because the only reason I could come up with is that he's having an affair. Period."

"When was the first time you had the thought that your husband had changed."

I knew about the not-where-he-says-he-is part, but maybe I needed to go back further.

She shrugged. "I don't know."

"Think. There must be a specific moment, something he said or did that had you suspicious."

Because it's neither normal nor healthy for people in a serious relationship to track each other.

I thought of Annie Carillo. The obsessive need of her husband to know where she was every minute of the day.

"Well," Brittney said after sipping her mojito, "I think it would have to be in February. We were out with friends, and they asked what our summer plans were. I mean, who stays *here* when it's a thousand degrees?"

Only millions of people…

"And Logan said we don't have plans. Not *we're thinking about it*, not *we haven't decided*, but he actually said we're staying in Scottsdale *all summer*."

"Did you ask him about it?"

"Of course! He was vague. Said he didn't want to leave, he had a new business venture, and he wanted to be on-site during the renovations for the resort. That's why you hire a general manager, so you *don't* have to do the day-to-day nonsense."

Or maybe he wanted to be on-site because he took pride in a multimillion-dollar renovation project.

"Maybe it was the truth," I suggested.

"He can do business *anywhere*. I told him I didn't want to stay, and he said I could do something if I wanted—alone! That's when I started thinking he was having an affair. Getting me out of town would be a big plus. So I watched him closely. Found out he wasn't in his office when that's where he was supposed to be. I tried to spice up our sex life, and I thought he liked it, but then he said I wore him out. I'm sure he has a slut on the side. I need to know who, and I want to put an end to it."

I didn't believe her. Yes, she wanted to know who, but I was 99 percent positive that Brittney wanted proof to get out of the prenup. She didn't want to be married to Logan Monroe. It seemed so clear to me now. Infidelity would give her a reason to walk with five million for every year they were married. They had just had their third anniversary, so she'd get fifteen million if Monroe cheated on her.

Finally, I said, "I don't think your husband is having an affair. Maybe your instincts are right and he's up to something—I don't know what." Though she wondered if it had to do with Jennifer White and Desert West Financial. "But if you want to keep me on, I'll give it an-other couple days."

"Thank you," she said, sounding relieved. "Tomor-row, Logan is supposed to be at his office meeting with investors on some golf thing he's working on. Ten a.m., then they're going to lunch—I'll find out where and text you. Then he said he had a cocktail meeting *here* at six thirty, which is why I wanted to come here, check out the place. He told me he was meeting someone. That's suspicious."

"Maybe if you just ask your husband specific ques-tions, he'll tell you."

"You're clearly not married," Brittney said. "I don't want him to know that I'm suspicious, and if I start asking questions, he'll think I am, and then he'll be sneakier."

My parents talked about everything. If Mom wanted to know who Dad was meeting without her, he'd tell her. They had busy careers separate from each other, but when they weren't working, they were together. They socialized together, they went to family events together, they *talked*. I had never once doubted that my parents loved each other.

Had Brittney ever loved Logan Monroe?

Reluctantly I said, "I'll see what I can learn tomor-row."

My instincts—and the evidence—said Monroe wasn't cheating. Maybe I was wrong. But what I really wanted to know is why Monroe didn't tell his wife about what happened today.

Something didn't add up.

Monday

Fourteen

Margo Angelhart

Fifty years ago, my grandparents, Hector and Margaret Morales, inherited a beautiful two-story Spanish colonial mansion in downtown Phoenix walking distance from St. Mary's Basilica and Chase Field. Built in 1907, five years before Arizona became a state, it had first been a residence, then a seminary, orphanage, and school. When Pop and Abuela took it over, it had been boarded up and in disrepair. They converted it to offices, and now half the building was Arizona Legal Services run by my Aunt Rita, and the other half was Angelhart Investigations.

I sat in my Jeep drinking iced coffee from my Yeti, staring at the back door of the historic building, working up the courage to enter.

I hated feeling liked I was about to be punished. Or humiliated. I didn't know why I was so nervous.

Family was complicated.

Even now, after everything that happened, I loved my family.

But being here, in front of the Angelhart offices that I'd been so excited to help create but was forced to walk away from, hurt.

Damn, it hurt.

I almost drove away.

Almost.

Angelharts didn't shirk our duties, didn't say *no* when we could say *yes.* My parents had instilled in all five of us kids a deep sense of family first—but also the value of community, service, standing up for what was right over what was popular or expedient. It didn't always make friends, but my dad was my role model. He'd lived his life by the principle of loving God and loving your neighbors.

Which is why when he lied and confessed to murder, I couldn't accept it. It wasn't him, wasn't my family, wasn't how I was raised. I couldn't back down, but every wall that could be erected blocked me, and the few pieces I had put together led nowhere.

Dammit.

Now or never.

I got out of my Jeep and went inside.

Jack was the only one there, and I was grateful.

"Hey."

"I got donuts," he said, motioning to a box on the table in the conference room. "Want coffee?"

"I have some." I held up my Army green Yeti.

He grimaced. Jack hated iced coffee. I lived on it.

I looked over the donuts. "Oh, these are Original Rainbow Donuts."

"Yep."

My favorite donut place, a small family business that closed whenever they ran out of donuts, which was almost always earlier than their posted hours every day. Had Jack picked them up just for me? A bribe or just being a good brother? I almost couldn't pick, but finally grabbed a crème-filled maple bar with bacon sprinkles. Took a bite. Moaned.

"Heavenly," I muttered.

Mom walked across the office and said, "Give me five minutes." She went into her office and I tried not to squirm. I had nothing to feel guilty about. But old habits die hard.

Jack, to his credit, didn't say anything. It wasn't like I didn't hang with my brother—six weeks ago Jack, his son Austin, Nico and I went to the opening day home game at Chase Field. D-backs beat the Dodgers, fun was had by all.

Tess walked into the conference room, her expression twisted in a scowl. "Endicott," she said, dropping her laptop on the table. "Why is Miriam Endicott involved in our case?"

It took me a second, then I realized that Tess had enhanced the photos I took yesterday of the two men and their vehicle driving away from Logan Monroe's rental.

"I thought it was Frank Sanchez on the mountain," I said. "Couldn't be sure."

"The other guy is Andy Drake," Tess said. "Also a licensed PI. Know him?"

I shook my head. Frank and I have had a few run-ins over the years when our cases collided, and once we'd even worked together when Miriam Endicott hired me for a project. I didn't really have an opinion of Frank. He was competent, straightforward, and we had never talked about anything other than business.

"What were they up to?" I wondered.

Miriam Endicott had run her late husband's private security business for the past ten years. When my mom was a prosecutor, she'd often butted heads with Roger Endicott who had made it his life's work to embarrass her department as well as Phoenix PD whenever possible. His lack of ethics was legendary, but when he withheld information from the court, his license was suspended for a year.

Miriam was as bad as her dead husband in many ways, but she had a few redeeming qualities—namely, she was the mother of Charlie Endicott, a man I once loved. I went through a rough patch after leaving the Army. Returning home, I no longer felt like I belonged and didn't really know what I wanted to do with the rest of my life. Then he walked into the bar I was tending and wham. I don't believe in love at first sight, but this was damn close. He was exactly what I needed to get my head on straight.

Charlie was truly one of the best guys I'd ever known. The first guy I genuinely loved—the kind of love that made me start to think that maybe I wanted to get married. That maybe there was one right person for everyone, and for me it was Charlie Endicott.

Then I lost him to the first girl he'd ever loved. Poetic, I suppose, if I weren't the odd-girl out.

Miriam sometimes tossed me cases. Not because she liked me. She did it because Miriam resented Mom opening up Angelhart Investigations, which was in direct competition to Endicott's own Trident Security Group. She also knew that my mom and I had a falling out. Miriam enjoyed twisting the knife in Mom's back. I ignored their rivalry. Miriam paid well and on time, that's all I cared about.

"So they were hired to watch the house?" Jack asked.

"Looks that way," Tess said. "Who hired them and why?"

"Million-dollar question." I finished my donut and drank more coffee.

Mom walked in. "I'm sorry I'm late," she said. "Jack filled me in on what happened yesterday."

Tess told her about Endicott's men watching the house, then said, "Nate's watching White's condo, but she hasn't been home."

Nate Lorenzo worked part-time for Angelhart. Former military, edgy, and probably suffering from PTSD. He grew up in our neighborhood so I had known him practically my entire life, though we didn't go to the same schools. I hadn't seen him for years after he enlisted in the Navy—mostly to get away from his parents, I thought.

Mom looked at her watch. "If she doesn't show up at work this morning, we'll need to assume she's on the run. Ideas about where she'd go? Our background check didn't yield any family, but she grew up in Florida, right?"

"Yes," Tess said, "and we put out feelers there when we first got the case, but so far zilch. Her emergency contact at work is her next-door neighbor. He's a pilot and hasn't been home in the last six days."

"Can I get a copy of her background?" I asked.

Silence around the table. I suppressed a flash of anger, and added, "If we're going to work together, I need to know what you know."

Mom looked at me, hesitated as if she didn't know how to talk to me. I didn't make it easy and took another donut, though I didn't really want it. Finally, Mom asked, "Of course. Tess will send you everything we have. You wrapped up the adultery investigation?"

"The wife wants me to follow him for a couple more days."

"Do you think he's romantically involved with White?"

"Nope, but if she wants to pay for my time, who am I to stop her? He's going to be at the Beverly's tonight at six thirty, and I said I'd check things out. The interesting thing is, it doesn't seem he told her about passing out or meeting White."

"Theories?"

I was uncomfortable in a collaborative role. For nearly eight years I'd been a one-woman shop. Margo Angelhart, Private Investigator. No one to answer to, no one to bounce ideas off. I didn't know if I wanted a partner—or partners—in this or any other investigation.

"When Tess and I spoke with Monroe yesterday," Jack said, "he was evasive on details, but said that Jennifer had interned for him and they'd kept in touch. He claimed he gave her the rental for a few days, agreed to meet her there to discuss something confidential, but claimed he didn't know what it was about. I didn't believe him."

"So even with all the cloak-and-dagger bullshit," I said, "someone else knew they were meeting there. That person drugged or poisoned them. I didn't know where Monroe was going until I followed him. But you knew because you accessed White's email."

"Company email," Tess clarified. "We had permission."

"It's still a good point," Jack said. "No one went in or out while we were watching until White arrived. We arrived thirty minutes before she did. Someone had to have set up the gas, poisoned the water, whatever happened, before then."

"Still no word on forensics?" Mom asked.

Jack shook his head.

"We owe our client a report," Mom said, "but without more information, any report would be vague. I don't want to be party to damaging someone's reputation without just cause. I'll hold them off for twenty-four hours."

"I want to know why Monroe didn't tell his wife about passing out," I said. I often talked to myself when working through problems. Maybe it would be nice to have a partner, but that wasn't going to happen. This case was a fluke, a one-off.

"Yet, you don't think he's screwing around," Tess said.

"I haven't almost since I started. The wife had some compelling reasons to believe that he was, all standard clues—not where he said he'd be, shift in personality, secretive. But after I saw nothing within seventy-two hours, I started thinking that she made the whole thing up—I only have her word that he lied to her."

"Why would she do that?"

"My first thought once I figured he was faithful was that she *wants* him to be cheating because of their prenup—she gets a lot more money if he strays. Maybe she figures all men cheat, therefore if she has him followed, she'll catch him. Then I realized after last night that the woman likes attention," I said. "Maybe he's not giving her the attention she thinks she deserves and she's trying to get a reaction from him. Or…" I stopped as a new idea popped into my head.

"Or she's accusing her husband of doing what she herself is doing," Mom said.

That was exactly what I'd been thinking. Sometimes, Mom and I were on the exact same wavelength. It made the last three years of tension that much more miserable.

"It's something like that," I said. "I don't know what's going on with her, but she wasn't completely truthful with me. It's like a game to her. Last night, she wanted to meet in public. At Beverly's, of all places. The first time we met was also in public, but a coffee place far from her house, little chance of being recognized."

"Beverly's is definitely not incognito," Tess said.

"Exactly." I shrugged. "Whatever she's thinking or planning, I'll check out Monroe's meeting tonight."

"Want company?" Jack said.

I almost said no, then shrugged. Hanging with Jack was always fun. "Sure."

Mom said, "We need to find Jennifer White. And I'm going to pay Miriam a visit."

I laughed. "Mom, she's not going to tell you anything. She's more likely to talk to me than you."

Mom obviously didn't believe it.

"At a minimum," I continued, "I'm the one who saw Frank Sanchez—I know Frank. I'll zoom in on the photo I took and ask her what the hell."

It was clear my mom didn't want me to do it, but she slowly nodded. "Very well."

As if she could have stopped me.

Mom left to take a call. It was clear to me that we had nothing else to discuss, so I headed out with a quick goodbye. The meeting hadn't been as bad as I'd thought, but lingering would make me uncomfortable. And honestly, this whole situation was depressing.

I was supposed to be part of Angelhart Investigations. I was the experienced investigator, I had helped build the business—and then *slam*. The proverbial door shut in my face.

As I was walking out, my cell phone rang.

"Hey," I answered as I stepped outside.

"Annie arrived safely in San Antonio," Rafe said.

"She wasn't supposed to make contact."

Damn, damn, damn.

Any contact with her old life put Annie in jeopardy.

"She didn't. My friend there wanted to make sure I knew she and the kids were safe."

I didn't need to know; I didn't want to know. Peter Carillo still loomed—free, angry, with resources. The fallout could be serious. Yet…there was also peace in knowing that Annie had made it all the way, that she hadn't had cold feet and backtracked.

"Okay. Good."

"Is everything okay?"

"Yeah, why?"

"You sound off."

"What, are priests psychic now?"

"No, but maybe uncles are."

"I'm fine. Working with Jack and Tess on a case, it's a bit on the weird side."

"I look forward to hearing about it."

"I'll tell all at the party. I gotta go, but I'll see you later, Uncle Rafe."

"Bless you, Margo."

"Right back at you," I said and ended the call.

"How's Uncle Rafe?" Jack asked.

I hit unlock on my car fob. I hadn't seen him exit the building.

"Good."

"I wasn't eavesdropping, but is everything okay?"

"Peachy."

Jack stared at her. "We're still family. We'll always be family."

"I know." That's why it hurt to be on opposite sides about something so fundamentally important to me. To them. I loved them, but we couldn't get beyond my dad's imprisonment. I would never understand how my mom could stand down.

Jack obviously wanted to say more, but he didn't. He was his mother's son, noble, loyal, always looking at the greater good. He, like everyone in the family, would argue with Ava Angelhart if they disagreed with her, but when Mom made a decision, Jack obeyed.

Most of the time, so did I.

"I miss—" I caught myself before I said something that opened up a bigger can of worms.

"Me, too," he said. "Margo, there will always be a desk for you here. Always."

It was an olive branch, so I didn't jump down his throat. "See you tonight."

Fifteen

Margo Angelhart

Trident Security Group was located in the pricey Bilt-more area. Everything was expensive—houses, commer-cial property, retail. Miriam Endicott's secure building also included a bank, a major insurance company, and several lawyers. Miriam's white Mercedes was parked in her assigned slot, so I went up to the Trident suite on the fourth floor.

Miriam's bread and butter was corporate background checks. They had secured contracts with multiple major employers in order to score the nice digs. Ninety per-cent of the work could be done with a computer and a phone, and Trident employed six full-time researchers who worked in cubicles and did the bulk of the work. Anything that needed to be verified in the field went to Frank Sanchez or Justine Young, both licensed PIs who I knew and didn't love. Andy Drake must be a new guy or a temp.

I knew enough about Roger and Miriam Endicott—and their history with my mother—to know that they played dirty. That didn't actually bother me—sometimes doing the right thing meant breaking a few rules. But motive mattered, and the jury was still out on that. Miriam was a hard woman to figure out.

Sherry, the young office manager, raised a perfectly plucked eyebrow when she saw me. "I don't have an appointment on the books for you, Ms. Angelhart."

Her voice was high, almost childish. She was twenty-two with a boob job to take her perfectly acceptable C cups to DD, and regular lip filler to plump out her already full lips. Her makeup was perfect as any beauty store employee, her long hair naturally blond with excellent golden highlights. In the two years she had worked for Miriam, she had dated three baseball players, the son of a major sports team owner, and a neurosurgeon twice her age. I'd once made the mistake of thinking Sherry had no brains in her too-pretty head; now I knew better than to doubt the calculating woman. Sherry might be looking for a rich husband, but she had done a few jobs exceptionally well for Miriam. It helped when people saw what they wanted to see and assumed an airhead guppy when they were really dealing with a corporate shark.

"Nope, but I'm going in."

Sherry knew better than to try and stop me, but she picked up the phone and buzzed Miriam.

By the time I reached the corner office, Miriam was hanging up the receiver and had a smile on her weathered face.

"Margo. You could have called."

"So could you when Frank realized we were working parallel cases."

Miriam may have once been attractive, and she certainly was what someone might call *handsome* in a woman, but too much time in the sun had given her skin an unnatural permanent tan and wrinkles that had been only partially smoothed out with regular Botox treatments. Her gray hair was short, well-styled, and she dressed impeccably. But she looked older than my mom, despite being two years younger.

"Sit, please."

I did, after closing the door.

"What were you doing at Logan Monroe's rental property?" Miriam asked.

"What were *you* doing at Logan Monroe's rental property?" I countered.

Neither of us spoke. I wasn't in a rush, but I didn't want to dance around with Miriam all morning. "I saw Frank. Nearly a hundred degrees and they were in the boulders above the property, with binoculars. When I saw them, they bolted. Why would Frank run when he saw me?"

Miriam said, "They weren't running, they were leaving."

Not accurate, but I didn't argue.

"So you were hired to watch an empty house and when it was occupied, your men left."

"The house wasn't empty."

Frank left because he had spotted the ambulance, I'd bet my license on it. He would have known police would be next and he didn't want to answer any questions.

All night, I'd run through possibilities about who could have hired Miriam, but nothing had made sense. I'd thought for a brief second that Brittney Monroe may have hired them, but she didn't bite last night when I was feeling her out on the subject.

She could be lying. I suspected Brittney Monroe lied about a lot of things.

More likely that Desert West brought in a second investigator, but why hide up among the boulders? So that didn't quite fit, either. Unless someone at Desert West was involved in some sort of political shenanigans, something that Miriam always found herself in the middle of. Was Miriam involved in some sort of opposition research program? For who? Nothing in my research gave any hint that White or Monroe were running for office.

Could Jennifer White have hired them? Why?

Logan Monroe was an extremely wealthy man with a lot of friends...and more enemies. Maybe Miriam was gathering dirt on him for someone else, someone other than his wife. Like a business investor, a competitor.

Nothing felt quite right, but with Miriam's standard clientele of business and political movers and shakers, maybe it was some sort of opposition research on a rival. I didn't outright dismiss the idea.

"For the record," I said, deciding to give Miriam a small truth. "I've found no evidence that Logan Monroe is cheating on his wife."

Miriam laughed heartily. "I should have figured that's why you were there. Margo, dear, you're too good to be chasing cheaters around town."

Miriam didn't mention Jack. Could be that Frank hadn't seen him.

"Your case is over?" Miriam questioned.

"Not yet. Need to dot the i's, cross the t's, yada yada. Track down Ms. White and just confirm she's who she says she is."

A flash of surprise crossed Miriam's face, but she

was good, didn't give anything else away. She knew White, and she hadn't known I'd identified her.

"I suggest," Miriam said carefully, "that you focus on your business, and I focus on mine. We've had a good working relationship over the years. I would hate to have something come between us."

"Did you know when I arrived at the house both Ms. White and Mr. Monroe were unconscious?" A flicker in her eyes. Surprise that they were incapacitated? "The house was leased by Monroe's company, but sent to Ms. White's email. I deduce she was the likely target. If she's in danger, I should offer my services. Maybe even bring in the police."

Miriam turned angry.

"Stay out of it, Margo," she said sharply. "You have no idea what's going on, and you're going to create more trouble for everyone—including yourself."

"Trouble's my middle name."

I walked out.

So… Jennifer White. That was Miriam's interest. And she had been surprised that they were unconscious. That relieved me. I couldn't be certain Miriam had nothing to do with it, but that seemed to cross a legal line I didn't think Miriam would cross.

I wanted to know why Miriam was following Jennifer White, especially in light of yesterday's events.

After I started my Jeep, I called Tess. Her voice came through my car speakers. "Tess Angelhart."

"Found White yet?" I asked.

"Nope. Hasn't picked up her car in Paradise Valley, hasn't been back to her condo, but she called in sick for work."

I wasn't surprised. "Do you think White knows that her boss is investigating her?"

"Maybe. She told Monroe that she thought someone was following her. I don't think she spotted us. Jack, Nate, and I rotated shifts, different cars, different times, and I think it would be unlikely…but we can't rule it out."

Jack was too experienced to be caught tailing, but there was always a chance if the target was paranoid. And right now, everything Tess had told me—and what I had witnessed—showed Jennifer White to be both paranoid and scared.

"Miriam didn't spill everything," I said, "but she's tracking White. I don't think she was behind the drugging—she seemed genuinely surprised when I told her—but I can't discount it. What I know is that Miriam was hired to find, follow, or track White."

"She's certainly become popular this last week," Tess muttered.

"She called Monroe and wanted to show him something on her computer. She didn't plan to stay in the house—if she had luggage with her, she left it in her car. No food to prepare, and if she was in hiding, I think she would have bought groceries. So I'm thinking the computer is the key."

"All evidence points to her downloading the software. I think this meeting is proof, but Jack says it's not enough."

"Other people could want the information."

"There are easier ways to steal a laptop."

Much easier. "I have to check in on Monroe's whereabouts and dig into a few other things. Call me if you need me. And if you get a line on White, she hasn't seen me, so I can track her for you."

"I'm looking deeper into her family—our standard background found nothing suspicious, but there really wasn't much there. Also, she has no social media footprint."

Definitely odd for a twenty-six-year-old computer expert, I thought.

"No Instagram, no TikTok, no Facebook," Tess continued. "Even her personnel file is bare bones—high school in Miami, college in Austin, Texas. And she *never* had social media, even in college."

"Maybe Jennifer White isn't her name," I mumbled.

"What?" Tess said.

"Nothing."

"It's not nothing."

"No footprint, minimal background…maybe she changed her name." I thought of Annie and her new name. Running from her abusive spouse. April Carra would never have a social media platform. "Did you look into that?"

"No," Tess said. "I had no reason to believe she changed her name, but I can check court records."

Unless she did it illegally. If she was running from someone or something, she wouldn't have used legal channels.

"She interned for ComOne for a semester," Tess continued. "A tech company that at the time was owned by Logan Monroe, so that confirms his statement from yesterday. He lived in Austin then—six years ago. From there, she took a full-time job at ComOne for two years after graduation, then went to a Silicon Valley company—no ties to Monroe—for two years. That's where she made her money, I think—her position paid $250,000 a year plus stock options."

"Wow, we're in the wrong business," I said. "A quarter million for computer nerds? Wow, Lulu is going to support all of us when she graduates."

"True." Tess laughed. "Jennifer landed at Desert West just over a year ago and took a pay cut—making $150K a year. That's weird to me. Sure, cost of living here is cheaper than California, but not *that* much cheaper."

That *was* interesting. Why take a substantial pay cut?

"Did you check into her previous employer?"

"They had nothing but positive things to say, gave her glowing recommendations, but I did get one thing— when she gave two weeks' notice, she left. Said she had a family emergency and would take her sick and vacation time. Never came back to the office. There was a two-month employment lapse between when she left California until she signed on with Desert West."

"For a lot less money." Though $150K a year was nothing to sneeze at. "Do you have any idea where she was during those two months?"

"Nada. It's like she disappeared completely, then showed up in Phoenix with the job at Desert West. She bought the condo the same week she was hired. And the other weird thing—her references are all business. Even her personal references for the condo were related to work."

"Can you get a copy of her high school yearbooks?"

"I suppose, if it's important," Tess said. "But what would that accomplish?"

"The more information, the better," I said.

Maybe the odd behavior from Monroe was because

he was helping his former intern, not that he was cheating on his wife.

"How'd she leave the hospital?" I asked.

"We think she used Uber—her private account, so we can't get into it." Tess paused, then asked, "Do you think that Logan Monroe might have another place for her? Let's assume for a minute that she's in trouble or danger or helping Monroe steal from his old company. He gave her access to that rental—maybe he has another."

"I have a list of all his properties."

"How many are there?"

"A dozen."

"You can send me half."

"Theo is already checking them out. Just recon. But if you want to dig into the property records, that might help—which are rentals, short or long term, commercial, co-owners."

"Easy. I'll get on it."

"He could have put her up in a hotel," I mused. "Or at his resort. I'm following Monroe now. We'll find out what's going on."

Sixteen

Theo Washington

Theo had mapped out Logan Monroe's properties, both personal and corporate. No sense in wasting gas, he plotted the shortest route that would take him by each place in the greater Phoenix area. If Margo wanted him to check out the place he had in Flagstaff or the out-of-state properties, she was going to have to pay him in advance.

Theo drove his five-year-old Honda Civic to the property farthest south—a large parcel of undeveloped land south of the airport. Snapped a photo for Margo, but there was nothing here—just cacti and scraggly trees, garbage and fallen barbed wire. He then checked out the commercial building Monroe's company owned downtown—again, took pictures, but he couldn't imagine someone hiding out in the four-story office building. One of his companies occupied the top floor, and he leased out the other offices, but he didn't actually work here.

A guy who looked familiar walked by the building. Hispanic, shortish hair, stocky build. Theo would have taken a picture, but he turned into the building, the door swinging closed behind him. Maybe someone Theo had seen with Monroe? He'd been helping Margo track the guy for the last ten days. But Theo didn't think so. He would have followed, tried to ID him, but he was here to check properties and see where Monroe could be hiding a female computer expert.

Theo glanced at his list, then headed down Washington Street. He always got a kick seeing his name on the street sign. And in four weeks, he'd be starting his internship at the crime lab, right on the corner of Washington and 7th Ave.

He could have turned up 15th, but decided to continue down Washington. He passed the Sandra Day O'Connor US Courthouse. The huge building sort of creeped him out—it was too contemporary, glass and metal. Sure, clean and new, but just *too much*. It didn't fit with the Phoenix vibe. But what did these days? They were putting up so much new stuff, the old stuff seemed to just disappear. His grandma would talk about places she went as a kid that are no longer around and he wished he could go see them, just to have that connection with her.

The light was red at 7th. He stopped at the line, looked over at the crime lab. He'd toured it with his forensics class from Paradise Valley Community College, and then again with Margo's brother Nico. The internship was part of his AA degree program, but he knew that Margo had talked to her brother to help Theo get assigned to Nico's team. It meant everything to Theo that she had faith in him.

Three years ago, he couldn't have imagined he would be enrolled in community college or on the path to get-

ting a totally cool job doing something that could make
a difference. He'd been on the fast-track to major life
fuckup. Hanging with the wrong people, not giving a
shit about school, making every excuse under the sun
about why he had no options. His dad was in prison in
California, his mom was a drug addict who came and
went, he'd had two older brothers, now both dead—one
shot and killed while dealing drugs, one who died of
a drug overdose.

The only person who'd stuck with him was his
grandma. When he screwed up big-time, his grandma
came to him, said, "Do you want to live or do you want
to die, Theodore? Because that's your choice. You want
to die, I'm saying goodbye right now, because I don't
want to be burying anymore kids or grandkids. You
want to live, you have to stop doing what you're doing.
I'll help you. Right now, you make your choice."

"I want to live, Gramma."

"Okay. I know a girl who can help. You do exactly
what she says, and maybe this mistake can go away
when you turn eighteen next year. But you don't get no
more chances, understand?"

"Yes, Gramma."

"Good. I love you, Theodore. We're going to get
through this."

His grandma called Margo, Margo helped him work
out a restitution deal with the store he'd robbed, got
him probation, and if he didn't fuck up, his juvie record
would be wiped. Not sealed, but erased.

He followed the rules. Graduated from high school—
barely, but he'd done it. Actually did better at community college because the classes were more interesting
and he was paying for them with money he earned work-

ing for Margo and then for the last year being an Uber driver on the weekends. He lived with his grandma in her tiny house in Sunnyslope, not far from where Margo lived, and helped her with expenses. His grandma was almost sixty, worked at the high school cafeteria, liked her job because she said being around kids kept her young.

Theo knew he was lucky having his grandma in his corner. Too many of his friends didn't have anyone to help them when they screwed up, to set them on the right path. For the first time in his life, he was thinking about his future. He was excited about working in forensics.

Theo checked out several short-term rental houses in Paradise Valley and then Scottsdale. Jennifer White wasn't at any of them. Monroe also co-owned a small shopping mall in north Scottsdale with high-end restaurants and shops, and his main office where he actually worked was in the Scottsdale Quarter. No real place for someone to hide out in either location.

He avoided the 101 freeway, which had endless construction projects that added to delays, and took Carefree Highway across the north end of Phoenix to Desert Hills, a rural community with houses on large multi-acre lots where nearly everyone had a horse or two. Monroe owned a five-acre spread out here where his divorced sister lived with her two kids. It would be a good place to hide out, Theo figured, especially since it was next to impossible for him to stake out the place without being spotted. The narrow roads had no sidewalks, nowhere to park, and neighbors would be suspicious of a strange vehicle on the dead-end road.

Theo drove to the end, turned around, slowed down.

No activity outside, but there was a four-car garage with all doors closed. A barn was behind the house with an enclosed rink in between the two buildings, but he didn't see any horses. To him, this would be the best place to hide, and he made a quick note for Margo. She'd probably want to check it out herself.

As he approached the driveway, he saw a black SUV parked just outside the pillars. The same stocky Hispanic guy he'd seen downtown walked toward the house.

Theo stopped the car, zoomed in, and snapped several photos, then he left the neighborhood and the first place to pull over, he sent the pictures to Margo. The guy might have seen him, but he didn't pursue.

Thirty seconds later, she answered the phone.

"Where are you?"

"This is the horse ranch Monroe's sister is living at, in Desert Hills. I saw that guy at Monroe's headquarters on Washington. He's familiar, but I don't know why."

"Frank Sanchez. Works for Endicott. I'll bet he's also looking for Jennifer White."

"What do you want me to do?"

"How many places do you still have to check out?"

"The last six are all clustered near Westgate."

"Follow Frank if you can. Don't engage. If he spots you, disappear. Let me know where he goes and what he does."

"Okay, boss."

Seventeen

Peter Carillo

Peter slammed the laptop shut and rubbed his eyes.

It was all gone. Every message, every contact, every trace of Annie's existence had been erased. It was as if she had vanished from the face of the earth.

Not everything. He looked around the family room, his eyes bleary from too much bourbon, too much time staring at the computer screen. The pictures of his kids, Peter Junior and Marie. His perfect children. Playing at the park. Their Christmas portrait, when Marie was asleep in Annie's arms, a tiny infant. He had a perfect family and that woman, that *bitch*, stole it from him.

Why had Annie left him? Why had she taken their kids? Why had she deleted everything?

It made no sense.

He picked up the laptop and almost heaved it across the room, but stopped. No. He couldn't. No violence. He needed to call the police, report this. Annie had kidnapped his children. She was unstable.

Yes. Unstable. Hadn't she been acting odd, ever since

Marie had been born? His mother had even mentioned it to him. He had dismissed it then, but maybe…maybe he hadn't really dismissed the idea that his wife was suffering from postpartum depression. No, he hadn't dismissed it. In fact, he had encouraged her to see her doctor, talk to someone.

That's right… And she hadn't wanted to. He was worried, had every right to be worried! See what happened? What if…what if his children were in danger?

He took another gulp of bourbon straight from the bottle and paced the family room. He needed to figure this out, do it now, not wait.

She'd been missing for more than twenty-four hours. She'd left a note—that was good. He could say he was looking for her, calling friends, wanting to give her time… but now he's worried, very worried, because there's no sign of her.

Should he do it now? Tonight? Tomorrow?

He'd called Brian this morning, told him that Annie left yesterday, left a note that she wasn't coming back, and Brian said she would, that she loved him, asked what might have happened. Peter didn't know—but they had an argument about something stupid, something he couldn't remember, and now some of her clothes and some of the kids' clothes were gone. But she left her phone, laptop.

"She could have just needed a day or two to calm down," Brian had said. "Annie has always been a little high-strung. I'll talk to Natalie, see if they talked, let you know if she has an idea where to find her."

Peter had told Brian that he was probably right, left it at that.

Self-preservation.

Peter shook his head. He had nothing to worry about.

He loved his family, everyone knew that. He had a good job, a good income, was home when he wasn't working, was a good husband, a good father. Dammit, why had Annie put him in this position?

He walked through the house and stared out the front window, as if waiting for her to drive up. The street was lively; it was three thirty and though nearly a hundred degrees, the kids didn't seem to care. They were home from school, playing games on the low-traffic street. Laughter. He'd picked a perfect neighborhood to raise a family. Good schools, close to shopping, safe. A lot of cops lived in North Phoenix, unless they moved farther out of the city to Surprise or Goodyear or Chandler or Anthem.

Good neighborhood… Other neighbors had security cameras. He needed to talk to them, see if they had footage of who came to pick Annie up.

He needed to do that before he reported her missing. If he could find her tonight, then he wouldn't have to call anyone else. Wouldn't have to bring in law enforcement. The last thing he wanted was to be the subject of gossip. That his wife had left him, that he wasn't good enough. The whispers, the innuendos.

He glanced at the half-empty bottle in his hand. Winced. He shouldn't be drinking, especially in the middle of the day. He put the bottle back on the bar, started a pot of coffee, then went upstairs and showered. Dressed in shorts and a DPS polo shirt.

He would talk to every neighbor who had a security camera and find out who came to his house yesterday morning and took his wife and children.

A sense of determination washed over him.

And then he would do whatever it took to bring them home.

Eighteen

Margo Angelhart

"I forgot how much I liked this place," Jack said, looking around at the Beverly's ambiance.

"If you like overpaying for beer." I sipped my beer, a Church IPA like last night. Jack ordered something lighter. The appetizers were already gone—both of us had been famished. Steak bites and truffle fries. I could have eaten another round all by myself.

"It's Scottsdale," he said with a shrug. "You pay for atmosphere. So, who do you think was the target yesterday? Monroe or White?"

"The obvious answer is Monroe—he's important, he's wealthy, he has enemies. Yet…they were rendered unconscious, fresh air brought them around. Do you know the cause? Because it would have to be something heavy duty for them to be knocked out without much warning. And they both came around minutes after I aired out the house."

Jack shook his head, sipped his beer. "I'll call Nico

in the morning, see if he'll track it down—if they've even gotten to it. Major crimes go to the top."

Like every police department in America, staffing shortages affected every level, from street cops to forensics to support staff.

"White's the one who is acting squirrelly," I said. "Plus, Endicott's lead investigator was out doing what we were doing—tracking White by canvassing Monroe's property. That tells me they were hired to find her, talk to her, follow her…drug her? I don't know."

"Tess said you think she could have a false identity. That would be difficult to pull off, unless she has exceptionally good docs."

"Not impossible. Not even that difficult." I'd found someone to create three very real, but false, identities for Annie Carillo and her two kids, though I didn't mention that to Jack. "I don't see how the target is Monroe. He's been going about his business, meeting investors, friends, no unscheduled trips. Only his wife says he's acting weird and out of character. I'm wondering if she's just making up all this bullshit."

"Why would she?"

"Hell if I know. Relationships aren't my strong suit."

"Don't look at me," Jack mumbled.

Margo glanced at her brother. "No one serious?"

"Honestly, I'm just not interested in anyone. Rick got me out on a few double dates—oh, sorry."

"Don't apologize. He's your best friend."

"Just—well, he's not seeing anyone seriously, either."

"I don't care." Secretly, I was pleased. Then I told myself not to be happy.

Sergeant Rick Devlin. We were oil and water, fire and ice, all those clichés that basically meant that even though make-up sex between us was the best thing on earth—the kind of sex where fireworks went off and the angels sang—fighting was exhausting. We were two stubborn people set in our ways, neither wanting to give an inch.

Sometimes, I missed him.

"Anyway," Jack said, "I didn't like dating before I got married, and I like it less now. I even tried one of the dating apps."

I laughed; I couldn't help it. "You? Of all people, I can't imagine you on Tinder."

"Bite your tongue. Some other app, I don't even remember the name, but I deleted it. Went out on half a dozen dates in as many weeks and it was literally hell." He stared at his beer and I felt for him. "I loved Whitney. Even three years later, I can't just turn it off. I don't love her in the same way, not after everything, but she's the mother of my son."

I didn't like Whitney. Never had, even before they got married. It wasn't my place to tell him I didn't think she was good enough. At least Jack now has an amazing, fun-loving son. But with the son came his mother.

Whitney was selfish, demanding, and manipulative. She got them so deep into debt that Jack cashed out his Phoenix PD retirement to pay it off, then ended up paying penalties because he pulled money out early. Whitney left him when he told her not to take out any more credit. She refused marital counseling and demanded a divorce.

There was a lot of other shit that went down, but in the end, when the divorce was final, Jack came over to my place and we got drunk. He cried. I'd never seen Jack cry, not like that. It was humbling, and I wished I could take his pain away. I hated seeing my big brother so broken. But after, we were good. And once some time had passed, Jack put the pieces back together and found peace.

"You should call Rick," Jack said after several minutes of silence as we watched the room.

Fortunately, Logan Monroe walked in, so I didn't have to answer.

Logan glanced at his watch, then looked toward the bar. We were sitting in a corner booth near the entrance, both to be inconspicuous and because it was the best place to see most of the room. The dark lighting helped obscure us in case he looked too carefully, but he didn't even glance our way.

We'd already scoped out the place and identified three lone females. Jack had voted for the redhead; I thought the brunette with long hair in the corner drinking red wine because she looked classy and smart. And while the redhead was beautiful, she seemed…harder. Neither of us picked the cute short-haired brunette with multiple tattoos.

Logan raised his hand to the woman at the bar.

"He's meeting the redhead," Jack said.

"You were right."

"Can I get that in writing?" He grinned.

Jack won; I was paying for the beers.

Logan was dressed in what I called his business-casual look—comfortable slacks, a short-sleeved button-down shirt with a small repeating pattern. This one white with navy pinstripes. He must have dozens of the same style, just different colors and patterns.

I couldn't tell, based on his attire, whether this was a business meeting or a personal meeting. I had my phone out and discretely took pictures of both of them, then zoomed in on the woman.

The woman wasn't dressed for a business meeting. She wore a short royal blue dress that barely covered her slender well-shaped butt, with thin straps made of fake diamonds—this was Scottsdale, they could be real, but the dress didn't look upscale enough to include real diamonds. If I tried to walk in her heels, I'd break my neck.

The woman touched Logan; his arm, his hand. He didn't touch her. He pulled his hand back, and then seemed relieved when the bartender put a tall drink in front of him. It looked like a Coke with lime. Could have rum or bourbon in it, I supposed.

"He's not drinking," Jack said as if reading my mind. "I watched the bartender."

The woman was drinking white wine. She rose, motioned to a table, said something that my above-average lip-reading skills translated to, "Let's go over there."

Logan hesitated, then followed.

"He doesn't look happy," Jack said. "Like he got bad news?"

"Or the woman isn't who he expected," I offered.

The table they sat at was small with a curved leather seat that could comfortably sit four. Logan sat at the opposite end from her, and the redhead moved closer. There was nowhere for him to go without falling to the floor. They sat directly across from Jack and Margo now, but too far for her to hear the conversation.

"This is strange," Jack muttered. "Monroe doesn't look like he wants to be here, and I don't think he knows the woman."

The woman was definitely leaning in, flirting, while Logan was sitting rigid, as if he was looking for any reason to leave. But they *were* talking. The angle made it difficult for me to read them, but I made out a few words—none of which made sense without the context.

A man and woman approached the table and greeted Logan. He smiled, chatted a minute, introduced the woman. I strained to watch his lips. "This is Rachel. Friend." Something like that. Rachel a friend? Rachel Friend?

Jack put his hand on my knee and squeezed. "She just drugged his drink. Something liquid, she palmed it. Shit, he just gulped the Coke." The couple he spoke with walked away and exited the bar. "You distract the woman, I'm going to get Logan out of here."

"She needs to be held accountable," I said.

"First we intervene, then we'll talk to the manager. Let them know what went on. Our goal is to protect Logan. Go first."

I went over to Logan's table. "Rachel, right?"

The woman looked at me with wide surprised eyes. "Do I know you?"

"What, you don't remember? High school?"

"I'm on a date," she said. "Call me later."

"This isn't a date," Logan said. His voice sounded off, not quite slurred, but strange. "It's hot in here, let's go outside and talk."

"Great idea. I'll call an Uber," Rachel said.

"I have my car."

Rachel stared at me with an anger I didn't expect. "Excuse me, honey, we're leaving."

Jack took Logan's hand as he stood. "Logan, so good to see you again. Hey, I have a question about your new project."

Logan looked doubly confused as Jack led him away.

I leaned over and said to the woman, "We saw what you did. There are security cameras all over this place. You'll never be let back in, and if I have anything to say about it, you'll be prosecuted for assault."

"What the fuck?" The woman looked angry and panicked. She was loud enough that a few people glanced over, curious or concerned.

The bouncer—a discreet security guy who stood near the door and kept an eye on the room—took notice. Then Jack was talking to him, and the guy frowned, looked over at Rachel and me, said something to Jack, but I couldn't hear or see his lips.

"Stay," I said, then followed Jack out. I didn't expect Rachel to obey me, but she didn't follow.

I saw Jack sitting with Logan on a bench near the entrance. Logan had his head in his hands.

There was only one couple in the patio area because it was still too hot, even with the misters going. They sat under a vine-covered trellis in the far corner.

"Whatever she gave him must have been potent," I said. "He drank less than ten minutes ago.

"Security will talk to her, but I don't know what they can do other than ban her. I gave the guy my card."

"Do we need to take him to a hospital?" Margo asked.

"The best thing is to get him to puke. That's all they'd do there, unless he has an adverse reaction."

"No," Logan said. "I don't feel like puking. You're familiar. Who are you?" He looked at Jack, not me.

"Jack Angelhart, Private Investigator. I talked to you yesterday at your house in Paradise Valley."

"Jennifer," Logan said. "Yeah—her friend."

"What friend?"

"Rachel. She called me. Jennifer." He frowned, confused.

"Jennifer called you? Or Rachel?" I asked. "When?"

I had a bad feeling that Brittney had set me up—okay, set *Logan* up, but used me to do it.

"This afternoon. She had my private cell phone number."

"Who called you, Logan?"

"He's been drugged," Jack said. "He might not remember."

I understood how date-rape drugs worked. He might be confused, but he should remember who called him before he was roofied.

"Who called you?" I repeated.

"Rachel. Jennifer gave her my number."

"Is that what Rachel said?" I pressed. "That she was friends with Jennifer and Jennifer asked her to set up a meeting?"

"Yeah—she said they were friends."

"When did you talk to Rachel?"

"This afternoon. I rescheduled a meeting with an investor to be here." He frowned. "Why would she drug me? Are you sure?"

"How do you feel?" Jack asked.

"Fuzzy. My head feels thick. I didn't drink any alcohol." He rubbed his temples. "Are you sure?"

"I saw her put something in your drink," Jack said. "I spoke to security. They'll review the cameras if you want to prosecute, but she's already gone."

I looked around; I hadn't seen her leave.

Jack said, "We can't detain her, Margo. But we'll find out who she is. Logan, what did she say when you first got here?"

"I asked if Jennifer was okay. She said yes, that she would meet us soon. Ordered me a drink, but I declined. I ordered a Coke. I have an early day tomorrow." He frowned. "I can't remember what I'm supposed to do in the morning."

"Have you spoke to Jennifer since she was taken to the hospital yesterday?" I asked.

He almost didn't answer, then said, "I really don't know who you are."

"Jennifer left the hospital," Jack said. "She didn't go back to your rental or her condo. Is she in trouble?"

He didn't say anything.

I knew that it wasn't Jennifer who sent that woman here to meet Logan.

I motioned for Jack to step aside, then said quietly, "He can't drive home. You drive him, ask questions. I'm certain that Brittney set him up. When we met yesterday, she told me he had a meeting *here* at six thirty. But Logan said Rachel called him *today*."

"He could have been planning to meet his investor here."

I didn't buy that, and neither did Jack. The Beverly wasn't a place for business meetings. It's where you might take clients *after* work.

"I'll see what I can learn." He tossed me the keys to his truck. "What are you going to do with your case?"

"If Brittney set him up with that woman so I could get pics of them in a compromising position, I'll tell him."

"Can you? Ethically?"

"Yep. She lies to me, our contract is null and void. We need to find this Rachel and talk to her."

"I already sent her photo to Tess."

Nineteen

Jack Angelhart

Logan Monroe let Jack drive his Tesla to his house. Margo followed in Jack's truck. Logan had grown contemplative during the drive, repeating himself several times as if trying to keep clear what had happened that night. Jack let him work through it, knowing how he'd feel if he were in the same situation. Embarrassed, angry, confused.

Jack pulled into Logan's circular driveway in the gated Troon North area in the mountains above Scottsdale. "If you want to press charges," he said. "I witnessed the woman pour something into your drink. The bar has security footage, and the bouncer will save and flag the tapes."

"I don't know. Why would she drug me? Why would she lie about Jennifer?"

Jack didn't think it was wise to explain Margo's theory about his wife hiring someone to seduce him. There was no proof, even if she had good reason to believe it.

"Why did Jennifer ask you to meet with her yesterday?"

Logan didn't answer.

"Yesterday, someone poisoned you and Jennifer at your house. That person must have known that either you or Jennifer was going to be there. Then tonight, a woman drugged your drink at a bar—a woman who said she was there because Jennifer gave her your number. Something isn't adding up. You may be in danger."

"Not me."

What about a *woman drugged you* did he not understand?

"Jennifer found…some financial irregularities at Desert West. She wanted to show me the problem, walk me through it, see if she missed something."

"You two must be close," Jack said, thinking about the affair his wife suspected.

He didn't answer.

"Logan, I'm trying to help you."

"Jennifer interned for me in college, and then I helped her get a job with the company when she graduated college. I respect her, she's bright and exceptionally good at her job. I had already sold my half of Desert West when she was hired there, but I gave her a recommendation."

"So you're professionally close."

"Until yesterday I hadn't seen her since she first moved to Phoenix. We had coffee a week after she was hired at Desert West." He paused. "On Friday, she reached out to me and asked if I had a place for her to stay for a few days because she thought someone was following her. I offered my house in Paradise Valley."

"For free."

"Like I said, she sounded worried."

"Did she show you the problem she identified?"

"She started talking about numbers that didn't match

up and wanted me to look at raw code, but then she said she felt lightheaded, then collapsed. I tried to get her to the couch, but I started feeling woozy as well." He frowned.

"Are you okay?" Jack asked when Logan looked ill.

"I'm fine. Really."

"I'd like to check out your house, if you don't mind." Jack had told him yesterday that he'd been with Phoenix PD and was now a licensed PI, but he didn't know if Logan remembered. "Is your wife home?"

He shook his head. "She had plans."

"Do you know where Jennifer went after the hospital?"

He shook his head. "I offered another place—"

"So you talked to her."

"Last night. She called, said she had to get out of town for a while. I offered her a house or hotel room—I have a suite at my resort I use for clients—but she said someone might be able to find her again. She sounded scared, said that her past was haunting her. She promised to call as soon as she was settled. That's why..." His voice trailed off.

"You thought Rachel was telling the truth."

"Why would she lie?"

Either because Margo was right and Brittney had set him up, or Rachel was hired to drug Logan and find Jennifer's location.

Jack said, "You have my card, call me. I can help both you and Jennifer." Might be a conflict of interest, but he was now concerned about Logan Monroe's safety. The guy didn't act like a multimillionaire. He had no private security, other than a home alarm system; he was known in the business world, but he acted like an ordinary guy. Someone Jack could like.

"Okay," Logan said noncommittally.

"And you might want to tell your wife about what's going on, to make sure she's taking precautions."

"I did."

That surprised Jack, considering what Margo had said. "About yesterday?"

"Yes. She said it was probably a gas leak or a problem with the AC. I sent out an inspector today, should have a report tomorrow. I asked them to copy me in, not just the management company."

Margo was going to flip over that news. Why did Brittney lie to her?

Then, Logan said, "I'm worried about Jennifer. I would reach out to my old partner, but something Jennifer said has me wanting to talk to her first."

Gavin O'Keefe hadn't hired Angelhart, but he owned the company.

If Desert West was up to no good, why would they hire Angelhart to investigate? To cover up a crime? Jack had met personally with Ron Tucker, the CFO, and he didn't get any sign of deception from him.

Jack walked Logan into his house. The door didn't have a key; instead, a code let them in. "Do you mind if I look around?" Jack asked Logan.

"Go ahead." He glanced at his phone. "My wife is on her way home."

Jack sent Margo a text with that information, and then he looked through the house, turning on lights as he went.

The house was spacious—far too big for two people. But who was Jack to judge? His ex-wife would have liked the place—the windows, the view, the space, the expensive furnishings. The house itself was a tasteful blend of contemporary and Southwestern styles, warm, earthy tones with splashes of color. Jack had never cared about things. His parents weren't wealthy, though they did well enough to send five kids to Catholic school. While no one had wanted for anything, they didn't have extras. Jack bought his first car by working weekends and summers as a lifeguard at a country club for two years. Margo bought her first car by working as a caddy at the same place.

The one thing Jack wanted was a little space—a few acres in the hills, a couple of horses and big dogs who needed space to run. He was always looking for the right property, but he couldn't afford most of the ranches he'd seen, and the rare times a fixer-upper popped onto the market, it was gone before he could put in an offer. He'd take a flop if it was in the right area.

Jack cleared the house, then found Logan sitting at the kitchen bar drinking a bottle of water. The man looked uncomfortable, as if he didn't know what to do or say.

"I appreciate you helping me out, Mr. Angelhart," he said.

"Call me Jack." He sat across from Logan, looked him in the eyes. They were focused but bloodshot. "You doing okay?"

"Splitting headache, but I don't have that fuzziness anymore."

"Good."

"Do you need me to call you an Uber?"

"No, thank you, my partner followed in my truck. Logan, I want you to think hard about what's going on with Jennifer. If she's in danger, I can help. Have her call me. A man in your position could be at risk for kidnapping for ransom, extortion, any number of crimes."

"I can't imagine who would do anything like this. To me or Jennifer. She's a good kid. Very smart. If— if I don't hear from her, perhaps I can hire you to find her. I don't know why she would be in danger—her job doesn't entail state secrets or anything like that. But she was scared on the phone, and this thing tonight—what if that woman is looking for her? Lied to me, drugged me, thinking I know where she is?"

"All good questions. Call me, Logan. I want to help."

It would put Jack in an ethical dilemma, since he'd been hired by Desert West, but right now he was more worried about Jennifer White's well-being.

Jack let himself out. Margo was sitting in his truck in the driver's seat. He didn't ask her to move over; instead he opened the passenger door. He told her that Logan *had* told Brittney everything about yesterday. Margo sat there, quietly angry.

"And she told me *yesterday* he was going to be at the bar tonight," Margo said. "She set him up."

"So, we're waiting for Brittney, I presume?"

"You know me well."

"Rachel claimed Jennifer gave her Logan's number."

"Then how did Brittney know he would be there *yesterday* when Rachel didn't call Logan until *today*? That *bitch*."

"Rachel?"

"Her, too, but Brittney. I gave her Jennifer's name, said there was nothing romantic between them that I could see. That's when she told me about him coming to the bar tonight. I think she hired Rachel to drug him, so Rachel could make the moves and I could get the pictures."

"You can't prove it."

"She'll tell me," Margo said with complete confidence. "I have no problem going to Logan Monroe and telling him everything if Brittney lied to me or I think she's a threat to Logan."

"I like the guy." Jack said. "He seems genuine."

She shrugged. Margo had always been more cynical than most of the family, but never to the degree she was now. She'd changed three years ago when their dad went to prison. It wasn't just because their dad was *in* prison, it was because they hadn't fought for him. Just because Cooper Angelhart said to stand down, didn't mean they should stand down, Margo had said. And yet…they had. Because their dad asked.

It broke Margo's heart that the family turned their back on her need for the truth.

"I found no evidence that he's cheating on his wife," Margo said. "I can't figure out why she hired me to prove something that isn't true."

"Maybe she believes it," Jack said, "and doesn't want to accept that you couldn't find anything."

"Why? Really, wouldn't you be relieved to know that your spouse is faithful? Maybe she had bad relationships, maybe someone is pushing at her, urging her on, I don't know. But tonight was a setup, and that was all Brittney."

"We can't discount that Rachel is working for someone who is looking for Jennifer, and tried to get that information out of Monroe. It's definitely a trick Miriam Endicott would pull."

Margo shook her head. "Not Miriam's style. She's sneaky and will lie and her ethics are questionable, but she wouldn't drug the guy."

"Could she be willfully ignorant?"

"Like tell Rachel to get the info any way she can?" Margo nodded, conceding the point.

Jack looked at his phone. "Tess ID'd Rachel Roper."

"Is that a real name?"

"According to Tess, Rachel Roper is a physical therapist by day, an escort by night."

"A prostitute," Margo said flatly.

"Works a girlfriend-experience gig. They're not always prostitutes."

Margo snorted. "So Brittney hired a *girlfriend* for her husband."

"Or someone looking for Jennifer did."

"Nope, it was Brittney. I'm ninety-five percent certain."

Jack trusted Margo's expertise and instincts. Maybe because she'd spent three years of her six-year stint in the Army as an MP, or maybe because she was just wired that way. Jack had tried to get her to join Phoenix PD when she decided not to reenlist, but she said no, that she had her fill of "following stupid rules." He'd always wanted to know what happened—because something must have turned her off law enforcement—but she rarely talked about her time in the military, and he didn't push.

A car turned up the long driveway and one of the garage doors started to open. Just as the sporty convertible pulled into the garage bay, Margo jumped out without comment.

Twenty

Margo Angelhart

As the garage door started to close behind Brittney's car, I stuck my foot in front of the sensor to force the door to roll back up.

Brittney was already getting out of the car and jumped when she saw me walk through the opening.

"What the hell are you doing here? My husband is home!"

"No more lies. Tell me what the hell you're up to."

"Have you been drinking? Go away or I'll call security."

I had a couple of theories, but I went with the obvious. "You hired Rachel Roper to seduce your husband, at least to the point where you thought I might be able to get pictures of him in a compromising position. Problem? I'm good. I saw her drug him." Slight fib. Jack saw her, but there was no reason to bring my brother into it.

"What?" Brittney's eyes went wide. She glanced around as if looking for an escape. Score one for the PI.

"Cut the bullshit. You told me *yesterday* that Logan

was meeting someone tonight at The Beverly. Yet Rachel didn't call him until this afternoon. She dropped Jennifer White's name. That's where you fucked up. I put Jennifer's name in my report, and you knew that your husband was trying to help her. He told you about meeting with her—you neglected to tell me that. He told you about how he and Jennifer were rendered unconscious… You also neglected to share that with me. He even told you that he was meeting a friend of Jennifer's tonight—but you knew that, because you set the whole thing in motion."

Brittney glanced toward the door to the house, worry clouding her expression. "Why are you making all this up?"

But there was no venom in her words. Just a woman caught in a sticky web of lies, trying to think of a way to pull free.

"You put your husband in danger tonight," I said. "You're lucky my associate and I were there to help him. He could have been molested, he could have been robbed, he could have gotten behind the wheel of a car and killed someone."

"Did you tell him? Oh, my God, that's not what happened!"

"I didn't tell him that you set him up." I paused a fraction of a second, waiting for Brittney to jump in with a fierce denial. She was silent.

"I'm done," I said. "I'm sending you a report and my final bill. I expect prompt payment. My report will list everything I believe you did. If anything happens to your husband, I will turn it over to the police—along with photos of Rachel Roper drugging him."

"You can't do that. We have an NDA!"

I didn't usually work with a written contract, but when a client wanted me to sign an NDA, I had them sign a contract to protect myself. "Read the contract. It's very clear." I took a step closer to her. "Not only is there no evidence that your husband is cheating on you, but I think you made up the whole story. I don't know what game you're playing, what you want, or why you thought you could use me, but it's over."

I stared at her until she fidgeted, then I turned and strode back to Jack's truck. He'd moved over to the driver's seat, so I climbed in on the passenger side.

"Did you get Rachel's address?" I asked. I wanted to talk to her.

"No, but we have the name and number for the girl-friend experience. No one answered. I didn't leave a message."

"Damn. Okay, I guess we have nothing to do."

"It's nearly nine. Those appetizers were not a meal. I'm starving."

Food. What did she have at home? "I might be able to grill up a couple of sandwiches, if the bread isn't moldy."

"You owe me a beer. Let's go to North Mountain Brewing. I could use a good cheeseburger."

"Sold."

Twenty-One

Peter Carillo

Peter went to three houses on his street before he found exactly what he was looking for.

Mrs. Emily Carmichael lived across the street, three doors down. Carmichael was an eighty-year-old widow, and her son had installed security cameras after a string of robberies in the neighborhood last year. She was a nice-enough lady for a busybody, and knowing that Peter was a cop, she waved to him when she saw him.

He talked his way into her house to look at her computer, where the security footage was stored for two weeks before it auto-deleted. He knew this because he'd talked to Emily's son when he first installed the system.

He made up an excuse—that Annie had seen a prowler, but he didn't have a camera on the side of his garage. And to ease his wife's mind, he wanted to just check.

Emily hovered, chatting about her kids and grandkids and two great-grand kids. Peter blocked it all out while he searched the footage for Sunday morning at 7:00 a.m.

Then he watched.

He saw himself leaving. He fast-forwarded until seven thirty-two when a Jeep pulled into his driveway. A moment later, the garage door went up; the Jeep pulled in, and the door went down. Thirty-six minutes later, the Jeep left with Annie in the front seat. A woman was driving—a woman wearing a baseball cap. He couldn't see her face well, didn't recognize her.

The children had to be in the back, but he couldn't see them through the tinted windows.

He copied the clip and saved it to a flash drive, thanked Mrs. Carmichael while politely ignoring her questions, and left.

He had a license plate. An Arizona plate.

One of the perks of being a state trooper was taking home his patrol cruiser. Most cops didn't have such a privilege.

He sat in the car, turned on the laptop, and ran the plate. Yes, there would be a log of his action, every single thing he did in the system was logged, but no one looked at the information—there was no need to. If down the road someone did inquire, he'd come up with an excuse. He ran plates all the time—dozens, sometimes hundreds a day.

The Jeep was registered to Margaret Elizabeth Angelhart. She lived on North 14th Street in Sunnyslope, one of the oldest neighborhoods in Phoenix, near the Phoenix Mountains Preserve.

Why was that name familiar?

Angelhart.

Well, shit. He knew the name because there had been a prosecutor named Angelhart.

He shut down his work laptop and went inside to his

personal computer. Bringing up Google, he typed the name. It was an uncommon last name and all the top results were for Angelharts in Phoenix.

Cooper Angelhart went to prison three years ago for murder—killed a fellow doctor at the VA. Now Peter remembered the case. It had been wall-to-wall coverage for weeks. Cooper Angelhart was married to a lawyer, Ava, who was the daughter of retired judge Hector Morales. Peter didn't remember working with Ava when she'd been a prosecutor, but he found her biography on a website for Angelhart Investigations.

The woman was now a private investigator.

Ava Maria Morales Angelhart graduated from the University of Arizona with a degree in criminal justice and a minor in history. She attended law school at Arizona State University to be closer to home as she began her family with her husband, Cooper.

After law school, Ava took a job as a prosecutor for Maricopa County. Ten years later, she was appointed as County Attorney when George Fieldstone resigned following a heart attack. She was elected twice to the post, but declined to run for a third term. Instead, she and her sister, Rita Morales Garcia, opened their own law firm, Arizona Legal Services, where they handle a variety of cases both civil and criminal. Ava is the co-founder of Angelhart Investigations.

Who was Margaret? A kid? Grandkid? Did she work for the firm? Was a former prosecutor responsible for taking his wife and children from him?

It took him fifteen minutes of digging around on the internet because none of the Angelharts had a large digital footprint. He found Angelhart Investigations— but no Margaret. Ava, Jack—a former Phoenix PD officer—and Teresa were the principal investigators. Maybe this Margaret was a nobody, a secretary…

Why was she here? Where had she taken his kids? His wife?

After thirty more minutes of frustrating searches, he finally identified her. Margaret went by *Margo* and she, too, was a private investigator but didn't work for the family. A lone wolf, working from a tiny storefront near where she lived, likely not much more than a mail drop.

Margo Angelhart would know where his wife was. If she didn't cooperate, he would consider going to her mother.

Why? Why did you leave me, Annie?

Maybe he had *on occasion* been a bit rough on Annie when she irritated him. She understood what he liked, what he expected, what he expected of *her*. That was no reason to disappear with his children.

But, he didn't know what she might have told the private investigator. She may have lied, exaggerated, blew everything out of proportion.

Maybe Annie was at Margo's house.

Was that even a possibility? For Annie to leave him, take his children, to another house practically in his backyard? Why? To *punish* him for putting his foot down on her unacceptable, selfish behavior?

He didn't know what he would do to Annie when he found her. He loved her, didn't want to hurt her.

She couldn't leave him.

He took Annie's car, not his cruiser. Her practical

minivan—that he bought her because it was safe for her and the children—wouldn't stand out. It was still light outside, not yet eight in the evening. He headed down Highway 17 and navigated to Angelhart's house in the hills bordering the southwest boundary of the Phoenix Mountains Preserve.

He parked across the street and looked at the small, cinder block house. No lawn, just rocks and cacti, though someone kept it free of weeds. Potted plants on the small covered porch, a couple of chairs. He looked west—the front yard had a nice view of the sunset.

The garage was at the end of a narrow driveway to the left, and he couldn't see if anyone was home. He finished his coffee, exited the car, and walked to the front door. Knocked. No answer. He didn't hear anyone inside. He knocked again. Silence.

He tried the door. Locked.

Peter was nervous. Angelhart was a PI, likely had a weapon, and he wasn't in uniform. He needed to walk away now or he would be trespassing. He glanced around, didn't see any neighbors lurking, no one walking their dog.

She took your family from you.

Emboldened, letting the anger fuel him instead of his nerves, he walked around the side of the house to the back, grateful that it was near dark. There was a gate, but it didn't have a lock on it. He slipped into the backyard and immediately felt relief at the privacy— no one could see him here.

The backyard was mostly rocks with a couple trees that provided shade, much needed in Phoenix. The cracked patio had seen better days, but the woman kept the yard tidy. A small peanut-shaped swimming pool was clean, and a separate raised hot tub looked to be new. Two sliding glass doors led to the house; he tried both of them.

Locked.

He shook one of the doors. Dammit!

He studied the locks; they were old.

Be smart, Peter. Think.

He slipped on latex gloves and then wiped the doors that he'd touched. He checked all the windows—they were locked as well.

He went back to one of the sliding glass doors and looked inside.

A large bed, a dresser, white comforter, colorful pillows. Her bedroom was neat, her bed made. A night-light came from the adjoining bathroom, casting shadows in the rapidly diminishing light.

He studied the lock. Old, but he'd come prepared. Maybe he had known this was what it would come to for answers.

Taking a screwdriver from his pocket, he removed the handle on the door. Then he used the narrow end of the tool and inserted it in the center hole, wiggled it until he found the lock mechanism, and pushed it down.

He smiled as he put the handle back on the door and opened it. He quickly stepped inside, listened. No one was here.

The house was under twelve hundred square feet and had been updated. Margo Angelhart was a tidy woman. The floors were fake hardwood. Easy to clean and maintain. Her bedroom was a bedroom—no desk, no papers, no clutter. Pictures on the walls of friends and family, he supposed. A large print of the Grand Canyon. As he looked closer, he saw that a family was centered in the photo, though the picture focused on the beauty of the north rim.

A man and woman, five young children. He picked out the teenage Margo—he had her driver's license memorized. She had dark blond hair, lightened from the sun.

He glanced through her drawers; nothing of particular interest other than a .38 in the nightstand. A stack of books, a mix of fiction and nonfiction. The bathroom was barely big enough for a shower, sink, toilet. Down the short hall was another bathroom and then a small bedroom in the front of the house. This had a couch, desk, laptop.

He opened the laptop. It was off, not asleep.

He closed it. Looked through the drawers. Banking, financial documents, insurance documents, everything well-organized. Files for what he presumed were clients.

He looked through them, didn't see his wife's name anywhere.

He grew angrier with each passing minute.

The office had bookshelves, a filing cabinet, more pictures, many with Margo in uniform. Army, he determined upon closer inspection, when she was much younger.

Peter frowned. Why would this woman, this private investigator who'd been in the Army, a woman with connections to law enforcement and the DA's office and a criminal defense lawyer and God knew who else, why would she take Annie?

Why would she help Annie disappear?

His wife had lied. Plain and simple, she had made up some bullshit story to convince some do-gooder bitch to help her screw with *him*. The man who had taken care of her for *seven years*. The man who had provided, given her a home, done more for her than anyone! Her mother was dead, her father a deadbeat. She'd been barely scraping by working at that coffee shop, living with a pot-smoking roommate in a crappy apartment when he met her, when he fell in love with her, when he promised to love and protect her for the rest of their lives.

He pounded his fist on the desk. The knickknacks and photo frames jumped; one fell over. He righted it, looked again around the room. Lots of books, framed pictures, a cork board with notes and snapshots. He scanned them; they all seemed personal.

Order balloons for Austin's birthday.

Call Grandma A on Sunday.

Confirm Sat. party.

A wall calendar looked out of place; it was from St. Dominic's Catholic Church. Above the calendar was a simple carved wood crucifix mounted on the wall. He flipped through the calendar's pages. Here she had written birthdays, anniversaries. Her birthday was at the end of this month; someone named Austin was two days later. An anniversary this weekend. June, July, August... In September, there were four birthdays in a row—Adam (21st), Uncle Rafe (24th), Mom (25th) and Josie (27th), then an anniversary on the 30th—Uncle Tom & Aunt April, #34.

Every month had at least one birthday or family event. How much family could one person have?

He opened the closet. It was smaller than the closet in her bedroom, but just as organized. Shelves with more books, office supplies, a couple warm coats and sweaters hanging in plastic bags. A tall narrow safe. Guns? Papers? Information about his wife?

He didn't even attempt to open the safe.

Peter walked through the rest of the house. It was as tidy and organized as the bedroom and office. He could respect a woman who kept a clean space. He opened the refrigerator, frowned. The door was filled with beer, the shelves practically bare. Some fruit in the drawers, a few condiments on the top shelf, a container of leftovers—some sort of stew—not much else.

The kitchen opened into the eating area and family room. It looked like someone had taken out some walls and opened the place up. There was even a large laundry room off the kitchen with built-in cabinets, a counter, and walk-in closet that had been converted into a pantry. She stocked a lot of staples—at least twenty gallons of water, canned food, flour, cereal, the top shelf packed with military rations, another shelf with stacks of ammo—at least 500 rounds each of .38, .357, .45, 9mm, 30-30 rifle ammo as well as more than a thousand rounds of 5.56, used in the popular AR-15. Paranoid or prepared? A quick glance told him she wouldn't have to leave her house for weeks if she was under siege.

He hated this woman—she'd taken his wife—but he was certainly intrigued by anyone who was both organized and disciplined.

Margo Angelhart was his adversary. He would need to be cautious when dealing with her.

The side door from the laundry led to the driveway and the garage. Peter unbolted the door and exited, doubly cautious. He didn't hear or see anyone. The sun was down, a thin red line to the west. The night was so clear he could see the remaining glow framing the White Tank Mountains twenty-five miles away.

He would check out her storefront, see if it was legit,

find out if she had anyone working for her. Maybe he could pick up some clue. Something to tell him where this woman, this *bitch*, took Annie.

First things first. He needed to report that Annie was missing. He should have done it today, but he had hoped she'd come back on her own. Now? He had no choice. She was missing and he was concerned about her and the safety of his children.

Because Annie Carillo was mentally ill. That's the only reason she would leave him.

He headed home. Who would believe him? He had to be clear, focused in how he answered questions. Annie was ill, certainly. In fact, he'd noticed a change in her behavior and personality after Marie was born. He had wanted her to go to the doctor. Perhaps she suffered from postpartum depression. She wouldn't go to the doctor... Yes, it all came clear to Peter as he drove.

Annie was sick. She needed help.

Why hadn't he called the police right away? They would ask...

Because she left him a note... He thought she would return. Called friends. But now he's very worried.

He smiled. He would find her or the police would find her. She would come home. He would be the best, most attentive, most loving husband in the world. He'd take a leave of absence, have his mother move in to help with the children. When the time was right, when enough months had passed that Annie thought he'd forgiven her, he would punish his wife.

Annie was not going to get away with putting him through this hell.

Twenty-Two

Margo Angelhart

At 10:30 p.m., Jack dropped me off at home.

I loved my little house. I fixed it up myself with Jack's help, hiring a professional contractor to tackle the big projects like updating the kitchen. While I still had some items left on my to-do list—for when I had extra time and money—my home had become my sanctuary.

I headed straight to my home office, planning to do more research on both Jennifer White and Brittney Monroe. But as soon as I switched on the light, I froze.

Someone had been in my office.

Everything on my desk had been moved, my files had been looked through. It wouldn't be obvious to anyone but me, but I kept my space organized. It was as if someone had picked up every item and put them down in a slightly different place.

First thought? Brittney Monroe had hired someone to investigate *me*.

Hand on my gun, I slowly turned around the room. I didn't expect that someone was still here—I didn't sense another human breathing—but I didn't assume anything.

The closet door was open an inch.

I pulled my gun—the lightweight Smith & Wesson 9mm, which I preferred when carrying concealed—and searched the entire house. The sliding door that went into the backyard was unlocked. I squatted and inspected the handle; each screw was loose. Someone had removed the handle, opened the door, then replaced the handle.

I checked every other door in the house; the dead bolt in the laundry room was undone. The intruder came in through my bedroom slider, and left through the laundry room.

The only things of value that weren't locked in my safe were my generous supply of ammunition, computer, television, and a couple pieces of decent jewelry. Nothing was missing.

Someone had broken in, but hadn't taken anything. And based on moving my stuff, not securing the back door or the deadbolt, the intruder wanted me to know that he had breached my home.

If so, why not leave a note? Make more of a mess? Most people wouldn't notice small disturbances in their space; I wasn't most people.

I was angry. Someone had come into *my* home and gone through *my* things. Not a thief, not family. A stranger with an unknown motive.

I called Theo, who had a key. He would tell me if he came by, but I couldn't think of anyone else.

He answered on the first ring. "Yo, Angel, what's up?"

A video game played in the background.

"Did you come by my house tonight?"

"Your house? Nope. You need something?"

"Just covering my bases." I hesitated, then said, "Someone broke in."

"No shit? You need me there? I can be there in ten."

"No, I can handle it, I just wanted to make sure it wasn't you."

"I wouldn't, not without giving you a heads-up. You okay?"

"Just mad."

"Your guns all there?"

"Yep."

"Nothing was taken? Not even all that ammo you have stashed in the laundry room?"

"Nope."

"Weird."

Very. "I'll talk to you tomorrow."

I was about to end the call when Theo said, "You think the asshole found you?"

"You're going to have to be more specific," I said. "I know a lot of assholes."

"The one who beats his wife. You told me to keep an eye out, right? Just in case, you said. So I have. Haven't seen anything, but maybe you need to keep an eye out. It was you who fucked with him. Not that he didn't deserve it. How would he know where you live?"

I stared at the ceiling, a litany of swear words running through my head, though I only uttered one. "Fuck. Watch your back, Theo." I ended the call.

That was fast, but Theo was right. Peter Carillo was a cop. I'd been careful, didn't drive by the front of his house, but what if he talked to neighbors? What if someone else caught my Jeep on camera?

Any cop could run my license plate and get my name,

address, driver's license, social, driving restrictions. There would be a log, but that log was only accessible to certain people in the department. I couldn't just call a beat cop like my cousin Josie to find out who'd run my plates, I'd need someone higher up.

Like my sometimes-boyfriend, Phoenix PD Sergeant Rick Devlin.

I hadn't talked to Rick in months. While Jack knew more cops than I did, I didn't want to bring my family into this. Annie Carillo was my case, and I needed to take care of my own.

If State Trooper Peter Carillo had run my plates, then he had most likely broken in to find out where his wife was. Maybe he thought she was here.

And I had to figure out what to do about it, because proving he broke in would be next to impossible.

Tuesday

Twenty-Three

Peter Carillo

Two Phoenix PD officers responded to Peter's missing persons call Tuesday morning. They stood in his kitchen while he sat at his table, hands around a mug of cold coffee. His head pounded from lack of sleep, and his heart hurt from missing his family. He kept going over *why, why, why* and alternating between angry and sad.

His friend Brian had come over for support. And, Peter thought, to corroborate everything Peter said. He was right to tell Brian immediately about Annie walking out. But he didn't tell his friend about Margo Angelhart. He wouldn't understand why Peter had gone to her house *or* why Peter decided to withhold that information from the investigating officers. Angelhart was Peter's angle to pursue. If they found out about her on their own, fine, but for now, she was Peter's best bet to get Annie back under his roof where he could control her.

Officer Ritchie looked twelve and his badge number suggested he'd only recently graduated from the academy. Officer Archie Nunez was in his thirties, a training officer with a good reputation. Their paths had crossed in the field a few times over the years, but Peter didn't know him well.

Peter explained everything—that he'd tried Annie during the day, but she hadn't answered. That he knew she was going to a fair to see Natalie, Brian's wife, so he didn't think much about it until he came home and she and the kids were gone, but her car was here. He gave them the note—he had debated that for hours. But if he hid the note from them, then the police might think that *he* had done something to his family.

He would never hurt his family. He loved them.

He claimed he thought she took Uber, maybe went to a hotel because she was mad about something, but he checked their joint credit card and she hadn't charged anything. He gave all the statements and bank records to the police, so they could see he wasn't lying.

"What does this mean?" Nunez asked, pointing to the first line of the short note. "*You hurt me one time too many.*" He looked at Peter as if *he* was a suspect. As if *he* had done something wrong.

"I don't know," he said. *Less is more*, he told himself. Don't over talk. Don't say anything that can get you in trouble.

"Did you have a fight recently? Maybe Saturday night? Sunday morning, before you went to work?"

"No. We don't fight. I mean, we argue like everyone about stupid things, but we don't fight."

Brian said, "Tell them, Peter."

"Tell us what?" Nunez asked.

"I—I have been asking Annie to see a doctor."

"Is she sick?"

He shook his head. "Ever since Marie was born, Annie

has been...different. I didn't think much of anything about it, just the stress of having an infant and a toddler. PJ is almost four, he's a handful. My mom comes over to help around the house and with the kids a few days a week when I'm working, and she told me that Annie has signs of postpartum depression. My mom is a retired nurse. I mentioned it to Annie, and she got so mad at me. She broke a vase my mom had given us, stormed upstairs. I let her calm down, but she refused to see a doctor."

"When was this?" Nunez asked.

"She broke the vase six, seven weeks ago? But I'd noticed her behavior change shortly after I went back to work after paternity leave—I took two weeks off to help with PJ and the baby, and then my mom stayed here for a couple weeks."

"Is Annie on any medications?"

"Not currently. She'd been on anxiety medication years ago, but not since she was pregnant with PJ."

"We're going to look around, if you don't mind."

"Of course. I've called everyone I can think of, talked to some of the neighbors. I just don't know why she'd leave, and I'm worried about my kids. I've been reading about postpartum depression. I'm terrified that she might hurt them. Hurt herself."

"Let's not make assumptions. We'll take a look around, then go from there. Does she have family? Have you contacted them? Even if they're in another state, maybe she went to visit."

Peter shook his head. "She's an only child. Her dad left when she was young, her mother died before we married. I don't know anything about her dad's family, she never talks about him. Her mom had a brother, but they weren't close—he lives in Montana or Wyoming. I've never met him. He didn't even come to our wedding."

"Okay. Stay put, we'll be right back." Nunez motioned for Ritchie to follow.

Brian sat next to Peter. "She'll be back."

"I don't know. What if—what if something happened?" His voice cracked, and he felt the heat of tears, squeezed his eyes shut.

"Don't think that," Brian said firmly. "Natalie is calling everyone we can think of. Annie will come home, I know it. Whatever she's thinking, she's going to come back and work things out."

"I hope you're right, Brian. I'm frantic. I don't know what else to do."

Several minutes later, the two officers returned to the kitchen. Nunez said, "We're going to talk to your neighbors."

"I already did," Peter said.

"Maybe we can help refresh their memories. We'll check security cameras in the area."

"I asked, no one saw anything."

"It doesn't hurt for us to follow-up. Since she didn't take her car, and didn't take a taxi, maybe someone picked her up. You have a camera on your door—have you checked it?"

"Yes." Of course, he checked it! It was the first thing he'd done. "You can look at the footage, there's nothing from Sunday."

"Okay. Save it, a detective may want to see it. We'll put out a welfare check on the kids, but since your wife isn't under a doctor's care, and there's no diagnosis for PPD, I don't know that if we find her, we can compel her to return."

Peter's hands fisted. "My children!"

"You're married, not legally separated, and unless the kids are in danger, she can go where she wants. There's no parental kidnapping law in Arizona. You might want to talk to a lawyer. You can petition the court for—"

"Just find them. Please." Peter knew the law. It was bullshit. In no just world could a wife just *leave* with his children without telling him, without letting him see his kids. Yes, he could petition the court for visitation and yes, he could fight for custody, but the woman had *just walked away.* He didn't want a divorce. He wanted his family back.

And when he found her, she would return. She would have no choice but to come back to him.

Brian touched his arm and it was all Peter could do not to slap his hand away.

"We all understand that you're worried," Brian said, "but Arch is doing everything he can. Getting a lawyer would be good. You can document Annie's emotional state, for one. You have a lot of options."

"Nothing matters if we can't find them," Peter said. This wasn't going the way he thought it would. His word—his *statement* that his wife was mentally unwell should hold weight. It should hold *all* the weight.

"I'm going to walk Arch out, okay? I'm coming right back. Have faith, Peter."

Faith. What had that ever done for him?

Twenty-Four

Officer Archie Nunez

Brian Nichols came out of the house and motioned Nunez over as he was about to get in his patrol car. Nunez told Ritchie, his rookie who only had two more weeks of probation, to start typing up the report. Then he closed the door and turned to Brian.

"Have something to add?" Nunez said.

"I'm sick about this. I've known Annie since she and Peter got together, she's terrific. They both are. I'm PJ's godfather. My wife is calling around, and I'll let you know if she hears anything. This has thrown Peter. Annie is a great wife and mother. She can be a little high-strung sometimes, but…" Nunez waited for Brian to continue. "I didn't want to say this in front of him. Do you think there could be foul play?"

"Do you think that Mr. Carillo has something to do with her disappearance?"

Brian's eyes widened. "No! He worships the ground she walks on. Peter and I have been friends for nearly ten years, since we went through the academy together.

I was their best man, I *know* them. They've always seemed happy. Annie is a sweetheart."

"But you said high-strung."

"You know what I mean."

"Not really."

"She gets upset if like, um, she overcooks dinner or a cake doesn't turn out perfect. A perfectionist, not high-strung. She was in a book club for a while, but quit. She told Nat the women made her feel stupid because she was a stay-at-home mom. I'm sure they didn't do it on purpose—I know a couple of the girls. One is my neighbor."

"Name?"

Brian looked at him oddly. "What?"

"The neighbor who knows Annie from the book club."

"I'm sure Natalie will call them." Nunez just stared at Brian, waiting. "Kris Madera," he said after a brief hesitation. "She lives across the street from me. I'm just a few blocks over from here."

Nunez made notes.

"Was their marriage good?"

"Yeah, real good. We have barbecues and dinner all the time. I've never seen anything weird. That's why I'm thinking foul play, since her car is here."

"The car seats aren't," Nunez said.

"What do you mean?"

"We checked the house, the garage. The car is here, but the car seats—I assume she has two, one for the baby and one for the toddler—are not in the minivan. Do they have another vehicle?"

"No." Brian frowned. Had he not known that? Had Carillo not noticed? Or did he notice and not say anything.

"We don't know what happened, but there is no sign that Mrs. Carillo left under duress. At first glance, it seems that a friend picked up her and the kids. She left her phone behind. She doesn't want to be found right now, but in my experience marital spats take a few days to work themselves out. We'll look into this. If the kids are in danger, we'll bring in CPS, but there have been no calls to CPS, no record that the family has had any problems, no calls for service to this address.

"If your wife talks to her, or finds someone who has, I know you'll want to tell Carillo, but also call me. I'll talk to Annie. See what's going on, where her head is at, make sure the kids are safe."

"Thank you." Brian shook his hand. "I'm sure you're right, and Annie will come home on her own in a couple of days. Peter is just really worried. This came out of left field, you know?"

Nunez nodded and watched Brian go back inside.

Marital problems never come out of left field, he thought as he climbed into the patrol and pulled away from the curb.

"Aren't we going to talk to neighbors?" Ritchie said.

"We will. But I want to talk to Natalie Nichols first."

"Okay, why?"

"According to both Carillo and Nichols, Natalie is Annie's closest friend. I want to see who she called. Maybe she knows something more but doesn't want to say in front of her husband or Carillo."

"You don't think that something happened to her and the kids, do you? I didn't see any evidence of violence."

"I think she left of her own free will. Natalie Nichols may know why."

Twenty-Five

Margo Angelhart

Late last night, I drove by St. Dominic's and cruised through the surrounding neighborhood, looking for either Carillo's DPS cruiser or the family minivan. He wasn't there, which made me feel marginally better. There was no clear way to connect me to Rafe, and less Rafe to Annie.

I parked outside the rectory for an hour, just to make sure my uncle was safe. He lived there with two other priests—a young priest, who was just ordained last year, and a retired priest. All quiet. Finally, at two in the morning, I went home, showered, and slept uneasily for a few hours.

After morning coffee and a bagel, I again circled St. Dominic and the neighborhood until I was confident that Carillo wasn't staking out the church.

Tess had left a message for me to come to the office this morning, but I texted her that I had things to do. She'd wanted to join me to talk to Rachel Roper, but Rachel drugging Logan Monroe was my cross to bear—I needed to confirm that Brittney hired her, then to figure out why. I thought I knew—divorce settlement—but I wasn't positive. I needed the truth, and Brittney Monroe wasn't going to give it to me.

After calling Rachel's work for her schedule—pretending to be an existing client to see if she could "squeeze me in" this morning—I learned that she came in at eleven. That gave me plenty of time to hit Costco when it opened.

Last night while watching Uncle Rafe's place, I had researched security systems. I didn't need—nor could I afford—an alarm service. But surveillance? Most home camera systems recorded anyone who approached—even people who walked by the front of the house with their dog. I was more interested in people who approached my door—front, side, and back.

If Peter Carillo came to my house again, I wanted to know about it. If I'd thought of this before, I could nail him now—he would have a lot of explaining to do. Would he return? I doubted it.

Still, I bought a system with cameras that could connect to my phone and alert me in real-time if anyone entered the house—or even if someone came to the door to deliver a package. Though I was pretty handy and the instructions were clear, it took more than an hour to install. By the time I left and arrived at Rachel's work in north Peoria, it was noon.

Foothill Physical Therapy was a large building at the end of a new strip mall in upscale northern Peoria, in the hills above Highway 101. It was a nice community—if you liked big houses that all looked alike packed close together. FPT had the trappings of a gym, but with less equipment and added tables for muscle massage.

I'd had physical therapy twice. The first, when I was sixteen and tore my ACL during the championship soccer game, which we won 2–1. The second, two years after I left the Army, I was in the middle of my annual two-week Army Reserves training. During a drill—an obstacle drill I've done hundreds of times—my body went one way and my ankle went the other. *Snap.* It was a clean break, but I worked my ass off to be mobile as soon as possible.

I hated being out of commission.

The AC hit me hard when I walked into the building. Such was life living in the desert—it could be a hundred degrees outside but you needed a sweater when you went indoors. I had a light blazer on to conceal my weapon. Arizona was an open-carry state, but I preferred discretion.

The receptionist smiled. "Appointment?"

"Rachel."

She looked at the book. "Mrs. Thomas?"

"Margo Angelhart. I need five minutes of her time." I saw Rachel on the far side of the large room working with an athletic kid wearing a knee brace.

"She has an appointment—"

"Tell her it's about last night. Please, I would appreciate it."

More flies with honey. But if the receptionist balked, I'd push back. I had no time for games. If Rachel thought I'd tell her colleagues about her moonlighting as a paid girlfriend? All the better.

"I'll see if she can step away."

"Thank you," I said with a friendly smile. I watched as the receptionist spoke to Rachel, who looked over at me with a stunned expression. I waved. Surprise!

She quickly approached me and said in a low voice, "You can't be here."

"I'm here."

"This is my work. Go."

"I'm here about Brittney."

Her face paled. "I need ten minutes," she said. "*Please.*"

"I'll wait outside."

Rachel looked shaken when she walked back to her client. She also didn't look like the hardened vixen she'd appeared last night. Her long shiny red hair was pulled back, she wore no makeup, and she dressed comfortably in shorts and a blue Foothill Therapy polo shirt.

I left the building and stood under the awning where I could watch the door.

I saw the teen leave eleven minutes later, then Rachel came out.

"I only have five minutes between clients. You *really* shouldn't be here."

"Tell me what happened," I said.

She looked scared. "I could be fired. *Arrested.*"

You should have thought of that before you drugged someone. But I didn't say it.

"If you don't go back to The Beverly, they're not going to go after you. And if you don't do it again, I won't have any reason to come after you. Tell me the truth. That's how you protect yourself."

"I *can't.*"

"I'm not a cop. I'm not the aggrieved party. I can't file a complaint. But if you don't tell me exactly how you ended up at The Beverly last night and why you drugged Monroe, I'll make sure that *he* files a complaint. I think the police will listen to him, don't you?"

Rachel paled even more. I hoped she didn't faint.

"Damn her," Rachel muttered. "Britt and I went to high school together. Not friends, but we knew each other. She heard that I worked for a girlfriend experience—we're *not* escorts. I don't sleep with the guys, I'm just a hired date. For weddings and business events. I made a thousand bucks—more than I make here in two weeks!—for a weekend at the Waste Management golf tournament last year. Just to be arm candy for a nerd. Britt said her husband was having an affair but the PI she hired couldn't prove it. She gave me a sob story and I fell for it."

"That doesn't explain why you roofied him," I said.

Rachel winced. "She paid my date rate, and said she'd pay me $500 if I could get him to make a pass. Someone would get the picture. That's it. She was in tears."

"And you drugged him why?" I asked.

She glared at me. "I didn't."

"I'm not recording this conversation," I said.

She wasn't going to admit it. "Anyway," Rachel continued, "I could tell he was not into me—color me shocked." She flipped her sleek red ponytail over her shoulder. "He wanted to know about this Jennifer. She wasn't returning his calls. I told him she was fine, thought Britt was right, he was all into this Jennifer chick, then he said something weird, like he was worried about her safety and she needed to call him. Wanted to know how to reach her because she wasn't returning his calls."

Though I suspected I knew the answer, I asked, "Why was he asking *you* about Jennifer?"

"Britt said to drop her name when I called to make the date."

"You didn't tell Logan it was a date," I said.

She didn't say anything at first.

"Rachel, this is important. Brittney hired you to set up her husband. You can't be okay with this."

"I'm not. It just—the way she talked, it didn't seem like a big deal."

"What did you tell Logan so he agreed to meet with you?"

"I said Jennifer asked me to call, wanted us to get together to talk. That was it."

"Have you met Jennifer?"

"Don't even know who she is." She twirled the end of her ponytail in her fingers, tears in her eyes. "Britt said give him a little boost if he didn't seem interested. I swear, I've never done anything like that before. I wasn't going to sleep with him. God, I'm not a prostitute or anything. I just was going to let him kiss me, maybe get to second base, let the PI—you—get a couple pictures. That was it. I swear."

Rachel was in a near-panic and I believed her. Still, I pushed. "What did Brittney tell you about Jennifer?"

"Only that her husband was obsessed with her and she wanted to find out how long they'd been involved. That was it."

So nothing I said to Brittney sunk in—that Logan wasn't having an affair, with Jennifer or anyone. She set him up.

Rachel pleaded. "I'm telling you the truth. I've never done anything like this before and I swear to God I'll never do it again."

Rachel was scared enough not to do something like this in the future, at least for a while. I hoped this near-miss with a sexual assault case would keep her clean for the rest of her life.

"What did you give him?" I asked.

She hesitated.

"Some drugs have serious side effects. He deserves to know."

"I have a prescription for lorazepam. It's legit, but I don't use it anymore. I dissolved a double dose in water."

"Throw them away. And steer clear of Logan Monroe."

Rachel went back inside. Yeah, I believed her, but her excuses were pathetic.

Brittney Monroe was worse. When I found no evidence that Logan was committing adultery, she hired Rachel to seduce her husband so that she could divorce him for cheating on her and walk away with fifteen million dollars.

Something didn't fit. Maybe I'm more devious or smarter than Brittney, but if it were me and I wanted to set up my husband, I would have set everything in motion *before* hiring the private investigator. I would have a similar sob story—*oh, he's changed, he's lying to me, he's ignoring me, blah, blah*—but I would have had Rachel (well, someone smarter and wiser than Rachel) already in the wings so that the first time my PI went to follow him, there would be something to photograph.

There were plenty of people who could be hired for nefarious purposes.

Which is why this whole charade with Brittney was giving me a headache. Ten days of nothing…then I give her a name of a female business associate and suddenly that's the name Brittney drops to set up her husband? And she didn't think I'd pick up on it?

I called Tess.

"What have you found on Jennifer White?"

"Nothing new. Did Rachel admit everything?"

"Yep. Brittney hired her, wanted the money shot with her husband making it with another woman." Which I didn't get because there was no money shot to be had.

"Why would she want to sabotage her own marriage?"

There were a lot of reasons people no longer wanted to be married, but Tess still believed in true love and happily-ever-after. Even when I was mad at her, which was often, I never wanted to burst her bubble.

"For Brittney, it's about money. She gets more in the divorce if he cheats."

"Just money? There has to be something else."

"Why?"

"I don't know—it seems so *crass*."

It *was* crass, but it was also common. "Yeah, I think it is just about money. Maybe she never loved him, maybe she did but he's a jerk, maybe she just got tired of being tied down to one man, maybe she found someone else. Don't know, don't care."

Not completely true—I didn't care about Brittney Monroe, but I wanted the truth.

I hated being used.

I shifted the conversation back to Jennifer White. "Learn anything about Desert West?"

"Jack's there now. Are you coming to the office?"

She sounded almost hopeful. "Miss me?" I said.

"I thought you wanted to help find Jennifer."

"I do, but I have something to follow up on. I'll call you when I'm done."

Twenty-Six

Jack Angelhart

Jack sat across from Desert West Financial CFO Ronald Tucker in Ron's private office early Tuesday afternoon.

"Sorry to drop in last minute," Jack said, accepting the water bottle that Ron offered him.

"I'm glad I was in," Ron said. "I'm leaving this evening with our CEO to meet with investors." He glanced at the door.

"Are we waiting for someone?"

"The assistant CFO. But go ahead, I can fill him in later. I read your report and am a bit confused. You believe that Jennifer is the only one who could have downloaded the software, but have no evidence?"

"Correct. At this point, you may want to lock her out of the office, the computers, until you question her. We don't think she's sold any proprietary information, and there's no sign that she's planning to do so, but again, her behavior has been suspicious so it has to be your call." Jack wasn't sold on not telling Ron about Jennifer's meeting with Monroe, but both his mother and Margo wanted to hold it back until they knew more.

"I don't know what to do," Ron said. "I don't want her to be guilty of anything. There may be a logical explanation."

Maybe, Jack thought, but Ron didn't seem to be a decisive CFO. Jack would have already confronted Jennifer with the information they had. "Our staff went through the logs you provided, but my partner thinks we need to review the on-site logs. An expert can assess whether the logs were tampered with only if they can access the hard drive. We'd like to bring in our in-house computer expert."

"Anything you need, you have," Ron said. "I'm leaving for Las Vegas tonight with the CEO, Gavin O'Keefe, since we have a long line of meetings. I'll be back Thursday afternoon, and then I'll talk to Jennifer. It would help if you were there, to outline what you've found and why her actions are concerning."

"I'll be there."

That seemed to relieve him. "Thank you. Brad can get you set up for tonight."

"It would be best if no one, not even your most trusted employee, knows what we're doing here," Jack said.

Ron seemed surprised, then agreed. "Building security will then need to let you in."

"Okay. One more question. I went through the records you gave me and there is only one contact for Ms. White—her neighbor. Do you know anything about her family?"

"She doesn't talk about her family," Ron said.

"Did you know she took a pay cut when she left her last job?"

"Yes. She said that the stress was difficult to manage with her last employer, and she preferred our smaller, more relaxed environment. She also came highly recommended by Mr. Logan Monroe, who had owned the company with Mr. O'Keefe until about eighteen months ago."

Confirming what Jack knew without him asking. Suspicious, or conversational?

"And the split between Mr. Monroe and Mr. O'Keefe was amicable enough that you accepted his recommendation?"

"They've been friends for more than a decade. Logan wasn't really interested in the financial sector. We buy and sell loans. It's a profitable niche market. I think the rote tasks bored Logan. Gavin doesn't interfere in the day-to-day management, but is hands-on at the macro level, such as investor and client meetings. Logan is more of an innovator. Is there a reason you're asking?"

"I'm verifying what I've learned about Ms. White. She interned for Mr. Monroe, and he recommended her for this job."

"She more than proved herself. That's why I'm having a hard time believing she'd steal from us."

Jack rose. "What time does your staff leave?"

"Generally everyone is gone by five—our office is open from six a.m. to five p.m. to handle both East and West Coast transactions."

"My people will be here at five thirty, if you can make sure your staff is all gone?"

"Yes, and I'll let security know."

"Thank you," Jack said.

"How long do you need?"

"A few hours." Lulu said it wouldn't take long, and Jack hoped they had the answers tonight.

"You'll let me know as soon as you know?" Ron said. "Call me, no matter the time. I'm losing sleep over this."

Jack agreed, thanked Ron, and left. He sent Tess the details; she would alert Luisa, the Angelhart secret weapon. Jack grinned. His little sister was a whiz with computers, thanks to the military.

Jack slid into his truck just as his phone vibrated with a text message. He assumed it was Tess confirming. He was wrong.

The message was from Logan Monroe.

Can you meet this afternoon? I need to hire you.

Twenty-Seven

Margo Angelhart

I sent Jack's call to voice mail, but followed with a quick text that I'd call in a few.

I'd just arrived at the Cactus Park police precinct because I needed to confirm that Carillo ran my plates. That meant talking to Rick.

Sergeant Rick Devlin worked swing shift in the 900, a long narrow precinct bordering Glendale west of the I-17 corridor. I had debated going to his house in Anthem, but decided after three months of no contact, showing up on his doorstep wasn't the best idea.

So here I was, outside his precinct and hoping it was open.

Phoenix PD was so understaffed that they often didn't have the people to handle walk-ins. They were understaffed three years ago when Jack left, and they were no better off now. Phoenix was the fifth largest city in the US and had half as many officers per capita as the fourth largest city—and a *third* as many officers as the sixth largest city.

So staffing precincts for walk-in traffic was one of the first luxuries to go.

Just because Rick was a sergeant didn't mean he sat at his desk all day—he was often in the field, responding for backup or whenever a ranked officer was needed at a crime scene. But, because he was a sergeant, he was always in the precinct at the beginning of his shift.

I arrived at ten minutes before two, when he would officially be on duty, and was fortunate that the precinct was open, manned by a very pregnant woman in leggings, a filmy blouse, and lightweight jacket. My guess, a cop on light duty.

"Hi, I'm here to see Sergeant Devlin," I said. "Margo Angelhart."

"Angelhart? You know Jack?" She had a New York or New Jersey accent. I know they're different, but linguistics are not in my skill set. I can tell the difference between the west, the east, and the south, and that's about it.

"My brother."

Angelhart is not a common name. I was related to every Angelhart I'd ever met.

"How's he doing?"

"Good. You worked with him?"

"Eight years ago, before he got his gold shield, he was my FTO. Back when I only had one kid and thought that was it. You talk to him often?"

"Just had burgers and beer last night."

"Next time you see him, tell him Fitz got knocked up again."

"You're Fitz."

"Eleanor Fitzpatrick, a mouthful."

"Try Margaret Angelhart ten times fast."

Fitz laughed. "I saw Dev come in, but let me see if he's free."

She rose, put a hand on her back. "I swear, this is the last kid I'm popping out. 'Course, I said that four years ago with number two. It just gets harder the older I get."

There was a time I wanted kids. That's what happens when you grow up in a great family—you want to make a great family of your own. But I was on the verge of turning thirty-three and didn't have a steady boyfriend, let alone a husband, and I wasn't going to do it alone. I'd thought Charlie Endicott was the one, then he wasn't. For a while, I thought Rick Devlin was the one.

He wasn't. At least, the jury's still out. And the longer the jury was out, the less likely we'd make it work.

Rick came out with Fitz and stared at me. I wanted to melt. He was just as sexy as I remembered, and the way he looked at me as if he was surprised and pleased and confused all at the same time had me twisted up inside.

Rick was one of the few men who ever tied me in knots like this.

"Have a sec?" I asked.

Unspoken, *in private.*

"Of course." He walked me through the back. He glanced at my hip. "You carrying?"

"My usual." It was always a good idea to tell cops when you had a weapon, especially in their own house.

Rick and I had been to the range together many times. We were competitive. But win or lose, whatever we bet usually ensured we *both* won.

Rick was one of those guys I was super attracted to. All fit and lean and muscular with deep blue eyes the color of dawn, a square jaw, and dark hair that was always just over regulation length and curled at his collar.

Rick could have been a model. Knowing Police and Fire had a sometimes not-so-friendly rivalry, I once teased him he was so gorgeous he could be on the cover of the next Phoenix Firefighter calendar. He pretended to be angry and proceeded to do things to me in bed that he claimed no fireman was capable of.

I had to stop thinking about Rick and sex or I was going to make another huge mistake.

I'd promised myself three months ago when we had it out that I would not come back without a sincere apology coming out of this man's mouth. A bit of groveling would be nice. Hence, we hadn't spoken in three months.

Rick found a small conference room for us and closed the door. "I assume you want privacy."

"I really want a computer."

"You look good, Margo."

"Liar."

He smiled, shook his head. "I didn't think you'd want me to comment on the dark circles under your eyes."

"I like honesty," I said and returned his grin. "A lot of late nights this week. I need a favor."

"We haven't talked in three months and you want a favor."

"We haven't talked because you haven't called to apologize," I said, losing the smile. "I don't like asking you for a favor, but I don't have anyone else to go to."

He didn't say anything for a minute and he didn't avert his eyes. I refused to fidget. I stared back at him, as casually as I could.

"It depends," Rick finally said. "I'll help if I can."

I had thought the entire morning as I was installing my new security system about how much to tell Rick.

He would know if I was lying—or at least suspect—and be less likely to help. But I didn't want to tell him everything. I knew him, and he would go after Peter Carillo.

Maybe I wanted him to, but not when it could jeopardize Rick's career.

"Can you find out if someone ran my plates? It would be recent—the last forty-eight hours. Law enforcement, but not Phoenix PD."

That surprised him. "Why?"

"I'll tell you if the answer is yes, you'll do it."

"I don't want to know if you've committed a crime, Margo. Don't put me in that position."

"I didn't commit a crime."

Rick and I had three fundamental problems in our relationship. One of them? He didn't like how I sometimes crossed the line. I would argue I walked the line, but he didn't concur. We had dealt with this conflict by, essentially, ignoring it.

He motioned for me to follow him to his cubicle.

"It's quiet."

"Everyone's on patrol."

"I thought you'd be in briefings."

"They staggered swing. Hell, last year they fucked up the entire schedule. And we're still seriously short."

"I know. It sucks."

"We need more good cops. With your background, you'd be fast-tracked."

"Don't start again."

When I left the Army, Jack tried to get me to join Phoenix PD. Being a female *and* former military *and* military police was like a trifecta of positives. I seriously considered it after two years of bartending while building my fledgling PI practice, but then I got my first big case and I knew then and there, being a PI was my calling. I'd had enough of the rules and regulations in the military, and being in law enforcement would be more of the same.

I liked my job, I liked making my own hours, and I especially liked not having to follow other people's rules.

"Can't help it," he said with a half grin and logged into his computer. "Let me think about how to do this— what agency, do you know?"

"DPS."

He typed quickly, but only using four fingers—the middle and index fingers on each hand.

Then he stopped. "I'm trusting you, Margo. Because everything I do generates a record, and I don't want to have to explain this to my LT."

"I didn't commit a crime."

He turned back to the computer. "Your plates."

I rattled off my license plate number.

He stared at the screen.

"Yes."

"Yes, someone at DPS ran my plates?"

"Monday afternoon, just after seventeen hundred."

"Shit. Is there any way for him to go back and erase his search history?"

"Every search is logged. It can't be erased." Rick looked back at the computer, printed the sheet. He stared at it, frowned. "Wait, we had a report come in this morning with this name." He closed down the database he was in and brought up the briefing sheet. "Trooper Carillo filled a missing persons report on his wife and two kids. Do you know about this?"

The bastard filed a report. I thought he might—when

your wife runs away with your kids without a trace, you have to say something to someone otherwise you might be considered a suspect in their disappearance.

But what did I tell Rick? I technically hadn't committed a crime. Annie was the mother of those two kids, and she was still married to Carillo. If he wanted to fight his wife for abandonment or denying him access to his children, he had to go to court. He'd probably win, but it wouldn't happen overnight, and by the time he had a judgment, Annie would be deep in her new identity two states away.

"Can I see the report?"

"You promised to tell me."

"I will. But Rick—you have to make me a promise."

"What the fuck, Margo? Changing the rules?"

"I know you, and I don't want you to do something stupid."

"Are you in trouble?"

"No."

"Then just tell me."

I glanced around, but the only person in the bullpen was a detective on the far side of the room, and she was on the phone.

"Carillo's wife hired me."

"Why?"

"To protect her."

Rick's eyes darkened, his voice turning so low it was almost a whisper. He grabbed my wrist. "Are you telling me that Carillo hurts his wife?"

I should have found someone other than Rick to get the information from. I knew his story, knew about his childhood.

"Rick." I didn't raise my voice, but I glanced at where he held my arm tight.

He immediately let go, looked almost panicked.

This was our second fundamental problem. Rick had been raised by an abusive father and alcoholic mother. He feared he would turn violent, that it ran in his genes. He became a cop to help victims, but sometimes, his anger overcame him when faced with certain cases. He'd been suspended once for excessive force when he was called to a scene where a belligerent man had blackened the eye of his teenage son, then broke his arm right in front of Rick and his partner. At the same time, when he worked a domestic violence case, he could almost always talk the victim into getting help.

I didn't want to give him a reason to go after Carillo.

"He ran your plates," Rick said calmly. "So he knows you helped her."

"I was careful, but he's sneaky. He monitors all external doors—when they open and close—so he knew when Annie last left the house. He probably talked to the neighbors, looked at their security cameras. He could have run every car that drove down his street around the time his garage opened." I did not tell Rick that Carillo was in my house. I wasn't certain I could talk him down from going after the man, and I had no proof. If I had proof, I would have filed charges against him.

I held out my hand. "Can I see the report, please?"

Rick hit print, then handed me the paper when it popped off his printer. I read quickly.

"Fuck him," I said. "He's making claims that I know are not true."

"What claims?"

"Annie isn't depressed—postpartum? What the hell?

That's just to make it sound like she might be a danger to her kids."

"Is she?"

"No."

"Where is she?"

"I don't know." Technically, I didn't know *exactly* where she was, only the city and the person she met when she arrived. "I didn't want to know. She's gone, she's not coming back."

"He can go to court."

"Let him."

"What did he do to her?"

I looked at him, really looked. "Do not go after him, Rick. I have a plan." Sort of. Not really. More, thinking about making a plan.

"What did he do to her?" Rick repeated slowly. Anger lit his eyes but his voice was cool, calm.

"Complete and total control over her life. Tracked her through her phone. Knew when she left the house and when she came home. Separated her from her friends. Repeatedly raped her. Every morning she woke up to him forcing himself into her. When she said no, he punished her—but never left a mark on her body where it could be seen. She started planning to leave when she found out she was pregnant with Marie. She hid grocery money. But she didn't know how to leave him without him being able to find her or get custody. When he accused her of flirting with a waiter, she finally reached out for help. She fears for her life."

"Arizona has some of the toughest domestic violence laws in the country. Why didn't you bring her to me?"

He meant to say to the police, but he didn't. Because he personalized these cases.

"Because Carillo is a cop and she doesn't trust the system. She feared he would get visitation and either take her kids or turn them against her. He's sadistic and cruel. She has no family—her mother's dead, father lives out of state and she hasn't talked to him in years, grandparents are dead, no siblings. She had friends, until Carillo. She had a job, until Carillo. She believes that only by disappearing will she live."

"And he knows you helped her."

"He can't surprise me because now that I know he knows, I'm prepared."

"A man like this—he'll come after you."

"I hope he does."

"Dammit, Margo!" Rick glanced around to make sure no one heard him. He lowered his voice. "Margo, listen to me—you are tough and capable and I'd bet on you any day of the week in a fair fight. But a man with a badge who hurts his wife isn't going to play fair when you screw with him."

I was doubly glad I hadn't told Rick about the break-in.

Rick continued. "He needs to be fired."

"Good luck with that," I said.

"I have resources. I can get Annie into a safe shelter, get her a good lawyer—your aunt, she's taken cases like this pro bono."

"Annie isn't coming back. I can't reach her. I don't have her number, don't know where she is."

"It's the kids—someone reports the kids and we'll have to go and make sure they're okay, put it in the system. He'll know where they are, can still get to them. She needs to testify. I know it's hard, but—"

"Not going to happen. She left the state." I winced. I hadn't meant to say that, but Rick probably suspected

I knew more about Annie's whereabouts than I'd admitted to him.

He stared at me. "You gave her money, didn't you?"

I didn't answer. He knew me, and I didn't want to argue with him about my finances.

"Rick, I got this. Thank you—I mean it—for helping me."

"Does Jack know?"

I shook my head.

"He needs to know."

"No, he doesn't. Look," I added before he could argue with me, "if I get any sense that Carillo is going to do something rash, I'll talk to Jack. Right now, there is nothing against Carillo. I'll find something. Because you and I both know that his wife isn't the only one he hurt."

"I'll look at his record."

"You don't—" The look on his face had me stopping mid-sentence. "Okay. Don't do anything stupid."

"Double for you."

I rose, turned to leave, then looked back over my shoulder. "Tell Sam I said hi."

He nodded, but didn't say anything.

I left. Samantha Devlin was our third fundamental problem. Rick's thirteen-year-old daughter had come to me three months ago for help with a cyberbully. She hadn't wanted to tell her dad, and I hadn't told him. I had mistakenly believed because Rick and I were on a more serious spin in our on-again, off-again relationship that he trusted me with his daughter.

He found out and told me that I wasn't her mother and had no right to keep something like a cyberbully from him. It hurt. He was partly right—I should have told him, or pushed Sam to tell him what was going on.

But I had been a thirteen-year-old girl and there were some things that thirteen-year-old girls were not comfortable telling their fathers—especially a first kiss and the subsequent rumors and lies that followed online. He was right—but what he said cut deep. I love Sam. And Rick cut her out of my life.

Some things Rick and I could overcome.

Some things, we couldn't.

I called Jack as I left the station.

"You rang?" I said.

"I thought you were helping us."

"I have other cases."

"I'm here with Logan. If you're willing to help, I could use it. Tess and Luisa are working another angle."

Jack, wanting my help. Did he really need it, or was this another stunt to get me to join the family business?

Still…if Jack was helping Logan, I could find out more about him and his relationship with Brittney, try to figure out why she'd hired me in the first place.

Brittney wanted a divorce with as much money as she could get, which meant proving adultery. But my gut told me she knew he wasn't cheating, so why hire me *before* she set him up with Rachel? Maybe she'd tried to set him up at the beginning but it hadn't worked? She hadn't even *known* about Jennifer until after Logan met with her.

There were genuinely stupid people in the world. And increasingly, I suspected Brittney was one of them. Unless she had some brilliant endgame in mind that I just couldn't see yet.

"Okay," I said. "Text me when and where."

Twenty-Eight

Peter Carillo

Peter finally told Brian to leave late that afternoon. He needed to be alone. Too much pressure, too many people asking questions. He couldn't *think*.

But the pain that Annie had put him in was worse than anything. All because she was throwing a temper tantrum.

His mom called and Peter didn't want to talk to her, but he answered. "There's no news," he said.

"I know. A detective came to talk to me. I told you not to call the police. You're the police. She'll be back. Annie doesn't have two brain cells to rub together, she wouldn't know how to take care of those kids without your paycheck and support."

"Something could have happened to them."

"She's jerking your chain, like she always does. Didn't I tell you, Peter? Didn't I tell you when you married her that she was going to lead you around by your dick?"

Peter put his head down on the table and willed his mother to stop talking. But she continued. She went on and on about how he wasn't a strong enough man to keep Annie. How he had failed everyone because she left *with his kids*.

"What did you tell the detective?" Peter finally asked.

"I told them exactly what we talked about. That woman has a screw loose."

"I hope you didn't say it like that. They'll think you don't like her."

His mother sighed dramatically. "I know how to talk to people, Peter. And I explained that I shared your concerns about Annie. I know the signs of postpartum depression well enough—I was a nurse, after all."

She'd actually listened to him when he called her last night. Small blessing. "Thank you, Mom."

"Do you want me to come out? I'll be there tomorrow morning."

"I'm fine."

"You're not fine. I can tell. I'm your mother. You're drinking too much. When was the last time you ate?"

He stared at the near-empty bottle of bourbon. He'd drank most of it last night, but he'd finish it now. "Brian got me a sandwich from the deli."

"A deli sandwich? I'll be there tomorrow. I'll cook you a real meal."

"Please don't." He didn't know if he could handle his mother's criticisms, not now.

"Why don't you want me?"

She sounded hurt. Dammit, why did she do this to him?

"Of course, I want you here, Mom, but I have things to do. People I need to talk to. I've taken the week off, I have plenty of sick time. I'm going to find her."

"You'd better. Those kids are your children, *my* grandchildren, and she crossed the line."

He finally got off the phone and stared at his empty house. He turned on the television to the sports channel just to have voices.

Where did Annie go? She didn't have money, and if Margo Angelhart had money, it didn't show. Maybe the bitch gave Annie money for a plane ticket, but what about a house? Food? Annie couldn't support the kids. Were they going to be living on the street?

Or was Annie with another man?

Both ideas made him physically ill. He drained the bourbon, then went to the garage to toss the bottle in the recycling bin.

There had to be something here to give him an *idea* about where she had gone. He'd already searched the house, even the kids' rooms. Peter stood in the garage and stared at her car. Maybe…maybe there was something in her car that could give him a direction. A receipt. A scrawled phone number. *Anything*.

He opened all the doors, looked under the seats, between the seats, in the glove compartment box, the middle console, everywhere. The car was immaculate.

He sat in the driver's seat and thought. Where had she gone? How did she get there?

Credit cards.

He had logged in and looked at the last few days of charges, searching for hotel, airfare, gas outside of the area. There had been nothing. But what about months ago? What if she had this planned *for months*? He didn't look at the charge details unless the bill seemed unusually large.

He slammed the doors, went inside and logged into

their credit card account. He looked at every charge for the last six months and didn't see anything unusual.

Then he checked their joint checking account. This was the card Annie used for gasoline and groceries. He went through each expense starting with her last one—she'd gone to Walmart the day before she disappeared and spent $229.31. Food? Clothing? It was a larger amount than normal. Buying stuff with his money in order to disappear?

He scrolled back, back, back, growing frustrated, angry, uncertain.

Then straightened when he saw something out of the ordinary.

Three months ago, on the last Sunday of February, Annie had filled up the car with gas at a station on Dunlap and Highway 17.

Dunlap was the exit he'd taken to get to Angelhart's house.

His wife had been planning to leave him for *three months*. She'd plotted and schemed and *lied* to him for *months*.

He brought up a map of Sunnyslope, from the freeway to Angelhart's house. Stared, trying to find another reason for Annie to have been down there. As he zoomed in, he saw it.

St. Dominic's Catholic Church

He'd seen a calendar from the church in Angelhart's office. That made sense—Annie liked going to church. She took the kids to one closer to the house, but Sunnyslope... This felt familiar to him.

Something in the back of his mind told him St. Dominic's was more important than he'd realized yesterday. Hadn't Annie told him that her grandparents had lived in Sunnyslope? That they'd been married in a little church there?

He needed to research the church, find out what connection, if any, there was to Annie or her family. Maybe that's how she found the PI, through someone at the church. A secretary, a parishioner. A priest?

Would a *priest* take his children away from him?

Peter found the St. Dominic's website and read about the parish and the people who worked there.

Did one of them know where Annie was?

He would find out.

Twenty-Nine

Margo Angelhart

Logan Monroe had a suite of offices in the Scottsdale Quarter. Convenient with ample parking, great restaurants, and easy access to the 101 and small Scottsdale Airport.

When I arrived, I went to the top floor—the fourth floor—in a building near the Apple Store and across from the small palm-tree lined park in the center of the Quarter. At night the trees were lit with tiny white lights and it was quite pretty. With restaurants, shopping, and a theater, it made the area great for date nights. Not that I'd had a date in a while.

Logan was one of the investors in the Quarter, and leased a small office suite on the top floor of one of the buildings. When I entered, there was no receptionist, but I spotted Jack and Logan through the open door that led to the corner office. Logan didn't know the meaning of the word *security*.

"Want something to drink?" Logan asked when I stepped in. "I have soda and water. No coffee, sorry— I don't drink it."

"Water would be great, thanks," I said.

He opened a mini-fridge in his office that was stocked with Coke and water. He might not drink coffee, but the sugar and caffeine in the fully loaded Coke would give a jolt.

"I already told your brother what I know," he said.

"Tell Margo," Jack said. "Because if anyone can find Jennifer, it's my sister."

I was surprised by the praise—not because I hadn't earned it, but because Jack was just as capable as me.

"You work together, though, right?" Logan looked down at Jack's card. "Angelhart Investigations."

Jack and I both said, "Sometimes" and I added, "I have my own shingle, but all the same credentials."

Jack gave me a quick rundown on how Logan and Jennifer ended up at Logan's house in Paradise Valley, then he said, "We haven't been able to locate Jennifer, and that lends credence that she's in hiding, and that whoever poisoned them was targeting her."

I asked Logan, "How did you and Jennifer communicate in the days leading up to Sunday's meeting? Phone? Email?"

"Text," Logan said. "The last time I heard from her—again, text message—was Sunday night. She promised to call me when she was settled."

"And she hasn't contacted you?"

He shook his head. "That's why I'm worried."

"Do you have any idea who drugged you and Jennifer?" I asked.

Logan shook his head, and Jack said, "I talked to my contact at the crime lab this morning. They found three canisters of nitrogen in the ventilation system."

That stunned me. "Nitrogen? That could have killed them."

Jack nodded. "Margo saved your lives," he said. "You and Jennifer could have been asphyxiated."

Logan nodded. "The police called me this morning with a report—they're treating this as an attempted murder. I gave them all the information I had, but it's not much. They promised it's a priority for them."

It probably was, I thought, but an investigation like this would take time and they didn't have much to go on. "Did anyone know you were going there Sunday?" I asked.

He shook his head. "The police asked the same thing. No one—except Jennifer. But it wasn't her."

"You're certain."

"Why would Jennifer try to kill me? She was exposed as well."

I leaned toward agreeing with Logan's assessment, and Jack said, "It would have taken someone an hour or more to set up the canisters. There were no prints, and the police are working on tracing them but they're commonly available at retailers and online. I was watching Jennifer and she was only there ten minutes before you arrived. She didn't have time. And get this—the canisters were set on a remote, not a timer. Someone triggered them *after* you entered the house."

"What was the range?" I asked.

"They had to be close according to the lab."

I thought about Frank Sanchez on the mountain and Jack must have read my mind because he said, "Closer than the mountain. I think someone was in the house. I relayed my theory to the detective, and he's following up."

"Wouldn't they be affected?" I asked.

"Not if they had oxygen with them," Jack said. "As the intended victim, you should be able to get more info than me."

"This doesn't make any sense," Logan said.

It was just starting to make some sense to me, but I still had too many missing pieces.

"You told me yesterday that you and Jennifer hadn't discussed why she wanted to meet you, but that's not correct," Jack prompted.

Logan turned to me. "I told your brother that I didn't share information because I didn't know him, but I made some calls and you both come highly recommended. Even my lawyer gave the thumbs-up, and Carmen doesn't like many people."

"Carmen Delarosa?" I said.

"You know her?"

"She's hired me a couple of times." Carmen was a bulldog. She fought hard for her clients every step of the way, to the point that people who went up against her called her a bitch, often to her face. She took it as a badge of honor. And Logan was right—Carmen didn't like people. But she disliked some people more than others.

"When I arrived at the house on Sunday, Jennifer had her laptop open. She got right to the point. She had downloaded raw code that she said shows that every transaction that went through Desert West diverted between forty-nine and ninety-nine cents into an account not controlled by the company. She's not an accountant, but has enough computer and math skills that she saw the unusual pattern."

"Why didn't she tell the CFO?" Jack asked.

"She didn't know who had set up the transfer. It had to be done internally, and she felt that Tucker should have realized it, so couldn't discount that he might have been the one to have stolen the money. *If* the money was stolen. The line item was a processing fee, and it didn't stand out on its face. When you have a hundred-thousand-dollar transaction, a ninety-nine-cent processing fee is nothing. That alone should have raised red flags, but again when people think of pennies, they don't think they're losing anything."

"But all those pennies in the same pot adds up," I said.

"Exactly," Logan said. "Jennifer believes that over a million dollars was taken, but she doesn't know how long this had been going on. When I sold my half of the company to Gavin eighteen months ago, there had been a full audit, and I checked the paperwork—this processing fee *wasn't* there. Which means it was added after I sold."

"What was her theory?" Jack asked.

"We didn't get that far," Logan said. "She explained about the fee, then brought up the files and wanted me to look at the code—thought maybe I would see something because I had more experience than she did. That's when she fainted."

Jack and I exchanged a glance. We were thinking the same thing. Whoever used the nitrogen to knock out Logan and Jennifer wanted her laptop because she had evidence of corporate theft. They waited in the house until Jennifer was unconscious and intended to either destroy or steal the laptop. But then I showed up and foiled their plan.

"The data she downloaded must have been what

alerted the CFO that someone on staff had taken proprietary information from the office," Jack said. "Then he hired me."

Logan said, "Jennifer told me she'd contact me yesterday, which is why I met with Rachel at the bar last night. I can't believe that she lied about knowing Jennifer. Maybe she drugged me to find out where Jennifer is."

"She doesn't know anything about Jennifer," I said, "nor is she a threat to her."

His brows knit together. "How do you know?"

"I talked to Rachel today. She won't bother you again."

He looked confused. "Why did she do it?"

I wanted to tell him that his wife was trying to catch him with another woman, but I refrained. The NDA was null and void at this point, but until I knew exactly what was going on with Brittney, I wanted to keep it to myself.

I didn't answer Logan's question, hopefully he'd think I assumed it was hypothetical.

"I wanted to hire Jack to find Jennifer, but he said he had a conflict," Logan continued.

"I was hired by Desert West. I can't take money from you to, essentially, do the same thing."

"But they hired you to find out who downloaded information—oh." Logan realized the conflict. "I just told you that Jennifer downloaded the data."

"If what she told you is accurate, she didn't do anything to harm the company, but I still need to talk to her and verify the information she has, and she'll have to explain to her employer," Jack said. "Having you vouch for me would help, which is a long way of saying I will be looking for her."

Logan turned to me. "But I can hire *you* to find Jennifer, correct?"

"You can, but Jack is already looking for her—"

"I feel responsible," Logan said. "I helped Jennifer get the job with Desert West, and she came to me for help. Now she's missing. She hasn't returned my calls or messages."

I asked, "Do you know anything about her family?"

He shook his head. "She never talked about her childhood. I had a sense that it wasn't a pleasant one, but she didn't say anything about it. I didn't pry."

"Do you know if she has brothers or sisters? If her parents are still alive?"

He shook his head. "I really have no idea."

Jack shot me a confused look, which I ignored.

"Do you know why she left her position in Silicon Valley? She took a substantial pay cut to work for Desert West."

"I didn't know that," he said.

"You recommended Jennifer to Desert West, even though you no longer owned the company?"

"Gavin and I are friends. He remembered her from Texas and was thrilled to bring her on."

"Gavin O'Keefe also worked with you in Texas?"

"We both still own that company through our investors group. I really don't understand what you want to know," Logan said.

"Jennifer has no social media footprint. No known friends or family. She seems to be a lone wolf—she works, goes to the gym, goes home."

"Jennifer has always been introverted," Logan said. "I understand that. It took me a long time to learn how to be social, and I still don't particularly like social situations, unless I know the people."

"Can you think of anyone she's close to? At work, in Texas, from college?"

He shook his head. "I like Jennifer, but we're not social friends. She considered me a mentor when she interned for me. We worked together almost every day for a semester. I moved to Arizona before she graduated and started at the company full-time."

"Was she close to anyone in your old company? A friend, a colleague, a roommate?"

He was about to say no, then tilted his head and said, "Maybe Davis. Davis Balicki. He's the IT manager and they were friendly."

"How friendly?"

"Friends. Davis is married with kids. But he took her under his wing. She may have contacted him if she was in trouble." He pulled out his phone. "I can give you his contact information."

"Can you reach out to him? He knows you, and he might not tell a stranger where she is."

He didn't hesitate and hit Davis's number. He put the phone on speaker.

"Hello?" Davis said.

"Davis, it's Logan Monroe."

After a minute of small talk, Logan asked, "You remember Jennifer White?"

"Of course."

"She reached out to me last week to help her with a project, and now I can't reach her. She sounded upset and I'm worried. Has she reached out to you?"

"We talked a couple of weeks ago," Davis said.

"About?" Logan pushed.

"She asked about algorithms. She was analyzing a glitch in software and saw something that appeared to be a randomizing algorithm that shouldn't be in the code, but she wasn't certain because it had unfamiliar properties. We worked through a couple of problems, then she said she had a handle on it."

I scrawled a note with a couple questions I wanted him to ask and slid it over to Logan.

Instead, Logan said, "Davis, I'm here with two private investigators. They have some questions for you."

"Anything I can do, Logan, anything. I hope she's okay."

"Mr. Balicki, I'm Margo Angelhart," I said. "Does Jennifer have any friends that she would reach out to if she wanted to get away? Maybe in Austin, where she used to work?"

"Me," he said. "She used to come over for dinner when she lived here, we keep in touch, but I don't know any of her friends. Jennifer is very reserved. Private."

"What about a former roommate?"

"As far as I know, she's always lived alone."

"Do you know anything about her parents?"

"She doesn't talk about them. She'd come over to my house for barbecues if it was just my family and not a party. My wife is good at getting people to share, and that's when I learned her mother died when she was young and she left home when she was eighteen, hasn't spoken to her father since. Didn't say anything more about it. I had a feeling she might have been in an abusive home, so I didn't push."

That might explain why she didn't have social media. If her father was still trying to influence or abuse her— verbal and emotional abuse could be as bad as physical abuse. But there had to be more. She'd left home eight years ago. Shouldn't she have found a niche, a group, a few friends? I couldn't imagine not having friends and family. I could be grumpy and standoffish at times, but I thrived in the Army because my team was like family. And after growing up in a large family, silence was not always comfortable.

"If she calls you or shows up at your house," I said, "please let me or Logan know. Tell her that we can help, whatever is going on."

"I will. And when you talk to her, please let me know so I don't worry."

Logan ended the call and said, "I feel helpless. I'm not someone who usually feels helpless."

"She may have dumped her electronics to avoid being tracked," Jack said, "or she's ignoring your calls and messages. Send her another—email, text, every way you have of reaching her. She trusts you, so I think she'll listen to you more than anyone. Tell her that you've hired Margo Angelhart to protect her. Anything she needs to feel safe."

I glanced at my brother. "Me?"

"Do you handle personal security?" Logan asked.

"Yes, but—"

"Margo is a former Army MP and has been trained in personal security, she's capable," Jack said. "I would do it, but I have to ask Jennifer questions about the data she downloaded. Margo doesn't. If Jennifer is truly in fear of an external threat, she'll need someone to protect her. But until we know what that threat is, we're floundering.

"In the meantime, Tess and Luisa—my other sisters—

are doing a deep dive into the Desert West computer systems. You've seen the data that Jennifer had, right?"

"Part of it, but only for a few minutes."

"Still, you might be able to help narrow their search to avoid them wasting time. Based on what Jennifer showed you, do you think someone is embezzling from the company?"

"I didn't make that leap. It was odd, but it could have been a coding error. Without a full audit and computer security check, we can't know. Gavin should be made aware of this."

"Right now, the only person in house who knows that I've been hired and why is Ron Tucker, the CFO. The fewer people who know, the better. The important thing is to find Jennifer and analyze the information she has. Because if someone is embezzling money, they may be trying to cover their tracks, and that's why Jennifer thinks she's being followed."

"Anything you need from me, let me know."

Jack could be right. Jennifer's paranoia could be directly related to her discovery at work. But I still thought it was more than a little odd that she had no social media, that her background was murky, and she had no close friends.

And who hired Miriam Endicott?

There was something else going on in Jennifer's life, I was certain. Whether it was potentially dangerous was anyone's guess.

Thirty

The Thief

The thief glanced at caller ID and declined the call for the third time. He didn't need the pressure right now. And they wouldn't be in this situation if it weren't for her.

If he didn't love her so much, he'd have killed her for her stupidity.

He had to focus on the problem at hand. He didn't know how much time he had. He'd waited until everyone else had left, then went into his boss's office. Now, reading through his boss's email, he realized Desert West had put private investigators on retainer to look into the illegal downloading of proprietary information.

On the surface, that wasn't a problem—he had already worked on laying the trail to frame Jennifer White, and with her unusual and erratic behavior no one should question it. Anything she said would be suspect. But this email indicated that the PI was bringing in a computer expert to analyze data directly from the server. *That* could potentially expose him.

Hoping for more information, he clicked on the report in the email. If he knew exactly what they planned to do, he might be able to cover his tracks.

Dammit, it was password-protected.

He didn't need this, not now. Jennifer was gone, and with her the evidence of his crime. He needed her laptop. He needed to stay on top of these so-called *experts*.

Sunday, when he lost Jennifer and the laptop, he'd returned to the office and, near tears, ended his "processing fee" program. All that cash flow...gone. He'd taken time to rewrite the code to erase the program, but it was a Band-Aid fix. He didn't have the time or—he admitted to himself—the skill to backtrack over the last fourteen months of potential evidence.

It wasn't fair! That bitch had stumbled on his brilliant plan and ruined everything.

And now, someone from Angelhart Investigations was coming in.

He couldn't let them download the data. While the program was no longer running, and he'd left a trail pointing at Jennifer White, they *might* be able to trace everything to him.

He'd been successful for more than a year and *wham*! Jennifer White puts her nose in software she should never have seen and destroys him.

"Calm down," he told himself.

"Excuse me?" The building security guard was walking through the office.

"Sorry, I'm just gathering up work."

"You need to be out of the office by five thirty because building maintenance is setting bug bombs," the guard said. "No one comes in until five thirty tomorrow morning."

It was a farce he now realized, but he went along with it. "Yes, I know, sorry. Work never ends." He smiled. He was the last one here and felt stuck.

The guard looked at his watch. "Five minutes, okay?"

"Yeah—thanks."

The guard walked away to check the other offices.

Be calm. They're not setting off bug poison.

He looked up at the ceiling. Desert West had the entire third floor. The fourth floor was partly vacant.

He had an idea.

He said good bye to the guard and rushed down to the parking garage. Popped his trunk and extracted—carefully—the last nitrogen canister. He hoped it was enough—he'd release it in the vent above the main computer room where they would be working. He grabbed his gym bag. It didn't have clothes or shoes; instead, it had supplies for just such an emergency.

Desperate times, desperate measures.

He used the elevator and bypassed the lobby, going directly to the fourth floor. By the time he reached the empty office, he was sweating and his hands were nearly raw from carrying the heavy metal canister.

He broke the lock and quickly went inside. Closed the door. Waited. Heard nothing.

He would wait until the investigators were in the office, then he would put them into a deep sleep, go downstairs, and finish destroying the evidence.

Yes, he would need to completely wipe the Desert West Financial server. It would damage the business, but sacrifices had to be made. They would recover eventually. And if he did it right, all fingers would point to Jennifer White, like he originally intended.

He wiped his brow. He was sweating. The AC wasn't on up here.

He looked at his phone. His girlfriend had called him seven times.

Even though he was still angry with her, he called her back. Listened to her rant, then cry.

"I love you, but I can't live like this," she wailed.

"Whatever you want to do," he said calmly, "don't."

"Don't be mean."

"Let me handle it. I have another plan, but I have to go. I'll call you tomorrow."

He ended the call and sighed.

If he didn't love Brittney Monroe so much, he would have killed her Sunday with his bare hands.

Thirty-One

Tess Angelhart

Tess was good with research using all the tools at her disposal, but her younger sister Luisa was a computer whiz. She'd always been smart, and had done something related to cybersecurity in the Marines. Luisa didn't talk much about her time in the Marines. She'd left last summer and enrolled at ASU studying psychology and computer science. She'd said that psychology was interesting, and computers were easy. Based on how her fingers flew across the keyboard, computers were certainly easy for Luisa.

"I don't even need to be here," Tess said after an hour.

"Don't be silly."

Tess let her sister work, not wanting to mess with her rhythm.

"Have you and Gabriel talked about a date yet?" Luisa asked a few minutes later.

Tess moaned. "Please, don't start. Everyone is asking, and I don't want to rush."

"I'm not nagging. You said yes, you want to marry him, why are you hesitating?"

"I'm not! I love Gabriel."

Tess loved him with everything she had. She knew why she was scared. She'd been engaged twice before. And twice before, her fiancé had left her. The first time had hurt, but she'd been young and accepted that he wasn't the right man. But the second time? She'd been head over heels in love, they'd set a date, she'd bought a wedding dress, they had mailed the invitations...and he said he couldn't go through with it. That he loved her, but he wasn't in love with her. She had no idea what that even meant. She'd begged him not to leave her, feeling small and stupid then, and especially now thinking about it.

It had taken her a year before she could even think of going out with another man. And then her father was arrested and her family fell apart. Her mother needed her, her brothers and sisters. She was resigned to being single for the rest of her life.

And then came Gabriel.

She kept expecting him to leave.

"I know you're scared," Luisa said simply. "But I've seen the way he looks at you. He loves you."

"I know."

"Do you?"

"He's perfect."

"No one is perfect, but Gabriel Rubio comes close." Luisa smiled. "Don't let the losers who came before kill your chance for happiness."

Tess rolled her eyes. "Now you sound like Margo."

"I'm glad we're working with her on this."

"I don't know," Tess said. "She's smart, and she has real good instincts. But she's a maverick."

"That's not always a bad thing."

"Not always a good thing, either."

"April," Luisa said.

"What?" Tess was confused.

"You met Gabriel in April, right? Next April is eleven months away and will be your two-year anniversary, of sorts. It's spring, not too hot, not too cold."

"I don't know," she said.

"Think about it."

Luisa frowned at the computer, tapped a few keys, frowned deeper.

"Someone installed a virus," she said.

"Like a virus in an email when you click on a bad link?"

"It's not an accident," Luisa said. "Someone intentionally downloaded a worm that ate all the data."

"How can it just be gone?" Tess yawned. It was only seven thirty, but she was exhausted. It had been a long week.

"It's gone *here*, but I can recreate the data from the archives. We can't do it tonight but it tells me someone knows the data will lead back to him, or her."

Tess had more questions, but she couldn't think clearly. "I'm going to find the break room. I need coffee."

Luisa frowned. "Wait," she said.

"What?" Tess rubbed her temples. She had a splitting headache. It seemed to come on suddenly, and it pounded.

Luisa didn't answer. She rose from her seat and looked at the ceiling, so Tess looked at the ceiling. She had no idea what she was looking at. Luisa started walking around, then stopped as if to listen.

"We have to get out of here," she said. "Drop to the floor, crawl to the door."

The room began to spin and Tess could barely hear Luisa.

"Do it," Luisa commanded, rushing over to Tess and pulling her down. Luisa grabbed her backpack, strapped it over her shoulders, and started crawling across the room to the door, urging Tess to move faster.

Tess tried.

"Whdya see?"

"I heard something—a hissing. You're yawning, your words are slurred, I'm lightheaded. There's gas coming from the vent in the corner."

"Like at Logan Monroe's house on Sunday," she muttered, or thought she did.

"I smell something," Luisa said. "Smoke, upstairs."

Tess didn't smell anything until they were halfway across the room. Then a pungent scent came from the ceiling, followed by smoke coming in through the vents. But her eyes were droopy, she was dizzy even though she was practically on the floor.

"Tess, move it," Luisa ordered.

She tried to tell Luisa that she was going as fast as she could, but her words were jumbled.

A moment later, the fire alarm pierced the silence, a high-pitched trill that made her jump. She moved faster, then collapsed. She tried to get up, but her arms and legs were slow and heavy.

She smelled burning—like a campfire, but more pungent. She kept moving, or thought she was moving, but Luisa was yelling at her over the sound of the alarms. Then suddenly, Luisa picked her up and had her over her shoulder. The first thing Tess thought was Luisa was way too small to carry her—Tess had at least four inches and forty pounds on her. But Luisa carried her easily.

They stumbled as they exited the office. The security guard ran up the stairs, coughing, and said, "You're the only two in the building, the fire department is on their way. Where's the fire?"

Luisa said, "Fourth floor."

Then the sprinklers came on and showered them and everything in Desert West Financial with a torrent of water.

Thirty-Two

Margo Angelhart

Jack came over to my house at nine Tuesday night with his laptop and a six pack of one of my favorite beers from Four Peaks Brewing, their year-round specialty Double Knot IPA.

"You really love me," I said and grabbed the six pack. "Want one?"

"I'll waste half of it. I don't know how you can drink IPAs."

"A meal in a bottle," I said. My favorite beer was Four Peaks seasonal porter, but I had to wait until October for it. The Double Knot was a close second.

I pulled out a bottle, put the rest in the fridge, and found a Coors Light in the back—it's what Rick drinks the rare times he drinks, so I usually kept some around. Thinking of Rick reminded me of our conversation today. It hadn't been as bad as I thought it would be.

I handed Jack the can and popped open my bottle, took a long swallow. "Did you get it?"

Jack and Tess had been working with a PI in Florida to obtain the yearbooks from Jennifer White's high school.

"Photos only," Jack said. "The school wouldn't give him hard copies. And even finding her high school was difficult—it's nowhere on her employment documents, and Tess finagled it out of her college. The problem? She lied on her résumé. No Jennifer White graduated from this high school. But I considered your theory that Jennifer White isn't her real name. Maybe she did graduate from this school, but not under that name."

"Don't businesses confirm all this? Run backgrounds?"

"College, maybe—get her transcript or just a copy of her degree. But unless she's going for a job that needs security clearance, no one is going to confirm her high school information. They might not even ask for it."

Jack opened his laptop and downloaded a large file from a cloud account.

"How does she get into college on a fake name?" I wondered.

"She's a computer expert. Maybe she falsified her transcripts. Almost everything is digital these days and someone who knows the system might be able to do it. Or hack in? I asked Logan about her skills, and he said she's more than capable. She has the ability now, but at eighteen?" He shrugged.

"Or someone did it for her," I said.

Jack brought up the most recent yearbook. "This is the year she graduated high school, according to her résumé with Desert West. This coincides with when she would have started college as well."

The Miami PI had done a decent job with the photos, taking clear pictures without any glare. The senior class had 520 graduates, and there was a total of 2,123 kids in the school. Jack first looked at all the *W*'s in all four grades and there was no Jennifer White.

So we started through the yearbook, looking at every senior female.

"Stop," I said. "That's her."

"What?"

I pointed to a blond girl with thick glasses. Under the picture was the name *Virginia Bonetti*.

Jack stared. "It could be, but—"

"She dyed her hair darker and wears contacts. But that's her."

I didn't doubt it. I pulled up my laptop and started searching the name while Jack continued to scroll through the yearbook photos. "She started at the school her sophomore year," he said as he finished going through the yearbooks. "She's not photographed or listed in her freshman year."

"Okay," I muttered as I scrolled through Google first. I had access to paid databases that most PIs used, but Google was always my first stop for basic information. "And she's dead."

"What?" Jack turned my laptop so he could read with me.

Teenager killed in boating accident week after high school graduation

A tragic boating accident outside Key Biscayne took the life of eighteen-year-old Virginia Bonetti on Sunday when a fire on the boat forced the occupants to jump into the ocean before the boat exploded.

The Coast Guard arrived twenty minutes after the explosion and rescued Vincent Bonetti and his sixteen-year-old son Thomas. After an extensive search, the body of Bonetti's eighteen-year-old daughter Virginia was not recovered. She is presumed to have drowned.

The family went out for the day on Bonetti's forty-foot yacht when, an hour after they left the dock, mechanical failure stopped the vessel. A fire started and Bonetti called the Coast Guard for assistance, but the fire spread fast and the family was forced to evacuate. Bonetti put his children on the lifeboat and pushed it off while he attempted to put out the fire, but it spread close to the fuel tank and he jumped as the boat exploded. The lifeboat capsized by the force of the explosion, and Thomas Bonetti found his father unconscious in the water. The teenager managed to right the lifeboat and pull in his father, but Virginia never surfaced.

Bonetti is currently in a medically induced coma while the doctors wait for swelling on his brain to go down.

Two weeks later, a follow-up to the article revealed that Bonetti was recovering at home and that the Coast Guard halted search efforts after a tropical storm moved in. A spokesman stated that Virginia Bonetti was presumed dead and they would send notices to all coastal agencies should they find remains. The Bonetti family set a memorial date at St. Elizabeth's.

The cause of the fire is still under investigation.

"She faked her death," I said.

"You can't be certain—"

"I am."

Jack was skeptical, so I continued. "There is no lapse between her high school graduation and when she started college in Texas. If she was injured, suffered from amnesia, whatever, there would have been a lag. A semester, maybe a year. But if she rolled up alive on shore, someone would have known who she was. Hospitals and police would have checked missing persons. And she's using a completely different name. She changed her appearance. She has no social media profile, no friends. She made one stupid mistake."

"Only one," Jack said sarcastically.

"She used her real high school to get into college. I don't know how she did it, maybe she created a fake high school transcript? Found a way to use the school to send it to the college? Used her own transcript to get into college, but somehow changed the name in the system? You and I both know that if someone is determined, they can disappear and take another identity. But it's her." I tapped Jack's screen.

He nodded. "You're right."

"She needs a social security number, needs to be able to pass basic checks," I muttered. "I wonder if Jennifer White is a real person? The best way to assume a different identity is to take an existing one."

"Tess should be able to find the trail, now that we know where to look."

I saved all the articles, then searched Vincent Bonetti. "Her father is a wealthy developer in Miami. Some hints of shady deals, but no big headlines, no public arrests. That's just a cursory look."

Jennifer White was twenty-six—Virginia Bonetti would have been twenty-six as well.

"This is interesting," Jack said. "I'm reading the obituary—Virginia was born on February 4th. According to her employee file, Jennifer White's DOB is January 18th of the same year. Two weeks earlier."

"Maybe the real White was born on January 18th."

Jack did his own search and a minute later said, "Wow."

"What?"

He turned his screen toward me. I scanned an article from a newspaper in Orlando, Florida. The obituary of a thirteen-year-old girl, Jennifer White, who died along with her family in a house fire the day after Christmas.

Her birthday was January 18.

"No coincidence," I said. "She took the name of a dead child. That's creepy. Can you get the PI in Miami to find out more about the Bonettis?"

"Do you think this is important?"

"Yes," I said. "Very important. Is there a problem?"

"No, I can justify the expense."

"Well, Logan Monroe wants to hire me to find Jennifer West."

"But he didn't."

Not caring that it was nearly ten, I dialed Logan's cell phone. He answered on the second ring. "Did you find her?" he asked before even saying hello.

"I have a lead. But there's some expenses I may incur, and I need to make sure you will cover them."

"Absolutely. Anything, bill me. Do you need an advance?"

"No, I trust you're good for it."

"What's the lead?"

I didn't want to share too much over the phone, so I said vaguely, "Florida. When I know something definitive, I'll let you know. Thanks, Logan."

I ended the call and smiled at my brother. "Bill me for the PI, but I'm going to want to talk to him. Send me his contact info."

"It's one in the morning there."

"I'll wait a few hours."

Jack sent me his contact and when it came through on my phone, I saved it and added a few notes.

"This is a turn I wasn't expecting," Jack said. Then his phone rang. "Hey, Lu, did you find something?"

As he listened, his face grew dark and I leaned forward and whispered, "What?"

He didn't respond, and I couldn't hear what my sister was saying. Jack said, "I'll be right there."

He jumped up, started to pack his laptop. "A fire in the building that houses Desert West. It's serious. Lu, Tess, and the guard were the only ones in the building at the time, and they're fine. But Tess and Lu were drugged. Lu managed to get Tess out of the building before they passed out."

"You're sure they're okay?"

"Lu said they were, but I want to make sure."

"I'm going with you."

Jack didn't argue.

Thirty-Three

Peter Carillo

Peter drove to St. Dominic's church Tuesday night in the minivan, not his patrol car. It was quiet. Too late for school or evening mass. He parked across the dead-end street and stared, willing Annie to come out of one of the buildings and run to him.

Was Annie even here? He couldn't see her living in the rectory, a small house on the far corner of the property.

He might be wrong about Annie's grandparents being married here, but he'd seen the St. Dominic's calendar on the wall of the private investigator. That couldn't be a coincidence.

Peter didn't know quite what it meant, not yet. He wanted to talk to the staff here—maybe the secretary, or even the priest. A priest wouldn't lie to him.

He thought about his approach. He could canvass the neighborhood—in uniform—ask if anyone had seen his wife. Show pictures. Tell them she was troubled, suffering from postpartum depression. He needed to bring her home, get her help. People generally wanted to help, especially when children were involved.

He knew exactly what to say and how to say it.

This stupid, ridiculous game of Annie's had gone too far. She had been gone for more than forty-eight hours. What did she hope to accomplish? What did she expect from him? That he would just say fine and go about his life? Didn't she realize she had gutted him? She might as well have put a gun to his head and pulled the trigger. He felt dead inside.

The bitch who helped his wife leave didn't live far from the church. Five minutes later, he was in front of her house. Lights were off, he didn't think she was home, and he had already confirmed there was nothing of value to him inside.

He considered waiting for her, but her street was narrow, the houses were close to the road, and the neighborhood—though old—seemed to be well-maintained, like people cared about their property. People might notice if he parked here too long.

He didn't want to confront Margo Angelhart on her turf. He needed to talk to her away from her house, away from people. Assess her, figure out why she decided to fuck with him.

This bitch had ruined his life. She couldn't get away with it.

He wouldn't let her get away with it.

Thirty-Four

Rick Devlin

Rick Devlin walked into his house in Anthem, north of Phoenix, at 11:15 that evening. He'd lived here since his wife had walked out on them eight years ago. It was a safe community for a single dad to raise a young daughter.

He greeted his two German shepherds, Max and Lucy. They were brother and sister and he'd raised and trained them since they were pups.

He gave the shepherds dog biscuits and told them they were good dogs for watching the house, then he went to check on his daughter. He was home earlier than normal, and Sam—who should have been asleep—was still reading.

"It's after eleven," he said.

She put her book down. "You're early."

He kissed her forehead. "You have school tomorrow."

"Graduation rehearsal. *Boring.* And we don't have to be at school until ten."

"Then graduation on Friday—not boring."

One reason Rick continued to work the swing shift

was because he had a coveted Monday through Thursday schedule—no weekends. Sam had played softball since she was ten. Her team had tournaments twice a month, and his schedule enabled him to go to all her games, even when they traveled to southern California or Colorado. He sometimes picked up overtime—he'd worked two straight weeks during the Super Bowl in Glendale last year—but he spent as much time with Sam as possible. All his overtime pay went into Sam's college fund.

She wrinkled her nose. "It feels dumb to graduate from eighth grade and then go back to the same school for ninth grade."

"It's a rite of passage."

Sam went to a charter school in Anthem that served kids from K–12. It was a program that focused on classical education with a lot of reading, writing, and discussion. Caroline had selected the school for Sam even though Rick was concerned they were pushing their young child to achieve too much too early. But Sam thrived there and he had never moved her. Consistency was important, especially after the divorce.

"Otto is coming by when he gets off shift." Clive Otter was a senior deputy with Maricopa County Sheriff's Department and lived in the gated Anthem neighborhood on the other side of the main road. Otto and his wife, Mickey, were the primary reason Rick finally relented and let Sam stay home alone. They were five minutes away in an emergency.

Company wasn't a common occurrence on a work night, and Sam knew it.

"Is something wrong?"

"Nope."

"*Dad.*"

He'd made a promise to Sam never to lie to her. Good or bad, he told her the truth, even when it was uncomfortable. He might tell her too much sometimes, but he would rather she had information to make informed decisions than go into the world wearing rose-colored glasses.

"Nothing is wrong. I'm asking Otto to help with an investigation."

She lit up. "What kind of investigation?"

Sam had always been far too interested in his job. Rick hoped she didn't want to be a cop.

"There's a trooper I have some concerns about, and Otto knows most of them. I'm going to pick his brain."

"Oh. Okay. I won't bother you." She yawned. "But… ten more minutes? Please? I want to finish my chapter."

"Since you have a late start tomorrow, fine." He kissed her again. "By the way, Margo came by the precinct today. She says hi."

Sam's face lit up, then immediately clouded. "When are you going to let her come by?"

He didn't want this conversation now. "Sam—"

"Look, I get it, you and Margo aren't together anymore. But why do I have to cut her out of my life, too? I like Margo. I mean, you don't hate her, do you?"

"Of course not." Quite the opposite.

"Can I invite her to the graduation party?"

They were having a party Sunday afternoon here at the house.

"You can invite anyone you want. It's your party."

She gave him *the look*—her head tilted, her eyes slightly narrowed, her lips in a tight line.

"You want me to ask her."

"She's not going to come if she thinks you don't want her here."

It was a complicated situation and Rick didn't want to discuss it with his daughter. Margo had crossed a line and Rick was still angry about it. Yet... Sam didn't have a mom around. Mickey Otter was a good role model, but she had four boys under ten that kept her very busy, and a part-time job at the hospital. Margo had given Sam time—something no other woman had given his daughter since Caroline left when she was six.

"Alright. I'll invite her."

"Thanks, Dad." She smiled, revealing faint dimples. He loved his kid more than anything in the world.

"Ten minutes."

She gave him a thumbs-up and turned back to her book.

Otto arrived just before midnight. He was a large black man who loved being a cop as much as he loved being a dad. Otto loved everything about life and Rick was grateful for his friendship.

"Have a beer for your best friend?" Otto grinned widely.

"Sure, and one for you, too." Rick pulled out a light beer and handed it to Otto, then grabbed one for himself, though he probably wouldn't finish it.

They went outside. The evening was perfect, no wind, a comfortable seventy-five degrees. Rick enjoyed his yard. It was shaped like a slice of pie—no front yard to speak of since he was on the curve of the cul-de-sac—but the backyard was wide and relaxing. Open space behind them, a large outdoor kitchen which he used often, covered patio, small pool with hot tub, established trees—desert willows along the back interspersed with paloverde, and lemon trees along the side that produced some of the biggest lemons Rick had ever seen. And grass. Grass in the desert was a luxury, but he had an L-shaped patch, part of which went under the dog run.

Max and Lucy came out with them and sat at Rick's feet.

"What's wrong?" Otto asked as he leaned back in the cushioned Adirondack chair and looked out at the garden lights.

He told Otto what Margo had said about Peter Carillo. "Do you know him? He's thirty-one, been with DPS for eight years."

"Carillo— Yeah, I think I do. Margo helped his wife disappear?"

"He's abusive. He raped her."

"Allegedly."

"Don't."

"Just saying, anyone can make accusations about anyone."

"Margo investigated her allegations, she believes her. Margo isn't knee-jerk—she's not going to help someone who's making shit up."

"No, no she wouldn't." Otto sipped his beer, his long broad body stretched out, his face unreadable in the dim lighting.

A few years older than Rick, Otto was a thoughtful man, wise, disciplined. They'd met on the job more than a decade ago and had been friends ever since.

"Carillo patrols mostly the north end of the valley. I've worked a couple scenes with him. Meticulous. Not chatty, but friendly."

"I need more."

"Like?"

"Complaints. Over and above the typical bullshit complaints. Reprimands. The guy was abusing his wife. Margo said he raped her repeatedly. She wasn't allowed to say *not tonight, honey*. A man like that isn't going to be a saint on the street."

"Hmm."

Rick didn't know if Otto agreed with him. He waited, didn't push. Drained his beer. He didn't get another. His father was an alcoholic, and Rick didn't want to end up the same way, chasing beer with bourbon every night until his mood turned dark and violent.

"I'll talk to Jesse." Jesse Otter, Otto's brother, was a lieutenant with DPS. He would have access to personnel records of all troopers, and would know if there were quiet concerns about Carillo that didn't make it into his file. "I'll leave Margo out of it, because if she knows where the woman is, she can be compelled by the court to testify. I'm sure Carillo will be petitioning the court for custody or abandonment."

"Margo says she doesn't know where Annie is." Rick wasn't positive he believed her. He also wondered if she would lie under oath. She could lose her license, be prosecuted, or jailed for contempt. But Margo was a rock—she couldn't be swayed if she thought she was right. He admired her loyalty as much as he was frustrated with her stubbornness.

"Still, I don't want to put her in the spotlight," Otto said.

"I appreciate it."

"Might take me a day or two."

"Anything you can learn would be great. I don't want to go to his supervisor, since I don't have cause to ask about him. And I don't know Jesse well enough to go to him with this." The lieutenant wasn't as friendly as his brother.

"Is Margo in danger?"

Otto liked Margo. She had that way with people. She could be cynical and surly, but befriended people easier than anyone Rick knew.

He missed her. Seeing her today reminded him how much he missed her. But it was over.

"He ran her plates without cause. Hasn't confronted her yet, but it's only a matter of time. Detective Sullivan out of the 200 is assigned to his wife's missing persons case. I read the report. No sign of foul play, no air travel. She left her passport at home, as well as her phone, her credit cards, wedding ring. Took the kids, didn't take her car."

"Margo."

"Yes."

"I'll let you know what I find out." He rose, dropped his beer bottle in a plastic can on the back porch. Rick followed suit, walked Otto to the door.

"Thanks, buddy," Rick said. "Best to Mickey."

"Anytime."

Rick double checked all the doors, brought the dogs in, showered, and went to bed. He didn't sleep for a long time.

He'd couldn't stop thinking about Margo.

Thoughts about the case faded away to thoughts about the last time he'd seen her—the fight, his anger, her anger, the overwhelming sensation that he was losing something he desperately wanted.

But there was no going back.

Some things couldn't be forgiven, and Sam was the most important person on earth to Rick.

Thirty-Five

The Thief

He watched the firefighters and police from the ridge above Desert West Financial. He'd bought himself a little time. He hoped it was enough time to turn this miserable situation around.

It had been his idea to set Logan up for cheating, knowing that Brittney would get far more money in the divorce. Between the millions he had stolen from the company and the millions Brittney would get when she left Logan, they could go anywhere they wanted and start their own business, their own life.

But Brittney had screwed everything up. She'd jumped the gun, brought in some PI to track Logan before he'd had time to set up the honey trap. It was Brittney's PI who had screwed up his plans to destroy Jennifer White's laptop.

He would just have to convince Brittney to leave her husband now and take the three million she'd earned for the three years they'd been married. Maybe...a little extra. Drain a couple of their joint accounts—it wasn't a crime, right? Not while they were still married.

But he wanted her to leave Logan *now*. He was tired of sharing the woman he loved with another man.

Brittney had to make some decisions. Because right now, he wasn't positive he would come away clean after this situation with Desert West. They would need extra money to disappear for a while, in case someone looked too closely at him.

Money made the world go around, and Logan had far more than he needed. And if Brittney didn't want to take it from him?

Well, maybe they'd have to find another way to take everything Logan Monroe had.

Wednesday

Thirty-Six

Officer Archie Nunez

Nunez pulled up in front of Kris Madera's house. He lived in a similar cookie-cutter home out in Buckeye, the only place he could afford ten years ago when he and Melinda married. They'd made it their own, and his wife did a great job decorating with lots of color and photos of them and their kid, Sophie, and their large extended family. They'd tried for more kids, but no luck. Still, they were happy, content, and Sophie was the light of their lives.

He'd been thinking about Peter Carillo and his family since he interviewed the man and his friends yesterday morning. He'd have been destroyed if Melinda and Sophie left him, especially if he didn't know where they'd gone.

Nunez and Ritchie had talked to Natalie Nichols the day before. She had been making calls to neighbors, but admitted most of the calls were to her own friends, because Annie didn't socialize much. PJ wasn't in school yet, and Annie was introverted. Her neighbors said the same thing. Annie Carillo was nice, polite, standoffish, attentive to her kids, helpful when asked, and always brought the most delicious desserts to neighborhood parties. Her behavior at the parties? Everyone used the same word: nice. A nice, young, quiet, shy mom.

Nunez had tried to speak with Kris Madera, the woman who ran the book club, but she hadn't been home yesterday.

Madera's house looked like the reverse floor plan of the Nichols' home with more character: a Baby Yoda decal in the front window, balls for every sport littering the front porch, and a basketball hoop installed over the garage door. Nunez knocked on the door and immediately heard someone inside.

A woman in her late thirties opened the door. Nunez introduced himself. "Is there a problem?" she asked, looking out at the street as if expecting to see crime scene tape or a car accident.

"No, ma'am. Do you have a minute? It's about one of your neighbors."

"Oh—Annie. Yes, come in. Nat left a voice mail for me, said you might come by. I meant to call her back, but I've been swamped getting ready for summer classes. I teach at GCU." She unlocked her screen door and held it open for them. "Can I get you a bottled water?"

"No, thank you."

For the record, Nunez confirmed her name and that she lived here with her two minor sons.

"When Nat and Brian married and bought the house, she and I became friendly and I invited her to join my book club. She brought Annie for a while. We actually just drink wine and talk about books and life." She shrugged, gave him a small smile. "There's twelve of us in the club, but usually only six or seven come each month. We're all moms, so life is busy."

"And you meet here?"

"Usually. I'm divorced, so it's easy for me to have it here, and Josh—my ex—has the boys every other weekend. Most of the other women have kids younger than mine, so they just want to escape for a couple hours and be with other women, you know?" She raised her eyebrows.

"My wife has a Bunco group. They've been playing practically since we got married," Nunez said.

"*Exactly*." She nodded. "We need a few hours with no demands on our time. I love my boys to death, but sometimes—well, anyway. Annie. Nat said she left and no one knows where she is. What can I do?"

"When was the last time you spoke with Annie?"

She thought on it. "Months," she finally said. "I thought she loved book club, and honestly? She needed it. PJ is a great kid, but she's with him 24/7. She doesn't work—not that I think there's anything wrong with that, it's great she can stay home with the kids while they're little, I wish I could have. But we all need a break sometimes, you know? And book club was her only break. I thought she was coming out of her shell.

"Then about the time she announced she was pregnant again, she stopped coming. Nat said she had morning sickness. After Marie was born, I went over there with one of the other girls—Donnell. We brought her a present for the baby, and a stack of books to read for herself. She cried. She said she missed the book club and the gifts were so thoughtful. I told her come back and bring the baby."

"Did she come?"

"No. She always had an excuse, so I talked to Nat and Nat didn't really know what was going on, but then Nat can be a little clueless."

"How so?" he asked. Kris Madera was a wealth of information and clearly didn't mind talking.

"Not so much clueless, as scattered. She started her own business making specialty oils and vinegars. You know, garlic-infused olive oil and raspberry-flavored vinegar, things like that. It's good—she goes to local farmer's markets and craft fairs and sells out. She and Brian have been trying to get pregnant, and I think the business keeps her mind off the fact she's not."

"You said months—do you remember when?"

"Well—we brought over the baby present right before Halloween, I think. Marie was born in September. And Annie made homemade strawberry jam for Christmas and hand-delivered it. We chatted for a bit about the kids. Then—" she looked up as if trying to remember "—I saw her at Nat's during spring break. My boys had a baseball tournament in Tucson and I went over to see if Nat could feed our cats for a few days, water my plants." She motioned vaguely toward the breakfast nook where there were a dozen plants, mostly thriving. "Annie was there with the kids."

"Was that middle of March?"

"Yes, week of the 14th."

Nunez made a note. Two months ago.

"How was she then?"

"The same." She frowned. "I remember Nat was trying to convince Annie to work her business with her, saying that it would be great to do it together, Nat could make more product if she had a partner, that sort of thing. Annie said Peter wouldn't like it because it would take time away from the kids."

She rolled her eyes.

Nunez had a little tingle. "You didn't believe her?"

"I believed her. Look—I don't think Annie has a backbone. Peter seems to be a good guy, worships the ground she walks on. Good dad, from what Nat says. They do a lot of things on his days off—go to the zoo, park, things like that. He even walks the kids at night. Told me once when I was out in the street playing catch with the boys that it gives Annie time to take a bath and relax. I thought that was thoughtful. I mean, what woman doesn't love a hot bubble bath without calls of mommy, mommy, mommy?"

She hesitated, then added, "But if Peter told Annie he didn't think something was a good idea, she wouldn't do it. I had a feeling—not because she said anything— that Peter didn't like her coming to the book club every month. And that's why she stopped coming. Maybe she grew a backbone and stood up for herself, and realized that Peter was too controlling."

"Controlling." Interesting word choice. "How so?"

"He had a say in everything. They're married, sure, and maybe I'm not one to talk. Josh and I were married for fifteen years and it wasn't all bad, but if Josh tried to tell me what to do and not do with my free time? I would have put my foot down. Of course, I've always been independent. Anyway, I just think Annie wasn't happy."

"She wasn't happy in her marriage?"

"I suggested she see a marriage counselor. Confessed that if Josh and I had done it when problems started, we might have been able to save our marriage before everything got out of hand." She frowned. "You know, that was about the time she stopped coming to book club. I probably overstepped. I didn't think about that at the time. I have no filter."

Maybe not, but Kris Madera had given Nunez a much better picture of Peter and Annie's marriage.

"Thank you for your time." He handed her his card. "If you think of anything else, or know of someone else we can speak with, let me know."

He left, and Nunez called Sullivan as he pulled away from the curb. He relayed the key points in the conversation and Sullivan said, "Sounds like she just wanted to get away. But it bugs me that she didn't use her credit cards, hasn't accessed her bank, didn't fly anywhere. Who picked her up? Get any vibes from who you spoke with?"

"No. Everyone I talked to said she was shy, quiet, friendly, a good mother. Stunned she left." Nunez paused. "This might be a leap, but is there any indication that the husband might have done something?"

He was intentionally vague. He didn't want to put his suspicions on paper, and wasn't certain about giving voice to them.

Sullivan considered, said carefully, "You reported that you didn't see any indication of foul play."

"None. And the girlfriend, Nichols, said the handwriting on the note was Annie's. None of the neighbors saw him Sunday after he left for work, not until he came home Sunday night. We could check his vehicle log."

"You think something is off."

"It's been seventy-two hours since anyone has seen or heard from Annie or her kids. She really could have just left her husband and disappeared, but she would have needed someone to help her."

"Canvass the neighbors again. See if anyone has security footage. Carillo gave us her phone—she wiped it at eight in the morning, which suggests that she planned this and didn't want anyone to know what she had been looking at, where she made reservations. She may have applied for a credit card in her name that Carillo doesn't know about, maybe a separate bank account."

Nunez hadn't thought of that. He should have.

"Keep talking to people," Sullivan continued. "Someone might remember something. I'll go over to the house this afternoon and talk to Carillo. Take a look around, see if anything feels off. Tell him what his options are. With no sign of foul play and clear signs that she left willingly, this is a family court issue."

Nunez said, "Not one person said she was happy. They didn't say she *wasn't* happy, but it just struck me as odd."

"Maybe Carillo is right and she's suffering from postpartum depression. It can be serious and debilitating. Maybe she is a threat to the kids, or to herself, but we need someone else to corroborate Carillo's statement. We'll find her. It'll just take time."

Nunez ended the call. This whole thing felt off to him, and he didn't know why.

But right then, he got a hot call of a burglary in progress, so couldn't follow up with Carillo's neighbors.

He'd return this afternoon.

Thirty-Seven

Margo Angelhart

Theo came by my house early Wednesday morning. He was a tall clean-shaven black kid with a conservative haircut and easygoing manner.

"Why are you here?" I asked when I opened the door. "I'm on my way out."

"Thought you might want backup." He grinned broadly. Theo was a hard person to get angry with, but right now I was irritated.

"I don't need backup."

"You need someone to watch your ass with that angry cop running around."

"I should never have told you about that," I muttered.

"Seriously."

"I'm helping Jack with a case, and I need to go—without you."

I bolted the front door, checked my new security system to make sure it was functioning, and motioned for Theo to follow me to the side door.

"This is nice," he said, running his finger along

the server that ran the six security cameras. I slapped his hand.

"Don't touch."

"Maybe you should have—"

"Don't say it. Because yes, I should have had this in place before someone broke into my house."

"It's the barn door, baby. My grams always said no use closing the barn door after the horse has gone."

"I'm familiar with the expression." I grabbed my favorite folding KA-BAR knife from a drawer in the kitchen, stuffed it into my front pocket. "Let's go."

"Seriously, Margo, I want to help."

"You already did, and I don't need help today. Don't you have class?"

"Only Tuesdays and Thursdays."

Which I knew.

We walked out to the driveway and I locked the dead-bolt. "Theo, I have a lead on Jennifer White, and I don't want or need company. But thanks."

"I'm bored. Give me something to do. And not busy work."

I considered, then said, "Go to my office. Check my mail. Talk to the other businesses, show them a photo of Peter Carillo and ask if they've seen him or the minivan anytime since Monday. I think the Orozcos have a security camera, so ask if you can check the feed. I know the liquor store has cameras, but Manny is an asshole, so 50/50 if he'll let you look. Document everything if there's anything to document, and then let me know what you find. Good?"

"Sounds like busy work."

"It's not. I was going to do it yesterday but got side-tracked with Jack's case." I wasn't lying.

"Alright, fine, but you need me for something else? Call."

"I promise."

Theo climbed into his car—a practical Honda that just didn't quite fit the kid—and I followed him out of the neighborhood. He turned left, toward my office. I went straight, toward the Biltmore area.

I wasn't lying when I said I had a lead on Jennifer, but it was a thin lead. One that I had to follow myself.

Miriam Endicott wasn't expecting me, but I walked right in anyway. She wasn't going to like what I had to say, but I didn't care.

She was in a meeting with a client, but Sherry alerted her and she was leaving her office as I approached. She closed the door. "Next time you walk past my receptionist without an appointment, I will have you arrested."

"Vincent Bonetti."

She flinched and I knew I was right. She scowled. "Out."

"He hired you to find his daughter, who is presumed dead."

Miriam grabbed my arm and pulled me into an empty office, closed the door. I stared at her hand gripping my bicep. "Three, two…"

She dropped it. "Stay out of my business," Miriam said.

"There's a reason Virginia faked her death," I said. "Leading her father to her isn't right."

"You don't know anything about this case," Miriam said through clenched teeth.

"Enlighten me."

"I'm under no obligation to *enlighten* you about anything."

"You're on the wrong side this time."

Miriam crossed her arms. "Perhaps *you* are." She paused,

looked at me, her nose tilted up at an angle so sharp I wanted to break it. "You know, Margo," she said conversationally, "it might not be such a coincidence we're on opposite sides of this."

"What the hell does that mean?"

I'd thought a lot last night about who Jennifer/Virginia *really* was—why she faked her death, why she was on the run, whether she was in danger...or if she was dangerous.

I wouldn't have the answers until I talked to her.

"If you think about it, you'll figure it out. You should be asking yourself, why now? Why was *my firm*— the largest, most successful, most professional in the state—hired to find a woman presumed dead?"

"See you around," I said and turned to leave.

Miriam grabbed me again and this time I did slap her hand. She winced. I hadn't meant to hit her so hard, but I don't like being grabbed, so I didn't apologize. "Margo, let this go."

"You know me better than that."

I walked out.

I knew what Miriam had meant. It didn't take a rocket scientist to read between the lines. Why now?

Because Angelhart Investigations had been hired by Desert West and started running a background on Jennifer White. That background check took them to Florida. Poking around may have alerted her father that his daughter was still alive, though I wasn't quite sure how since she was using a different identity. Being out-of-state and a wealthy businessman, he would hire a company that catered to wealthy businesses.

I didn't know why Jennifer had faked her death— if she was the threat or her father—but Jennifer was the one with answers. I had to find her before Miriam.

Thirty-Eight

Theo Washington

Theo unlocked the door to Margo's office near the corner of Cave Creek and East Hatcher. Her narrow space was wedged between a barbershop and a take-out pizza place. One end was a mini-mart, the other a drive-through liquor store. There were a few other small businesses—including a Mexican diner owned by one of Margo's cousins. He couldn't keep her family straight. He thought the Orozcos were her grandfather's sister's family, and there were more of them than there were Morales and Angelhart combined.

He had his grandma and an uncle who lived in Colorado who he hadn't seen in years. His dad had been in and out of jail for years, but Theo barely remembered him. Didn't even know if he was dead or alive. His mom, an addict, walked out when he was ten. He didn't know if she was dead or alive, either. His grams had never left. She gave him a home, had rules he mostly followed (at least the important ones), and she loved him. She could be a bear at times, but he never doubted that she would be there for him no matter what.

But Margo? It seemed she was related to half the people in Phoenix. Her family had welcomed him as if he were one of theirs, even invited him and his grams over for Thanksgiving last year. His grams was nervous, wore her Sunday best, but everyone was real cool to her and raved over her peach pie.

Theo didn't really understand what had happened three years ago when Margo and her mom had it out. He hadn't known Margo then. All he knew was that it had something to do with her dad going to prison for murder. Margo said he was innocent and Theo made a crack that everyone said they were innocent. She had stared at him so hard his mouth went dry.

Now he knew more about Cooper Angelhart. And he felt for Margo, he really did, but if her dad pled guilty, maybe he was. Maybe it was Margo who needed to accept it. He never said that to her. He liked his job, and he liked Margo. Cooper Angelhart was an off-limits subject.

The pizza place wasn't open, but he could smell Mexican food and his stomach growled. They were open for breakfast and lunch. The neighborhood went to shit at night, but during the day wasn't too bad. He'd grab a breakfast burrito and put it on Margo's tab when he talked to the Orozcos about their security cameras.

Margo had a shit-ton of mail. Did she ever come to her office? There was at least two weeks' worth of crap here.

He sorted through it. Most of it was junk. He tossed it all, except two envelopes that looked like business (though were probably junk, too) and then checked her messages.

Margo gave clients her business card, which had this number and her cell number. She retrieved messages remotely, but people usually called her cell. There were currently two on the machine. An actual answering machine instead of a digital service. Why she had it, he didn't know.

He grabbed a pen from the drawer and the sticky pad on the desk and hit Play.

The first was a hang-up a couple seconds after the beep. Whatever. He deleted it. The second call was also a hang-up, but the caller stayed on for several seconds, breathing.

Creepy. Theo saved it because it was unusual and Margo always said to watch for anything out of the ordinary.

He locked the door and walked three stores down to the Mexican diner. His stomach did a flip of excitement. He didn't think they'd remember him, but the short chubby woman behind the counter smiled. "Theo! I haven't seen you in weeks."

"Hi, Miz Orozco."

"The usual breakfast burrito?"

"You remember?"

"Carne asada, the works, no jalapeños, extra cheese."

He grinned. He liked Mexican food, just not too spicy. "Perfect."

She rapidly called his order into the kitchen in Spanish. "I'll put it on Margo's tab."

"Appreciate it, ma'am. Margo wanted me to talk to you about your security camera."

"That girl," Mrs. Orozco shook her head, but smiled.

"Yes, we listened to her, we make sure it's working all the time. Tell her not to worry. We've had no trouble for months."

"Would you mind if I look at the recordings for the last couple days?"

Her expression turned to alarm. "Has something happened?"

"Naw, not at all. Margo just wants me to check to see if someone has come by when she wasn't here." He was vague and Mrs. Orozco looked at him suspiciously, but he didn't want to worry her.

"Margo takes so many risks, all the time." She waved her arms around dramatically, then clutched the small gold crucifix she wore. "We pray for her every night. She nearly died saving Homer and my boy, Michael." She kissed her cross before stuffing it back under her blouse.

That was before Theo's time, but he'd heard the story from the Orozcos at least three times, and again from Margo's grandpa over Thanksgiving. Margo said everyone exaggerated, that she didn't nearly die. But she saved the Orozcos from an armed robber, and Theo liked hearing the story. At least the first couple of times.

"Margo is one of a kind," Theo said. "She's fine, just wanted me to check a few things, if you don't mind."

"Not at all, not at all. Follow me, I'll bring your breakfast to you in the back, okay?"

"Great."

She showed Theo to the computer that ran the security cameras. She didn't know how to use it, but gave him the login and password; that was all he needed.

The system didn't have any bells and whistles, but was a good basic package. Two cameras, front and back.

Digital video was stored on the computer for seven days, then erased. An alarm system when they were closed, a panic button if there was trouble during the day.

Theo ran through the feed fast, starting with Monday afternoon. If Carillo broke into Margo's house Monday night, he could have come here right before or after. He looked specifically for the blue minivan.

Mrs. Orozco gave him his burrito, and he ate it while watching the video. She also brought him a Coke, remembering he didn't like the diet crap.

He almost missed the minivan because he was enjoying his breakfast, and had to rewind.

At 10:07 p.m., the only business open on the strip mall was the drive-through liquor store, which closed at eleven during the week. The minivan had turned into the strip mall from Hatcher, based on the fact that it moved from south to north on the camera. He couldn't see the driver, but the vehicle moved slowly, as if looking for an address. Theo froze the image just as the van was about to move out of sight. He could make out part of the license plate. It ended in 1284. If he had a better computer, he might be able to make out the letters that preceded the numbers, but from here they were just a blurry blob.

He pulled out the note Margo had given him with Carillo's physical description, vehicles, and license. Those numbers matched the minivan.

The van returned after five minutes. And now Theo could see the driver's face. Sure looked like the asshole Margo had described.

He copied the file and sent it to himself and Margo with a quick explanation, then he continued his review.

The van didn't show up again.

When Theo was done an hour later, he brought his plate to the front counter.

Mrs. Orozco asked, "Did you find what you needed?"

"Yep. Thanks so much."

"Good, good. You still hungry?"

"I'm stuffed. It was great."

"Let me refill your Coke." She held out her hand and he handed her the disposable cup. She topped it off and handed it back to him. "Tell Margo don't be a stranger. You, too. And bring your grandma in sometime, my treat."

"She'd like that, thanks."

Theo left and called Margo. "Did you get my message?"

"Looking at it now. It's him, isn't it?"

"Yeah. The image is pretty clear, and I could read part of the license plate."

"Okay. I have one more thing for you."

"Awesome. Give it to me."

"I'm texting you a number. Her name is Cora Mannigan, and she manages a condo complex in Scottsdale. Between eleven and noon I'll send you a text that says *now*. Call her and tell her you're looking for a condo for your grandma. Ask a lot of questions about the complex. Anything you can think of. Availability, pets, gym, stores, restaurants, view. She'll ask you to come in and look. Tell her you're out of the area and need to get a list together or something. Make it up, I don't care, just keep her on the phone as long as you can. When I text you again, give her my spam email to send more information and hang up."

He laughed. "Sounds like fun."

"After, go home and study. You have finals next week."

"Yes, *mother*," he said. "Jeez, Angel, I have damn near straight A's."

"What class don't you have an A in?"

"Statistics. Don't know why I need a stupid statistics class. I have an A in fucking Chemistry III, that should be good enough."

"If you get stuck, text Luisa. She's the math whiz in the family."

Luisa Angelhart was hot. If she were just a few years younger, he would be in love. She was Gorgeous with a capital *G*. But she scared him as much as Margo. Maybe more. She had this piercing gaze that he swore looked deep into his soul and knew all his secrets. He wondered if she'd handled interrogations for the Marines, because one look and he'd confess anything she asked.

He didn't want to get involved with any woman who could read his mind.

"Will do," he simply said, then cleared his throat.

"Be ready." Margo hung up.

Thirty-Nine

Margo Angelhart

I'd told Jack last night that I didn't need him today in my search for Jennifer White, aka Virginia Bonetti. He was dealing with the fallout from the fire at Desert West. Clearly, someone set the fire to prevent Tess and Luisa from figuring out what Jennifer had already downloaded. If Logan was right, someone was stealing from the company, and it wasn't Jennifer.

The main reason I didn't want Jack with me was because I planned to lie. A lot. Jack had many skills, but he couldn't lie to save his life. When he was sixteen, Mom and Dad went away to one of Dad's medical conferences in Seattle. It coincided with their anniversary, so they left a day early. Mom had sent Luisa, who was only six, to stay with family, but left Jack in charge of the rest of us. Jack loved being in charge, but he was also very responsible. Most of the time.

This weekend, however, our cousins Mateo and Grace—fifteen-year-old twins—convinced Jack to have a "small pool party." Because our parents had said explicitly no parties, Jack bribed Tess, Nico, and me—he'd do Tess's and Nico's chores for a week *and* pick me up from softball practice for the next month. No more riding my bike a mile home in the heat.

The bash that was supposed to have "a dozen" people had more than sixty. There was alcohol—which made Tess super nervous. The party was fun for everyone but those of us who had to clean up and make the house immaculate for the return of our parents—and decide who would take the fall for the giant dent in the BBQ and the mailbox that had been knocked over.

Tess, Nico, and I kept our faces straight when Mom and Dad got home, but one look at Jack and Mom said, "What happened?"

He spilled everything.

Jack has no poker face.

Me? I had no problem with spinning tales. It made me a good detective.

I had considered just breaking into her condo, but there were too many security cameras and I didn't know anything about her neighbors. So after Jack left, I created a brilliant cover as a real estate appraiser. Because Jack had given me the file on Jennifer from Desert West, I had her email address and could easily clone it. I sent a message from Jennifer to the manager, asking her to let me—Margo Angelhart, Appraiser—into the condo on this day and time because I (Jennifer) was out of town for work. "Jennifer" gave her a phone number (a burner I had for just such emergencies) if necessary.

One problem: Frank Sanchez. He followed me as soon as I left Miriam's office. It took me longer than I expected to lose him, and I was ten minutes late.

The manager, Cora Mannigan, was distraught when I arrived.

"Is Ms. White selling? She didn't tell me she wanted to sell. She said she loved her condo."

Cora was in her fifties and impeccably dressed with real diamonds in her ears—probably—and no wedding ring. My guess: a divorcée living off her alimony but bored so took the job. Probably owned a condo in the complex and knew everyone and their business.

"She's looking to refinance and wanted an appraisal," I said. "I was told she did some remodeling when she first moved in."

"*Yes,*" Cora said. "She updated the kitchen and it's *gorgeous*, especially the subway tile she selected, plus replaced the awful carpets with beautiful tile and wood floors."

"I need pictures for my files, so I can give her the best value on her condo."

I handed her my business card. I'd made eight— that's what the sheet feeder in my printer could handle— on nice linen paper. No color, but the paper was top-of-the-line. And in some businesses—like real estate appraisers—the simpler, the better. Classy block font, PO Box, phone number, license number (fake), and email.

"I used to work for Thompson Pierce," I said, mentioning the largest real estate company in the valley with multiple offices that would be next to impossible for her to verify, "but started my own business a year ago. I need to make my own hours because I'm helping my mom take care of my grandmother."

"That's so wonderful you're able to do that," Cora said. She started walking toward the elevator and I refrained from a fist pump that I had sold her on my temporary identity.

We rode the elevator to the top floor—the sixth—with Cora chatting about the amenities of the condo complex.

I asked, "Do you know Jennifer well?"

"No, I can't say that I do. I've met her, of course. I make a point to talk to all the owners, and we have a homeowners association meeting once a month that I run. It's one of my main responsibilities. You should know, for your appraisal, that our HOA is on top of everything. The fees are reasonable for a complex this size. We have two pools—indoor and outdoor—and the dog park, the—oh, here we are," she said when I stopped in front of Jennifer's door. I knew her unit number and I was certain that Cora would have continued walking to the end of the hall if I hadn't stopped.

Cora smiled and knocked. "Just to make sure she didn't come back early."

"Did she tell you about her trip?"

"No, I didn't even know she was gone until she emailed. She works so hard."

No one came to the door, so Cora opened it up. "Here you go. This kitchen is just amazing!"

It was, I concurred—bright and functional. A little *too* bright for me, but with lots of counter space and gorgeous green subway tiles. But it was the view that was truly stunning. The mountains east of Scottsdale were crisp and clear in the mid-morning light. A wide covered balcony that curved around the corner so she had a view to the north and east. Sunrises would be spectacular.

I sent the message to Theo, then took out my camera.

I made a point to ask Cora to move a few feet with just enough frustration to still be polite, but a little annoyed.

She pulled her phone from her pocket and answered. "Kierland Prime Condominiums, Cora Mannigan speaking, how may I help you?" She listened intently, and then said, "Oh, lovely! I can arrange a tour, and we have six units currently for sale. They go quickly—oh. Yes."

I motioned for Cora to move again so I could get a different angle, then pulled a tape measure from my pocket and started measuring.

"One moment, Mr. Washington." Cora turned to me, a bit flustered. "I need to go to my computer, but it won't take long. Are you okay for a couple minutes?"

"Yes," I said. "I should be done in twenty minutes or so. I'll see you on my way out."

She nodded, clearly distracted, and left the condo. *Score another one for the PI*, I thought.

I kept my camera around my neck and my tape measure in my pocket just in case she came back sooner than I expected.

Jennifer White was a tidy minimalist. The furniture was high-end, but basic. The condo had a large master suite and a small den. Her desktop was empty—no computer, but I didn't expect to find one. Many people only had laptops these days. I looked through the drawers—tax forms, food flyers, a lot of computer magazines, spec sheets, software documentation. A bookshelf was filled with mysteries, history books, and computer books. No photographs of friends or family—not one.

I was looking for any clue as to where Jennifer might have gone to hide out for a few days, and nothing at her desk jumped out at me.

I walked through the condo, searching for something,

anything, fearing that my brilliant idea was a dud. I found her hobby pretty quickly—video games. She had two different gaming systems and dozens of disks. I had played many of them. I wasn't as into gaming as my younger brother and sister, but I could hold my own, and a few of my Army buds and I played *Warzone* a couple times a month. It was a good way to have fun and keep in touch.

Jennifer had all the *Call of Duty* games, which I understood, and a bunch of games I'd never heard of. The games got me thinking about communicating online, and then I had an idea.

I called Logan Monroe as I searched her bedroom. He answered on the first ring. "Are you on Discord?"

"Of course."

"Is Jennifer?"

"Yes! My teams use it all the time. I'll reach out and—"

"Not yet. Add me and I'll reach out. She'll see we're connected and might respond."

"But she doesn't know you."

"And she hasn't returned your calls in two days." I paused. "We'll do it together, at your office, thirty minutes." I was only a few minutes from his office. I gave him my Discord name and ended the call when he agreed to meet me. I hoped he didn't jump the gun. Jennifer was agitated and scared and I needed to find the best way to convince her to trust me.

I went through Jennifer's bedroom. Her bed was made. On her nightstand were several books—all nonfiction, including a book on the history of Arizona, and another on Arizona historic places. I picked it up. A bookmark had been inserted at the chapter about Bisbee, a historic mining town near the border with a population of five thousand. That might mean nothing, but I'd seen a shelf of books in her den by J.A. Jance who wrote a series set in Bisbee.

Here, too, there were no pictures of people. I went into the closet.

Gold mine.

On the top shelf above her neatly hung clothes (she even hung up her T-shirts) was a large metal lockbox. I took it off the shelf and brought it to her bed. Less than ten seconds later I had the wimpy lock opened. With one ear listening for Cora Mannigan, I opened the box and looked inside.

Clippings from the disappearance of Virginia Bonetti. Articles about Vincent Bonetti that had been printed from the computer—about the explosion on his yacht, his recovery, his business. Nothing jumped out at me other than Jennifer had been tracking her father since she faked her death.

But there were also articles about the fire that killed Jennifer White, presumably the girl whose identity she had assumed. Plus a file folder with an arson report.

I didn't have time to read it all, so took pictures of every page with my phone.

Under it all was a faded Polaroid photograph of two girls—one blonde and one brunette, wearing the same soccer uniform with pigtails and ribbons. They were about nine or ten. On the white part under the photo was written in ink:

Jenny and me, BFF.

Little hearts had been drawn on either side of the words.

One other thin folder revealed an autopsy report for Abigail Bonetti, dated twenty years ago. I took a pic-

ture to read later. A photo under the single page was of a
very young Jennifer—or rather Virginia—and a toddler
with a woman who looked so much like Jennifer now
that I suspected it was her mother. Nothing was written on the back, but there was residue as if it had been
ripped from a photo album.

I was carefully putting everything back when I received a text from Theo.

She's sending me stuff and said she had to go. Watch
out.

I left the bedroom and went out to the balcony, taking pictures of the view. Cora walked in a minute later,
breathless. "I'm so sorry! That young man could just
talk *forever* about his grandma. Sweet boy, but I just
don't have the time."

"No worries from me. I have all the measurements,
the pictures, and a list of questions for Ms. White to
answer. Walk me out?"

Cora beamed, chatted all the way down. I said goodbye and called Theo as I walked to my car. "You did
great."

"I did, didn't I?" he gloated. "You got what you
needed?"

"The jackpot."

Once I turned on my Jeep and sat with the AC blowing at me, I sent Nico a picture of the autopsy report and
asked him for the layman's version. I then called Tess.

"How are you feeling?"

"Fine. I was fine last night, too, but Jack called Gabriel." Dr. Gabriel Rubio, Tess's fiancé. "So now Gabriel
is worried. I am *fine*."

"I know you are, and that's why I have something for you to do."

"I need something because Gabriel made me stay home."

I frowned. It's sweet that he's concerned, but no one could make me do anything I didn't want to.

"It's computer work and phone calls."

"Give it to me. And if I need to go to the office, I will."

I told her what I found and Tess knew what to do. "I'll send you pictures of everything in her lockbox. I have a lead on locating fake Jennifer."

I hoped.

Forty

Jack Angelhart

Jack used his connections to push the link between what happened with Logan and Jennifer on Sunday in Paradise Valley to what happened to Tess and Luisa last night.

Phoenix PD Detectives Lopez and Capelle were the lead investigators, but the Phoenix Fire Arson Investigation unit were in charge of the structure. They hadn't issued an official report, but determined arson because accelerant had been detected.

Jack knew Detective Wendy Lopez—she'd been a senior detective before he got his shield. She was fifty, smart, sassy, and had raised three boys. Two were in college, one in the police academy. Her husband taught high school math and coached football, and when they socialized, he and Jack could talk for hours about sports.

She'd wanted him to come to the station to chat, but he knew better—he said he couldn't leave his office and she agreed to meet him. He wasn't concerned about any liability or crime on his part, but he didn't want to see former friends and colleagues. No one had an issue with him, but his father's crime hung over him and he didn't want to field questions.

After small talk to catch up and introductions to Detective Capelle who Jack didn't know, Jack gave Wendy as much detail into their investigation as he could and explained why Tess and Luisa were there after hours. There was no reason to hold anything back, especially since he'd already talked to Ron Tucker and told him about Logan Monroe's involvement.

"Someone tried to kill my sisters," Jack said when he was done. "They were drugged before the fire started."

"A nitrogen canister was found on the fourth floor," Wendy said.

"The same thing happened to Monroe and White on Sunday. You can compare the canisters. This time, the guy sets a fire? If my sisters had been unconscious, they could have been killed." The thought made his stomach churn.

"Slow down. I'm not saying you're wrong, only that we don't have all the facts yet. I talked to both Luisa and Tess, got their statements, talked to the security guard. What I want to know is more about this Jennifer White. No one can find her. That seems suspicious, don't you think? She called out sick this week and now no one can reach her."

Jack collected his thoughts. He was still emotional over Tess and Lu's near miss.

"No," Jack said flatly. "I'm more worried for her safety."

"You need to see it from my perspective. I spoke to Mr. Tucker this morning. He corroborated everything you just told me about your investigation into Jennifer White."

Carefully, Jack said, "Yes, we have evidence that she downloaded proprietary software, but we haven't determined what she intended to do with it. Our investigation has led us to believe that Jennifer became suspicious of code written into the company financial software and was trying to back-trace the source."

"But she was the individual who broke company policy."

"Yes, but only because she uncovered a larger crime." Jack hoped he wasn't overstepping here. He trusted Logan's assessment, but maybe he was wrong to do so without more evidence.

"That's really not for me to say—that's up to Mr. Tucker and his company on how he wants to handle his employees. But someone set this fire, and Jennifer White is the only person we haven't spoken with."

"Wendy, I'm not going to tell you how to do your job—"

"But, you're going to tell me how to do my job."

"Someone erased the files from Desert West before we got there. Luisa said it would only delay the inevitable, that the archive is off-site. Jennifer is a computer expert, so she would know that."

"Yet, this has bought her time to disappear."

"After what happened Sunday, she's scared."

"According to Officer Cameron, she left the hospital against staff recommendation. In fact, she slipped out without telling anyone. You haven't spoken to her, so you don't really know what's in her head."

Jack understood Wendy's strategy, and he would have approached the case the same way. Jennifer had a lot of explaining to do, but he was certain there was a lot more to this than even they had figured out.

"We're looking for her," Jack said.

"Call me if you find her first."

He wasn't going to find her because he wasn't looking—Margo was. But Wendy didn't have to know that. Jack wasn't a good liar, so he stuck to what he could back up.

"What do *you* think is going on here, Mr. Angelhart?" Capelle asked his first question. Still green behind the ears, Jack doubted he had more than a year with his shield, and he was too young to have spent more than a couple years in uniform.

"I can't say."

"Can't or won't?"

Jack didn't like the confrontational tone of Wendy's partner. He preferred Wendy's straightforward approach.

"You've spoken to all the employees?" Jack said.

"Yes, in person or by phone. We asked them to come down to the station to give a formal statement about where they were last night, when they left the office, if they saw anyone suspicious. So far everyone has cooperated. Except Jennifer White."

Jack had an idea he needed to pursue, but without Wendy and Capelle hounding him. "If I find her, I'll tell her to contact you. Fair?"

"If she fled the scene to avoid prosecution, don't help her," Wendy said. "You were a great cop, Jack, and you're a solid PI. Don't jeopardize your license."

"That threat is not warranted," he said, angry.

"Didn't mean it as a threat," she said. "Truce."

He didn't acknowledge her olive branch. "Are we done?"

"Sure."

He stood. "I'll walk you out."

"What do you know about Logan Monroe's relationship with Jennifer White?" Capelle asked without getting up.

"She used to intern for him, and he recommended her for the position at Desert West."

"Don't you think it's odd that they were meeting at a vacant house?"

"No."

"I do."

Jack shrugged.

"Monroe gave a statement to Officer Cameron that Jennifer asked to meet with him for advice about a computer code," Wendy said. "Do you think that was the code she illegally downloaded from Desert West?"

Jack didn't respond.

"Look, corporate espionage is way out of my wheelhouse," Wendy continued. "But arson and attempted murder? That's what I care about. Like you said, someone tried to kill your sisters—or, someone didn't know they were inside and set the fire in order to destroy evidence of a crime."

"I'm sure you'll find out who did it," Jack said, "with all the security cameras in the building."

"That's the thing—the cameras were wiped out shortly before the fire started. We have no idea who might have been on the fourth floor, or how they left the building. The security guard didn't see anyone, but he left his post to help your sisters. Anyone could have walked out through the front before Fire got there—or drove out the garage."

Jack had another idea. He needed them to leave so he could do his job.

"Well, you know what you're doing, Wendy. I won't keep you."

She motioned for Capelle to get up, and they started to leave. Wendy looked back at Jack and said, "Always good to see you, Jack. Wish you were still on the force."

"Thanks. Best to Mike and the boys."

She tipped an imaginary hat and walked out.

Jack called Margo as soon as they left the building. "Two detectives want to talk to Logan about Jennifer White. I don't think he's a good liar."

"Probably about as good as you. But we'll be out of here in ten."

"What are you doing?"

"We got Jennifer to reach out. Talking to her now. More later."

She hung up before Jack could ask her more.

He was thinking about the security cameras that went out, and the structure of Desert West. Someone had set the fire *hours* after the building was empty, except for the guard, Tess, and Luisa. That meant they were on the fourth floor before the building was closed.

They may have disabled the security cameras when they came down, but what about when they went up?

He called Luisa as he jumped into his truck. "Sis, I need your expertise. Meet me at Desert West."

Forty-One

Margo Angelhart

Discord worked.

It took a bit of finesse, but finally Jennifer responded to my message on the chat platform.

How do I know you are who you say you are?

"Got her," I said to Logan. We both sat behind his desk at his computer in his Scottsdale office. "What's something that I can tell her so she knows I'm here with you and I'm one of the good guys?"

"Tell her I'm here and I'm still upset that she surpassed my ELO at online chess."

I typed it in and a minute later, she responded.

Jennifer: You're with Logan?

Margo: Yes. We're sitting in his office. He hired me to find and protect you.

Jennifer: Why?

Margo: He's worried because he hasn't been able to reach you, you're not returning his calls or messages.

Jennifer: I don't want to drag him into this.

Margo: You already did when you showed him the data from Desert West. I don't care about that right now. I know who you really are.

No response. "Can you trace this?" I said to Logan. "Like, trace her IP address so we know where she is?"

"No. I mean, I could try, but she'll have a VPN, which is difficult to trace."

I had to trust Logan on that; tech was not my strength. I refocused my attention on convincing fake Jennifer to trust me.

Margo: Your name is Virginia Bonetti. Jennifer White was your best friend until she was killed when you were both freshmen in high school. Your family moved from Orlando to Miami. I don't know why—yet—but you don't think it was an accident, like the fire investigators determined. I also have your mother's autopsy report.

No response. I waited a beat, then continued.

Margo: You told Logan that someone was following you. I tracked down the individual to a local PI, who I believe was hired by your father. I know you're scared—I can help you. Logan will help you.

No response. What other angle could I use?

Margo: Someone saturated Logan's house with nitrogen to knock you out in order to steal your laptop. That's our best guess. They could have killed you. Then last night, someone set fire to the Desert West building after they wiped the system. Three people were inside.

Jennifer: Are they okay? Was anyone hurt?

Bingo!

Margo: Not seriously. But someone at Desert West is trying to cover their tracks. I don't know if you're in danger from your father, but you are definitely in danger from this guy. Do you suspect someone specific?

No response, but I hoped she was thinking.

Jennifer: If I'm wrong, I could ruin his life.

Margo: I will prove it one way or the other. Call me, Jennifer. Let me help you.

I typed in my cell number and waited. She didn't respond to my Discord message, nor did my phone ring.

"Dammit!" I said. Where had I gone wrong?

"I'll try to trace the connection," Logan said. He started typing and code flashed by, making my head pound. I stood and paced.

"I might know where she is," I said. "Not specifically, but she had books on Arizona history and had marked Bisbee. Plus, she has nearly every J.A. Jance book—she writes mysteries about a cop in Bisbee. I can go down there, ask around, but if I'm wrong it's going to waste a full day."

"Hmm," he said as if he barely heard me.

Two minutes later, as I seriously considered jumping in my car and driving to Bisbee, my cell phone rang.

"Who's this?" Jennifer said.

"Margo Angelhart."

"Okay. Don't put me on speaker. Logan's in the room with you, right?"

"Yes."

"I don't want to hurt him."

"Okay."

This was a very strange call. I almost stepped from the room, but then Jennifer started talking fast, and I didn't want to miss anything.

"Last month I started looking at this report that seemed off to me. I brought it to Mr. Tucker's attention, but he was distracted—he's going through a divorce and has been kind of out of it for months. He told me to do whatever I needed to do, but I don't think he understood the seriousness of the situation. I found a secret account. Pennies of *every* transaction were sent to the account, and I couldn't figure out why. The account wasn't in our annual audit, so I knew something was wrong, but I didn't know specifically *what* was wrong. It's not unusual to have automated splits—like your cell phone bill will have a few pennies going to state taxes, to federal taxes, to different surcharges. That's all automatic—some are a flat fee, some are a percentage of your total bill, which is calculated automatically by the program. So on the surface, the line item isn't suspicious."

Her clear explanation helped me visualize the situation.

"But," Jennifer continued, "I couldn't figure out where this money was going or why it was diverted, so I downloaded the source code. I didn't think about calling Logan then because he's so busy." Her voice grew even quieter, as if she was afraid Logan could hear. "Then… I saw his wife."

Suddenly, I had part of the answer I was looking for, even before Jennifer spoke.

"Where?" I asked.

"At the airport. She was with someone I work with."

"Tucker?"

"No—no, of course not."

Tucker was logical, I thought. "Then who?"

"Brad Parsons," she whispered. "He's the assistant CFO. They were—um—*involved*."

"Okay." I avoided Logan's questioning gaze. "And then?"

"Mr. O'Keefe had said once that Brittney married Logan for his money and Logan would eventually figure it out. I learned later, from Mr. O'Keefe's personal assistant Gwen, that Brittney had worked at Desert West, and that's how she met Logan. She implied that Brittney had been involved with Brad first, but he didn't make the big bucks. Her words. I wasn't around then and you know how gossip is, so I didn't think about it. But after the airport, I was angry and suspicious. I didn't immediately think it was Brad, but when I was looking at the data again and traced the programming to Mr. Tucker's office, I thought it had to be Brad."

"Not Tucker?"

"No. The coding came from his computer, but after hours, and Mr. Tucker doesn't come in at night."

"Do you have proof?" I asked bluntly.

"I have all the data on my laptop, but I can't prove Brad created the account or the code. I hoped that Logan could. But I should have told him everything from the beginning. I don't want to hurt him. He's a really good guy and he gave me my first real job."

Logan was trying to get my attention; I ignored him.

"You told Logan that you were scared, that you thought someone was following you. Do you think it was this Brad?"

"I don't know. Two men followed me at least twice, I just got a weird vibe. They were watching me last week—I saw them once outside work, and once outside my condo. I got paranoid—you said you know what I did."

"Yes."

"I've done a good job covering my tracks, but my father is resourceful. I thought maybe they worked for him…but after what happened Sunday, I thought Brad might have hired them to get my laptop. The evidence of what was going on. So—I really don't know who hired them, but it freaked me out and after being drugged, I had to get away."

I asked Jennifer, "Where are you now?"

She didn't say anything.

"Jennifer, I can help you. You're in danger, and you can't hide forever. If you need to disappear, I can even help you with that." *With a little money from Logan Monroe*, I thought. "Are you in Bisbee?"

A gasp. "How do you know?"

"Good guess." Nice to know I hadn't lost my touch when I searched her apartment. "Tell me where, and we can be there in a couple hours. You don't want to come back here alone until we know what's going on."

"I'll send you the address."

Forty-Two

Jack Angelhart

Jack left Luisa in the security office to review the footage while he met with Ron Tucker in a temporary office on the first floor. The fire department had determined the building was secure and allowed staff into the first and second floors, but the top two were blocked off for the investigation.

"Gavin O'Keefe will be back tonight," Tucker said. "I need to have answers by then."

Tucker looked exhausted. He probably hadn't slept last night after the authorities contacted him.

"We're working on it," Jack said.

"The police told me they interviewed all the staff except for Jennifer White. Maybe you were wrong, I was wrong, I shouldn't have trusted my instincts about her. I just—I can't see her doing this." He shook his head. "I don't know what to think anymore."

"My colleague found Jennifer. She left for personal reasons, but will be here to talk to the police tomorrow."

Tucker took off his glasses and rubbed his eyes. "I've

spent all day getting the office halfway functional in a space a third of the size. We have responsibilities, and thank God our primary server is off-site, or we would have lost millions of dollars. As it is, it's going to take us a week to be fully operational, and without Jennifer here to help facilitate IT, I don't know how we're going to handle the load."

Jack didn't have an answer, so didn't say anything to that. "How long has Brad Parsons worked for you?"

Tucker looked confused at the change of subject. "Since the beginning. He helped set up the office six years ago when Mr. Monroe and Mr. O'Keefe launched the venture."

"You were here then?"

"Yes. I have experience with financial start-ups."

"Does Mr. Parsons normally work nights?"

"We're a financial services company. We operate primarily expanded bankers hours."

"Jennifer has evidence that someone may have been stealing money off every transaction, charging a *processing fee* ranging from a few cents to ninety-nine cents. She confirmed that she was responsible for the download that alerted you that something was wrong, because she planned to analyze the code on her own time."

"Why didn't she come to me?"

"She claims she did, but you told her to fix the problem. She said you've been going through a divorce."

At first, he looked angry, then his face fell. "I remember the conversation now. Honestly, I wasn't paying much attention, and trusted Jennifer to figure it out. Then I forgot. The divorce—anyway, I shouldn't have let my personal problems interfere with my job. But what does this have to do with Brad Parsons?"

"Jennifer will bring you her analysis." Jack didn't want to share what he'd learned about Brad Parsons, especially since Jennifer had no hard evidence Parsons had stolen the money.

"But you asked about Brad."

Jack said, "When we first looked at all employees, only Jennifer stood out. Now we're digging deeper into Parsons. I suggest that you lock him out of the system and change your password. Right now, I have no evidence that he is responsible for the theft, but between my team and Ms. White, we'll get to the truth."

A knock on the door and Tucker said, "Come in."

Luisa stepped in. "I found something."

Jack introduced Luisa to Tucker.

"I looked at the security feeds from this building as well as the entire business complex and every business within a block radius that has cameras," Luisa said. "Brad Parsons's vehicle was in the garage until cameras went out at nine twenty p.m. That's when I estimate he set the fire and left, after the attempt to gas Tess and myself failed. Then at nine thirty-seven, his car drove past the coffee shop on the southwest corner—I matched his vehicle to their feed at that time. I can't tell if he's driving, but the police may have better tools."

"The police have the video as well?" Tucker asked.

"Yes, the security officer said they have copies of everything, and I assume they also checked surrounding businesses, though Jack can tell them about the coffee shop if they haven't looked yet."

"The 9-1-1 call came in at nine forty-one p.m., which gave him the time to get out of the building before the fire spread," Jack said.

"The arson investigator hasn't issued his report,"

Luisa said, "and I couldn't get too close to the flash-point, but I took a look and it seems he accessed the ventilation shaft from the fourth floor to ensure the fire spread to the Desert West offices. It wasn't the fire that destroyed equipment, but the water from the sprinkler system. The investigator is testing the accelerant, but it's likely a gasoline compound."

"Brad," Tucker said in shock. "He's been here from the beginning, working up from receptionist to my assistant to assistant CFO. I mean, I work with him every day. I can't believe he would do this. I need to talk to Gavin."

Luisa said, "He may have thought the water would destroy the computer systems and files, and he's right—but your archives are stored off-site."

"Yes," Tucker said. "The IT department is already working to restore our systems. Well, the two team members who are left, since Jennifer is still missing."

"Last night I uncovered a virus in the system," Luisa said. "I isolated it, but it erased everything I wanted to look at. However, it's doubtful that the virus could have affected the archives. I can help your IT staff reverse engineer the bug so it doesn't corrupt your system when you reinstall your software."

Jack knew his sister was smart, but he hadn't quite realized how smart.

"Thank you," Tucker said. "Have you already met the staff?"

"Yes, I'm working with Kevin Gorman."

"Okay, good. Thank you so much, Ms. Angelhart." She nodded and left.

Yep, Jack was impressed by his little sister. He some-times forgot she was all grown up. "You need to tell the police everything you know. Corporate espionage is one thing," Jack said, "but Parsons—and I'll stake my reputation that he is responsible—set fire to a building with people inside. The police are going to want to interview him about his whereabouts, and they will arrest him if they find evidence."

Tucker nodded, though he looked miserable. "Let's call them now."

Forty-Three

Margo Angelhart

I generally consider myself brave. Bugs don't bother me. I can dispatch a spider or scorpion with ease. I served in the Army and went through Basic Training, which was no piece of cake, especially for an arrogant eighteen-year-old who thought she was in amazing shape. I was deployed for six months during my first enlistment and had been under enemy fire—especially not fun when you were in a "peace" zone. Blood doesn't freak me out, nor do broken bones, rattlesnakes, hiking Camelback Mountain, or encountering a javelina at sunset.

But planes? I hate flying. I don't know why; it's nothing I can explain. I've never flown in a plane that had serious trouble nor have I seen a plane crash. But every time I flew, my heart raced, my head ached, and I could picture myself tumbling to earth.

Logan convinced me that it would save time if he flew us down to Bisbee in his Cessna. One hour each way, as opposed to a seven-hour round trip by car.

I followed the philosophy that being brave didn't

mean not being afraid; it meant doing something even when you were scared. Like climbing into Logan Monroe's tiny Cessna and letting him—a man I just met—fly us down to Bisbee.

Saving time notwithstanding, I would much rather drive.

I told Logan everything Jennifer said on the phone as soon as we were in the air. He hadn't spoken since. He didn't ask questions, stomp his feet, or insist it wasn't true, didn't really show much of any reaction—except sadness. His dark eyes were full of such sorrow that I half wished I hadn't said anything.

But he should know. He deserved to know. Jennifer might not want to break his heart, but the truth was generally better than lies. Especially *this* truth that may put him in danger.

Twenty minutes into the flight, Logan finally spoke. "Were you at my rental house on Sunday because Brittney thought I was having an affair with Jennifer?"

He'd made the connection. He must have been thinking about it for the last few days.

"She hired me to prove you were having an affair. She didn't know about Jennifer."

"I've never cheated on my wife."

"I believe you."

"You do? Most people I meet seem to think that affairs are commonplace and it's a surprise when someone doesn't cheat on their spouse."

"I'm generally cynical and believe the worst about most people, but I followed you for over a week and got no vibe, no hint, that you were unfaithful. I told your wife. She didn't want to believe me."

"Do you believe Jennifer? About Brittney and Brad?"

I did, but instead said, "Jennifer sounded sincere." I paused, trying to find a tactful way to say what I was thinking, then decided that blunt was best. "After you were drugged Monday night, I tracked down Rachel Roper, the woman you met with. Brittney hired her to put you in a position where I could take compromising pictures. Brittney insisted on an NDA. I have one I use—mums the word, unless my client commits a crime or willfully lies to me, then the contract is null and void. Thus, I have no problem sharing the information with you. Brittney was an accessory to assault— drugging someone without their knowledge or consent is a crime."

Logan was silent for several minutes. I preferred talking, because it kept my mind off the fact that we were in a tin can flying at least two hundred miles an hour *way* aboveground.

"Why?" he said so quietly I almost didn't hear him.

"Ask her."

"I don't know if I'd be able to believe her."

"What I think and what I know are different things. I can give you the facts, but I can't tell you her reasons."

"But Jennifer thinks my wife was cheating on me."

"It's an old trick—an unfaithful spouse accuses the faithful spouse of adultery and walks away." I shrugged. "Maybe she believed it. But she *wanted* to believe it, because when I told her you weren't a cheater, she insisted you were just too sneaky for me to catch. *No one* is too sneaky for me."

He barked out a gruff laugh.

I let him have his time, even though now I was hyperaware that we were over the middle of the desert.

If we crashed, would anyone find our bodies? Would there be anything *to* find?

"When we got married," Logan finally said, "I told Brittney I wanted children. Two, maybe more, but at least two. I'm thirty-eight, I don't want to be an old man with babies. Brittney's twenty-nine. She said she wanted kids, too, just wanted to wait a couple of years so we could enjoy being newlyweds. I was fine with that. As soon as I started talking about it a few months ago, things changed. I knew it, but I didn't want to believe it."

He looked so sad that for a minute I was no longer terrified of dying in a fiery crash.

He continued. "I know people can change. That people can want different things at different times. But I made it clear from the beginning that this was important to me. I thought it was important to Brittney. She told me exactly what I wanted to hear." He paused, added, "That she would set up something like this—to give herself a reason to divorce me? I just don't understand. If she doesn't love me, I would give her a divorce."

It surprised me that someone so smart in the business world, who had made hundreds of millions of dollars because of his unique ideas and raw intelligence, could be so ignorant when it came to human nature. Not everyone was capable of doing what Brittney had done but, sometimes, even the people you loved disappointed you.

"Did you know that she had been involved with Brad Parsons before you married?" I asked.

"She told me after we started seeing each other that they'd gone out a few times but it hadn't been serious."

"Now you know and can decide what to do."

"I already have."

That surprised me. He seemed to be so torn up and upset that I didn't think he'd reached the point where he *could* make a decision.

"I already directed my lawyer to draw up divorce papers. I'll give her a no-fault divorce. Per our prenup she'll receive three million dollars, plus I'll give her the house. I didn't like the house, anyway."

I laughed. I couldn't help myself.

He frowned at me.

"I'm sorry," I said. "I was laughing at the situation. You are nothing like I thought you would be."

"Most people aren't," he said. "For what it's worth, when I hired you to find Jennifer, I had no doubt that you would."

"You don't know me, but I appreciate your confidence."

"I researched you Sunday night, after you showed up at the house. If I weren't so worried about Jennifer, I would have figured out then what Brittney was doing. But one thing I don't understand. You have your own business, but your family also has a PI business. Why aren't you under their wing?"

"Long story."

He glanced at his watch. "We have twenty minutes."

"Short version—my mom and I have a different way of doing things."

"You and Jack work well together. The unspoken commentary was loud."

I laughed. "It was?"

Now Logan smiled and relaxed. "I read people well. I have to. Maybe not so well in my personal life, but in business, I'm rarely wrong."

* * *

Jennifer White was staying in a nondescript motel that provided individual cabins around a cement and cactus courtyard. I liked that my instincts were right—between the book on her nightstand and her affection for J.A. Jance, I'd been sure she had decided to hide out in Bisbee. Too bad I couldn't have sleuthed my way here instead of having her give me the address.

The room was clean, private, and dark. A small kitchenette with a mini-fridge, two-burner stove, and plate-sized sink along one wall, and a small table with two chairs, a queen bed, dresser, and television filling the rest of the space.

"Were you followed?" she asked, glancing out the door.

Jennifer was nervous, had bitten her fingernails down to the quick, and—based on her overflowing trash can—seemed to be living on chips and energy drinks.

"We flew my plane," Logan said.

"Oh. Yeah. Okay."

"It's being fueled now. Come back with us. You can stay at my house."

"He'll find me."

"You have to trust us," I said, moving to close the door. I flipped on the overhead light and blinked as my eyes adjusted from the bright sun outside. I motioned for Jennifer and Logan to sit, then leaned against the counter and said, "You told me about Parsons. I filled Logan in."

Jennifer looked at him, her face filled with concern. "I'm *so* sorry. I didn't know what to say, how to say it."

"I'll be okay," Logan said. "I'm worried about you."

Jennifer offered soda or water. I waved her down and

grabbed three water bottles from the mini-fridge, put two on the table and kept one for myself.

"You have two problems," I said. "The first is Brad Parsons. The police talked to him like all the staff, but now they have more information."

"What if I'm wrong?" she asked.

"Then you're wrong. But we have to look, right? Because *someone* stole money from Desert West and *someone* drugged you and Logan on Sunday and *someone* set fire to the Desert West offices last night. Right now, you're the only employee the police haven't spoken with, and that makes you look guilty."

"I didn't!"

"I believe you. When did you arrive down here?"

"Tuesday morning. I stayed at my condo Monday night—there's a back way in—and I took a taxi and paid cash, walked a lot to get there. I needed to think, and my condo is pretty secure. But I didn't feel safe— so much was going on, and after Sunday... It was just best that I keep you out of it," she said to Logan.

"We're going to have to address what's going on at Desert West," I said, "and you'll need to talk to the police at some point, but if you can prove you were here last night, that's a good alibi."

"I think I can." She frowned. "I mean, I checked in here, but I paid cash—no credit cards."

"Would the manager remember you?"

"Yeah—I paid him five hundred upfront. I have a receipt."

"How did you get down here?"

"Uber," she said.

"Uber?" I repeated. That would cost a small fortune for a more than three-hour drive.

"I took an Uber to the airport, then a bus from there to Tucson, then an Uber here. Probably stupid, because someone could find me, but I was feeling lost and didn't know what to do."

"There will be a record, a driver, receipts. That's good. We'll put everything together, get your alibi in order," I said, not wanting to distract her from our primary focus. "But first, tell us about your family. Why you faked your death and are hiding from your father."

She looked at her chewed fingernails, saw one that wasn't chomped on completely, and went at it.

"Jennifer," Logan said, "please trust us—we want to help."

She took a deep breath. "I've always been the smart kid. Straight A's, gifted program, the whole nine yards. I didn't have a lot of friends because of it. And because my dad was very overprotective. When I was little, I didn't know why." She frowned. "Anyway, Jenny was my best friend. Her dad worked for my dad, so we knew each other forever, but we also loved each other. Like sisters. We did everything together." She didn't look at us, staring at a blank space on the wall over Logan's shoulder. I didn't push—she'd probably never talked about what happened eight years ago.

"My mom died when I was seven. A freak accident, they said. But she was murdered."

"Your father?" I asked, thinking that was a justifiable reason to want to run from your family.

She shook her head. "He loved her. In his way, he loved all of us. But my dad works for the Leone crime family. You've probably never heard of them—they're based in Florida. There's a long history about when and how they left New York before my grandfather was even born—my mom's maiden name was Leone." She stopped suddenly, and I didn't know if she was thinking about the past or wondering if she should stop talking.

"I don't care who your family is," Logan said. "We are not our parents."

"I don't know," she murmured. "Maybe not, but the sins of our fathers and all that."

I was about to interject, then Logan said firmly, "I don't believe that."

A moment later, Jennifer said, "I had a wonderful life growing up, until I learned the truth. My mom was murdered by a rival of the Leone family. Killed because of her family business. My dad and grandfather retaliated. For years, I lived in a fortress. Jenny and I talked about it, about being scared about losing each other, losing our families. But I was also angry and sad because my mom was gone—I didn't understand why then—and my dad kept going, just kept getting deeper and deeper into a pit he couldn't get out of. Jenny and I figured out what our fathers did and we talked about changing our names and going to college in Europe where we could be new people. Sometimes, we even talked about running away...and then Jenny and her whole family were killed."

Her voice cracked, but she didn't cry.

"The fire?" I asked, considering the information I'd found in her lockbox.

She nodded. "Just like my mom, enemies of my father and the Leones killed my best friend and her family. I hated my father for it. He didn't protect them, didn't protect my mother, just continued down this path of violence and rage. He retaliated—you can read about it. The nightclub bombing? That was my dad. He paid them back, but he didn't care if innocent people died. I snapped. I was fourteen, and I couldn't handle it anymore. I told my father that I was going to the feds, that I would tell them everything, that I had proof, which I didn't, other than things I heard and saw. My dad said if I spoke a word, we'd all be dead because the Leones had someone in the FBI. He didn't yell, didn't cry. He was so damn matter-of-fact about it. *Virginia*, he said in this too-calm voice, *we will all be killed if you talk to anyone*. Then he apologized, said that he was sorry, but this was his life and I had to accept it."

Every family was different. I'd like to say I didn't understand, couldn't understand, but though I hadn't lived in her shoes, I knew that family was complicated. Criminal families? More so.

"I don't remember exactly when I came up with the idea to fake my death... I just wanted to disappear. Thought about running away, but I was smart and knew I needed money and a plan. In high school, I learned that I was really good with computers, and I started thinking about what I would need to do, how to prepare. Then I realized I was good with money. I hacked—" She stopped talking.

"Jennifer, I'm not a cop," I said, "and I'm not going to rat you out for any crimes, unless you killed someone. So tell me the truth."

"I've never killed anyone," she said.

"Good. You hacked what?"

"I couldn't steal money from my dad—he might find out—but his country club? They had so much money—I suspect they were laundering it, but I don't know for sure. Anyway, I stole a hundred thousand from them over two years. Put it in a secure account, and then hired someone to create a Jennifer White identity for me. It was easier because she was real, had never worked but had a social security number. I had a driver's license and bank account in her name."

Definitely a smart girl, I thought.

"The hard part was messing with the electronics on the boat, so the only real answer was to build a bomb," Jennifer said. "I hoped the police would investigate, so that maybe they'd figure out exactly who my dad was and what he did for a living. The only way I could be free was if everyone thought I was dead, but I didn't want anyone to die—so I had to create a perfect plan. Not just the bomb, but create a leak in the boat so that we had to leave it. I didn't want my dad or brother on the boat when it exploded. I wasn't trying to kill him. I hated what he did, but I loved him."

"How did you get to college? What about records? Tuition?" Logan asked.

"That was easy. I hacked into the Texas system, created my application, my transcripts, and gave myself a scholarship. I was sure I'd forgotten something or would trigger security but nothing happened. I showed up, had a single dorm room—I didn't want a roommate, didn't want to make friends—and I had my nest egg in case I needed to run. I guess I need to disappear now." She sounded weary. I would be, too.

I was pretty certain that Vincent Bonetti found her because of Angelhart's background check on Jennifer White, but I didn't know exactly how.

"We'll figure it out," I said. "First you need to go back and talk to your boss and the police."

"But if my dad is coming—I don't know what he'll do."

"Is he a threat to you?" I asked.

"I don't know. He's probably furious at me. I hurt him. I'm scared even if my dad doesn't come for me, that people will find out who I am and then I'll be in danger from his enemies." She closed her eyes. "My dad loved me, I know that, but I was miserable and scared for years, especially after Jenny died. I can't live like that again."

I didn't blame her. "Okay. We'll figure it out."

Logan leaned forward, took one of her hands, and said, "Jennifer, I am your friend. I'm here to help. Do you believe me?"

She nodded.

"I hired Margo to not only find you, but to help you, and the only way we can help is if you tell us everything."

"Why did you leave the job in California?" I asked. "It was sudden and you told them you had a family emergency."

"It was a great company—I loved working there— but they were moving the entire business to Florida. That was just too close to my family, I couldn't risk it. My boss wanted me to go out with a small group early to set up the IT department because there would be a few months where we'd have offices on both coasts. I kind of panicked, told him I had a family emergency and quit. I didn't handle it well. Then I reached out to Logan once I got my head on straight, and he helped me get the job in Phoenix."

"Your dad may have been alerted because Desert West hired Angelhart Investigations," I said. Might as well come clean, since she'd figure it out eventually. "They ran a background on you starting two weeks ago. They found nothing, but one of their feelers may have tipped him off." And though I wasn't part of the business, I said, "I'll ask them to show you what they did. Maybe you'll see something that we don't."

"Jennifer White only exists on paper," she said. "Which is really all you need for a job. But if something tipped my dad, it's because something touched his business— or the business Uncle Jimmy used to run. I had to put my parents' names on some documents early on, and I used Uncle Jimmy and Aunt Maureen, said they were deceased so no one would ever try to find them."

"I don't know for certain," I said, "but I think the background check alerted him, and he hired a local firm to confirm your identity. That's why you saw two men outside your work and house." Frank and Andy, I thought.

"I don't know what to do," she said.

"First, he can't make you do anything you don't want to," I said. "He can manipulate you, which isn't a crime, or threaten you, which may be a crime. But you said he was responsible for a bombing?"

"Yes. To avenge Uncle Jimmy and his family, my father had all those people in the nightclub killed because the club was owned by his enemies."

"Can you prove it?" I asked.

She shook her head. "I overheard my father planning the bombing. I don't know who he was speaking with, but I'd recognize him. And I thought, how could my father bring a killer into our home? That's when I knew my father himself was a killer."

A plan started to form, but I didn't know if it would work, or if Jennifer would go along with it. "If you saw your father in person, do you think he would hurt you?" I asked. "Like take a gun out and shoot you?"

"No." She bit her lip. "Maybe. I don't know. He loved me, but I hurt him."

"I can help you disappear," Logan said.

"Before we go there," I interjected, "we need to resolve the situation at Desert West and determine if Brad Parsons is a threat. Because right now, he's the top suspect—at least to me and my brother Jack—in both poisoning the two of you on Sunday, and the arson last night. And you, Jennifer, are the only person with the evidence of his crime."

"But I can't prove it was him!"

"Fortunately, I have a sister as smart as you, and she's working on it. Between her and your copy of the code, that should put Parsons in jail for theft at a minimum—but there could be other charges, like attempted murder." I glanced at Logan. If Brittney was part of Parsons's plans, she could go down for accessory. Did Logan realize this?

"Okay," Jennifer said quietly. "And the police want to talk to me. I'm scared."

"Of your father?"

She shook her head. "If the police find out I'm Virginia Bonetti, I'll get in trouble for faking my death."

"Maybe, maybe not," I said. "It's complicated. Did you receive insurance money?"

"No, I was dead. I don't know if my father did. I mean, the boat would have been insured…"

"But you didn't profit. Your father would have to go after you civilly if he collected insurance money and then had to pay it back. Don't talk without a lawyer. I know a good one who will help. We'll prove you were nowhere near the fire, and less is more—don't answer any questions they don't ask. Your lawyer will guide you through it."

"Okay," she said, sounding young and defeated.

"Chin up," Logan said. "You can stay with me."

"She needs protection," I said. "I have a place where she'll be safe and no one would think to look for her there."

I picked up my phone and hit a familiar number.

"Mom, I have someone who needs help."

Forty-Four

Peter Carillo

The priest had light brown skin and black hair, of average height and slight build.

Peter had waited until the children left for the day and the younger priest had gone into a meeting in the social hall, leaving Father Raphael Morales—the *uncle* of Margo Angelhart—alone in the church.

And he fumed.

Detective Sullivan had come to his house with two uniformed cops. They searched his home... They treated him as if he were a criminal, as if *he* had done something to Annie and his children. Peter had to sit there and watch. In the end, Sullivan said Annie would probably come back on her own.

You should get a lawyer to help you through the family court process.

Family court. *Family court.* How could Annie do this to him? Take his kids and make him file in a court to get them back? It wasn't right.

Finally, the person who'd been talking *forever* to

the priest left the church. Peter went inside. Father Raphael Morales was straightening the missals stacked on a table in the vestibule.

"Father Morales?" he said.

The priest turned and said, "Yes, may I help you?"

Peter wore his uniform because it commanded respect. Authority commanded compliance.

"I'm looking for my wife. I think you know where she is."

The priest's eyes darkened and he took a small step back. "I don't know you. I'm sorry."

Yes he did, Peter thought. *You know exactly who I am and what I want.*

"My wife is Annie Carillo. Her grandparents were parishioners here before they died." Peter had looked up the marriage records this morning; her grandparents had been married in this little church. His instincts had been correct.

The priest remained silent.

"Tell me where she is."

"I can't help you."

"Yes you can, Father," Peter said, working on keeping his voice calm, but firm. "She was here on February 27th. I found the gas receipt. I found your church bulletin in the recycling bin. She was here, and *you* are related to the woman who took her from my house on Sunday."

"I do not feel comfortable with this conversation, Mr. Carillo. I'd like you to leave."

Peter waved his arms around. "This is God's church, is it not? This is for everyone, or is that a lie?"

"Please leave or I will have to contact the police."

Peter laughed, put his hand on his gun. He enjoyed watching the arrogant priest flinch.

"Tell me where my wife is, Father Morales. We are married in the church—it's a sacrament that can't be broken by man, yet you are preventing me from being with my wife. How can you wear that collar when you are a liar?"

Peter wanted to grab the man and shake him until he answered. But he didn't. He had too much control, too much honor to beg.

"I'm calling the police," the priest said. He turned and started to walk away, toward the altar.

"Just tell me the truth! I can't live without my family."

The door opened and the young minister who Peter had seen earlier, walked in along with a small group of eighth graders. He said to Peter, "Officer, is something wrong?"

Dammit. Peter could have made Morales talk. He just needed more time, needed to explain. Surely a man of God would understand that a wife couldn't just walk away from her wedding vows? From the sacrament of marriage?

Now the man wouldn't speak. But he would be alone again, and Peter would return for answers.

"I'll come back later," he said and left.

Forty-Five

Margo Angelhart

As soon as I had Jennifer secure and confident that Logan would fill my mom in on the situation, I rushed over to St. Dominic's.

It was late, after eight, and I knocked on the door. The young priest, Father Eduardo Diaz who I knew fairly well from spending time here, answered the door.

"You didn't ask who it was," I said.

He pointed to the security hole in the door. "I'm glad you're here, Margo. Rafe was very concerned about your safety."

I didn't want to remind him that I knew how to take care of myself. Instead, I walked over to where Rafe was sitting in the small living room. The only sign that he was concerned was a cocktail glass half-filled with golden liquid on the table next to him. Rafe was known to partake in a shot of Reposado tequila on occasion when relaxing…or worried.

"Uncle Rafe, what happened?"

"I told you on the phone. He came here, tried to intimidate me, I told him I would call the police, and he left."

Father Diaz cleared his throat, and Rafe shot him a narrowed glare.

"What did you leave out?" I asked.

"He didn't leave until Ed walked in, but he didn't make any move toward me. He believes I know where his wife is, and that I should tell him. I told him I couldn't help him and I wasn't comfortable with his presence."

Leave it to Uncle Rafe to get out of a difficult situation without actually lying.

"The man had a threatening presence," Father Diaz said.

"Did he outright threaten either of you?" I asked.

"No," Rafe said. "He was angry and he was demanding, but he didn't verbally threaten me."

I latched onto the word *verbally*.

"But?" I asked. "Do not lie to me, what did he do?"

"He was wearing his uniform and he made a point of putting his hand on his gun—I believe to intimidate me."

I barely refrained from swearing. It was a threat, clear as day, and my uncle was giving Peter Carillo far too much grace.

"I'll stay here tonight—"

"No," Rafe said before I could finish my sentence. "I don't need anyone to watch over me. We will keep the house locked and be mindful of any visitors. I will not live in fear."

"Did Jack leave?"

I had called Jack as soon as Rafe called me, which was only an hour ago. I was angry that Rafe waited hours to tell me what happened, but he hadn't wanted to worry me. It was Father Diaz who convinced him to let me know.

I asked Jack to check on things, but I didn't give him

any details, other than someone had come to the church and acted in a threatening manner.

"He's walking around, making sure everything is secure," Father Diaz said.

Then Rafe said, "Carillo knows you helped Annie leave him."

I knew that, but I hadn't told Rafe. I hadn't wanted to worry him.

"You don't seem surprised."

"I'm not." Lie of omission, maybe, but I didn't want to put any of this weight on Rafe.

There was a knock at the door and before Father Diaz could get up, I motioned him to sit and walked over, looked out the peephole.

Jack.

I opened the door.

"Hey, thanks for coming, but I got it from here."

Jack ignored me and walked in. "Uncle Rafe, everything is secure and I called in a favor to have Phoenix PD increase patrols in the neighborhood."

"They do not need to do that."

"An unknown man came in and threatened you, and you don't know if he'll return." Jack stared at Rafe. "You know who he is."

"Yes. His wife left him and he believes I know where she is."

Jack glanced at me, his face unreadable. Then he turned to Rafe. "And Margo is aware of the situation?"

"Yes, she is."

"Care to tell me the whole story?"

"I think Margo needs to tell you," Rafe said. "I have early mass tomorrow, so I need to retreat to my room.

We will make sure the house is secure, and be on alert for any trouble."

"I don't trust that Margo will tell me the truth," Jack said through clenched teeth.

"She will," Rafe said. He got up, walked over to where Jack and I stood uncomfortably next to each other. He put his hand on my arm, looked me in the eye. "It's not weak to ask for help." He kissed my cheek, then kissed Jack, and walked to the back of the house.

"I'll make sure he's okay," Father Diaz said. "For what it's worth, Margo, you did the right thing. Don't let this trouble deter you from your path."

He walked us to the door. Talking with Father Diaz always made me a little uncomfortable. I'd known Rafe my entire life, he was my uncle and ten years older than me. Every other priest I'd had was gray or bald. But Father Diaz was the first priest I knew well who was *younger* than me, by two years.

"Call me if you see him, even if he doesn't set foot on the grounds."

"I will, Rafe will."

"And if he threatens you in any way, call the police."

He nodded, and I made sure I heard the deadbolt slide closed.

"What's going on?" Jack demanded.

I headed toward my Jeep and Jack followed. "Margo, don't you dare walk away from me. Are you in trouble?"

"No," I said. "Come to my house, I'll explain everything."

Fifteen minutes later, we were sitting in my living room. Jack had noticed the security cameras immediately, but didn't comment. In fact, he didn't say anything, waiting for me to talk. He'd been angry earlier, true, but Jack was usually even-tempered, and he was doing his best to remain so now.

"Three months ago, Rafe met a woman after Sunday mass. He'd never seen her before. She stayed after— her young children had fallen asleep in the pew, and she was silently crying. He went to her, and she told him her husband was abusive and she was scared. He told her to go to the police, and that he would help her and the kids get into a shelter that night. She said she couldn't go to the police because her husband was in law enforcement."

Jack's face fell. "Jesus, Mary, and Joseph," he muttered. I almost smiled. That proclamation was the closest our dad had ever gotten to swearing. Jack reminded me so much of our dad. Not so much physically—Jack was a bit darker, taller, broader—but personality. Having him here was surprisingly comforting.

"She made Rafe promise not to go to the police, didn't tell him her name, just that her grandparents had been parishioners and she came here to pray for guidance. Rafe gave her my card, told her to call me. He told me that night what he'd done, and I waited. It took her a week to call. Her name is Annie Carillo, her husband is a trooper, and he abuses her regularly."

I told my brother about the rapes, the emotional abuse, the control. The system was flawed—they could protect Annie to a certain degree, but it was a he said/she said with no proof of abuse, no physical injuries. Without that evidence, the court wouldn't deny Peter Carillo visitation rights if she left him, and Annie feared that he would come after her someday, when she least expected it.

"I believed her. More, I believed he would kill her

for divorcing him. She needed to disappear, and I made it happen."

Jack didn't say anything for a long time. So long that I started to get angry. "What would you have done? Told her to go to court, get a restraining order? A restraining order is paper. It's a deterrent for someone who hasn't yet gotten violent. It's no deterrent to a man who told his wife he would kill her if she ever left him."

"I don't know what I would have done," Jack said. "Is she safe?"

"Yes. I don't know where she is, or what her new name is." Okay, the second part was a lie. But I would absolutely swear in a court of law if I was forced to that I didn't, that I gave her a sealed envelope with the documents. In fact, depending on how I worded it, it wouldn't be a lie—because I did give her a sealed envelope.

"I need a beer," he muttered and got up. He went to my refrigerator, opened it. "You have no food."

"I've been busy."

He grabbed a light beer for himself, a dark beer for me. I took it, though I didn't really want it.

He drained half the beer and said, "Okay, how did Peter Carillo find out you helped his wife?"

"I don't know exactly, but he ran my plates."

"He ran your *plates*?"

"So I'm thinking he went through his neighbor's cameras. I talked to Rick about it, he confirmed that Carillo ran my plates, and there's a missing persons report about Annie and her kids. She left a note and there are no signs of foul play. My guess is his next step is family court. He can claim abandonment or that she's denying him access to his children. But it's a civil matter, not criminal, and that puts it lower on the priority list."

"He knows that," Jack said. "Which is why he went to Rafe."

I didn't want to tell Jack everything. I'd kept it from Rick and from Rafe, but now that Carillo went to the church, I needed help.

"Peter Carillo is a tightly wound abusive husband who is also a cop," I said. "That he threatened Rafe—maybe not explicitly, but implied—tells me he's losing his control, and I don't know what he'll do."

"Is that why you got the security cameras?"

"I got the security cameras because Carillo broke into my house."

"What the *fuck*?"

Now I knew Jack was truly angry.

"Why didn't you call the police?"

"Because I can't prove it. He didn't take anything. He didn't leave a note. He unscrewed the handle on my sliding glass door and put it back on. The only reason I knew that someone was in here was because some things had been moved on my desk, the door handle was loose, and the deadbolt wasn't engaged. So I bought security cameras and installed them."

"When?"

"Monday night. I noticed when I got back from our dinner."

"And you didn't tell me?"

"What could you do?"

"Protect you."

"I don't need your protection, and Carillo isn't coming back. There's no information about Annie here. If he does, I'll be ready for him."

"You told Rick?"

"No."

"But—"

"I told Rick that I helped Annie, but I didn't tell him that her husband broke in. Rick can be a loose cannon, and I couldn't risk him doing something foolish and ruin his career. Or worse."

Jack didn't say anything; he knew about Rick's childhood, just like I did.

"Rick is working the law enforcement angle, calling a few people to see what we can learn about Carillo's behavior on the job. He probably called Otto."

"Good," Jack said.

"And," I continued, "he will get what he can get. I'm being careful. I don't know how he figured out Rafe helped Annie, but the man isn't stupid. He could have logged every place Annie went. She only went to the church once, but once is enough."

Jack stared at me so long I almost squirmed. Then he said, "Why didn't you tell me?"

"There was no need to."

"I'm your brother."

"I'm an adult. I mean," I said quickly as I realized that was a childish thing to say, "I've been working on my own for a long time. I was working through this, I've had cases like this before, and I didn't want to worry anyone needlessly."

"I care about you, Margo. There's no doubt in my mind that you can handle any situation that is thrown your way, but as Rafe said, asking for help doesn't make you weak."

"I know," I said, and he was right. "And I would have if things got out of hand."

"Breaking into your house means things are *way* out of hand," Jack said.

He wasn't wrong.

Jack continued. "We're working together this week—I thought we did well together."

"We did, but that doesn't change anything. Annie is my case. My responsibility. I'm telling you now because, yeah, you need to know—he went after Rafe."

Jack didn't say anything.

"So," I said, feeling a bit uncomfortable, "do you have any ideas that I haven't thought of? How to take Peter Carillo off the board?"

He shook his head. "It was just a matter of time before he found out you helped his wife. He'll always be a threat to you. You know it, I know it."

"Unless," I said carefully, "we can make him lose it."

"*No.*"

How did Jack know what I was thinking?

"In a situation where we have the control."

"I'm not putting you out as bait, and there's no way he's going to bite."

I disagreed with my brother. "Going to a church and confronting a priest is the first sign that he's unraveling. It'll continue. We may not have to do anything and he'll fall apart and do something stupid. I'd rather he do something stupid that I can control, instead of where innocent people might get hurt."

Jack didn't say anything for a long minute. Then, "Let's see what Rick has learned and then maybe we'll come up with an idea that doesn't include tying you to train tracks."

I laughed; I couldn't help it. Jack smiled.

"We *do* work well together, Margo," he said. "I want you to join us. We're family."

"Jack—"

"Don't say no. Not yet."

So I didn't say no.

Forty-Six

Brad Parsons

If Brittney hadn't screwed up everything by hiring a private investigator to follow her husband, none of this would have happened. He would have retrieved Jennifer's computer on Sunday as planned, and any suspicions about him would have died.

Brad paced his townhouse, craving a Scotch, but knowing that alcohol would muddle his mind. He needed a clear plan.

It was Brad's idea to set Logan up, but he'd had a *plan* and Brittney jumped the gun. Why had he even told her about his idea in the first place?

Because you had just had the best sex of your life in Logan Monroe's bed with Logan Monroe's wife and you wanted her all to yourself.

He should have known better. Brittney was beautiful and charming and fun and adventurous, but she wasn't smart. She'd loved the idea, and Brad *thought* he'd convinced her to wait until he set things in motion. He hadn't told her that Jennifer White may have uncovered his processing fee scam; he'd wanted to fix the situation first.

But Brittney went and hired a private investigator without thinking it through. When she told him Sunday night, Brad realized it was Brittney's PI who had screwed up his plans.

Britt, listen to me. Fire the PI. Get rid of her. We need to hire a prostitute to set him up. Someone we pay, and then we'll know when and where they'll be, and we can bring in a PI to take pictures. This is a process, baby, a process.

She'd sulked, but he coddled her—even though he was worried about Jennifer White and her damn computer.

And then Brittney fucked everything up again.

You told me to hire a prostitute!

I said we needed a plan and then we'd hire someone. Shit, Brittney!

She'd started crying and he couldn't stand the tears.

Now Jennifer was in the wind *with* the evidence of his crime, and Brittney was going to get nothing but three million from Logan in the divorce. Unless Logan learned that Brad and Brittney had been together. Where was her patience? He had patience. He'd been waiting for three years while the woman he loved beyond all measure was married to another man. He'd been embezzling money for more than a year because he was patient.

But Brittney thought she was a whole lot smarter than she actually was, and now Brad was paying for it.

Worse, Britt was going home to Logan. She'd rolled out of Brad's bed at eight to roll into her husband's.

Which *really* made him mad, on multiple levels. Brittney was his, had always been his. When Logan

Monroe asked her out, she was still Brad's. They had planned for her to seduce him so that Brad could find his weak spot. But Brad didn't expect her to marry the man.

Don't you see? We'll have half the money!

No, they wouldn't, because she'd signed a ridiculous prenup. But Brittney convinced him that she loved Brad alone, and it would only be *a year or two.*

It had been three. Still, Brad hadn't really complained. Logan traveled a lot on business and Brad stayed at the house. Brittney paid for all his luxuries, they went out to dinner (not where anyone would see them), to the theater, and sometimes even went away for the weekend to New York when Brittney told Logan she was visiting her mom.

Brad liked that Brittney spent Logan's money on him.

Even now, when she screwed up everything, he loved her. He couldn't get enough of her. When he took her to bed this afternoon—after nearly throwing her off the balcony listening to her sob story about how her PI couldn't get photos of Logan and a woman—he reminded himself that they were still screwing behind Monroe's back.

He poured himself one finger of Scotch. Just one, because he had to figure out how he was going to find Jennifer, destroy the evidence, and frame her for the theft. Because now that he'd destroyed the office and Tucker had brought in some computer expert, the theft was going to be discovered. If they accused him, he would deny it. They'd never be able to prove it because they'd never find the money. He'd left no fingerprints in cyberspace. But he didn't have enough to just *leave*—they needed a large chunk from Monroe, and the three million that Brittney would get in a divorce now wouldn't last very long, plus it would take months to even get that money.

Brad loved his townhouse in Scottsdale, near the shopping district of Desert Ridge, where he had a view of McDowell Mountain from the expansive balcony off his bedroom. The narrow, contemporary four-story home had cost him a small fortune, but it was worth it. He walked up to the balcony because he needed fresh air, needed to *think*.

What he *really* needed was Monroe's money. It wasn't fair that he had so much and Brad had to fight and scrape for *scraps* that men like Logan Monroe shared with their benevolent *bonuses*.

Bullshit.

At least he knew Brittney preferred his bed to her husband's.

Brad recognized that he'd become obsessed about Brittney and Monroe's love life. He'd told Brittney to record herself having sex with Monroe. She made three different recordings, each one better than the last as she started acting up for the camera. The last time, she'd set up her phone to record her on top, so Brad could watch her face and her breasts bounce with each thrust. When she orgasmed, she looked right at the camera and blew him a kiss. Right with Monroe underneath her and the nerd didn't even know what she was doing.

That video always gave Brad a hard-on. *Thinking* about it gave him a hard-on, which went limp when he thought about how Brittney had put their entire plan in jeopardy.

Brad hated Monroe and wanted everything he had. His wife. His house. His bank accounts. He had his wife, he'd get his house—and if Brittney didn't fuck up the one thing he'd told her to do when she got home, he'd have Monroe's money.

He just had to wait for her to call.

His phone rang as he was about to pour his second Scotch. He answered, surprised that Brittney had actually done what he'd told her so quickly.

It wasn't Brittney.

"Brad?" the female voice said, quiet and nervous.

He looked at the caller ID. "Tammy?"

"Hi. Um, I'm at your gate. Can I come in?"

Tammy was Gavin O'Keefe's temporary assistant. Gavin's regular assistant, Gwen, was a ball-breaker and on maternity leave. Tammy had been there for the last two months. She was young, sweet, efficient, and cute. Not hot, but attractive with the innocent girl-next-door vibe. She had a crush on Brad. He'd encouraged it because he needed information from O'Keefe's office, and Tammy got it for him. He'd nearly slept with her once, but stopped himself, realizing that when he didn't want to see her again, she might turn vindictive and tell Gavin what he'd been asking her to do.

His restraint had earned him far more than he expected—Tammy thought he was a "total gentleman" and was now half in love with him. He'd made up an excuse, that he couldn't get involved with someone in the office, but when Gwen returned, then maybe they could go out.

He never planned to, but he definitely liked the benefit of information. Without Tammy, he would never have known that Jennifer had been prying into his business.

That Tammy had shown up here at his townhouse was very worrisome.

"Of course," he said automatically. "I'll release the gate. I'm in the middle of the second row, number twenty-four."

He walked downstairs, typed the code to open the complex gate, and waited for Tammy to drive up in her MINI Cooper. She walked up his short walkway with a nervous smile. "I'm so sorry to come here without calling first, but I didn't know what to do, and after everything that happened last night—it's just awful."

He motioned her inside.

The entry level had an office perfectly set up for a work-from-home arrangement, but he led Tammy up the stairs to the main living level—living room, dining, kitchen. The place was large and comfortable and all his.

"This is beautiful," she said, taking in his contemporary decor, her mouth slightly open.

He didn't want small talk, but needed to be polite. She had information for him, and information was power.

"Can I get you a drink?" he asked.

"No, no, thank you," she said, flustered again. "I shouldn't have come, but…"

Her voice trailed and he said, "Tell me what's wrong. I talked to Ron this morning, he was justifiably upset, but our data is archived and the IT department will fix it. Though I heard Jennifer is still AWOL."

"I'm so glad you talked to Mr. Tucker." She smiled, as if his comment answered a question for her.

He hadn't actually spoken to Ron. Ron had sent out an email stating that each staff member would be interviewed by detectives and to cooperate, and no one needed to come into the office except for the IT department. Brad had talked to a Detective Capelle, told him what time he had left (5:20 p.m.) and where he'd gone (home) and who he was with (no one—he was working from home on a project). No way they could confirm any of it either way, he figured.

Brad hadn't been concerned about all that—until now. Until Tammy walked into his townhouse, face etched with worry.

"Gwen is coming back part-time starting tomorrow—can you believe it?"

"Gavin has always depended on her." Damn. Brad had hoped he'd be long gone before that battle-ax returned.

"Mr. Tucker said I still have my job because she's part-time for a few months."

"Good."

He wanted to scream at her. *Why the fuck are you here, Tammy?*

Instead of yelling, he said with fake concern, "What's troubling you?" He was surprised his voice was so calm. He would have reached out and caressed her shoulder in affection if he didn't fear he would squeeze too hard.

"I think…" she began, then straightened her spine. "I think that Jennifer White is trying to get you fired."

He didn't say a word.

Tammy continued. "Mr. Tucker was very concerned about her when she called in sick, and I overheard him talking to Mr. O'Keefe about data that she had downloaded without permission. He made it sound like a…*a crime.*" She whispered the word.

"If it's proprietary data, it *is* a crime," he said.

"He brought in a private investigator, Jack Angelhart—I spoke to Mr. Angelhart today. He talked to all the staff."

He didn't talk to me. But Brad nodded. "And?"

"And some of his questions—he made it sound like Jennifer was investigating someone in the office. Remember when you told me last month that Jennifer was prickly and didn't like you for no reason?"

He nodded. Of course he remembered. He was working to set up his innocence in case Jennifer figured out what he'd done before he could clean it up.

"Well, Jennifer called and talked to Mr. Tucker and Mr. O'Keefe after hours tonight on a conference call. I was there only because I was waiting for my car to be done from the shop down the street. I didn't hear anything, but *then* the police came in and Mr. Tucker said something—I didn't hear all of it—but he mentioned your name, and it sounded like Jennifer had been talking about you. And that's not right."

That. *Bitch.*

"I will straighten it out," he said.

"Please, don't say I said anything," Tammy said. "I just think you should know."

"Thank you. Ron and I have worked together for years, since we helped start Desert West. We'll figure out what's going on."

He walked her back downstairs and watched her leave. He could tell that she wanted to stay, and any other night he might have wined and dined her, seen how far he could take it. He would have liked to have had sex with her at least once—she was young and inexperienced, but that could be a turn-on.

But definitely not tonight.

He stared at his phone. Brittney had better not fuck this up because Brad was going to have to leave town sooner rather than later.

And he needed Logan's money to do it.

Forty-Seven

Margo Angelhart

Jack was double-checking my new security system and deeming it as good as I could get without an alarm company when Rick drove up. He wasn't in uniform.

"Jack," Rick said with a nod. He glanced at me as if gauging why my brother was here so late.

"He knows," I said. "Carillo went after Uncle Rafe at the church."

"Is he okay?"

"Yes." I motioned for Rick to come in, offered him a beer.

"No, thanks," Rick said. "What happened? I didn't see a dispatch to the church."

"No crime. He intimidated Rafe, wanted to know where his wife was. He didn't leave when Rafe asked him to, but when the other priest came in, he walked out."

Jack said, "I asked a buddy of mine to keep an eye on the church for the next couple of days. And I checked out the property. Margo and I are trying to figure out what to do about Carillo. She said you were asking around."

"That's why I'm here. Otto called in favors and I got this."

He dropped a file on the counter.

"What is it?"

"A copy of his personnel file. Every complaint against him. Normally, I'd say most of it is bullshit—a guy gets pulled over for a DUI and files a complaint that the cop who pulled him over was a prick. Nothing that's going to make me look twice. He doesn't have an unusual pattern of excessive force—no more complaints than average. He's never discharged his firearm in the line of duty. But...there are two complaints that were settled but I think warrant a second look."

Now I opened the file, started to look through as Rick continued.

"They were both complaints by fellow cops," Rick said. "One was a deputy who Otto knows. He filed a complaint that Carillo didn't go to a call he'd been assigned. He wouldn't have filed the complaint, but it was the third time another trooper had to cover for him, and it was a particularly difficult situation, so he brought it to their command. Carillo was reprimanded, but nothing else came from it."

"We've all known cops who keyed in to a call but never followed through," Jack said.

Rick shrugged and nodded at the same time. "The other complaint was from a female trooper."

"Sexual harassment?" Jack asked.

"No—general harassment. Most female cops take ribbings like anyone. Sometimes it's gender-based, but they let it roll off."

I'd gone through it as an MP. No one—man or woman—was safe from being teased, but once you established that you had a thick skin, the teasing pretty much ended or became playful jabs, much of it to blow off steam in high-stress situations. But some people were assholes and didn't know when to stop.

"This time, the trooper felt that he had singled her out. Made inappropriate—not sexual—comments, such as now that she was married, maybe she should find a less dangerous job."

"That's...odd," Jack said.

"Her husband is also a cop, a deputy with Maricopa. They met on the job. And that's what stands out to me—Carillo worked with this woman for two years with no issues, but after she got married, Carillo started singling her out for harassment. But the kicker—the cause for the complaint—was when she called for backup in a DUI situation and he was first on scene. He let her take lead, and as she approached the driver, he became belligerent and hit her. She ended up taking him down, but Carillo didn't step in to help. She had a split lip and black eye. Carillo stood there and watched, told her that she looked like she could handle it."

"Bastard," I muttered.

"Her husband nearly went after Carillo—a couple cops had to hold him back—and in the end, the trooper transferred to Glendale PD. Carillo got a mark on his record and a one-week suspension."

"Does he have problems with other female officers or troopers?" Jack asked. "I thought that bullshit was mostly gone."

"You'll always have a few numbnuts who don't like female cops, but the training process is rigorous and most cops who have gone through the academy together don't have issues because everyone has to pass the same tests."

"Considering how he treated his wife," I said, "he probably has this warped worldview that once a woman gets married, her life should focus completely on her husband."

"That's my take," Rick said, "especially after I talked to Officer Nunez. He's been helping Sullivan with the investigation into Annie's disappearance. He didn't put this in his report, but told me off-the-record that Carillo appeared to have separated Annie from friends, that he frowned on her doing anything without him. No one has seen physical abuse. The common theme is that Carillo worshipped Annie...but Annie was quiet, introverted, and generally skittish."

"How does this help keep Carillo away from Rafe and Margo?" Jack asked.

"He's losing it," I said. "Breaking in here, confronting Rafe, threatening him—" I stopped when I saw the expression on Rick's face. *Shit.*

Slowly, he said, "He broke into your house?"

"I can't prove it." *Damn, damn, damn.*

"Is that why you put cameras up?" His voice was too calm.

"I want to set him up," I said. "He's going to cross the line."

"He's already crossed the line," Rick exclaimed. "Why didn't you file a police report? Get it on record?"

"Because he didn't take anything and I had no proof that it was him."

"CSI could have printed the place. Talked to neighbors."

"I talked to my neighbors. They didn't see anyone or

anything. He's not stupid, Rick—he likely wore gloves. I have nothing here that can lead him to Annie, and I can't prove he broke in. Drop it."

Rick glanced at Jack, but didn't say anything else.

"I've been thinking about how to get him to trip up," I said. "Going after Rafe was a mistake—a big one. I don't know that he'll do that again."

"He could go after you," Rick said.

"He's doesn't want to jeopardize his job or risk being arrested, so whatever he does, he's going to be subtle. If I can get him to escalate—in a controlled environment—that would be the best of all worlds. I'm thinking on it. Jack and I already talked, and he'll back me up." I glanced at my brother. *Always*, he mouthed.

Out loud, Jack said, "The more we can learn about the investigation into Annie, the better."

"Sullivan doesn't know you're involved—yet," Rick said. "He and Nunez are going through security cameras in the neighborhood, but Sullivan thinks the best option for Carillo is to file in family court."

"He'll do it, go through the motions," I said, "but it won't be enough for him. Too slow, too bureaucratic, and since he doesn't know where Annie is, it's going to take months—years—to find her, if they do. I need to be visible, in his face."

"What do you mean by that?" Rick asked.

"Be someplace he can see me to channel his anger and frustration."

Rick shook his head. "There has to be a better way."

"I don't know exactly what I'm going to do," I said, "but if you have ideas, I'm all ears."

No one had an idea. Rick said, "Just don't do anything tonight, okay? Give me a day or two to dig around, and between the three of us, we should be able to come up with something that doesn't put your head on the chopping block."

"Not tonight," I agreed.

Rick got up to leave.

"Hold on," I said and ran into my bedroom.

I retrieved a small, wrapped present I'd had for months. I was going to mail it to Sam for her graduation, but kept going back and forth on that, and now her graduation was in two days. Here, I had Jack as a buffer. I wasn't usually timid about anything in my life, but the situation with Rick and his daughter and our fight three months ago had shifted things.

I handed Rick the purple-wrapped package—purple was Sam's favorite color. He stared at it quizzically.

"For Sam. Her graduation. I got it a long time ago. It's been in my closet."

He put it down. "Why don't you bring it to her? Graduation is Friday morning. We're having a party Sunday afternoon at the house."

"I don't know," I mumbled. Damn, I hated feeling this way.

"Sam wants you to come."

But did Rick? That was the million-dollar question. "We'll see—just take the present, okay? And if I can come, I'll be there."

"Fair enough," Rick said. He turned to Jack. "You'll be there?"

"Wouldn't miss it."

"Great."

The whole conversation was awkward and weird, and I just wanted Jack and Rick to leave.

"Jack, I'll see you at Mom's in the morning, okay?

Wrap up your case with a pretty bow." I smiled, though I couldn't help but think if Jack hadn't been here, where would Rick and I be right now? In bed? Or fighting?

Fifty-fifty.

Jack walked out with Rick, and I could breathe again.

Thursday

Forty-Eight

Tess Angelhart

Tess brought pastries over to her mom's house early Thursday morning. "Is she awake?"

Her mom nodded, sipped her coffee. "I heard her, but she hasn't come out yet."

"Jack and Margo are on their way." Tess poured her own mug of coffee, then sorted the sweets onto a plate she'd grabbed from the top shelf. When she was a teenager, she hated being the tallest girl in the family by far—sisters and cousins. Even her brother Nico was an inch shorter than her. Now? She'd grown into her gangly limbs and liked being able to use all the shelves in the kitchen.

She sat at the kitchen table with an apple fritter. "Did you talk to her?" She took a bite and savored the sugar.

"Yes. I'll represent her during her interview with the police about the fire, but I don't expect anything to come from it." Ava sat down, selected a plain croissant with her manicured fingers. "She has a solid, verifiable alibi and I'll shut down questioning if it veers too far off that path."

Tess wouldn't want to be a cop on the other side of the table from her mother. Ava Angelhart was a rare attorney who performed exceptionally well whether for the prosecution or the defense. If she believed in you, she was your greatest advocate.

"What do you think?" Tess asked.

"About the fire?"

"About her family. Faking her death."

"If she was honest with Margo," Ava said, "then she must have been both grieving and conniving to pull it off. Death—especially violent death—changes you."

Tess glanced up as Jennifer walked into the kitchen. She wasn't certain if Jennifer heard her mother's entire comment until Jennifer said, "I told Margo the truth. Not the entire truth, there's much more, but I didn't lie." She gestured toward the coffeepot. "May I?"

Ava nodded, and Jennifer poured herself a cup. She sat at the far end of the farm-style kitchen table in a bright nook that looked out to the pristine backyard. The Angelhart family had spent hundreds—thousands—of hours around this table. Their formal dining room had long ago been converted into the home office that Ava used—and once shared with her husband.

Her mom had more patience than Tess, so Tess asked Jennifer, "What did you leave out yesterday?"

It took Jennifer a minute, then she spoke. "I told Margo the big things. The retaliation. The murders." She stared at her coffee. "What I didn't say was all the little things, the security around the house, the men that came and went, some I never saw again and didn't know why. The lies my dad told me, and how I miss my brother. The guilt I feel because I never followed through on my threat to tell the FBI after the nightclub bombing. Because I didn't know if my dad lied to me about a bad agent who would have us killed. My little brother—I couldn't live with myself if something happened to him."

"You were fourteen," Ava said. "Traumatized, angry—your decisions then were clouded by youth and grief. Your decisions today are what matters."

"I can't prove anything."

"You may know things you don't realize you know. That bombing was twelve years ago. There is no statute of limitations on murder."

"But my family has people in law enforcement, people in government who help them."

"You're in Arizona," Ava said. "I know people here, and I know who I trust. The question is, do you trust me to keep you safe?"

Jennifer didn't say anything.

Ava laughed lightly. "Not me, personally, I promise you. But I can get you real protection. If you decide to go down this path, I'd contact an assistant US attorney I know—we went to law school together and have worked well over the years when our cases crossed. He is ethical and honest. He'd assess whether he can open an investigation into your allegations, and call in the US Marshals to provide protection if warranted. That would mean putting everything you know on the record, under penalty of perjury. I need to do a little research, but I'm almost positive any crimes you have committed—the identity theft, the hacking—have passed the statute of limitations. But going this route won't be easy. You may have to leave Arizona, take another name, build a new life."

"I'd have to do that anyway," Jennifer said quietly,

staring into her mug. "My dad knows that I'm here, that I'm using Jennifer's name, so he can find me anywhere."

"I suspect," Ava said, "that Margo is correct in her assessment that when we started investigating the employees at Desert West, that triggered something that alerted your father or made him suspicious, and he then hired Miriam to find you, confirm your identity."

Jennifer nodded. "He'd want confirmation. He could send someone. Or maybe come himself." She visibly shivered and held her mug as if it were grounding her.

"You told Margo he wouldn't hurt you," Ava said. "How certain are you?"

She hesitated. "I don't *think* he would. I'm his daughter. But I really don't know. He's believed I was dead for eight years. How does that change a person?"

"What about your other family? Your brother, aunts, uncles?"

"My mother was an only child, and we never really socialized with my dad's family. My grandfather—my mom's dad—died four years ago."

"How'd you find out?" Tess asked.

"I set up Google alerts about the family. I expected over the years that my dad would go to prison eventually, or be killed. If—if he had died, I planned to reach out to my brother. Anyway, I saw the obituary. Heart attack. He was eighty-two."

"I'm sorry to hear that," Ava said.

"I hate what my dad did—the crime, the violence, the arrogance of it all. But...he wasn't always that way. He treated me and my brother well, loved us. We played games—my dad and I loved cards, and my grandfather would play chess with my brother. They'd both come to my soccer games and cheer me on, and to my brother's baseball games. I remember how proud they were when my brother made a game-saving dive to catch a ball in center. Right before Jenny and her family were killed." Her voice cracked and Ava put her hand on Jennifer's arm.

"No one is all good or all bad," Ava said. "It's sometimes difficult to reconcile people we know with things they do. It doesn't make you a bad person to fondly remember the good times with people who loved you."

"I just don't see how they could love me and put our family in danger like they did. I can't forgive that."

"That's okay. Maybe now that you can talk about it with someone, it'll help you come to terms with your past and navigate your future."

Tess admired the way her mother always had the right words, the right tone for difficult situations.

"So, what now?" Jennifer asked.

"Jack is contacting the detectives and letting them know that they can interview you here, in my home. We won't be telling them anything about your family situation. Margo said you already called your employer about what you had been doing with the files, but you'll need to talk to them again, answer all questions."

"Logan was on the call with me. If he didn't back me, I don't know what they would have thought."

"They would have eventually discovered the truth, but having someone in your corner helps. We're all going to help you get through this."

"Thank you." Jennifer's voice cracked.

Ava patted her arm, then rose. "With your permission, I'll contact the federal lawyer I mentioned and start the ball rolling."

"Okay," Jennifer said with a nod. "Okay."

Forty-Nine

Peter Carillo

Peter listened to the lawyer go over his options. Frank Bollinger worked in family law. A *divorce* lawyer. A *custody* lawyer. A lawyer that Peter never in a million years thought he would have to consult. He sat in the small conference room, back straight, heartbroken, angry and deeply sad that Annie would do this to him, to their family.

Blah, blah, blah. That's what Peter heard. Rehashing everything Detective Sullivan had already told him. That it's a process, that it takes time, that he has options. Completely dismissing Peter's concerns about Annie's mental health and the safety of his children.

"Without independent corroboration, we won't get an emergency hearing," Bollinger was saying. "And even when we do get a hearing, without her address we won't be able to subpoena her to produce the kids."

He didn't speak—*couldn't* speak. None of this was fair. What about his rights? As a husband? A father?

"There is one option we have," Bollinger said. "Your

wife could be charged with federal kidnapping if she took the kids over state lines. Right now, because it's only been a few days, I don't know that the FBI will look at it, but we can definitely reach out to the local FBI office and ask them to open an investigation. Phoenix PD may pass it along to them in a few days, but in my experience, without evidence that she left the state, Phoenix will drag their feet."

He didn't want the FBI involved. He didn't want *anyone* involved, but Annie had left him no choice.

"The private investigator knows where she is," Peter said. "Why can't we force her to talk? Subpoena her?"

"There is no cause to do so, but if she aided in the kidnapping of minors, the FBI may be able to bring her in for questioning and possibly charge her with obstruction. It's a bit of a delicate situation. Do you have any idea where Annie might have gone?"

He shook his head. "Her father lives in Montana. He left her mother when she was young and as far as I know, she hasn't spoken to him in years." It was possible, he supposed, because she had proven to be a deceptive, lying bitch.

Bollinger took notes. "It's a place to start. Have you reached out to him?"

"I don't know how to contact him."

"Do you have a name? Last known address?"

"Chris Correa. When he left Phoenix, he moved to Bozeman. Annie was thirteen at the time. But that's all I know."

He wrote down the information. "I'll have my investigator track him down and if she's there, then we might be able to compel her to return, or go to the FBI. I would suggest that we start the process rolling in state court— but it'll take time to get before a judge. We'll need that time to track her down. Once we have her location, we might be able to expedite the hearing—but the FBI would be the best option to get the kids back. They can go anywhere in the states." He paused, then asked, "Does she have friends or family in Mexico?"

"Not that I know of."

"You've talked to her friends locally, but does she have friends elsewhere? Relatives? A distant cousin?"

He shook his head. "Her mom died when she was nineteen. She's never talked about any family."

Peter didn't want to bring in the FBI. He wanted to find Annie on his own, and all he could think about was forcing Margo Angelhart to tell him. Put the fear of God into her...

The fear of God.

The priest was involved. He had talked to Annie—Peter was positive. There was nothing at Angelhart's home pointing to Annie's location, but the priest might have records.

Peter knew the church schedule, when they had masses and school, but he would watch the place for a while. There were at least two priests. During school hours would be best, because the priests would likely be in the classrooms, but would there be staff in the rectory? Where would Father Morales keep such information? Did he have a private office? Maybe in his bedroom. A safe?

"Peter, are you listening?"

He nodded, though he had no idea what Bollinger had been saying.

"I'm going to prepare the papers, but hold off filing until after my investigator talks to Annie's father, on the chance that she is there. When we file, it'll be a few weeks before we get a hearing, and that gives us time to have a private investigator track her down."

Private investigator. Like Margo Angelhart. The bitch who took his wife.

"Okay," he said.

"We don't know where Annie is, and you have no proof that Annie is a danger to the kids, so I suggest you file for a divorce. Since she has left your home and is unreachable, the divorce would likely be granted. The court would then appoint an investigator to find her."

"I don't want a divorce."

"This might be the best way to get your children back. Once you're divorced, then you have the right to custody of your children, and she can't withhold the right without violating a court order."

He didn't want a divorce, but he wanted his kids. Was this the only way to get them?

"Okay," he said, "and we can do it right away?"

"It'll take a few months. Six to nine months, but—"

"Months? *Months?* My baby will be walking! My son might not even remember me! I can't wait *months*!"

Bollinger stared at him. "There's no quick fix here. Even if we bring in the FBI, it'll take them time to find her, and that's *after* they determine she's left the state. If she's keeping a low profile—changed her name, keeps moving—finding Annie will take time. My recommendation is that you work this both ways—file for divorce and while it's pending I can work to get custody rights, which will put her immediately in violation. But like I said—it'll take a few months."

Months. Peter couldn't believe Annie was doing this to him.

"Once we contact the FBI, they'll interview you,

look at your bank records, credit cards, computers. They have more resources than Phoenix PD. She may be arrested, depending on the circumstances."

"Hold off on the FBI for now." That was too much, and he couldn't focus on what he needed to do if he was worried about some asshole federal agent getting into his business. "I just want my family back. Let's just give it a little time first, then we can talk about it."

Bollinger nodded.

"I don't want a divorce, but I want my kids, and if that's the only way..."

"It may be. Just because you start the paperwork, doesn't mean you have to sign. We should get the process started as soon as possible. If you think of anything else—a friend from high school, a cousin, anyone—let me know and I'll find them. If she accesses your bank account, credit cards, or you get a call verifying anything like her identity or employment—let me know."

"I will. Thank you."

He wouldn't, of course. He would find out where she was and bring his wife and children home.

Bollinger prattled on about nothing Peter cared about as he walked him to the door. Then the lawyer said, "My experience tells me that in situations like this, the wife comes home within a week. If you haven't heard from her by Monday, we might want to rethink calling in the FBI."

"Okay," he said, though he didn't want the FBI involved at all.

Not when he finally had a plan.

Fifty

Margo Angelhart

I didn't make it to my mom's Thursday morning. Instead, I sat through morning mass at St. Dominic's with the elementary kids and a handful of people from the community who came every morning—mostly older women who wore veils.

If Peter Carillo showed up, I didn't want trouble. Not with the kids here. But he didn't show, and I doubted he would return during school hours. I touched base with Rafe and as I was leaving, Jack called.

"Sorry I didn't make it to Mom's," I said. "I decided to stay at the church for a bit and make sure Carillo didn't show. How'd Jennifer do with the police?"

"Great. I'm taking her now to Desert West to turn over her information to Tucker. Luisa is meeting us there. Jennifer said she can't prove it was Parsons, but she has a compelling case based on process of elimination. Wendy is heading over to talk to him again, considering they found what Lu and I found—his car was in the garage right before the fire started. He has a lot of explaining to do, though there's no physical evidence tying him to the arson. CSI is still processing."

"I'm going to check in with Logan. He stayed at his resort last night. Which is pretty damn cool. You own an elite resort with a private condo, wife cheats on you, head over for a little R and R."

"Go easy with him, Margo."

That confused me. "What do you mean by that?"

"He just found out that his wife not only was having an affair, but she tried to set him up. He's going to have complex emotions. Sometimes your bedside manner is a bit…indelicate."

I wanted to laugh. Indelicate? "You mean I'm too blunt."

"I can hear you now, Margo. *Logan, she's a bitch, get over it.*"

I winced. I think I called Jack's ex a bitch before he was ready to hear it. I guess my bedside manner is a bit *indelicate.*

"I call 'em as I see 'em," I said lightly. "But I'll try to be sensitive."

Now Jack laughed. "You do that." Then, in a more serious tone, he said, "Be careful, Margo. You know what I mean."

I did. "Back at you." I ended the call.

After checking in with my uncle after Mass, I was heading to North Scottsdale when my phone gave off an odd chime. I looked down as soon as I hit the stop sign. My new security system alerted me that someone was on my front porch. A uniformed officer and a plainclothes, probably a detective. I didn't recognize either of them.

I turned right rather than left and three minutes later

was pulling into my driveway. The two cops were back in their cars, but hadn't left yet.

I parked in my driveway and walked to the curb, curious. They each got out of their vehicles. The detective approached me first. "Margo Angelhart?"

"Yes. You?"

"Detective Grant Sullivan. This is Officer Archie Nunez. Do you have a minute?"

"Sure. My brother was on the force, until three years ago. Worked out of the 900."

"Jack," Nunez said with a nod. "I didn't know him well, but the name sounded familiar."

"I know Jack," Sullivan said. "He doing good?"

"Yeah. If you came by last night, you could have had beers with us."

I leaned against my Jeep. I knew why they were here— Detective Sullivan was the primary on the Annie Carillo "disappearance"—but I wanted him to talk first.

This day was going to come, and I'd gone round and round with how to respond. No lies—but I didn't plan on telling the whole truth. I really wanted to tell Sullivan that Peter Carillo was an abusive prick, but I hadn't seen the abuse—the marital rape or emotional manipulation. Only Annie could testify to that. I *could* tell them but then they'd want to speak to Annie.

"What can I help you with?" I asked.

Detective Sullivan said, "We're investigating a missing woman, Annie Carillo. Do you know her?"

"I do."

"When was the last time you saw her?"

"Sunday."

He wasn't expecting my prompt answer, but I knew if they were here, they saw me or my Jeep on a security camera. No way Carillo would have told them, though he may have pointed them in the right direction.

"What was her state of mind?"

I shrugged.

"Was she upset? Angry?"

"I couldn't say."

"Did you see her kids? She has a boy, nearly four, and a baby, eight months."

"I did."

"Were they healthy? Well cared for?"

I wasn't exactly sure where they were going with this, but considering what Carillo had told them in the official report about postpartum depression, I suspected they were trying to ascertain whether she was a danger to her children.

"They were kids. PJ was chatty and running around, happy, the baby a chunky, bright-eyed little girl. Annie dotes on them and every time I've seen her with them, she's been an excellent mom."

"Annie left her house Sunday morning, with her children. Did she tell you where she was going?"

"No." Getting into the gray area, but Annie didn't tell me where she was going. I gave her the address in a sealed envelope because I didn't want to know. I knew she was headed to San Antonio, but that could have been a stop—maybe they had another destination for her. I didn't want to know that, either.

Rafe knew, but there was no reason for the police to talk to him.

"Ms. Angelhart, I viewed security footage from one of the Carillos' neighbors, and it showed Annie in the front seat of your car." He gestured to the Jeep. "I couldn't tell if the kids were in the back seat because of your tinted windows, but I assume they were."

I didn't say anything because he didn't ask a question.

"It's not a crime for a woman to leave her husband and not tell him where she's going," Sullivan said, "but they are his kids, too."

Again, no question, so I remained silent.

"Where did you take Annie?"

"She doesn't want me to tell anyone."

"Her husband just wants to know that his wife and his kids are safe."

I didn't say anything.

"Mr. Carillo is concerned that she's a danger to herself and the kids."

When I didn't answer, he said, "Why don't you want to cooperate?"

"I am."

His expression changed just a fraction, but I could see the irritation flit across his face.

Officer Nunez asked, "Are Annie and the kids safe?"

Now she is. "Yes."

"Mr. Carillo plans to petition the court to compel his wife to return with his kids," Sullivan said. "I will be required to give a copy of my report to the judge, and he may subpoena you to testify as to where Annie is."

I doubted the court would subpoena me, and if they did, it would be months from now. I said, "I will answer all questions under oath truthfully. Including the *fact* that I do not know where Annie is." I pushed off from the Jeep. "My mother used to be the district attorney of Maricopa County. I know the process."

Neither cop showed a reaction; Sullivan had been a

cop long enough that he'd likely worked with my mother's office, though she'd left more than a decade ago.

He held out his card. "Call me if you want to share more information."

Odd comment. I took the card, slipped it into my back pocket. "Detective, did you tell Carillo you saw my car on security cameras?"

If he was surprised by the question, he didn't show it. He nodded toward the uniformed officer. "Archie reviewed the footage from several neighbors, ran the plates, identified you last night at end of shift, so we came out first thing this morning."

"You didn't answer my question."

"You didn't answer mine."

"I answered every question you asked. I can't answer unasked questions."

He hesitated, then smiled. "Fair enough." He glanced at Nunez. "Have you discussed this with Carillo?"

"Not yet. I have another question, though. Ms. Angelhart, do you personally know Peter Carillo? Or just his wife?"

"Just Annie."

"How long have you known her?"

"Nearly three months."

"How'd you meet?"

I smiled. I couldn't help it. It was a smart question, and Nunez clearly had a reason for asking.

I didn't answer the question. "I have an appointment, so you'll have to excuse me."

"We might be talking again," Sullivan said.

"I look forward to it."

Fifty-One

Officer Archie Nunez

Nunez watched the PI walk down her driveway and let herself in through the side door without looking back at them.

"You think she was lying about knowing where Annie is?" Sullivan asked.

"I don't know. She didn't have any problem not answering questions she didn't want to, so I don't know why she would lie."

"My gut? Annie was tired of marriage, wanted a break, and Angelhart drove her to the airport."

"We checked the airlines. She didn't fly anywhere." It was difficult to get fake IDs—not impossible, but that seemed a step too far for someone who wanted to leave her husband. "She doesn't have family, all her friends are here—what few she has. But she reached out to a private investigator months ago."

"You think there's something more here. Like what?"

Nunez wasn't certain where he was going with this, but something didn't feel right about this whole thing. "Carillo was drinking pretty heavily the other night."

"Devil's advocate? His wife had just left him, took the kids, and he doesn't know where she is."

"Yeah, but—I don't know. He wouldn't be the first cop to have a drinking problem."

"And she left him because he was a drunk? Why not put that in the note?" Sullivan frowned.

"Yeah," Nunez said, "the note bothered me. *You hurt me one time too many.* It can be taken in different ways, you know?"

"The first thing I did was check hospitals, shelters," Sullivan said. "No emergency room or urgent care visits. No one mentioned broken bones, bruises, anything like that. I couldn't get her doctor to talk to me, which isn't surprising, but doctors are mandatory reporters. If he thought she was being abused, he would have been compelled to file a report."

Nunez had been a cop for fifteen years, but he couldn't quite shake that he was missing something here. It was an overall impression after talking to Annie's friends and neighbors—especially Ms. Madera from the book club—that Annie was timid and scared. No one said she was scared, but it was a feeling he'd gotten based on what people *had* said.

"I'd like to talk to Annie Carillo," Nunez said. "I think there is more to the story than she put in that brief note."

"Someone knows where she is," Sullivan said. "We just need to find the right person."

Fifty-Two

Margo Angelhart

I put Peter Carillo out of my mind as I drove to Logan Monroe's elite golf resort, Saguaro Springs, just west of Scottsdale and north of the 101, though the lack of a Scottsdale zip code didn't mean it was any less fancy. The main hotel had three floors where every room was a suite. Multiple buildings on the edge of the green that blended into the surroundings each had four to eight condos or townhouses, which catered primarily to wealthy snowbirds.

I'd been here exactly once—fifteen years ago for my senior prom.

Saguaro Springs also offered golf memberships, spa services, indoor and outdoor swimming pools, and had three bars and two restaurants for members and resort guests.

Arizonians loved their golf. My dad tried with all of us, but only Lu and Jack took up the sport. Jack to socialize and hang with friends, Lu because she was competitive and liked to win. So did I—which is why I didn't play golf.

When Brittney first hired me and I researched Logan, I learned he had bought the resort three years ago with an investor group that included two retired baseball players and a former Arizona congresswoman. They'd gotten a steal because the previous ownership group had mismanaged it. They'd done major renovations and apparently it was now in the black. No small feat. I didn't know how hands-on Logan was, but he maintained a townhouse on the far side of the golf course that he used for friends and family—and now himself.

Even though temperatures were starting to creep up, it was still a respectable eighty degrees at ten in the morning, so the morning golfers dotted the landscape with their twosomes and foursomes, covered carts providing relief from direct sun when needed.

I hesitated, bumps rising on my skin, telling me someone was watching me. Could just be someone playing golf, maybe someone I knew, maybe staff. I looked around the area a second time, didn't see anyone acting suspicious or staring at me.

A private patio led to Logan's door. Putting aside the odd feeling, I knocked.

Logan came to the door. Dark circles under his eyes told me he hadn't slept much. "Did we have a meeting?" he asked, confused.

"I wanted to check on you. Everything okay?"

He motioned for me to follow him inside. The ground floor of the townhouse was a single room set up as an office, with sliders that looked out at the golf course. He went up the stairs and I followed. The second floor had a large great room, full kitchen, and what appeared to be two bedrooms off the living area. A small deck in the front, a larger one in the back. He'd been working at the kitchen counter—his laptop was open beside three phones, and a stack of what appeared to be proposals, all bound and professional. The one he seemed to be in the middle of reading was neither bound nor professional-looking, but had a clear sheet cover like I used in school for essays.

"You're busy," I stated the obvious.

"Just going over potential projects."

"I really don't understand what you do."

He shrugged. "A lot of different things. These," he waved to the stack, "are ideas that people want funded. Most are blah. But I'm considering one of them."

"And you just give them money?"

"A bit more complicated than that, but close enough."

He sat on the couch; I stood by the window and looked out. A foursome was fifty yards away, two men and two women, all over sixty. They were doing more talking than golfing.

"Is Jennifer okay?" Logan asked. "Did she talk to the police?"

"All went well," I said. "And Jack will stick with her until we know more about the threat from her father— or from Brad Parsons. Have you talked to Brittney?"

"Last night when I told her I wouldn't be home. She's been calling and texting me all morning."

"Can I see?" I asked.

He pulled yet another phone from his pocket and handed it to me. Nineteen phone calls between yesterday at three—about the time I was talking to Logan at his office—and this morning. He'd answered only the first call yesterday, and made one outgoing call to Brittney last night at seven, right before we left Bisbee.

I opened his text messages with Brittney. Most were from her. There was a slew of them yesterday asking when he was going to be home, insisting that they needed to talk, that she had a bad feeling something was wrong. It was after that series that he had called her. After the call, she texted him multiple times asking why he wasn't picking up his phone, she was worried, she was going to call the police if he didn't talk to her right now. He'd responded once at 10:10 p.m.

I'm tired and have an early morning meeting. I will talk to you tomorrow.

She responded immediately.

I love you, baby. I miss you.

He hadn't responded. Yep, he definitely believed that Brittney was involved with Brad Parsons.

Then the messages started up again this morning, along with several unanswered phone calls.

I handed him back his phone.

"I called Gavin last night after the conference call with Jennifer," Logan said. "I told him everything—he needed to know because Desert West is his business, and he needs to protect himself and his employees. He and Ron had already taken some steps, but they're hiring a forensic auditor—someone recommended by your mother—who should be able to figure out exactly what happened and how much money was stolen. I hope they'll be able to prove that Parsons did it. He's not answering Ron's calls."

"You told him about Jennifer's family?"

"No details, just that she had a major family upheaval and she'd tell him when she could." Logan paused, looked at the wall, not at me. "Gavin said he suspected that Brittney and Brad were still involved, but he didn't want to say something in case he was wrong. I don't understand why he wouldn't tell me—did he think I was so weak and thin-skinned that I couldn't handle it? Did everyone know except me?"

"We trust the people we love," I said. "It's as simple as that. That's not on you."

"My parents were married for forty-five years before my dad died. That's what I wanted."

It's what I wanted, too. I had my parents as an example, and I would rather be single than settle for someone I didn't think would stick.

"I think I'm supposed to say maybe you should go to counseling, or give her a second chance."

He tilted his head and looked as if he were confused. "Supposed to say?"

"Jack thinks I have no tact. And if you want to give her a second chance, go for it. But the woman tried to set you up—she hired someone to put you in a compromising position because, I believe, she wanted to use the photos in a divorce. She gave me a copy of your prenup. She gets more money if you cheat."

Even though I was in the clear to share with Logan because Brittney had lied to me, I was still uncomfortable. "I guess I should go," I said, feeling awkward. "If you need me for anything, you have my number. Remember—be careful. We don't know what's going on with Parsons right now, and last I heard, the police haven't talked to him yet."

Logan's phone vibrated on the table. He sighed as he reached for it. "I'm going to have to talk to her sometime. And I need to get some things from the house—I'd rather do it when she's not there, but I might not have a choice."

I wasn't going to let him go alone. There was too much we didn't know about Brittney and Brad Parsons. Parsons set a fire and risked lives to conceal his involvement in embezzlement. Would he be willing to go even further?

But I didn't say that to Logan. He picked up his phone, answered. "Yes."

He sounded weary and irritated at the same time.

Brittney spoke so loud that I could hear most of what she said.

"Logan! Finally! I need to see you... Please?" Some of her words were too soft for me to hear, but I understood the tone.

"I'll be home in an hour," he said. "I'm packing for a business trip."

I didn't know if he was lying or not.

"When?"

"Tonight."

"Baby, we have the dinner with the McCarthys tonight."

"You'll have to go without me." He rubbed his eyes. I gathered he hadn't told her he'd asked his attorney to file divorce papers.

"I'll join you."

"No," he said without explanation. "I need to go." He ended the call. "I can't do this."

"Can't do what?"

He tossed his hands in the air. "Everything."

"Of course you can," I said firmly. "You're a self-made multimillionaire, and you can't tell your wife that you're leaving her because she cheated on you?"

"I've never done emotional confrontation well. She'll be served with the papers this afternoon."

"Maybe," I said, "you should stay here until after?"

"I'm giving her the house. I don't want to go back after she knows. There's a few things that are important to me that I need to get in case—well, in case she gets emotional."

I raised an eyebrow. Emotional or violent, I wanted to ask, but didn't.

"I'll go with you."

"You don't need to do that."

I did. I'd witnessed too many volatile situations and Brittney was a wild card. "Domestic situations sometimes turn bad real fast."

"Brittney isn't violent. I don't want to make this harder on her than it is."

"Harder on *her*?" I asked, flummoxed. He was thinking about his lying, cheating wife and worrying about how she was going to take the split?

"Have you been through anything like this?" Logan asked.

"I've never been married."

"A bad breakup?"

I thought about Charlie, when he told me his ex-girlfriend had moved back to Phoenix. He cared about me, and he didn't know if it would work out with her, but when he saw her, all the same feelings returned and he couldn't in good faith continue to see me knowing he had feelings for another woman. He was mature and honest, and I waited until I was home alone to cry. With Rick? I definitely didn't act as mature. He chastised me for giving Sam advice without consulting him, without telling him about the cyberbully, and reminded me that I was not her mother. I walked away and hadn't spoken to him until this week.

Was it a sign of maturity that I'd been so angry and hurt that I just buried it?

"Personally, no. My breakups have been more or less straightforward. But my brother went through a tough divorce, and he has a son, making it ten times worse for everyone. All you can do is what you can do—but you need to do it. Something my dad always says, meaning ignoring a problem doesn't solve anything."

"I thought Brittney was the one. I didn't have many serious girlfriends because I'm busy and don't like dating. It's exhausting. I meet investors and idea people all over the world." He motioned to the huge stack of proposals next to his computer. "I love what I do. I'm really good at finding businesses on the cusp and turning them around. It takes time and Brittney seemed to accept that I'm gone half the year."

Probably because she was screwing Brad Parsons, but I didn't say that.

"Was it all a lie?" he asked, more to himself than me.

But I answered anyway. "You don't know what was in her head when she said yes to your proposal. What you know now is based on her actions. If you want to see a marriage counselor, fine. But I'll tell you this: if my husband hired someone to honey trap me—whatever the reason—I would absolutely walk away. If you want to give her a second chance, you're a better person than me." Or an idiot, but I didn't say that, either. "I'm coming with you. Just in case."

"Maybe stay outside? I don't want a confrontation if I can avoid it."

"Fine," I reluctantly agreed. "But I've observed a lot of splits and it rarely goes as planned. And another thing? You should lock all your financial accounts, then change your passwords and install two-factor authorization. Bank accounts, investments, anything you have that she can get into."

He gave me a sad smile. "I already did."

Okay, he wasn't an idiot.

Fifty-Three

Margo Angelhart

Logan's house was quiet. He'd told Brittney that he would be home to pack, but she wasn't here. Odd.

According to his lawyer, she hadn't been served yet. The process server had the paperwork as of ten minutes ago, but it could take a few hours—or a few days, if she decided to hide.

Logan was more than generous in giving her the house. I wouldn't have given her the time of day.

Over the last two weeks, since I first took the case, I had learned a lot about Logan. I'd gone from thinking him a cheater (every adultery case I have taken in the eight years since I've been a PI resulted in a cheating spouse, so believing it wasn't difficult) to being innocent but with secrets.

But the more I learned about him, the more I thought that he was the real deal—a smart, slightly awkward introvert known for being honest and respected in his circles. He donated to charities—not obscene sums of money, but generous enough to be recognized. His preferred charity was Phoenix Children's Hospital, which received half his charitable contributions, and I'll admit that endeared him to me. Not just because my dad had been a doctor, but because Nico had spent many nights there as a kid when they were trying to figure out what was wrong with him.

I had also dug into Monroe's past—he'd grown up in a typical middle-class family in a farming community outside San Antonio, Texas. He had a brother and a sister and his parents were married until his dad died, and his brother ran the family ranch. He'd dropped out of college when he and Gavin O'Keefe sold a video game they had designed to a major gaming company. O'Keefe moved to Phoenix with his long-time girlfriend, now wife, and Monroe founded a small gaming company with a group of investors. It grew, and he lived in Austin running it and other ventures during the time Jennifer interned for him six years ago.

Honestly, Logan didn't seem to have much time for an affair with anyone, but I'd caught more than one cheating spouse screwing a colleague. At the beginning, I'd considered he had a mistress in another city, but to date haven't found any evidence of an out-of-state lover.

I didn't believe Brittney intentionally lied until Sunday, and now? I thought she set this entire thing in motion. Because of Brad and his embezzlement? Did she want the money because he was on the hotseat?

I couldn't figure out what her endgame was—other than getting more money out of her husband. Maybe that was all she needed. Maybe she didn't know about Brad's embezzlement and wanted to bring money to their relationship. Or, she knew about the embezzlement and wanted more. Yeah, that was probably closer to the truth. After all, greed breeds greed.

Though there were cacti everywhere, most of the properties had paloverde and sycamore trees for shade. I parked under a grouping on the north side of the property and turned off the ignition. I rolled down all my windows to let the light wind push the warm air around. Logan said he'd be about thirty minutes.

When my phone chirped, I glanced at the caller ID. Miriam Endicott?

"Miriam, this is a surprise," I answered.

"We need to talk."

"So talk."

"Face-to-face."

"About?"

"Not over the phone."

"Then goodbye."

"Stop—dammit, Margo, this is a serious and delicate situation."

"What situation would that be?"

"You know exactly what I'm talking about."

"You must have started the conversation without me."

Miriam didn't say anything for a long ten seconds. I could picture her sitting rigid at her desk, hand grasping her phone, mouth tight and angry. Wanting to hang up but not able to because score one for me—she needed something and only I could get it for her.

"Margo," Miriam said, attempting to keep her voice calm and collected, though I heard anger vibrating underneath the cool shield, "I would like to facilitate a meeting between Jennifer White and her father."

"Why call me?"

The feeling of being watched at the golf course…

Had Miriam been following me? No, not me—Logan. I would have known if I had a tail.

"I know you have her."

"Have her? Like, holding her against her will?"

"Don't be cute."

"I wouldn't think of it."

What was Miriam's game? Jennifer didn't want anything to do with her father—yet she hadn't been terrified, just worried, concerned, and feeling serious guilt for putting her father and brother through the grief of her death.

"Neutral territory. I thought you might agree to Ava's office."

That surprised me. Miriam detested my mother, and that she would even suggest meeting there told me either she was up to something or she really was in a bind.

I tried to weigh what Miriam really wanted, and I suppose I took too long to respond, because Miriam continued.

"Vincent Bonetti arrived in Arizona yesterday morning. I had hoped to make contact with Jennifer and arrange a meeting, but you found her first."

"What do I win?"

"Dammit, Margo! This is serious."

"I don't know what you want from me, Miriam."

"I want you to bring Jennifer to talk with her father. Just a conversation."

Right. Just a conversation. "And I have some prime Scottsdale oceanfront property you might be interested in."

"I don't know what she told you—"

"Okay, you want serious? I know who Jennifer is, I know what she did, and she is scared. Meeting with her daddy? Not going to happen."

"You talk to him," Miriam said quickly. "Listen to him. Then you'll understand he means her no harm."

"I'll think about it."

A car came up the road. It slowed and turned into Logan's driveway. Brittney's Range Rover, but she was in the passenger seat. I couldn't see who was driving. The garage door started to rise.

"He knows she's here," Miriam said, "and I know she doesn't have the money to disappear again. Does she want to be on the run for the rest of her life, especially when there is no need to be running? Her father is no threat to her. He just wants to see her."

Interesting. I wanted to know more, because I agreed with Miriam that running should be the last option. But I didn't have time to discuss as the car pulled into Brittney's slot in the four-car garage, next to Logan's Tesla.

"I'll call you back," I said, then hung up over her objections and silenced my phone.

The garage door was closing before I could see who was driving, and the garage was on the opposite side of the house from where I was sitting under the tree. I didn't like the situation, and immediately called Logan.

He didn't answer. I tried again. Again, no answer.

Dammit. Who had Brittney brought home? Would she have the audacity to bring Brad Parsons?

Yes, I thought, *yes she would.*

I jumped out of the Jeep and ran across the large cobblestone driveway. Dismissing the idea of knocking on the door—if they were up to something, I doubted Brittney would answer it—I ran to the garage door and waited a beat, to make sure they'd entered the house.

I used Logan's code for the garage and the door silently rolled open. I skirted past the cars and to the door that led inside the house.

Maybe nothing was wrong. Maybe Brittney wasn't up to something.

I didn't buy it. Why bring a third party to the house? Knowing that her husband was coming home to ostensibly pack for a business trip, she brings a friend by?

It just wasn't adding up for me.

I opened the door that led into the house. I hadn't been inside before, though I'd looked up the floor plans during my research phase. The garage opened into a small mud room that led to a laundry room bigger than my bedroom. Stop, listen. I didn't hear anything. Yeah, I knew the house was big, but shouldn't I hear voices? Conversation?

Cautious, I ventured out of the laundry room. Logan should be packing, so I imagined he'd be in his bedroom. The master suite was to the left. I went down the hall to double doors that were open.

The king-sized bed hadn't been made, the comforter on the floor, the sheet and blanket tangled at the bottom. Either Brittney was a restless sleeper, or two people had been here last night.

There was a sitting area and a small office off the bedroom, plus a giant—and I mean *humongous*— closet. Inside the closet two suitcases were open on luggage racks, both half-filled with men's clothes. The larger side of the closet was packed with more clothes than I had owned in my lifetime; Logan's side was also full, but appeared to have twenty or thirty button-down shirts all the same style with slightly different patterns. Half long-sleeved, half short. Slacks hanging on pant-hangers. Polo shirts pressed and hung in a rainbow of colors. A tuxedo and five suits in clear protective bags. In the two weeks I'd been tracking Logan, he'd worn a suit once.

The larger suitcase had shirts and pants neatly folded; the smaller one had shorts, boxers, socks, and two pairs of shoes.

But Logan wasn't here. A pile of workout clothes were on the table in the center of the closet, next to the bags, as if he'd been sorting through them when he left.

Where was he? Where was Brittney?

I stood just inside the bedroom door and listened for anything to tell me where they were. The house had good bones, good soundproofing, and there were no creaks or echoes, even with the tile floors. Nearly six thousand square feet on one story—except for a family room and Logan's office upstairs.

I suspected that's where they were, but then I heard Brittney in the kitchen.

"No, Logan, you can't!"

It was a wail, and I imagined that Logan had told her he was leaving her.

Logan said something too quiet for me to hear, but I wondered where Brittney's driver was. He hadn't stayed in the car. It had to be Parsons—who else?

"We're going to fix this!" Brittney said, her voice more angry than upset. "Dammit, Logan, please just listen to me!"

Where the hell was Parsons? In the kitchen witnessing this conversation between his lover and her husband? Doubtful.

Hiding? Had Brittney not told him that Logan was coming home? Was Parsons sneaking around, waiting for Logan to leave so he could take over the house?

Wow—sleep with the wife of a wealthy man and get a two-million-dollar house free and clear.

Nice gig, if you had no class or morals.

Still, it bugged me. I didn't like unknown variables, and not knowing exactly what was going on made my instincts twitch.

I shouldn't have let Logan go inside alone. I should have argued with him, insisted I stick to him like glue. So what that Brittney hadn't been served yet? She had been cheating on her husband for years with a man who had embezzled money and set fire to his place of employment. Brad Parsons was unstable and desperate— he had to know he couldn't get away with his crimes.

Damn. I sent Jack a quick message.

Parsons is at Logan's. I'm going in silent.

I didn't want him to worry when I silenced my phone and he couldn't immediately reach me.

Jack was at least twenty minutes away, but I was pretty certain he'd send the police if he didn't hear back from me quickly. Scottsdale PD had a damn good response time because—unlike Phoenix, they weren't severely understaffed.

I didn't think that Brittney was a danger to Logan, but I didn't like the idea of leaving him alone with her. I liked even less Parsons being able to get the drop on me.

Slowly, I peered into bedrooms and didn't see anyone. I headed to the staircase, which fortunately couldn't be seen from the kitchen.

Creeping up the wide steps, I kept my back against the wall because I didn't know for certain that Parsons was upstairs, and I wanted to keep the downstairs as well as the upper landing in my field of vision.

The kitchen was to my left—a large room that opened

into the downstairs family room and the informal dining. From the landing, I'd be able to see into all three rooms. But Brittney might be able to see me as well.

I was torn. I was here to protect Logan, but how could I protect him when I didn't have the two potential threats in line of sight?

Even if Brittney wasn't armed, there were a lot of weapons readily available in a kitchen.

I made my decision and went back downstairs. Get Logan to safety, then worry about Parsons.

I walked across the huge foyer, past the formal dining room that had likely never been used for meals, and stepped into the kitchen.

In two seconds I had assessed the situation. Brittney and Logan stood at opposite ends of the counter. Parsons wasn't in the room. No visible weapons.

"Logan, we need to go," I said.

Brittney stared at me, eyes wide. "What the hell are you doing here? Logan, you can't listen to anything this woman says. I hired her and she lied to me, lied about me. She's crazy."

I would have laughed if her comments weren't so pathetic.

"Where's Brad Parsons?" I asked Brittney.

"What are you talking about?"

She sounded believable; Logan looked confused. I wasn't buying her act.

"Who drove your car, Brittney?"

"Me. Of course. Logan, she's *literally* insane."

"Logan, come with me," I ordered, using my tough MP voice.

Brittney's voice had escalated, and there was no

doubt that it was because she wanted Parsons to hear the conversation.

I had to get Logan out of here.

Fortunately, Logan trusted me. He walked over even as Brittney told him to come back.

"What happened?" he asked me.

"I'm getting you out of here."

"I need to get my bags."

"We'll come back. I'm serious, something is weird." I steered him with my left hand down the back hall toward the garage because it was closer than the front door, leaving my right hand free to draw my gun if necessary. At every opening, I glanced to assess if there was a threat.

"Is Brad really here?" he asked.

"Someone was driving her car, my guess her boyfriend."

Brittney ran down the hall after us. As she reached for Logan, I put my arm out so she couldn't touch him. "Back off," I ordered.

"How dare you! This is my house."

Brittney looked panicked. She glanced upstairs and Logan knew exactly what I knew.

"What is he doing in my office?"

"No one is here, baby!"

Logan made a move away from me, toward the staircase.

I grabbed him. "Don't be stupid," I told him. "Your life is more valuable than anything you have in there."

I hadn't seen Logan angry until that moment. His eyes darkened, a vein in his neck throbbed.

Movement directly above me, at the top of the staircase, had me pushing Logan toward the hall.

"Go!"

A gunshot hit the wall inches above my head. Either Parsons was a bad shot or hadn't intended to hit me. I pulled my gun at the same time as I pushed Logan to go.

Brittney screamed. "Stop it! Stop it!"

She ran toward me and as I sidestepped I hit the wall, but stayed upright. I stuck my leg out to trip her and she fell forward, hitting her head on the wall. She lay there stunned.

I couldn't take the time to check her. There wasn't any blood and she wasn't dead. Logan turned and looked. "What? Britt—"

"Go!" I said.

Parsons was running down the stairs.

"I will kill you Monroe!" He fired another shot. Glass broke.

We weren't going to make it to the garage. The hall was too long, and we'd be sitting ducks. I pushed Logan into the first door on the left. It was a theater. Well, shit. The one room without windows to escape.

I locked the door. "The police are on their way."

To make sure of it, I dialed 9-1-1, put my phone on speaker while trying to assess the room for cover.

It was a sloped room with three tiers of four leather recliners each, all facing a large screen. I ran over to one and started to push it over. Logan came to help me.

The door rattled violently as Parsons tried to get in. He fired a bullet into the lock just as we pushed the chair against the door. The lock didn't give, but it wouldn't take much more to break it.

I pointed to an open door that led to a bathroom. "Go in there now. Lock the door."

From my phone, I heard, "9-1-1 operator, what is your emergency?"

"Shots fired at my location, suspect on premises."

Another gunshot and the door budged. Parsons pushed and the chair gave a half inch.

"What about you?" Logan asked, talking over the operator as the woman asked for more information. She had to have heard the gunshots.

"I have an idea."

Only part of an idea, but Logan couldn't be caught in the crossfire.

"Go," I ordered him. "Lock the door and don't stand next to it."

The door started to give under Parsons's weight.

"Parsons," I shouted as Logan did as I told him, "the police are on their way. Leave the premises."

He was ranting about Logan—everything Logan had done to him, taken from him. I hadn't met the man, but clearly he'd snapped. Maybe around the time of the arson fire? Had the police talked to him a second time? Did he know he was a suspect?

He'd come from upstairs. Maybe he'd come here to steal directly from Logan, then learned that Logan had changed all his passwords.

Dim, recessed lighting along the corners of the room provided basic illumination. A long narrow bar was built against the back wall with a refrigerator, popcorn machine, and ten different kinds of whiskey.

The operator kept talking and I slid my phone toward the front of the room. It stopped about two-thirds of the way down. Then I ran behind the bar and crouched. The bathroom door was on the right; Logan had thankfully closed it behind him.

I had one chance.

Parsons finally pushed the door open. I could hear Brittney sobbing in the background, begging Parsons to leave with her now. I blocked her out. Parsons stormed in, looked around.

"Where the fuck are you, Monroe? You ruined my life! You took everything from me. Everything! Now the police are looking for me, all because of you."

Parsons was clearly rewriting reality in his head as he somehow blamed Logan for his embezzlement and general life failures.

The operator said something indistinct, and Parsons rushed to the front of the theater, raised his gun, and fired multiple times into the backs of the leather chairs.

I flipped on the lights and said to Parsons who stood twenty feet away, his back to me, "Drop your weapon! Hands up or I will shoot!"

I wouldn't hesitate to fire if he turned his gun toward me, but I didn't want to kill him.

The next ten seconds moved excruciatingly slow.

Parsons didn't move. He didn't drop his gun, but he didn't turn to face me. He stood as if frozen, staring at the blank screen. Was he thinking if he could turn and get a shot off before I did? Considering if he should drop his gun and surrender? If he could stand there and wait me out?

Then Brittney ran into the room and made a beeline toward Parsons. "Brad, let's go, please."

"Get out of the way," I shouted as Brittney put herself between me and Parsons.

"You've ruined everything," Brittney screamed. "Everything! Just leave us alone. Come on, baby," she said to Parsons. "Let's go."

She put her arm around him and steered him toward the door. I kept the bar between me and them as a shield, my gun still focused on Parsons, watching his hands for any movement that he was going to shoot.

He let Brittney steer him out, his expression full of loss and defeat. But the gun remained tight in his grip. They walked out of the theater and I lost sight of them.

I went to the door, cautiously looked both ways, didn't see them. I considered going after them—Parsons definitely had a screw loose and he had a gun—but I'd committed to protecting Logan, so that meant sticking to him until Parsons was apprehended.

I knocked on the bathroom door. "Logan, you good?"

"What happened?"

"Brad had a temper tantrum then left with Brittney. Stay put."

"Come in here with me," he said through the door. "They could return."

"I'm fine. Just hold tight until the police get here."

I heard sirens. Because the house was set back from the road, they were probably closer than they sounded. Brittney and Parsons didn't have enough time to get out of the garage, let alone out of the neighborhood. They could easily return and create a hostage situation. I hoped they didn't do something stupid.

I ran to the front of the theater and retrieved my phone, then posted myself in the doorway, my back against the broken door frame, where I could see the hall to the left that led to the laundry room and garage, and the wider hall to the right where parts of the kitchen and family room were visible.

"Dispatch, you still there?" I asked.

"Police have arrived at the residence. Are there any injuries? Can you give me a status?"

She sounded a bit stressed, and I supposed when I didn't immediately come on the line after multiple gunshots, she may have thought I was dead.

"My name is Margo Angelhart. I'm a licensed private investigator. I'm partly secure in a downstairs room on the north side of the house with the homeowner, Logan Monroe. A man named Brad Parsons fired multiple rounds into the room, then left with Brittney Monroe. He has at least one weapon. I do not know if they are still in the house."

"Is Mrs. Monroe a hostage?"

"She left with him willingly." I didn't know what Parsons was thinking and I hoped Brittney knew what she was doing. "I am armed and protecting Mr. Monroe. Mr. Parsons threatened to kill him."

"I've let the responding officers know your status. Please stay on the line."

I put the phone down on the bar but left dispatch on speaker. The entire call would be recorded, including the gunshots and Parsons's rants about Monroe. Evidence for the prosecution.

How did it come down to this? How had Parsons gone from a nonviolent crime of embezzlement to assault to arson, and now to attempted murder? He spiraled quickly. Pressure from the police investigation into the arson? Pressure from Desert West and the exposure? That Jennifer had disappeared with evidence of his crime?

Whatever the reason, the man was unstable, and Brittney, somehow, had contributed to it.

What a waste.

The dispatcher said, "Ms. Angelhart?"

"Right here," I answered.

"I'm patching you through to Sergeant Ryan Daza who is outside the residence. One moment."

A second later, a male voice said, "Ms. Angelhart?"

"Yep."

"An officer has been outside for the last four minutes and no one has exited. How long since you last saw the suspects?"

I glanced at my watched. "Six minutes. There were two vehicles in the garage when I entered the house—a white Tesla registered to Logan Monroe, and a gray-blue Range Rover registered to Brittney Monroe. When they left the theater—the room I'm in with Mr. Monroe—they turned down the hall toward the garage. The garage code is pound 4512."

"The garage is open and there is only a Tesla inside. Do you have the plates for the Range Rover?"

I rattled them off from memory.

"Hold tight."

Two minutes later, Daza got back on the line. "We're coming in through the garage and the front door. Are you armed?"

"Yes."

"Please holster your weapon."

"Roger that."

I did as he instructed and less than ten seconds later I heard multiple people enter the house from both sides, then calls of "clear" as they moved through the house. A female officer stopped by the theater door, gun drawn, barrel angled down. "Angelhart?"

"Yes, ma'am."

"Where's Mr. Monroe?"

I gestured to the bathroom door on the far side of the room. "Secure."

"Okay, I'll stay here with you." She looked at the shot-up leather chairs and the destroyed door. "Anyone injured?"

"No."

She gestured to the gun on my hip. "Did you discharge your weapon?"

"No." I'm glad I hadn't. I loved my SIG and didn't want to have to surrender it for days or weeks or even years if there was a trial. I asked, "What's your name?"

"Liv Branson."

We chatted for a few minutes as Branson stayed on the door, then five minutes later she got the all-clear.

I walked over to the bathroom and knocked. "You can come out, Logan."

He opened the door looking both mildly irritated and very concerned. "What happened?"

"I don't know," I admitted, "but the house and grounds are clear."

He looked around the room and saw the destruction. "Brad did that?"

"Yep."

"I didn't realize how much he hated me."

"I don't think he was thinking with all brain cells."

"I need to check my office, see what he took."

"My guess—he couldn't get what he wanted, which is why he lost it," I said.

"Hold off on that, Mr. Monroe," Branson said. "My sergeant needs to get your statement first."

"Did you find them?"

She didn't respond. She was listening to her radio, then she said, "Please come with me."

Logan and I followed her to the kitchen. Several cops were still outside looking around, and Sergeant Ryan Daza approached. I knew it was him because of his stripes. Six feet tall, fit, mid-thirties.

"We've detained Mrs. Monroe and Mr. Parsons at the guard house," Daza said. "The first responding officer saw the Range Rover on the road, ran the plates, found it was registered to this house and since we didn't quite know what was going on, we instructed the guard house to lock the gate until an officer arrived."

"And?" I asked. "You detained, didn't arrest?"

"Mr. Monroe," Daza said, "can you please go with Officer Branson and give her your statement? I need to talk to Ms. Angelhart."

"Of course," Logan said. "I also need to check my office and computer to make sure nothing was stolen."

"Go ahead, but take Officer Branson with you."

Logan squeezed my arm. "Thank you, Margo. I mean it."

Logan led the officers upstairs to his office, and Daza turned to me.

"Why didn't you arrest them? You have the 9-1-1 call, so the dispatcher can confirm shots were fired. My statement—Parsons tried to kill Logan Monroe."

"Why don't you tell me exactly what happened, starting with when you arrived here?"

So I did, from the time I followed Logan to the house and waited outside, until Branson arrived in the doorway of the theater.

"Are you retained by Mr. Monroe? Personal security?"

"No. He hired me for another matter, but I was helping him today out of the kindness of my heart."

"Are you friends?"

"We just met on Sunday, but we've been working together this week."

"Are you sleeping with him?"

That irritated me. "No. Why the fuck do you ask?" I couldn't refrain from the anger. "I just told you we're working together, not screwing around."

"Mrs. Monroe claims that she informed her husband she was leaving him and asked Mr. Parsons to escort her so she could pick up some of her belongings. Then she claims that Mr. Monroe threatened them both so they left."

I stared at Daza, then burst out laughing. I couldn't help it.

Daza wasn't laughing.

"She claimed that you, Ms. Angelhart, were having an affair with her husband and that's why she was leaving him."

I tried to stop laughing, but I couldn't. Maybe it was the crash after the adrenaline rush, or maybe it was the absurdity of the situation, but I needed to laugh.

When I managed to stop, tears still in my eyes, I said, "Brittney Monroe hired me two weeks ago to prove her husband was having an affair. He wasn't. When I informed her of that fact, she asked me to follow him one more night. She hired a friend to drug him and attempt to seduce him. My brother partnered with me that night, we witnessed the crime, took Logan to safety, and I tracked down the woman the next day, who admitted that Brittney hired her. Logan didn't want to press charges, but decided to file for divorce. Brittney hasn't been served yet, but he started the process yesterday."

"Do you know Brad Parsons?"

"Never met him until today."

"Why did Mr. Monroe hire you?"

"That's confidential. He can tell you if he wants."

"But your work for his wife wasn't confidential?"

"Our NDA became null and void when she both lied to me and committed a crime. I have no professional or moral obligation to keep her confidence. I can prove she paid me."

"And Mr. Monroe can back up your statement?"

"I have not lied. I told the dispatcher and you that Parsons had a gun."

"It's not on him."

"Search the car, the garage, and every place in between. I didn't discharge my weapon."

"Okay. Sit tight, I need to make some calls."

"So do I."

He stepped out and I called Jack.

"I'm almost there, what happened? You okay?"

"Fine." I gave him a brief recap. "Where's Jennifer?"

"Back at Mom's. Tess is with her."

"I got a very interesting call before all this other shit went down. Vincent Bonetti is in Phoenix, and Miriam Endicott wants to arrange a meeting between him and Jennifer. And before you say no, I have an idea."

Fifty-Four

Theo Washington

Margo owed him big-time.

Watch the church, she said. Keep an eye on her uncle, she said.

So when Theo was done with classes for the day, he parked himself outside St. Dominic's under a big oak tree and rolled down the window. Laughter from kids running on the playground made him feel like a creep. Wouldn't it be just fabulous if a couple cops rolled up on him as he watched the kids play.

He didn't want to be here.

But it was Margo, and she'd made him cards that said he was an associate at Margo Angelhart Investigations. They looked pretty damn cool and official.

A rap on his window had him jumping. He immediately thought cop and that he would have to explain he wasn't a pervert, that he was working, really.

He turned and saw the priest standing there, his collar very white against the black shirt and slacks. "Hey, um, Father. You doing good?"

Rafe smiled and said, "I appreciate you keeping an eye on things, but I'm sure my niece didn't mean for you to sit out here all day."

"Margo would be here, but she's wrapping up another case. She'll relieve me later."

"Come in, have something cold to drink. I just made fresh iced tea. It's hot out here."

Without waiting for Theo's answer, he started back toward the rectory.

Theo hesitated only a second, then followed.

Margo told him to keep an eye on her Uncle Rafe, might as well do it inside with a refreshing drink.

Still, Theo took one more look down the street, just to make sure Carillo wasn't watching them.

All clear.

Fifty-Five

Virginia Bonetti aka Jennifer White

Jennifer had spent so long convincing herself that Virginia Bonetti was dead that she almost thought of herself as Jennifer White. She'd even adopted some of her dead best friend's mannerisms, like twirling her hair when she was nervous.

But as soon as she saw her father walk into the conference room with Margo and Jack Thursday evening, she remembered exactly who she was. She expected anger and fear; instead she felt a deep overwhelming sorrow.

Her father looked like a shell of his former self. His hair gray, thinning. He still dressed well in his lightweight custom-made Italian suit. But he'd lost weight, his suit hanging loosely on his gaunt body.

A memory flashed from long ago, before she knew her father and grandfather were criminals, before she knew that her mother had been murdered. When her best friend was still alive and the two families—the Whites and the Bonettis—had a barbeque one Fourth of July. She and Jenny were nine and swimming in the pool and she clearly remembered her dad laughing at something Jenny's dad had said, and the two of them looked so happy, as if they weren't the bad guys, as if they were just average normal dads on a normal holiday weekend.

She and Jenny were making plans for both the upcoming school year and a trip to North Carolina with Virginia's grandparents. A whole month in the mountains, no younger siblings, just her and Jenny and her grandparents.

The flash of young joy and excitement disappeared when she saw her brother walk into the room with Jack.

Jennifer was watching the room through a video camera. Her father didn't know she was here, didn't know she could hear everything he said. Ava Angelhart and her daughter Tess were with her, watching her, watching the room.

Jennifer stifled a sob as she realized that Tommy had grown into a man. He was twenty-four now—she had missed eight birthdays. He was so handsome, but he looked sad, too. She'd left him like she'd left her father. She'd left her little brother who she loved…but she hadn't trusted him with the truth. She feared he would stop her.

That she would have let him stop her.

Ava put a hand on her arm. "Who is that?" she asked quietly.

"Tommy. My brother." Her voice was a squeak, barely audible, but Ava took her hand, held it, and Jennifer felt better.

Margo offered coffee or water. Her dad took water. Tommy took nothing. They sat at the large table, prearranged so that Jennifer could watch her dad's face.

"I talked to Jennifer—Virginia—and she's not coming," Margo said. She put a water bottle in front of Jennifer's dad and sat down next to Jack. "You need to convince us that you're no threat to her, and we'll relay that to your daughter. Ultimately, any decision about how to proceed will be up to her."

He nodded once. "Thank you for your time. I'll get right to the point. You know that my daughter staged her death eight years ago and has taken another identity."

"Yes."

"And she told you about my business."

"I learned most on my own, but she filled in some holes."

"Virginia was always a smart girl," he said wistfully. "I hadn't even considered she hadn't died. Even though there was no body…" He took a deep breath, coughed, drank some water. "Jenny White was Virginia's best friend. She died just before their fourteenth birthdays."

"Died in an arson fire, correct?"

A nod. Jennifer saw the flash of pain and anger in her dad's eyes, then it was gone.

"Her father was my best friend. My…enemies…killed them."

His words were calm, cool, but Jennifer felt the heat of his eyes as he kept them firmly on Margo.

Margo said, "How did you find her?"

"Two weeks ago, a local investigator called my insurance agent to confirm the deaths of the Whites. Jimmy and I had used the same insurance firm, and my agent thought it was odd—he hadn't had inquiries about Jimmy or his family for years. The investigator told the agent he was tracking a woman named Jennifer White in Phoenix who had parents of the same name. White is very common, but my agent wanted to let me know, in case…well, in case someone was trying to mess with me. It made me wonder…" He shook his head. "I didn't believe that Virginia was alive, but I thought I should look into it. I hired Trident Security and asked them to locate Jennifer White, twenty-six, in Phoenix and provide me with a photo and fingerprints."

"And she did."

"The photo, yes, and the fingerprints were being run. But I didn't need them—I knew by the picture that it was Virginia. I asked Ms. Endicott to track her so I had information before I reached out. I didn't know how I would do so."

Fingerprints. How had they gotten them? Had they broken into her condo? Her work? Her car? Jennifer probably shouldn't be surprised.

"And then…?" Margo prompted.

"Thomas and I consulted and decided the best thing was to talk to Virginia face-to-face. But when we arrived on Monday, she was missing. I feared she had somehow found out I was here, that she ran and I would never be able to find her, to explain everything."

His voice cracked, and Jennifer sucked in her breath. Her dad looked like he was still grieving.

"What do you plan to do with Jennifer?"

"Do *with* her?" He shook his head. "Talk. Ask for her forgiveness. I would like her to come home."

Jennifer shook her head. She would never return to Florida. It was full of pain and grief and death. Never in a million years.

"But mostly," he said, "I want to see her, to tell her I am sorry about the life I gave her. It wasn't fair to her, or to Thomas. Her mother and I…we grew up the same, in families that, let's say, didn't always play by legal rules. We knew how hard it was, but we didn't face death as Virginia did. First my wife, my strong, beautiful wife, taken too soon. Then my best friend, murdered. And I didn't see what it did to my children. I don't know if I would have cared if I had seen, not at the time. Now I see everything clearly, and I want to make it right."

"How?" Margo asked bluntly.

It's what Jennifer would have asked.

"I love Virginia. With all my heart and soul, I love my daughter and I will beg for her forgiveness. For what I did, for what she suffered. Thomas was gracious enough to forgive me."

Her dad was crying. She had never seen him cry. Not after her mom died, not after the Whites were murdered, not ever. But tears rolled down his hollow cheeks.

Tommy took their dad's hand and squeezed it. For the first time, he spoke, "My dad is dying. We walked away from everything in Miami—*everything*," he repeated for emphasis. "We bought a hundred-acre ranch in Wyoming, and that's where we're going tomorrow. We want—both Dad and me—for Virginia to come with us. I want my family back."

Jennifer didn't notice she was crying until the tears dripped off her chin. She got up, almost fell down. Tess steadied her.

"Is it true?" Jennifer asked Ava, searching her eyes. "Is he dying?"

Ava nodded. "I spoke with Miriam Endicott earlier. He provided her with a copy of his medical records. They could have been falsified I suppose, but looking at him, I think they're accurate. He has pancreatic cancer and treatment has been unsuccessful. He has three to six months to live."

Jennifer had been terrified that her father would find a way to bring her home, to put her under his thumb. But she hadn't expected this.

"Are you ready?" Ava said.

Jennifer could only nod. She let Ava escort her down the hall and into the conference room and she stood there and stared at her brother, her father. She couldn't contain her flood of conflicting emotions, and on a sob said, "Daddy, is it true?"

He slowly stood, nodded. Took a step toward her, his face in pain. Emotional and physical pain. He was dying.

She ran to him and hugged him. Tommy, who towered over both of them, wrapped his long arms around both of them.

"I'm sorry," she cried. "I'm sorry. I just… I hurt. I couldn't live like that anymore. I felt…broken and lost and…" Her voice cracked.

"No apologies," her dad said. "You owe me nothing. I'm sorry that you were in so much pain, that you suffered because of my actions. I didn't think. I just… didn't realize how much you knew, what you saw, how you felt." He stepped back and looked at them. "I gave up the business, all of it, because Thomas asked me to. I can't promise you it won't be dangerous to stay with me now, I still have enemies, but because I've disengaged, they have no reason to come after me. I love you so much, Virginia. In the time I have left, I will do anything to make it up to you and Thomas."

Fifty-Six

Margo Angelhart

We left Jennifer alone in the conference room with her father and brother. My mom had tears in her eyes and went to her office, closed the door. I stood awkwardly with Jack and Tess.

"Well," I said. What else was there to say?

"You believe him?" Jack asked with a nod toward the closed door.

"You don't?"

"I believe that he believes what he's saying now, but old dogs, new tricks?" He shook his head. "Let's just say I'm skeptical."

Tess said, "Mom believes him. She's been on the phone all day with lawyers and doctors, and she says he's really dying."

"What about the US attorney she reached out to?" I asked. "Jennifer was going to talk to him, tell him everything."

"Divine intervention," Tess said. "He's in court all day, said he'd call back tonight. Mom can avoid his call for a day or two."

"But the guy is still a criminal. He had people killed," Jack said. "I don't know about just letting him walk away."

I had mixed feelings, too, but I said, "How long would it take the federal government to build a case against him? Against his associates? Years. Especially if there isn't an FBI investigation already open. He'll be dead, and Jennifer and her brother can't speak to the facts, only hearsay. What would be the point? I don't think he should get away with murder, but he's going to be dead before any trial." I shrugged. "I don't have the answers. Really, it's up to Jennifer at this point."

The system sometimes worked…and sometimes it didn't. Bonetti should pay for his crimes, but he wouldn't because he was dying. I didn't know what I would do in the same situation.

"It's about justice," Jack said. "This isn't justice."

I couldn't argue with him.

"He's dying," Tess said. "Like Margo said, by the time the government puts a case against him, he'll be gone. Thomas and Jennifer will be dragged through the public eye and asked questions they can't answer. Their lives would be, essentially, over."

The children of a killer. We all knew how that felt.

"Maybe," I said, "we push him a little. Get him on record, solve some cold cases."

"What would that accomplish?" Tess asked.

"Closure for families who might not know why their loved ones are dead or who killed them. Maybe he knows where bodies are buried. It doesn't hurt to ask him to do the right thing."

"He's not going to turn himself in," Jack said, "especially if there is no evidence of crimes he's committed."

"I don't expect him to. But maybe he agrees to put everything down and we release it upon his death? Like a death-bed confession? Mom would know how to put it together."

"If she has specific knowledge of a crime that has been committed, she has to go to the court," Tess said.

"Then he makes the video without her in the room," I said. "Look, they're leaving tomorrow. What are we supposed to do? Call the cops and have him arrested? For what?"

Mom came into the room and surprised me by saying, "I agree with Margo."

We all looked at her.

"I just got off the phone with the AUSA in Florida. There is no open investigation into Vincent Bonetti. My friend didn't know the name. He knew about the Leone crime family, but said they disbanded after the patriarch died a few years ago. They had never been able to build a solid case against any of them, and shelved the investigation when Bonetti's father-in-law died."

"Jennifer said her father was responsible for a nightclub bombing," Jack said. "I looked it up. Eight people were killed. *Eight.* Only three of those eight were known to be criminals, the others were innocent bystanders. And even if they were all criminals, that's vigilante justice."

"We have no evidence," Mom said, "and neither does Jennifer. If the FBI opens an investigation into Bonetti, we'll cooperate. But ultimately, it's only Jennifer's statement that her father was behind the bombing, and she doesn't have firsthand knowledge."

Sometimes the system worked.

And sometimes it didn't.

* * *

Thirty minutes later, Thomas and Vincent walked out of the conference room. I glanced through the open door to make sure Jennifer was still in there and in good health. She sat at the table, head in her hands, her face splotchy from tears that no longer ran.

Vincent took first Mom's hand, then Jack's, then mine. "Thank you."

"And?" I asked.

"Virginia has asked for tonight. I recognize it's a lot to ask of her, but I must be in Wyoming for a doctor's appointment tomorrow afternoon. I have a private plane and we're leaving at eight in the morning. I gave Virginia the details. Whatever decision she makes, I'll respect."

Thomas didn't look like he felt the same. "Dad, you need to go back to the hotel and rest. It's been a long day." He nodded to us, then steered his father out the door.

My mom watched them leave, then went into the conference room to check on Jennifer. I followed; Jack and Tess didn't. I guess I was always the nosy kid of the family.

Mom sat next to Jennifer and immediately the girl turned to hug her. "I don't know what to do," she said.

"What did your father say?"

"He has about six months to live. Stage four pancreatic cancer, like you said. He went through chemo already, doesn't want to do it again. Tommy showed me pictures of the ranch. It's beautiful. Sheep, horses, a heated chicken pen. Tommy's going to stay, even after dad d-d-dies." She took a deep breath. "He wants to work with his hands, and he loves animals. I didn't know—he wanted to be a veterinarian. Went to school for it, but when dad got sick, he quit, to take care of him. They planned to move to Wyoming because dad pulled out of the business and there were people trying to get him back in. And then they found out I was alive."

She took a deep breath, the conflict in her expression real.

"He wants me to forgive him so he can die in peace. I do—but—I don't know. I don't know anything anymore. Everything I believed is true—his business, what happened to my mother, my best friend, everything. For the first time, he told me the truth, and it hurts. But I love him. And I hate him. And I don't know."

"You don't hate him," Mom said quietly. "He is your father, and he treated you with love even though he's done some horrific things. But he loves you and your brother and I believe he wants to make up for raising you in a violent life. For your mother, for your friend. I don't know if I could forgive him if I were in your shoes, but I would definitely try. Because forgiveness is for *your* soul, not his."

When Jennifer didn't say anything, Mom said, "Do you believe he will hurt you? Physically hurt you?"

She shook her head. "No. He never did before. I was scared because of the people around him, what happens to people he loves."

"Very understandable. Do you believe that he told you the truth tonight?"

She didn't respond at first, tears in her eyes. "Yes," she finally said. "I do. Do you think Tommy can forgive me? For making him believe I was dead?"

"Sweetheart, he already has."

How my mom knew that, I didn't know. But when she said it, I knew she was right.

"I don't know what to do," Jennifer said, clearly miserable. "He should pay for his crimes, but he's dying. I want to forgive him, but…" She started crying and Mom reached out and pulled the young women to her again.

I watched my mom, saw flashes of my past. The advice my mom gave to us as kids. She never pushed, never told me what to do, but simply gave her counsel—from when I was six and so angry I hit Eric Garcia because he pulled up my skirt on the playground to when I was contemplating reenlisting eight years ago. The first time she said she couldn't fault me for hitting Eric, but every decision had consequences. Then she took me to a movie—a rare treat when we were little—the day I was suspended from school. Eric was suspended for two days, so I felt that was fair. School rules. Sometimes they could be broken, but you had to face the consequences, even when you were right.

And then when I was going back and forth about reenlisting. Some shit happened on base and I was angry—but I hadn't lashed out like I had when I hit Eric. I stored everything inside until it nearly killed me. I considered the Army not only my duty, but my second family. Yet… I felt betrayed by that family.

My mom is the one who gave me the idea to serve in the Reserves. To come home and find my true calling. "You needed the structure of the Army," she had said, "and the sense of belonging, accomplishment, duty, and honor. And I think you wanted to prove to yourself that you could be someone without the family name. It's hard to live up to expectations all the time."

At the time, I had never once thought I wanted to get away from my family. I loved my family, my brothers and sisters and parents and grandparents and aunts and uncles and dozens of cousins. The Angelhart/Morales clan was huge. Family was everything to me, and I was proud to be an Angelhart, proud of my parents. But when she said it, there was some truth. Who was I without the family? Was I special? Could I succeed without the name? Because no one in the Army cared if you were an Angelhart. My mother saw a truth I hadn't even acknowledged.

"Everything your father loved about the Army, you love about the Army," she had told me. "But both of you are independent—too independent to always follow rules. This can be a good thing, but it doesn't always conform to the structure of a bureaucracy. You have the discipline now that you didn't have at eighteen. Go to school, learn a trade, or find a calling. If you choose to reenlist, I will support you. But if you choose a different path, I will also support that decision."

So I didn't reenlist, opted for the Reserves, and while it took a while to get my PI business off the ground, I found that it was my calling. Working for myself was exactly what I needed, warts and all. Helping people like Annie Carillo and Logan Monroe. Two people couldn't be more different than the young abused mother and the wealthy entrepreneur, but they both needed my expertise. And when I helped them, I felt complete.

Maybe my mother understood me better than I thought.

Now Mom held Jennifer, patting her back as she would if Jennifer were her own daughter. As if Jennifer were me. Offering advice without pressure, with the foundation of nearly six decades of life experience.

I missed my mom. I missed what we had before my dad confessed to a murder he didn't commit. I missed our arguments, our laughter, our family dinners.

I didn't know how to forgive her, but I needed to find a way.

Jennifer's sobs turned to sniffles, then she pulled back, frowned at my mom's wet shirt. "I ruined your blouse," she said.

"You certainly did not," Mom said, wiping Jennifer's face.

"Can I—I don't want to impose, but can I stay at your house tonight? Just to get my head on straight and figure out what I want to do?"

"Of course."

Because that was also my mom. She could be a hard-ass in court, she was the disciplinarian in the house when we were growing up, and she had high expectations for all of us. But she would help anyone who asked.

"If you decide to go with your father, Jack will take you to the airport, make sure that everything is kosher, okay? You're not alone anymore, Jennifer. Or do you now want to be called Virginia?"

She looked surprised. "I honestly don't know."

"Then you will sleep on it. In the morning, you will know what is right."

My mom had been my role model my entire life, until three years ago when everything fell apart. Had she changed…or had I? Could I forgive my mom for—for what? For accepting a decision my father made to confess to murder? For not fighting for him? Not searching for answers? For the truth?

Jennifer hadn't known everything about her father and the reasons he made the decisions he made. There weren't a lot of comparisons between the Bonetti family and my own. The Bonettis were criminals. The Angelharts fought criminals. Yet…they were family, and decisions were made because of family. Vincent Bonetti was asking for forgiveness, even though he didn't believe he deserved it. He understood his daughter's grief—over the loss of her mother and her best friend. Their pain was tangible, the circumstances complex, but not the love. The love was simple, straightforward, real.

My mother caught my eye for a split second, and I thought for certain she could read my mind—like I believed when I was little and she always seemed to know when I snuck cookies to Jack when he was grounded, or when Tess and I found a lost dog and decided to keep him in the shed thinking no one would know, or when I hid Luisa's favorite stuffed animal because she ratted on me for breaking curfew.

I loved her. I missed her. I missed my family. Because even though I had relationships with everyone individually, the weight of my father's incarceration had suffocated me, strained the bond that had united us for so long. Because of me. Because *I* had walked away. Because I said I couldn't live with her decision to let it be.

I didn't know if I could abide by her dictum, but I knew that even if we were on different sides of the line, I wanted my family whole again.

We locked up the office and left. Thomas Bonetti was waiting outside, without his father, and Jennifer excused herself and walked over to him. He said something to her and she started crying again, then hugged him. My phone vibrated and I read the message. It was from Theo.

Your guy is here.

Fifty-Seven

Margo Angelhart

I followed Jack to St. Dominic's. We arrived twelve minutes after Theo's text, just after 9:00 p.m. I'd called Theo from the road and he hadn't answered, so I called Uncle Rafe and he hadn't answered, either. Fear crept into my head during the twelve-minute drive, and not because Jack far exceeded the speed limit on both Highway 51 and then the side streets leading to the church.

As soon as Jack exited his truck he said, "There was no call to 9-1-1. You said he called 9-1-1."

"I told him to," I said, fearing for Theo.

The church was lit up; I didn't know why.

"Funeral," Jack said, gesturing to a hearse parked right outside the main doors.

That didn't make me happy. It might explain why Uncle Rafe hadn't answered his phone, but not Theo.

"Check the church," Jack said. "I'll check the rectory. I asked for a patrol to meet us."

We parted and I walked around to the main entrance, then entered. The Mass was ending and Uncle Rafe was there, on the altar giving the final prayer. More than a hundred people filled the pews; none of them was Theo or Peter Carillo.

I left before Rafe saw me and scanned the street. Theo's car was parked under an oak tree where he had a clear view of the church and the rectory. But I couldn't see him.

That worried me.

I ran over to the vehicle; he wasn't there.

Jack called me.

"Come to the rectory," he said.

My stomach dropped and I ran across the parking lot, behind the church, and to the small house. I didn't knock, but walked right in.

"In the kitchen," I heard Jack call, and walked to the back of the house.

Theo sat at the table holding a baggie of ice on his head. A rag in his other hand had blood on it. Father Diaz was making fresh iced tea.

"Theo, what happened?"

"He got the drop on me."

"Carillo?"

"Yeah."

"You saw him?"

He didn't say anything.

"Theo," I snapped my fingers, "answer me."

"I saw him walk behind the church. At least, I thought I did. It was hard to see in the twilight. That's when I texted you. He came in here, and I was about to call 9-1-1, I swear, just like you told me, but then the priest was about to go inside and I had to stop him, tell him someone broke into the house. He said the door isn't locked. Who doesn't lock their doors?"

"Priests," Jack and I muttered at the same time.

"Don't blame the boy," Father Diaz said. "We lock up at night, but since I was at the social hall, I didn't see a need to lock the house. I was certain it was a parishioner who'd entered. I know there's been a bit of trouble, but I doubted that man would return. So I went in."

"And I ran around back, in case he ran out. And well, he did."

"Did you see him before he hit you?"

He didn't say anything.

"Shit," I muttered, then winced. I tried not to swear around priests. Didn't know if it was a mark against me, but it was best to avoid it.

"It was dark and I heard a sound and turned and *wham!* I was down and he ran. I mean, I can't swear it was Carillo. I *think* it was him, walking behind the church, but it was dark. I just can't swear to it. I'm sorry."

I squatted next to Theo, looked him in the eyes. They were focused and the pupils were the same size. "Don't apologize," I said. "I'm glad you're not seriously hurt, but you're going to have a whopper of a headache tonight."

"Did you see anything, Father?" Jack asked.

He shook his head, poured iced tea for everyone. I detested iced tea, but didn't say anything. "I left at seven thirty for a meeting at the social hall. I always turn off the lights, except the lamp in the entry. When I came in tonight, after encountering Theo, the office light was on. I called out and a man ran from the office and out the back door. He wore all black and I didn't see his face."

"Father, you shouldn't have come in alone when there was an intruder."

"We get a lot of visitors, even at this time of night. It's part of the job."

I knew that to be true, but I didn't like it.

"You should lock your door at all times," I said.

He didn't respond, and I doubted he would listen to me. I'd appeal to Uncle Rafe, but he, too, could be stubborn.

"What's in the office?" Jack asked.

"It's our personal office, not the church offices, which are attached to the main building."

My stomach fell. Carillo was looking for information about Annie. He thought Rafe knew where she was and that he might be able to find answers here, in the rectory. He intentionally came here when the priests were out; I didn't want to think about what might have happened if Rafe were here when he broke in.

"Did you check if anything was missing?" I asked as I was already on my way down the hall to the office.

Father Diaz followed me. We stood in the doorway— the room had double pocket doors, which were both open. Two desks against opposite walls, a small couch between them and a comfy chair in the corner. Narrow bookshelves were stuffed with books and files next to each desk, and a painting of the Holy Family was displayed directly above the couch. It was a cramped but cozy room.

"Can you tell if something's missing?"

"No," Diaz said slowly. He went to first his desk, then Rafe's. "He wasn't in here more than a few minutes. But—it looks like someone opened the drawers. They're not fully closed."

Uncle Rafe walked in and said, "What happened?"

"Peter Carrillo was here," I told him, "and searched

your desk. But only for a few minutes. Could he have found anything that might lead him to Annie?"

"No," Rafe said. "I assure you, there was nothing in here about anyone involved."

"Where's your computer?"

"Upstairs. I—I suppose if he accessed my computer he might be able to access emails, but…"

"He wasn't here long, but would you please check?"

Rafe didn't hesitate, heading straight upstairs to his room.

Jack hadn't said anything for several minutes. In fact, he was still in the kitchen with Theo. I went back and said, "I need help, Jack. I don't know what to do here. I'm afraid Carillo is so desperate someone is going to get seriously hurt."

A loud knock sounded on the door and Jack went to answer it, saying, "It's the police."

Rafe came down and said his laptop was undisturbed. I breathed easier. We didn't tell the police that Peter Carillo broke into the rectory because Theo couldn't swear it was him. He did, however, state that he saw a man approximately six feet tall who drove up in a blue minivan enter the rectory. Father Diaz confirmed that the door was unlocked, that someone had been in the office when he entered, and that the person ran out the back. The police took photos of Theo's head and said they would file a report, but without a license plate or description there was no way they'd be able to trace the assault to Carillo.

And I couldn't in good conscious ask Theo to lie.

I might have lied, had I been there during the attack. I might have rattled off Annie's plates to put the pressure on Carillo, have the police look closer at that bastard.

But I didn't say anything. After the police left, Jack and I walked Theo to his car and told him to be careful. "If you see Carillo, call me," I told him. "Don't take any chances."

"I don't have a death wish," Theo said. "That's why I want to work at the crime lab, not on the streets." He waved as he drove off.

As Jack and I walked back to the rectory to make sure both Rafe and Father Diaz knew to lock up *always*, I said, "This isn't going to stop until he hurts someone. We need to go on the offensive."

"Do you have an idea?"

I was beginning to, but I had no idea if it would work. "Maybe, but I need your help."

Jack glanced at me with a half-grin. "You don't even have to ask."

Friday

Fifty-Eight

Jack Angelhart

Margo's plan was so absurd that it just might work, Jack thought as he hooked up the camera and recorder in the rectory at St. Dominic's.

Convincing Uncle Rafe to be involved was the hard part, but Margo did the hard sell, explaining that if Carillo snuck in once when they weren't here, he might do it again.

"I'm not asking you to lie," she had told him last night when she came up with the plan.

"I feel like you are," he said.

"You want to mediate. Imply, but don't say that Annie is interested. He wants to believe it, so he'll come."

Jack hoped Margo was right, because they would only have one shot at this. If they screwed up, Peter Carillo would be a threat to people Jack loved—his uncle and his sister.

Jack wasn't certain that Margo had fully played out the odds, because she would ultimately be Carillo's target if they failed.

"Okay, we're good here," Jack said after testing the equipment.

Rafe didn't say anything.

"Talk to me. You're worried."

"Of course I am."

"I'm not going to let anything happen to you. That's why you're going to wear a Kevlar vest under your shirt."

Rafe frowned. He hadn't wanted to wear a vest, but Jack had talked him into it.

"Just as a precaution," Jack said, not for the first time. "Hopefully, it doesn't go that far."

"I feel I'm being deceptive."

"You're not. You can be as honest as the day is long—just don't tell him where Annie's relocated. In fact, the more honest you are, the more he'll talk. To justify, to beg, to threaten." Jack narrowed his eyes. "You don't feel sorry for him, do you?"

"Yes, I do," Rafe said. "Not for what he did to his wife, but because a man like him who turns to violence against those he purports to love must have been hurt in the past. He's still a man, still a child of God, and deserves forgiveness and mercy."

"If he asks for it," Jack said. "And means it." Which, in Jack's experience, wouldn't happen. Abusers and rapists like Peter Carillo would never ask for forgiveness from anyone—their victims or God.

"I told Margo I would make the call if I could truly mediate. I will not back down from my word."

"I know."

Margo's initial idea was that Rafe call Carillo, but then leave the rectory and let Margo handle him. Rafe declined. If he made the call, he would be here because he didn't want anyone hurt.

But if Rafe knew the other part of Margo's plan, he might not help at all. So Jack agreed to remain silent.

"Do you regret helping Annie?" Jack asked as he cleaned up his tools.

Rafe looked surprised that he had asked. "Of course not."

"Then that's it. A woman, a mother, was so desperate that she reached out to a man of God to help her because she trusted you. You gave her Margo's name because you trusted Margo could help. Trust us now, Uncle Rafe."

He nodded. "I do, Jack."

"I'm going to move my truck," Jack said. "We don't know how much he's been around watching the place, and he might know I'm Margo's brother. But I'll be here, out of sight, the whole time. And Father Diaz and O'Neil won't be here, correct?"

"No. Not until nine tonight."

The school had a half day and the kids were already off campus. Father Diaz and Father O'Neil were at a day-long retreat in Sun Valley that Uncle Rafe was supposed to be at, but he backed out at the last minute. There was always the off-chance that a parishioner would come by the rectory or the church seeking guidance, but they would cross that bridge when they came to it. The office had a closed sign, as well as the church, and because the retreat had been scheduled long ago, they had no Mass this evening.

Jack hoped no one showed up. His concern was about innocent bystanders. He would let Uncle Rafe worry about Carillo's soul.

"Then we're good," Jack said and left.

He put his toolbox behind the driver's seat of his

truck, then drove it around the block and parked. His cell phone rang. It was Rick.

"All good?" Jack answered.

"Why did you have to do this the day Sam graduates? I would be there."

"You can't, Rick. You know that." He was a cop, and if Carillo felt like he was being entrapped it could jeopardize the entire case against him. "Did you talk to Sullivan?"

"Yes, called him first thing this morning and said exactly what we discussed. That Margo, as a long-time friend, came to me concerned that Peter Carillo was following her, and I learned he'd looked up her license plate on Monday. I was going to call his boss, but noted that there was an investigation into his wife's disappearance and Sullivan was the lead detective."

"Good. Better that you keep your fingers as clean as possible."

"What are you two planning?"

"Better you don't know."

"Dammit, Jack."

"I'll see you at Sam's party on Sunday, okay?"

Rick grumbled, but said fine and hung up.

One down.

Jack arrived back at the rectory five minutes later. Rafe was right where he had left him, sitting in the kitchen, a glass of iced tea between his hands. "Ready?"

Rafe let out a breath, sipped the tea, put the glass down. His hand was shaking.

"Hey, Uncle Rafe, we're not going to let anything happen to you, okay? I promise."

"What about Mr. Carillo?"

"Neither Margo nor I want bloodshed."

Rafe walked to his office, picked up his phone, and dialed Peter Carillo's cell phone. As Jack had already told him, he put the call on speaker. Jack started the recording. Arizona state law allowed conversations to be recorded as long as at least one party knew they were being recorded. "Mr. Carillo?"

"Yes? Who's this?"

"This is Father Raphael Morales. You came by my church the other night asking about your wife, Annie."

Silence.

"Mr. Carillo, are you there?"

"Are you going to tell me where my wife is?"

"After you left, I've lain awake at night, trying to come up with a solution to your problem. I think the best thing at this point is to offer my services to mediate."

"Have you spoken to Annie? Has she agreed? Will she be there?"

"I don't know," Rafe said. "I have counseled hundreds of couples, but the common theme is that they believe their marriage is a sacrament and want to find a way back to each other, with God as their foundation. If you come in and talk, it would be a sign that you want to fix things in your marriage. Do you agree?"

"I need my family."

"I am free this afternoon at four thirty. Is that convenient for you?"

"Is Annie going to be there?"

"As I said, I don't know. This is a first step. You can't rush these things."

"Okay. But first, I want to confess."

Jack's heart dropped.

"You want to confess to me as a priest?"

"Yes. I'll be at the church at four thirty. Will you be in the confessional?"

"I will be there."

"Thank you, Father. I think...for the first time I believe I will get my family back."

Carillo hung up.

Jack refrained from swearing out loud, but a litany of *damn-shit-fuck* ran through his head.

"I am not going to deny anyone the right to reconciliation," Rafe told him.

"Just a slight change of plans," Jack said, knowing Margo would go ballistic. But they would tweak the plan as needed.

"Don't even think of wiring the church," Rafe said. "I consented to my office, but I will not consent to anyplace else."

"The goal is to bring him in here," Jack said. "And we need a plan to do that."

"I will ask him to come back with me after confession," Rafe said, "but I can't do more than that."

Jack looked at his watch. It was nearly three thirty. They had one hour to come up with another plan. He excused himself and walked outside, stood under a tree, dialed Margo. "Change of plans," he said.

Fifty-Nine

Peter Carillo

There were no cars at the church. No kids playing, no teachers, no parents.

Peter frowned. He drove slowly by the church and turned into the school drop-off roundabout. A sign with changeable letters read:

Monday–Friday: Middle school half days

Friday, May 23: All-school out at Noon

Monday, May 26: End-of-school-year fair

Tuesday, May 27: Eighth Grade Graduation, 7:00 p.m.

Okay, he thought. Kids were out early today. It would just be him and the priest.

Father Morales would tell him where Annie was before Peter left. He just had to convince him to talk.

He parked outside the main church entrance and walked in just before four thirty that afternoon. The church was quiet, smelled faintly of incense. Many churches had given up prayer candles, but St. Dominic's had an alcove just inside the main church doors with rows of candles, some lit. Peter walked over, put a dollar in the box, and lit a candle.

Bring Annie home to me.

He stared at the flickering flame but instead of finding peace, grew angry. Annie had used the church against him, her husband. She'd come here and a priest—a man who should know better—had helped her leave her husband. That was a greater sin than anything Peter had done, was it not? The priest had interfered with their sacrament of marriage, and damn him, he would make it right.

There were three confessionals against the eastern wall. One had a green light over the door. Peter walked over and opened the door, hit the switch that said occupied, and knelt by the thick screen. He couldn't see Father Morales on the other side, but he saw his shape, heard him breathe.

"Forgive me, Father, for I have sinned," Peter said. He hadn't been to confession in…a long time. Since before he married Annie. "It has been more than seven years since my last confession."

"It is good that you have sought to ease your burden. God knows our fears and our sins."

"I have been angry on the job. I am a police officer and people make me so angry. They're stupid and make poor decisions. Driving drunk, killing people. Last year I was the first responder to a scene on the highway, up north of Black Canyon City on 17, a wrong-way driver. Drunk as sin, hit a family. Killed everyone inside—mother, father, three kids in the back. Drunk driver survived. I wanted to kill him. I didn't. Sometimes I think I should have."

"Vengeance is mine, says the Lord our God," the

priest said. "Your job is stressful. Attending Mass regularly may help you find the peace you need."

"I have not been a perfect husband," Peter said, ignoring the priest. "I have a tough job, and my home is my sanctuary. My wife left me, took my children, and I was so angry."

"In times of stress, anger is a common reaction. How we channel that anger is important. We can give our pain, our stress, our anger to Jesus, who died for our sins."

"I've been thinking of what I might have done to deserve this."

The priest didn't say anything, and Peter continued. "I provided for my family. Gave them a good home, stability. I expected my wife to appreciate me. When she said no in our marital bed, I hurt her."

"We often say cruel things to the people we love the most. Asking God to forgive these words is a good step, provided you truly seek to curb the anger and avoid repeating the sin."

"I made love to her because she is my wife and she must submit. I didn't want to hurt her. For that I am sorry."

Silence again. What did a priest know about marriage and sex? He was celibate. He couldn't understand Peter's deep needs.

"I am sorry I hurt my wife. I didn't want to. I never want to, but she makes me so angry when she refuses, so I taught her she cannot refuse. When she refuses, there is punishment, because a wife must submit to her husband."

The priest said, "'Husbands, love your wives, even as Christ loved the church and handed himself over for her.'"

"No one loves his wife more than I love mine," Peter

said emphatically. "When I found out she left, I wanted to kill her. I wanted to put my hands around her neck until she couldn't speak, couldn't breathe, couldn't..." He stopped. "But I didn't. I am sorry for those bad thoughts. I would never kill my wife."

"Evil thoughts are the first step to evil acts. Do you know the Act of Contrition?"

"Most of it." He shrugged. Did it matter?

The priest started off, and Peter mumbled the prayer. How was this going to bring Annie back? Wasn't confession supposed to make you feel better? He'd thought about what to say while driving here. Okay, he could admit that he had scared Annie, and maybe that was wrong. But dammit, why did she make it so hard on him? He didn't want to hurt her—so yeah, he could confess that he *might* have hurt her, but he didn't mean to! She was his wife and she shouldn't make him jump through hoops for sex, for dinner on time, for her attention and her affection. It was her duty.

This wasn't helping. This wasn't bringing Annie back. This wasn't giving him peace of mind.

"The Act of Contrition is important," the priest said. "You must believe in your heart and your soul that you did wrong, in thoughts and words, in what you have done and what you have not done. You should reflect on the circumstances that have led you here today. Part of absolution is prayer, and in prayer comes reflection and grace. The church is open. Stay here as long as you need, say five decades of the rosary and reflect on the love God has for you, for your wife and children, and how you can show your love to God. I absolve you of your sins, in the name of the Father, and of the Son, and of the Holy Spirit."

"You said you would mediate between me and Annie."

"Yes. Stay here, pray, and when you're done, your sins will be forgiven and you can come to me with a clean heart."

"She's not here."

"I have not seen her yet."

Peter got up and left. He almost ran out of the church, but he stopped at the prayer candles. Stared at them. Knelt.

He didn't say the Rosary, or even one Hail Mary. He knelt and begged God to bring Annie back.

Bring her back or I will go get her. Your priest knows where she is. Make him tell me the truth.

Peter knelt at the candles until he heard the confessional door open. He then stood, turned, and faced Father Morales. "I'm ready to see Annie."

The priest said, "As I said, I don't know when or if she will come."

"You know how to reach her."

"She is aware that you want her to return."

"Then you'll call her."

"I don't feel comfortable putting pressure on her. Let's go to the rectory and talk."

Was he playing a game? Why did he want to leave? Why did he look nervous?

"Call her. Right here, right now."

"I don't have my cell phone."

Peter pulled out his phone.

"I don't know the number from memory. Mr. Carillo, please, I'll make us some coffee and we can discuss steps to take to repair your marriage. I believe in the Sacrament of Marriage. I detest divorce, and have worked with couples to save their marriages when it's possible. Let me help you."

Sixty

Margo Angelhart

"How long is he going to be in there?" I hated this new plan. It put Uncle Rafe right in the path of danger. The Kevlar wouldn't protect him against a head shot.

I hadn't really liked the old plan, either, but we had a lot more control in the rectory.

I had Jack on speaker while I sat in Uncle Rafe's car on the far side of the church, my Jeep parked next to Jack's truck two blocks away. "What if Uncle Rafe can't get him to the rectory? What if he suspects something?"

I wasn't usually so jumpy, but this was my uncle. Someone who abhorred violence, who was compassionate and kind and sometimes I thought I saw a halo over his head during Mass.

"Have faith."

"Really? You're pulling the faith card on me? God helps those who help themselves. And yet we're trusting Uncle Rafe's life to an abusive rapist."

I took a deep breath. What Jack really meant was to calm down, and so I forced myself to calm. Deep breath in, hold it, breathe out slowly. Repeat. I could practically feel my heart rate drop by the third deep breath.

"The door's opening," I said. "Okay. Uncle Rafe's walking with him toward the rectory. I'm calling Sullivan."

I ended the call with Jack and called Detective Sullivan.

He didn't answer his phone.

I was perplexed; I hadn't considered that he wouldn't be reachable. Rick had confirmed that he was on duty until six, which was one reason we planned this time.

I left a message. "This is Margo Angelhart, we spoke the other day about Annie Carillo. I am worried that her husband is following me. My uncle is a priest at St. Dominic's, and Carillo is here. Please call me back. I'm scared." I didn't sound scared, I sounded angry. But he didn't know me, so I thought it might pass as fear. I rattled off my number and the address of the church.

I texted Jack the status and watched as Carillo and Uncle Rafe walked toward the rectory. I didn't like Carillo's body language. He seemed…suspicious. Had he seen me, this far away? I didn't think so, not from this angle, but I could be wrong.

Had he cased the neighborhood, seen my Jeep? Maybe.

They stopped walking and Carillo said something to Uncle Rafe. They stared at each other. I couldn't read lips this far away. Something was definitely wrong.

Suddenly, Uncle Rafe turned with Carillo and walked toward Carillo's minivan.

No, no this wasn't in the plan—what was Uncle Rafe doing?

I called Jack. "Uncle Rafe is getting in his car! Wait— he's calling me."

I hit the record app on my phone, switched to Uncle Rafe. "Hello?" I said, forcing my voice to be calm. I didn't want to give anything away.

"Margo, don't be concerned," Uncle Rafe said.

Don't be *concerned?* I was beyond concerned.

Carillo got on the phone. "Father Morales has graciously agreed to help mediate between Annie and me. Bring her home. You told the detective that you didn't know where she was—I don't believe you. Father Morales and I will be waiting for her. Don't be long."

He ended the call and drove away with my uncle.

The phone switched back to Jack. "He's leaving with Rafe. I think they're going to his house. I'm following." I waited until Carillo left the parking lot before I started the car.

"Wait for me—"

"No time. I'll text you his address—get there. There's a park a block away that can't be seen from his house. I'll meet you there. If he goes somewhere else, I'll let you know."

"Don't confront him."

"I'm thinking."

"Call Annie, have her call him, buy time. I'll call 9-1-1—"

"No, that will spook him. He's armed, and we don't need a car chase. And I don't have her number. I can't call her even if I wanted to."

"I'll call Rick. Shit, it's the middle of Sam's graduation."

"Call Otto," I said. "I'll call Officer Nunez. He gave me his personal cell."

"Be careful, sis."

"I have an idea. Rafe can't lie, but I have no problem with it."

I ended the call, pulled Nunez's card from my wallet, and dialed.

"Hello," he said when he picked up.

"Archie Nunez?"

"Yep."

"This is Margo Angelhart. I tried Detective Sullivan, but he didn't answer."

"I'm off-duty right now."

Shit. "Peter Carillo kidnapped my uncle, Father Raphael Morales, from St. Dominic's. It's a long story, and I don't have time to go into details, but I'm following Carillo's blue minivan and I think he's going to his house in Norterra. He called me from Rafe's phone and expects me to bring his wife there, says that Rafe will mediate a conversation to fix their marriage or some such nonsense."

"Is Annie with you?"

"No. I don't know where she is, I didn't lie to you. I have no way of reaching her. Carillo is violent. He abused her, raped her."

"She can press charges and testify—"

"And he would still have access to their kids. He never hurt his kids. She has no physical proof that he abused her, no emergency room visits. He's a cop. Look, I know what I'm doing, and he would have eventually killed her. Now he has my uncle, and I don't know what he's going to do when I can't produce Annie. I'm going to his house. My brother, Jack Angelhart, used to be with Phoenix PD. He's following me. One of my closest friends is Clive Otter, a trooper whose brother is—"

"Jesse Otter, Captain of DPS."

"So we're reaching out to the right people, but if this goes through channels, he could hear, and that puts my uncle at greater risk. Please trust me."

"I live out in Avondale, I won't get there in time, but I can find Sullivan and fill him in."

"Thank you."

"I had a suspicion about why she left," Nunez said, "but nothing concrete."

"People see the truth when they look," I said and ended the call.

I had an idea. I didn't know if it would work, but it was the only idea I had.

I followed Peter Carillo until he got off the freeway toward his house. I pulled off at the next exit, then backtracked, turned into his neighborhood and stopped at the park. And waited for Jack so I could tell him my plan.

He wasn't going to like it.

Twenty minutes later, I knocked on Carillo's door. I could practically see him staring at me through the camera on his door, the one that he used to track not who came and went with packages, but his own wife.

He said through the speaker, "Door is unlocked. Come in."

I checked my watch, then entered.

Carillo grabbed me as soon as I walked in. "Where is my wife?" he demanded.

"She is going to call me in five minutes," I said. "Let me go."

He pushed me onto the dining room table and searched me. Took my gun out of my holster, my knife out of my pocket.

He missed my slim lightweight Kahr P380 I had

holstered around my ankle, concealed by my khakis. It wouldn't be super easy to get to, but I had drilled with it.

Uncle Rafe had the vest on under his shirt. Not that Kevlar was perfect protection, but it was definitely better than nothing. Cops were taught to shoot center mass to stop the threat—it was training that became part of their muscle memory so that they could act in the face of danger, adrenaline and anxiety. Still, stray bullets didn't abide by muscle memory, so I wanted to keep Rafe out of harm's way.

He put my gun and knife on the top of the dining hutch. I could get to them, but not without a step stool or climbing onto the table. He kept my phone with him.

"Family room," he ordered and motioned for me to go in front of him.

Rafe was sitting at the table in the nook between the family room and kitchen. His hands were folded on the table in front of him, and he looked okay—alive, healthy, uninjured.

But his eyes showed his concern. Not for himself, but for me.

He should have known I would come for him. He should never have left with Carillo—he *knew* that Jack and I were near. What had Carillo said that he went without fighting?

Carillo pushed me down to the floor, my back against the wall, and said, "Don't move." He looked at his watch. "You had better not be lying to me."

"Let the priest leave."

"Your uncle?"

"Yes, he's also my uncle. You've done a lot of miserable things in your life—I wouldn't tack threatening a man of God onto the list."

"You and this priest conspired to destroy my family."

"You destroyed your family, Peter. You did," I repeated. "You hurt Annie, and she couldn't take it anymore."

"I never hurt her. I love my wife."

"You hurt her all the time," I said. "You separated her from her friends. You punched her in the stomach when she didn't behave up to your standards. You raped her every day."

"I *never* raped my wife, you filthy liar!"

"She told me."

"We were married."

"You taught her she wasn't allowed to say no by hurting her when she didn't feel like spreading her legs for you."

He backhanded me. I didn't see it coming and I fell over. *Damn, that hurt.*

"Please, Mr. Carillo, there is no need for violence," Rafe said. "Sit down, let's talk."

He didn't sit. Instead, he paced, glaring at me. I much preferred his attention on me than on Rafe.

"We are *married*," Carillo said. "Annie is my *wife*. I gave her everything. A house. A car. Two children. I was here every night. I never cheated on her. I was a good husband. Unlike my father and her father, who both left their families. I would never leave her, leave my children. How could she do this to me?"

My cell phone rang.

Peter looked down at my phone in his hand. The caller ID should read *Annie C*. He immediately answered. "Annie?"

This was where the plan was iffy. Okay, the whole plan was iffy, but having Luisa call and pretend to be

Annie was the dangerous part. The plan was mine, but Jack improved on it, suggested that the connection be "poor" and Lu speak quietly as if her voice is coming through a tunnel. I gave her some things to say that would, hopefully, distract Carillo so I could get Rafe to safety.

I was, after all, wearing a wire. It was in a barrette in my hair, a place he didn't even think to check. When I said the magic word, the police would storm in.

I thought it would take weeks, months, to find something to take Peter Carillo down. All it took was five days before he cracked. He kidnapped a priest. He would be in jail for a long, long time.

"Annie, I can barely hear you. Speak up!"

He was straining to listen and walked to the opposite side of the living room. I sat up, braced my back against the wall so I could get to my feet quickly. He turned away and I started to pull my .380, but he turned around again.

"Where are you? I'll come and get you. You can't leave me."

He paced and went to the far side of the kitchen. I didn't like that Rafe was now between him and me. I needed Carillo on my side of the room.

"Get someplace where the phone works!" Carillo screamed and whirled around. "I have the priest here, the man who took you from me. You went to him?" Carillo stood next to Rafe.

I heard sobbing over the phone. Good. I'd told Luisa to cry if she couldn't think of what to say.

"I'm not going to hurt anybody," Carillo said. "Why would you think that? I've never hurt you."

He listened, frowned, then stared at me.

"That bitch told you to say that. I never raped you. Do not say that. We're married. It's not rape!"

Carillo was coming toward me. Good. Focus on me, not my uncle.

Carillo stared at me when he told *Annie*, "You're my wife. You are supposed to submit to me when and where I want. You can't change the rules. I gave you everything, *everything*... I can't hear you, dammit! I will find you. I don't care where you are, I will find you and my children and bring you home."

He threw the phone across the room. "Where is she?" he yelled at me. "I couldn't hear hardly anything. Where is she?"

He pulled me up and put his gun to my head.

I was angry and scared. He was too volatile, and I had no idea how to deal with him. "I don't know," I said calmly. "Put the gun down and let Father Morales go."

He pushed me against the wall, but I was expecting it and braced myself. Now he was close. Very close.

The perfect time to go on the offensive.

"Rafe, take cover," I shouted at my uncle as I kicked my boot deep into Carillo's groin. He grunted, bent over, but didn't drop his gun.

I took advantage of his momentary pain and kicked his legs out from under him. Rafe hadn't moved. I heard pounding on the front door; the police were ramming their way in.

I slammed my heel on the wrist of his hand that held the gun, forcing him to drop it. He did, and I tried to kick it away when he grabbed my ankle and pulled me down to the floor. He reached for the gun, and I brawled. He was bigger than me, and being on the floor wasn't to my advantage. Women could fight men, but not hand to hand. We had different tools, focusing on pain points and skills, but men were generally stronger and hand-to-hand was almost always a losing proposition.

But I couldn't get to my gun in my boot without making myself far more vulnerable.

I sprung up and away from him because he was focusing more on getting his gun than on me. But then he had it in his hand and aimed it at Rafe as the front door burst open.

I threw myself at Carillo because I knew down to my soul that in his rage he would kill my uncle.

He turned the gun toward me, but I didn't stop, even when he fired. Even when I felt a burn in my left arm. I punched him with the palm of my hand in the solar plexus, which knocked him to his knees and had him gasping for air.

By that time, the police were inside and had Carillo on his stomach, hands behind his back, putting handcuffs on him as he struggled to breathe.

I went to Rafe and hugged him tightly.

"Are you okay?" I asked. "He didn't hurt you, did he?"

"No," he said. He touched my arm. "You're bleeding."

"It's a scratch." I stared at him. "You knew Jack and I were at the church—why did you go with him? You could have signaled."

He shook his head. "I never thought I was scared to die. Death is a beginning, not an ending. I will be with our Heavenly Father. I know that with all my heart and soul. But when he told me he would kill me if I didn't come, I believed him. In that moment, I didn't want to die. I was selfish."

"No," I said. "You are human." I hugged him again. "I'm not ready to lose you, Uncle Rafe."

Jack came in, his face first panicked, then relieved. He hugged me, then squeezed Rafe's shoulder. He stared at my arm. "You need a paramedic."

"I've had worse."

"Humor me. There's an ambulance on the way."

"No," I moaned. "One condition—I don't want to go to the hospital. The paperwork alone will drive me to drink. I'll let the paramedic clean and tape the wound, okay?"

"I'm going to stand over you, and if it's worse than you say, you're going."

"It's not."

"We're going to have to talk to the police, give statements."

"Let's do it now," I said, "because there's no way I'm missing Pop and Abuela's party tomorrow."

I smiled at Uncle Rafe; he didn't smile back. He was still processing everything that had happened, and I wished I could tell him that it was absolutely normal to fear death, even when you believed in the afterlife.

I believed. Maybe not as strongly or devoutly as my uncle, but I sensed something else was out there. But I could wait for Heaven because I had my family, my community, my calling right here on earth.

And there were more people like Annie Carillo who needed my help. Because as my dad always told me, "If not you, who? If not now, when?"

Saturday

Sixty-One

Margo Angelhart

My grandparents are two of the most amazing people I know.

Abuela shared her advice and suggestions freely. So did Pops—he loved to talk about the law to anyone who wanted to listen. And we all loved spending time listening to them. They'd lived amazing lives and I felt grateful and sincerely blessed that I had been born to this family.

Both Pops and Abuela celebrated their 81st birthdays in February, but it was today, May 24th, that mattered more to both of them: sixty years of marriage. I wasn't surprised that Uncle Tom's restaurant was packed with friends and family—more than two hundred people showed up, and that didn't include kids under ten.

The only thing that would have made it perfect was if my dad were here. Three years in prison and the emptiness without him still physically hurt.

While I loved my family, so many crammed together laughing, talking, hugging—it became a bit overwhelming. I stepped out to the back patio and found Lu and Tess sharing a pitcher of Uncle Tom's killer margarita.

I walked over to the small table, sat down, and held out my empty glass. Lu grinned and filled me up.

"Cheers," I said and held my cup out. We clinked the plastic and all drank.

I hadn't felt so relaxed in a long, long time. I don't know if it was because Annie was finally safe—at least for the next five to ten years—or because I had reconnected with my siblings in a deeper way.

Talking with Lu and Tess was just like old times… and that they didn't hold a grudge that I had separated myself from many family events over the last three years made me feel like the decision to step back into the family fold was right.

I didn't feel guilty for anything. I was right—we should fight for the truth about what happened the day my dad allegedly killed Devin Klein. Why did he confess? There were so many unanswered questions that I didn't know if I could put it aside. But for the first time in three years, I realized how alone I'd been with my grief and anger.

I may not have faked my death like Virginia Bonetti, but I had shut out my family.

Gabriel Rubio came over, the too-handsome, too-perfect pediatric surgeon who would be marrying my sister whenever they set a date. He smiled warmly at all of us, kissed his fiancée, and said, "I'm so sorry I was late."

"Everyone knows you were working," Tess said with a smile.

Tess was the holdout. She had two failed relationships that had almost gotten to the altar, and she feared if she set a date, she'd lose Gabriel as well. She didn't talk of it, but both Lu and I knew this was the case. Maybe now that we were in a better place, I could push her. I was probably the only one who had the guts to withstand Tess's wrath when she was angry…or scared. I didn't sugarcoat the truth, or back down.

"Come with me to talk to your grandparents?" Gabriel said, taking her hand.

Tess rose, waved at Lu and me, then walked off.

Nico came over with his boyfriend. Quincy looked distinctly uncomfortable. I was trying to focus on what we had in common—Nico, our mutual love of guns, and… Hmm, I didn't think Quincy and I had anything else in common.

"I heard through the grapevine that you were shot by a cop," Nico said. "What happened?" He was looking me over carefully.

"Not shot. Grazed. Long story."

"Maybe you'll finally come over for dinner and tell us?" Nico said pointedly, putting me on the spot.

I looked at Quincy. He stared back, face rigid.

Dinner with me would annoy Quincy, so I agreed. "When and where?"

Nico smiled, leaned back. "Next Friday, Quincy's place. He's a great cook."

Not even neutral turf. *Only for Nico*, I thought.

"I'll be there."

Mom walked over, made chitchat with Nico and Quincy, who soon left to get more food, and then she said, "Luisa, would you round everyone up for the cake-cutting? I'll be right there to make the toast."

A not-so-subtle way to get rid of my sister and leave us alone.

Mom sat where Lu had been sitting.

"I wish you had told me about Annie Carillo from the beginning."

"I take a lot of cases I don't tell you about. I don't work for you."

"No, you don't. And I don't want you to work *for* me. I want you to work *with* me. And Jack and Tess. Jack has reminded me that Angelhart Investigations had originally been *our* idea, that we had created it to be a team. That we were strong together. And we are both stubborn."

I could have made a wry joke, but didn't. I was stubborn. "I get it from you," I said simply and she laughed.

"We butted heads a lot when you were growing up. Jack was always the leader, the mediator. He grew from a responsible boy to a wonderful man. And Tess, she is a people pleaser. Always wanting to make sure everyone is happy, that they have what they need. You—you are a contrarian. I don't think I have ever met anyone who could take any side of any issue and argue effectively. You would have made a great lawyer."

Now I laughed. "Hardly. Seven years of college?"

"Well, if you could have skipped all that."

My mom knew I detested classrooms and book-learning. I had to do things to learn things. I made it through high school because I had a good family who helped me when things got tough, and because I wasn't incapable of learning. I just had to want it bad enough. I managed to graduate with a 3.0 GPA and that was fine with me.

"Sometimes," my mom said, "I thought you argued with me just because you never wanted to agree with me. Then... I realized you were highlighting the flaws in my thinking, the holes in my ideas, making me dig down for the truth. It didn't matter what it was or even if you agreed with me, it actually helped. You helped me be a better lawyer, a better advocate for my clients *because* you are a contrarian."

"I live to serve," I said, half joking.

I remembered those arguments and friendly debates. It reminded me that family wasn't just the past, not simply memories of the good and the bad, but also the present, the future. Family meant something—it always had. Being here, in the middle of my big extended family celebrating the sixty-year union of two amazing people who connected each and every one of us, made me yearn for more. Crave what I had, that I had either given away…or ignored.

For too long, I'd felt as if they had turned their backs on me, but I was wrong. We had disagreed, my mother and I. And my brothers and sisters sided with her, not me. It hurt. I'd felt like the odd man out.

But in the end, ideas and issues and people came and went, but family stayed. Family had your back. Family was your lifeline.

With our family came unconditional love.

I had forgotten that. Mom and I may never agree on whether to prove dad's innocence, and I'd let that disagreement—no matter how fundamental—put a wedge in my family that had affected all of us, not just me and my mom. I'd put conditions on my mother's love that were unfair and unjust.

No longer.

I was home, even before my mom reminded me that Angelhart Investigations was our collective dream.

"You have sharp instincts and a deep compassion that is both tempered and enhanced by those instincts," my mom said. "You intuitively know what to do. I may not have helped Annie Carillo as you did."

"You would have."

"I don't know. I would have weighed the risks, likely opted for finding solutions within the system. And my need to work within the confines of the system may have gotten her killed. Or put her children at risk. But at the same time, the risks you take are dangerous. I would say I don't know where you get it, but I do. Your father has always taken risks. He's always stood up for what is right, even when he's suffered." She took a deep breath, let it out. "I want you to come with me tomorrow, to visit your father."

"I visit him all the time—did you think I didn't? That I turned my back on him?"

"Of course not. I know you see him nearly every week. But he's been depressed because he feels his decisions have divided us. I want to show him, not tell him, that we're united."

"I can't promise not to investigate Klein's murder. I won't promise."

"I know. And I'm not going to ask you to. But the answers may not be what you want or expect. And I am going to do what Cooper has asked me to do: stand down."

I didn't know how my mom could do that, could just not look for the truth, free her husband. But I did know how she could stand with my father and do what he asked of her. I had a feeling my father was going to try to convince me to stand down as well. Maybe he could…but I doubted it.

Maybe if I listened, I could read between the lines.

"Alright, I'll go."

I could actually feel the tension leave my mother's body. "I want to give him good news—that you will join me, Jack, and Tess at Angelhart Investigations."

I wanted it, but I didn't know how it would practically work.

"I'm used to working on my own, Mom. I'm used to taking cases that you might not take."

"I know. We're a partnership, not a dictatorship. And I might not agree with all your decisions, but I will always have your back. You take the cases you want, and you'll have the backup. Jack has been going through the motions the last few years. He misses being a cop, misses his family. Seeing his son every other weekend is slowly killing him. He needs you, needs us, more than he'll ever admit."

It hurt me when anyone in my family was in pain. And if I could help, even in a small way, I would.

"Okay," I said. "One day at time?"

My mom hugged me. I hugged her tightly back.

"I love you, Mom," I said.

"I love you, Margo." She leaned back and I saw tears in her eyes, but she was smiling. "Now, let's toast to the most successful marriage I know, and say a prayer that Tess finally sets a date for her wedding."

I followed my mom into the restaurant, listened to her speech and toast, talked to all my relatives, watched the kids play, and felt like I had truly come home.

* * * * *

Acknowledgments

Five years ago, I moved to Arizona and knew I wanted to set a series here. Arizona was nothing like I had thought it was on my visits over the years. I embraced the diversity of the environment, from the towering mountains to the deep valleys, and the snow in the north and the heat in the summer. I learned to love the cactus and appreciate the cleansing rain. Nowhere, even in my beloved California, are there more beautiful sunrises and sunsets. I believe in loving where you are when you are there, because nowhere is perfect. And I hope my five years of immersing myself in Arizona and, specifically, Phoenix shows in this story.

As always, my agent, Dan Conaway, and his amazing assistant, Chaim Lipskar, work hard to help me build my career. My editors at MIRA, April Osborn and the indispensable Dina Davis, who help me be the best storyteller I can be. Publicist Justine Sha, who helps get my books into the right hands. The copy editor, proofreader, and artist who all put their mark on my books. And, honestly, doesn't this book have an amazing cover? Thank you, all.

With every book I need to reach out to people who know more than I do.

First and foremost, Father Fernando Camou, the rector of Ss. Simon and Jude Cathedral in Phoenix. He took time out of his very busy schedule (including marrying my daughter and her husband in 2022 and then baptizing my grandson in 2023) to let me interview him about the priesthood, why he became a priest, some of the ethical challenges he faces, his background as a first-generation Mexican–American growing up in the Phoenix area, and more. While I wasn't writing a religious thriller, I wanted to get the details right, as well as have an understanding of Father Camou's background. I took some liberties, but I hope none too major. If I got anything majorly wrong, that's on me and me alone.

My daughter, Katie, a Phoenix PD officer, probably got annoyed by my many, many questions about a myriad of things, ranging from who responds to what crime to what a cop might do when faced with certain situations. She also explained how the reporting system worked, what is public and what is not, and drove me all around central Phoenix—good areas and bad—so that I could absorb the areas about which I was writing. I think for the first time she really understood my writing process—which is, truly, inexplicable.

My son Luke, for teaching me about Discord and what can and cannot be done through the platform. Also, everything I know about video games, I know because of my boys, Luke and Mark. Thanks for playing with me, even when you get tired of playing the same two games over and over...

My cousin DeeDee Gifford, supernurse, who always helps me with medical questions and has saved my butt on more than one occasion when I almost got something wrong. If I messed up, that's on me.

And as always, a special thanks to Wally and the gang at Crime Scene Writers who I can ask any questions and they'll answer. Thanks to Martin Roy Hill and Bob Mueller for information about the army, the military in general, and information about the military police. You helped make Margo's back story more real for me. And thanks to Lynn Balabanos, who gave me an absolutely terrific tutorial on family law.

I also want to give a special shout-out to Deputy Sheriff Travis Allred of the Millard County Sheriff's Office in Utah. My husband, Dan, got himself a flat tire in probably the worst possible place in the western US—a little valley a few miles across the Utah border from Nevada. Dan had a spare and a jack, and started to change the tire when he realized that the lug nut set included with the car didn't have the right size. With intermittent cell service, it took him an hour to finally get through to roadside assistance…and then it would take them more than four hours to get out there, well after dark. On the advice of our daughter the cop, Dan called 911 and Deputy Allred came out to help even though he was off duty, simply because he was closer. Good Samaritans exist.

And a super special thanks to my husband, Dan, for the great idea of the thief using nitrogen. He always comes through when I need him!